RULING SIKTHAND

THE CLECANIAN SERIES: BOOK SEVEN

This is a work of fiction. Names, characters, places, and incidents either are the product of the author's imagination or are used fictitiously. Any resemblance to actual persons, living or dead, events, or locales is entirely coincidental.

Copyright © 2023 by Victoria Aveline

All rights reserved. No part of this book may be reproduced or used in any manner without written permission of the copyright owner except for the use of quotations in a book review. For more information, address: victoriaaveline.com.

First paperback edition October 2023

Cover design by Mayhem Cover Creations

ISBN 978-1-958397-10-7

www.victoriaaveline.com

RULING SIKTHAND

THE CLECANIAN SERIES: BOOK SEVEN

USA TODAY BESTSELLING AUTHOR
VICTORIA AVELINE

1

Bad luck.

For the most part, Sophia had never thought of herself as someone prone to bad luck. But as she sat tied to a chair somewhere in the upper floors of Vrulatica—the Vertical City—with nothing to do but think back on the last three months, she had to reconsider.

One night, she'd been lounging in a pile of blankets in her backyard while watching *Let the Right One In*. George and Sarah had both bailed on her as usual, so she'd been sulking and annoyed by everything from the low hum of her projector to the slight curling of the white sheet she'd hung over a tree limb. At some point, she must have fallen asleep, because when she'd woken, she'd been on an entirely new planet. And she was…different.

The toothache she'd been grappling with for a week was gone. Her vision, which she'd had to correct with glasses since middle school, was crystal clear. And to her horror, the tattoos that covered her body had vanished.

Sophia frowned at the clear skin of her right hand where a small snake had once twined around a wishbone. Before her abduction she'd also had a four-leaf clover, a koi, and a horseshoe decorating her body, but now those had all been wiped away. Maybe that was why her fortunes had turned sour. She no longer had her tattoo talismans to protect her.

She still grieved for Earth, for her tattoos, and for the little remaining family she'd left behind light-years away, but she'd tried to make the best of things and settle into life on Clecania. She'd made friends, found a small house, and started learning the complex written language. She'd even agreed to tour the planet in an effort to introduce the world to humans. But then her fortunes had turned sour again.

Just when she'd thought, *Maybe I can be happy, maybe I can be useful, maybe I can make this planet my home*, the stony Vrulan king had gone and imprisoned her in a darkened tower straight out of a Dracula retelling.

Back on Earth, Sophia had been a graphic designer. She loved her job for the most part, but there was no simple equivalent here on Clecania. It wasn't like they had Photoshop on their mind-bogglingly advanced technology. Without a job or a purpose, she'd been left feeling a little rudderless, so when the Queen of Tremanta had asked for volunteers for a tour around the planet, Sophia had submitted her name.

Six months visiting otherworldly cities, working to spread knowledge and compassion for the abducted humans living on Clecania had felt like a worthy thing to do with her time. Especially considering she hadn't had anything else to do. She could only wallow alone in her house while staring up at an unfamiliar sky for so long before boredom ate away at her. Well, she wasn't bored anymore.

Explore the world, they said. It'll be fun, they said, she griped to herself as she wriggled beneath her restraints.

The tour had started off well. Cities beyond her wildest dreams and the interesting people that resided in them had left Sophia inspired and hopeful. She'd even started drawing ideas for tattoos again. They were only rough scribbles, yet the rising motivation to draw anything at all felt glorious compared to the apathy she'd been grappling with back in Tremanta.

But as the tour had gone on, murmurs of unrest arose. Humans were descendants of ancient Clecanians, their earliest ancestors arriving on Earth eons ago. Somehow, knowledge of the humans had been lost in time, so when a plague barreled through, wiping out a devastating number of Clecanian women and setting the planet on a path to extinction, the Clecanians hadn't known to look to Earth for a solution.

But they knew now.

Humans were a blessing wrapped in red tape. They were sexually compatible, fertile, and miraculously able to awaken long-dead mating instincts among the lonely Clecanian people. But Earth, a Class Four planet, was strictly off-limits. No visits or communication allowed. If a ship belonging to an Alliance species was found even *near* the Milky Way, the offenders could be thrown in jail indefinitely and their planet could face exile from the enforcing powers of the universe, the Galaxy Supervision Federation.

Currently, there were an estimated one hundred humans living on Clecania. Not enough to save the species from extinction. Not by a long shot. They needed access to Earth, which meant Clecania had to convince members of the Intergalactic Alliance—the lawmakers of the universe—to reclassify the human species.

The fate of an entire planet rested in what else but politics. And the Alliance representative from Clecania, the person who would need to bring this issue up for discussion, the Queen of Tremanta, had been utterly silent.

The Queen had sent Sophia and a group of other humans and Tremantian representatives out on this PR tour and then, for all intents and purposes, vanished. No communication with the Intergalactic Alliance. No explanation as to why she hadn't broached a case for the reclassification of Earth. Nothing.

Sophia couldn't blame the people of Clecania for being upset. How could they *not* be when a carrot of salvation was dangled before their eyes? Sophia and her traveling companions had been touring for less than a month when tension began infecting their visits.

During their scheduled panels in each city, wherein attending Clecanians had been welcome to ask the humans whatever they'd wanted, the questions had grown more and more pointed. Rather than ask about Earth or human customs, they'd asked about the Tremantian Queen.

Where was she? Why hadn't she responded to meeting requests from Clecanian leaders around the world? Why wasn't the reclassification of Earth being prioritized or expedited?

As the days passed, curiosity had turned into criticism and then anger.

Her group had muddled through, sidestepping questions they couldn't answer and working hard to charm those they met out of their worry. But that had all changed when they'd arrived in Vrulatica.

A vicious rumor about the Queen had circulated in time with their arrival, and King Sikthand, who'd been vocal in his criticism of the Queen, had snapped. Suddenly, Sophia and her group were no longer valued guests, but hostages, pawns held under lock and key until the Queen broke her silence.

Other cities across the planet had taken steps to force the Queen into action as well. Merinta had cut off all trade to Tremanta, as had Tuva, but King Sikthand had taken things a step too far. This wasn't merely a show of strength, this was a slap across the face. Sophia couldn't fathom what the Queen planned to do about it.

Fortunately, most of her group had fought their way out and escaped Vrulatica. *Unfortunately*, Sophia's streak of rotten luck had resurged when she was mere feet away from freedom, and her friends had been forced to leave her behind.

Sophia sighed, tipping her head back against her chair. King Sikthand only had one human and one Tremantian guard to negotiate with now. A good thing for her friends and the Queen. A bad thing for her.

Would the Queen put up a fight to get one guard and one measly human back? She doubted it.

Her gut churned at a sudden thought. Her friends *had* escaped, right? They'd gotten free of the room they'd been trapped in. She knew that much, at least.

Sophia had watched each human, guard, and Tremantian representative being lifted through a compartment in the ceiling as she'd clumsily fought the soldiers in the room, keeping them distracted so her group could sneak out.

When Heleax, the last Tremantian guard left standing, had all but shoved her toward the rope, she'd dropped her weapon and made a run for it. She'd been climbing upward, cursing her nights spent on her couch instead of at the gym, when the King's axe flew through the air, cleaving the rope in two. The deep ache in her back pulsed sharply at the reminder of her plummet to the ground.

Guards had collected her from the floor and dragged her kicking and screaming through the Vertical City before dumping her in this cold museum of a room. All her thrashing must have made them certain she'd tear apart whatever she could get her hands on the moment she was left alone, because they'd strapped her to the chair—ensuring her feet were doubly secure after she'd gotten in a satisfying kick to one's gut—then left.

Had her group made it out of the city? Or were they still fighting somewhere in Vrulatica? The Vertical City was so named because it was entirely contained within an enormous tower that stretched a mile into the sky. Only accessible from the outside by the beautiful flying creatures called malginash, Sophia wondered whether her friends had wrangled one and escaped.

Though Sophia couldn't tell exactly how long she'd been here, a nagging rumble in her belly told her it'd been hours at least. Long enough for the stabbing pain in her low spine to settle into a pulsing ache.

Not knowing what had happened was maddening. Heleax had been captured as well, but he'd been taken somewhere else. Had that been done on purpose to keep her isolated and anxious?

The room she'd been locked in was quiet and empty, but it was far from any cell she'd ever seen. On the contrary, it was a beautiful, if not dusty, bedroom. She had no idea how to interpret the decision to stow her *here*, of all places.

Vaguely, she recalled the king halting the soldier who'd hoisted her off the floor as he'd dragged her away. She couldn't tell what he'd said, but the soldier had changed direction after that. Almost like he'd been ordered to bring her here, to this opulent bedroom. Why?

With women being as scarce as they were, the Clecanians cherished females. Had the king wanted her to be brought here because it was more *comfortable* than a cell? Sophia wiggled her tingling fingers. Doubtful, if the leather bands digging into her wrists were any indication.

Besides, if he wanted her to be comfortable, why not lock her in one of the many guest rooms that had been set up for their arrival? They were less fancy, she thought as she studied the towering, vaulted ceiling, but at least they were clean. *This* room looked as if it hadn't been occupied in decades.

Every surface was covered with pale dust. Crooked black cloth shrouded the windows, and the thickest cobwebs she'd ever seen spotted the ceiling. Sophia didn't mind spiders, but she shuddered to imagine what could have spun thread so thick it could be used as a shoelace.

Dominating one side of the room was a bed. It had taken her a while to identify it as such since it was more of an ornate gazebo with a bed cocooned inside. The hint of a mattress peeked out from an opening maybe five feet wide. All other sides of the bed were made up of sculpted metal malginash. They were skillfully shown climbing over the top and sides of tree limbs, which bowed in to create a rounded sanctuary over the mattress. Sophia could only imagine how dark and cozy it must be to sleep in there when it was clean and piled high with soft pillows.

The only light in the room came from a round skylight overhead. The colored glass diluted the sunlight streaming through and lit the room in a moody red glow. Despite the dimness, she could make out four doors in the room. She cataloged them.

She'd been dragged through one. One was ajar and led into a bathroom, one was plain and closed next to the bathroom door, and the fourth was located on the wall directly across from the bed. It was the most ornamental of the bunch and stood larger than the rest. A curious lack of grime in front of the door hinted that it was used often, the dust on the floor brushed away as it might be when the door swept open. Another entrance maybe?

More time passed, and not a peep of sound floated through the walls. Her ears rang in the silence. She tested her restraints again and winced. The soldier hadn't tied them exceptionally tight, but hours of struggling had made her skin raw.

She shifted in her seat, and as she did, the chair creaked ever so slightly. Wood? No, not exactly. But not metal. She wiggled in the chair, trying to get it to groan again.

A few years ago, her friend Claire had forced Sophia and the rest of their friends to sit through a PowerPoint presentation outlining tips and tricks on how to survive if you were ever kidnapped or attacked. Her slides ranged from breaking duct tape to gouging eyes. It had been a wonderful night filled with drinking and laughing. They'd listened, half making fun of cautious Claire and half taking notes.

Now Sophia racked her brain, trying to recall if there'd been a slide about slamming a chair down so hard it broke or if she'd just seen that in the movies. After a few more minutes of tedious silence, she decided to go for it.

All she had to do was stand up and then fling herself down hard enough to break the chair. *Easy.*

Feet flat on the floor, but ankles tied to the legs of the chair, she tried to shift her weight so she could awkwardly stand, but barely made it a millimeter off the ground before gravity pulled her back down. *I need momentum.*

With a deep inhale, she used all her strength to explode forward. Her heels flattened against the smooth stone, and the chair lifted. For a brief moment, she was standing…but her body didn't stop.

Instead of balancing on her feet, her burst of energy sent her flying forward onto her toes. Before she knew it, she was barreling face-first toward the floor. At the last second, she angled her foot so her body twisted, and she landed on her shoulder. Dust billowed around her, making her cough and sneeze.

Sophia blinked toward the door and let out a low grumble. She was now sideways on the ground, stuck to a fully intact chair.

Just my luck.

2

The dramatic red light from the skylight above turned blue as Sophia lay on the ground, throwing the room into shades of steel and navy. She gazed up through the tinted glass. Maybe it was night now.

Albeit still on the floor, she'd managed to throw her weight around enough so that the chair tipped onto its back. It wasn't ideal, but at least she was lying on her back with her knees in the air and not on her shoulder with her neck pulling to one side.

She'd spent her time counting the tiles in the round stained-glass window high above. Blues and silvers glowed through the abstract design, reminding her of clouds on a stormy day. Hours ago, the tiles had shone red, though. She studied the glass until her eyes hurt but couldn't figure out how it was possible for the color to change.

Back on Earth, she'd painted the back window of her house with translucent glass paint to mimic the feeling of stained glass. In the city of Seattle, where she lived, the sun never seemed to shine on the window long enough for her to enjoy it, though.

Where she *used* to live, Sophia reminded herself. The house her grandparents had left her had likely been cleaned out and sold off by now. Unless they'd somehow tracked down her closest relative—her father. She hadn't heard from him in over twenty years, though, so she doubted it.

She turned her head and caught her reflection in the enormous dressing mirror affixed to the wall near the mysterious carved door. The mirror stood even taller than the door, its wide arching frame nine feet high at least.

Sophia blinked at herself. She'd avoided looking at her reflection for hours now. It was just too pathetic a sight. She was tied to a fallen chair, her skin dirty and scraped up from the fight and from the dusty floor. The grandeur of the space and the size of the chair made her look pitifully small. Light from above bathed her in blue and deepened all the valleys of her face. She looked like a gaunt ghost trapped underwater.

Her bladder seemed to grow fuller at the thought, and she glanced away. Had they forgotten her here? Would she die tied to an unbreakable chair on an alien planet covered in pee because she hadn't been worth remembering?

No. Even if these aliens didn't find her particularly remarkable, she was still human, and she doubted very much they'd forget about that. Humans were too valuable to treat poorly.

Sophia frowned. Had the icy king ordered her to be abandoned here? She wouldn't be surprised if he got off on throwing his power around. At dinner he'd sat higher than everyone else, glowering down at the human table.

Well, it had at least *felt* like he was glowering. She couldn't be certain, since he'd never actually taken off his masked helmet. When he deigned to appear at all, he prowled around, covered head to toe in armor. The only bit of his face she'd been able to spot beneath the metal plating of his helmet was a pale slice of hard jaw and his eerie glowing silver eyes. They were cold too.

Sophia pictured him again. How could an eye color feel so…sharp?

He'd be interesting to draw, she grudgingly admitted. She placed him beneath a beam of red light in her mind. The metal antlers of his masked helmet would glint with a blood-red lining. It wouldn't be a happy picture, but she might be able to capture his severity if she got the lighting right.

A noise louder than the pounding of her heart—the only sound she'd heard for hours now— roused her out of her thoughts. It grew louder.

Thump. Thump. Thump.

Her breath caught in her throat. *Footsteps.*

She craned her head back, gazing above her forehead to the door she'd been brought through hours before. Being alone had insulated her from her current predicament, her anger fading once there was no enemy to direct it toward. At the clink of metal on stone, a shiver shuddered down her spine.

This wasn't some LARP event where she was merely *pretending* to be a warrior maiden. This was real. She was locked in a tower in an alien city. Real soldiers with real blades took real orders from the very real, very terrifying king.

Fighting back had been the right move before, since it'd meant she'd been able to cause enough of a distraction to allow her group time to escape, but Sophia was no fighter. Not unless you considered live action role-play fighting *real* fighting, which would be ridiculous. A handful of weekends swinging around a foam sword had allowed her to be convincing enough to keep the soldiers confused as to whether or not she knew what she was doing. But her adrenaline was gone now—and with it, her bravado.

She was a hostage. If she was going to make it out of this situation, she had to be smart.

Thump. Thump. Thump.

She swallowed. She was a human and a female, which meant she had value on this planet. They wouldn't hurt her. If she cooperated and didn't try to swipe anyone's head off with an axe, she'd be fine.

The metal inner workings of the door whirred as it unlocked.

Damn. How she wished she wasn't on the floor right now.

The door swung open, and King Sikthand's silver eyes fell on her.

Sophia stopped breathing. She'd seen him from afar at dinner or skulking in the background as his Guild peppered them with questions. But now he was here...alone, and the cold shadow that clung to him only felt heavier and more menacing.

He froze halfway through the door, gaze fixed on her. That damn mask still covered his face. Black metal woven with chain and curled silver presented her with a beautifully intricate façade through which no humanity shone. A mix of antlers and horns sprung from the crown of the mask, and the pointed tips glinted in the dull blue light.

Sophia kept her face stony, not wanting to show how forcefully her fear had hit her. His outfit was made to cause this reaction. She had to keep reminding herself of that.

It was like Micah, the guy she'd pined over for years. When he wrapped himself in padding and costume armor, he transformed. Long brown hair, a scruffy beard, and an impressive control over prop swords had made her swoon. But when he took it all off, he was just Micah. A normal, nice guy who spent most of his time managing a landscaping company and chewed with his mouth open.

The razor-sharp horns, icy stare, and layers of pointed metal making the king's frame far bulkier than it likely was, were all designed to intimidate. *He's just a Micah underneath. Just a man—er, an alien.* He slowly stepped toward her, and she attempted to merge into the chair. *And a king. Okay, so underneath all that, he's an alien and a king, but also just a guy, right?*

Her heart thundered in her chest the closer he got. She wanted to be brave. Cooperative yet stoic. But his eyes...they were so harsh. They shone out of his mask so brightly she couldn't tell whether they were solid silver or contained whites and an iris like other Vrulans.

Her discomfort won out, and she averted her gaze, staring up at the ceiling while listening closely for every movement of his boots. He stopped at the top of her chair, looming over her head and blocking out the beam of light from above. She swallowed.

Silently, she contemplated how she was going to get her voice to work when he finally *did* speak, but he said nothing. Like a hunter examining an animal in a trap, he circled her until he came to her feet and stopped. Her fingers curled against her chair. She almost wished he'd ask how she ended up on the floor. Describing her clumsy fall might be embarrassing, but anything was better than this stifling silence.

He hunched over her and slid his hands under the arms of her chair. A shiver tore through her when the cool silver of his gloves brushed her skin. His grip tightened. At this distance she should feel his body heat, but he was just cold layers of metal. Like a dead thing. A zombie.

He straightened, still holding her chair, and lifted her as if doing no more than standing, then set her upright. *Okay, under the armor, he's just an alien and a king and laughably strong. But also just a guy?*

"Uh, thank you," she mumbled as he reached for the band at her wrist. His face was close now, yet all she could make out below the mask was the pale, chiseled line of his jaw.

Her breath caught when his gloved finger ran over the small indentations she'd left in the leather straps on her wrists. His eerie gaze lifted to hers in a silent question. She chewed on her lip, building the courage to explain. But he put it together himself before she could.

His focus drifted between her mouth and the marks on the leather. The line of his jaw tensed further.

She'd been gnawing on the straps like an animal, trying to bite her way free. Too bad she didn't have fangs like the Vrulans, or she might've been successful.

A choked squeak of pain escaped when he loosened the band and pulled the leather off her blistered skin a little too roughly.

Any remaining wisps of softness that clung to him fled. She tried to pull her now free hand away, but he held it firm and turned it slowly, examining the damage. His eyes glowed a little brighter.

"Thank you," she said pointedly, pulling her wrist from under his scrutiny.

A deep, noncommittal rumble sounded in his throat. His gaze lingered where her hand had been for a few moments before he slid his plated gloves off.

Her eyes caught on his hands as he tossed his gloves onto the ground. So severe. Pale skin, almost the shade of bone in the blue light, was decorated with thick black designs. They were geometric and harsh and somehow made his long fingers appear as if they could crush stone.

Though his movements were vastly gentler, Sophia still bit back a wince when he peeled the other leather strap away. On instinct, she almost thanked him again, but clamped down on the words before they got out. She'd literally said nothing to him except *thank you*, which was ridiculous considering he was the one who'd ordered her to be locked up in the first place.

"Where's the rest of my group?" she asked, her voice containing the merest whisper of demand. Her nerves won out when he froze while peering at her reddened skin, and she added, "Your...Your Majesty."

His gaze lifted to her, but he didn't appear angry—more surprised. After a tense moment of silence, he answered, "Gone."

Warm, deep, and smooth. Sophia's brain didn't have time to process how a voice like that could emerge from a man like this when he sank to one knee before her. Still reeling from the shiver his singular word had sent through her body, she was momentarily dumbfounded as to why he knelt between her feet. Then she recalled her legs were still tied.

Something brainless in her body roused at the sight of the enormous alien king kneeling in the filthy ground, but she silently smothered it.

Get a hold of yourself.

He finished undoing the knots at her ankles and stood. Sophia tried to stand too, but both her legs were asleep, and she immediately fell back into the chair.

"You're needed in the Guild chamber."

"Can I ask why, Your Majesty?" she asked as she shakily got to her feet. The scrape of metal on stone made her flinch. His long tail, also covered in armor, flicked across the ground. She'd learned this was an emotional response for the Vrulans—but *what* emotion, she didn't know. *Don't make him mad.*

His hand, which was gloved again, wrapped gently around her bicep as he guided her out of the room. "To discuss your stay in Vrulatica."

A frown curled her lips at the word *stay*. *My forcible confinement, you mean?*

He was silent for the rest of the walk through the buttressed hallway and out a large pair of ornate doors. A guard waited outside, and the king handed Sophia off, locked the doors, then sped ahead without a backward glance. The guard, whose grip was much tighter, guided her in the king's wake.

Why didn't he just send this guy to get me from the room? Sophia hadn't initially considered it, but why would the king of a whole ass city have seen fit to retrieve her all by himself? Especially when he'd brought a guard to walk her most of the way anyway. She shrugged it off as they neared what must be the Guild chamber.

Two arched doors were thrown wide. Six chairs sat embedded within the perimeter of the room in a semicircle. In the center, a throne sat higher than the others. It was built of carved towers of black rock. A crescent sliver of a window was set above the head of the throne. Light poured in from the thin segment of glass like the sun seconds from being overtaken during an eclipse.

As the king sauntered into the chamber, the occupants buzzed to life. There were about twenty people all huddled in smaller groups throughout the room as if they were having semi-private meetings. Sophia recognized the Guild, the six officials of the city who worked under the king to run Vrulatica. They'd briefly introduced themselves when her group had first arrived, but she couldn't remember their names.

Non-Guild members, those she could only assume were underlings for the heads of the Guild, broke away as the king neared his throne. Cushioned benches lined the walls on the opposite side of the raised seats of power, and in the center of the room, right where Sophia was being dragged, was a single chair. The guard's tight grip on her arm forced her to stay standing when she tried to sit in the chair. His voice was stern—but not cruel—when he whispered, "Wait."

The king took his seat while the rest of the room remained standing. She stared up at the sharp decorative points dripping down from the ceiling's architecture and swallowed.

The Guild's seats were raised in such a way that the six guildmembers were all peering down at her. Placed against their ornate perches in this gothic room, Sophia couldn't shake the feeling she was being judged by looming gargoyles.

Her shoulders curled forward.

They stood silently rather than sitting, clearly waiting for something to happen. The king was the only one moving, slipping off his gloves. His hands were even harsher without the blue light shining on them. Her nape tingled when he undid the clasps of his helmet.

"Down," her guard hissed. Sophia's head snapped around with a start, and she realized the faces of everyone in the room were dipped to the floor. She did the same.

The hollow knell of the king's helmet hitting stone echoed through the room. It must weigh a ton. Curiosity to see what his face looked like burned in her. She forced her gaze to remain locked on a crack in the stone to keep herself from peeking on instinct.

"I bestow my trust." Though Sophia had only heard him speak through the echoing metal of his mask, she knew exactly who the deep, smooth voice came from.

A chorused reply floated from the occupants of the room. "And we ours." The guard spoke the words too and gave her a little nudge. She peered at her guard and saw he was facing forward again.

"And we—" She raised her head, rushing to repeat the greeting, but her gasp sucked up her words.

King Sikthand's face was just as unnerving as the rest of him.

The race of people from this city, the Vrulans, had an interesting feature known as a hood. A triangular section of skin that began at their temples and came to a point somewhere between their top lip and chin. Men typically had longer hoods than women. A Vrulan's hood was often a different color than their skin, and their beauty was attributed to how harmonious their coloring was. Bronze skin with a golden hood. Gray skin with a charcoal hood. Sophia had found them interesting to look at, but the king's appearance was…unsettling.

Hair, white and thick, was pulled back from his face and braided in a haphazard way that didn't align with his tidy armor or brutalist hand tattoos. His skin was ghostly pale, almost as light as his hair, and his hood was the darkest black she'd ever seen. The contrast made his glowing silver eyes and bright fangs so striking that he was difficult to look at.

The scrape of metal against stone rocked her out of her stupor. She sucked in a breath, realizing she hadn't in quite some time. His lips thinned.

Oh shit, I'm staring. Sophia quickly looked away. The rest of the Vrulans shot her pitying glances, and whispers skittered to her ears from the lower representatives seated behind her.

The source of the scraping noise revealed itself when she saw the metal tip of the king's long tail swishing back and forth near the base of his throne. With a quick swallow to lubricate her throat, she steeled herself and stared up at him again. "And we ours," she repeated in barely more than a squeak.

She tried to keep her focus trained on his eyes, but her gaze roved over his face despite her efforts. He was just too damn interesting to look at.

He flicked his wrist, and everybody in the room sat. After an unsure moment, Sophia sat as well.

"The room is open." The king declared as he relaxed back into his chair. She tried to ignore the way his gaze remained glued to her, as if he were punishing Sophia for gawking at him by directing his considerable intensity toward her. She avoided his eyes and kept herself from fidgeting.

A harsh clang made her flinch. A beautiful woman clothed in teal tapped her metal-adorned tail against a silver panel on her chair, indicating she wanted to speak.

She looked at Sophia through glittering white lashes. Though the woman didn't exactly smile, there was enough kindness in her expression to make Sophia's shoulders relax a fraction.

"My name is Madam Kalos. I'm the head of trade and international relations. I have some unfortunate news I need to deliver."

"Are my friends okay? Did they make it to the desert? What happened to them?" The words burst from her before she could contain them. The king's tail scraped against the floor again. She glanced his way for a split second. Annoyance mixed with her fear at his stony stare. What? She wasn't allowed to ask questions either?

Madam Kalos' gaze lit with sympathy, and Sophia braced herself, biting her lip to keep silent. "We have no information on your traveling party. As far as we know, they left unharmed, but we haven't had news of them since."

She couldn't help but notice the hesitation Madam Kalos put on the word *left*. Like it hadn't been an escape. As if they'd simply walked out the door after a pleasant, if not short, stay.

Madam Kalos continued, "This is regarding the Tremantian Queen. A message came through yesterday. The Queen has died. There's an unconfirmed assumption that she was assassinated."

The words hung in the air, but Sophia couldn't quite process them. Ears buzzing, her hands lifted to the arms of her chair, and she ran her palms along the smooth surface over and over, trying to make sense of what this woman was telling her. "Assassinated," she whispered, more to herself.

"Our reports are preliminary, but it seems there was…evidence of harm."

Sophia's hand lifted to her chest. That poor woman. She hadn't interacted with the Queen as much as some of the other humans had, but she'd gotten the impression that the Queen always tried her best to protect them while remaining fair to her people. And now someone had killed her for it? Why?

Anger ignited in her chest, and her focus snapped to Sikthand. *Him.*

Clecanians the world over had already been stewing in impatience, waiting for the Queen to make more bold moves where Earth was concerned. King Sikthand's decision to make a flashy statement by holding their traveling party hostage might've been the spark of inspiration some asshole needed to take matters into their own hands.

The king raised a brow at her glare.

"Based on evidence found in her home, the belief is she was killed some time ago…before your arrival in our city." A man on the king's right chimed in. He was more unkempt than the rest of the Guild. Burly with coppery red hair and a deep bronze hood. It was obvious his words were an attempt to assure her that whatever happened to the Queen had not been a result of the king or Guild, but that did nothing to cool Sophia's indignation.

The king might not have killed her, but people like him had. People who viewed humans as cattle and Earth as a planet ripe for harvest. The Queen had been the only leader Sophia had heard of that seemed concerned with the terrible impact they might have on humans. The only one to want to think through a strategy that would result in peace for everyone.

"We realize this must be difficult to hear." Madam Kalos' voice was softer, but it sounded artificial to Sophia's ears. "Your friends remain missing, and we can only assume they chose not to return to Tremanta after hearing the news. The Guild has agreed that until a new leader is chosen and negotiations can be reopened, you will remain here."

"I'll be *detained* here, you mean," Sophia hissed.

"Yes." The king's voice was level, but it rattled through her as if he'd bellowed the word. "You will stay because it is in the best interest of my city and, though you choose not to believe it, you as well."

"And what about Heleax?" she challenged, earning a few whispers. "Why isn't he here being told all of this?"

"He'll remain in the dungeons," Madam Kalos answered as if this were obvious. "He's a soldier of Tremanta. You're just a human caught in an international conflict. There's no reason for your stay to be any more unpleasant than it already is. You may not be allowed to leave," she continued, "but you're free to explore the city."

"Are you a soldier, female?" The copper-haired man eyed her suspiciously. Sophia almost snorted. "I've had conflicting reports from my males. Some say you fought during your party's escape."

Sophia had bluffed her way through the fight earlier today, but the element of surprise and the knowledge the soldiers were forbidden from harming the humans had been the reason for that. If a soldier came at her intending to injure, she'd be laid out before she had time to lift a weapon.

"No. I'm not a soldier." Her lack of further explanation seemed to frustrate Copperhead. The thought that he suspected she might be secretly deadly gave her a petty sense of enjoyment.

"She's human." Sophia glanced at the man to her right who'd spoken. "She should submit herself to our marriage ceremony," he drawled, his curling black beard quivering as he spoke. There was no hint of suggestion in his voice but plenty of annoyance. He'd clearly argued this many times over.

A tennis ball lodged itself in her throat. She met the king's hard stare and prepared to beg. They couldn't make her marry someone, could they?

"There are quite a few laws that forbid forcing a female into marriage, even if she is an alien female—as I've told you repeatedly." The woman glaring at the black bearded man was too beautiful for words. Her skin was bronze, her hood golden, and her long silvery hair looked like it'd been infused with moonlight. *Gorgeous and the voice of reason. Thank God.*

Not ready to let the issue of her friend go, Sophia inhaled a determined breath. "Heleax should be allowed out of the dungeons." She lifted her chin. "Or you should lock me up with him." Maybe she could bluster her way into getting him freed. Then they could figure out an escape plan.

Another member of the Guild, who was clad in a shockingly drab outfit compared to the rest, chuckled. "Prideful little being, isn't she?"

The king's scowl never wavered.

"Nonsense," Madam Kalos scoffed. She addressed the group, ignoring Sophia. "Are we settled on where she'll be staying?"

"The market district sees the most traffic. More opportunities for her to be recognized."

"Yes, but if we hope for a valuable exchange between the new Tremantian ruler, do we want to take the chance of her being recognized? The soldier would be our only bargaining chip, since she'd need to stay with her mate."

"I don't—" Sophia tried to interject, but the Guild's heated discussion continued on.

"If there's even a remote possibility one of our citizens could recognize a mate, we should support that possibility."

"There are some agreeable rooms available in lowcity. Our miners and metalsmiths rarely travel skyward. They deserve a chance at recognition as well. She could have—"

Sophia shot to her feet, anger boiling inside her and showing itself in her watering eyes. They said she wasn't a prisoner but immediately followed up that assurance by verbally passing her around. Not one of them was asking what she wanted or even glancing her way as they argued about her.

Well, no one except *him*. The king hadn't looked away.

She didn't like his stare, knew it was meant to intimidate, but in this moment, she couldn't help but draw comfort from it. He, at least, saw her.

"Quiet." King Sikthand's voice boomed around the room, and silence fell. His tail curled over his thigh as he worked through some thought. Finally, he spoke. "She will remain where I put her."

"But sire, those are the queen's quarters. Wouldn't it be…" The voice of the guildmember in drab clothing died out as the king shot him a lethal look.

"It's the only place that vermin doesn't have access," he growled, baring his fangs.

Vermin? Who is he talking about?

A few guildmembers looked concerned, but remained silent.

"I've heard your suggestions. This is what I've decided." The finality in his statement was palpable. Without pause, the Guild nodded their assent. They might have some input in the ruling of Vrulatica, but Sikthand had final say, and it was clear they either feared him or respected him enough not to argue.

"Speaker Besith has assigned a chaperone." The king nodded toward the man with the curling beard. *Great, a babysitter. I bet he picked someone super friendly,* Sophia groused as she took in his mild sneer. "He will show you the city, and more importantly, he will make sure you understand which areas of Vrulatica are off-limits. If you try to leave or pressure any citizen into aiding you in some misguided attempt to flee, I will punish you." The king took in the stubborn tension of her shoulders and added, "If that doesn't deter the defiance I see in you, know that I have no qualms with punishing Heleax for your mistakes. Am I understood?"

Sophia's jaw was tensed so hard it popped. She couldn't bring herself to answer.

The king leaned forward, and the room cooled a degree. He rested his elbows on the arms of his throne, every inch the icy-hearted ruler. "I will not place you in the dungeon, but I don't see any problem locking you in your rooms for weeks on end. Freedom. Confinement. I don't care either way." The sharp tip of his tail flicked behind his calf. "So, I ask again. Am. I. Understood?"

It would do her no good to get herself locked in her room just to spite him in this moment, though she wanted to. Badly.

Ruling Sikthand

"I understand," she gritted out through clenched teeth.

3

∞

If sitting before the Guild and listening to them decide her future while she remained obedient wasn't humiliating enough, the king had also decided to make her wait outside the chamber as they discussed the rest of the topics on their docket.

Her stoic guard had borne the brunt of her ire in the form of incessant questions, of which he'd answered very few. After an hour of interrogation, though, he was beginning to crack. His steel-blue eyes drifted toward the sealed door more and more often, and the sound of clinking metal echoed through the hall as he fidgeted.

The only piece of information he'd deigned to share was that they were to wait in the silent hall until the king was done. Like a damn dog leashed outside a store. But why? Did he want to speak with her more? Doubtful. Was this just some kind of perverse power move? A way to say, *Fuck you for questioning me?*

It didn't matter why in the long run, only that he *could* do it. As long as she lived in this city, she was under his control. The sheer helplessness made her want to scream.

What could she do, though? Escape? Vrulatica was aptly named the Vertical City, and right now she was near the top. As far as she knew, all travel in and out of the city was done using malginash. Even if she could somehow get her hands on one of the winged creatures, she wouldn't know how to fly one. And even if by some miracle she *could* fly one, she wouldn't know which direction to go. Red desert surrounded the city as far as the eye could see.

The sad truth was that even if she somehow made it out of Vrulatica and found a cruiser to commandeer, she didn't know what awaited her in Tremanta. If her friends hadn't gone back, there must be a reason.

She didn't expect anyone to save her. She wasn't really in danger anyway. No, for now, she had to bide her time.

Maybe she could splash a coat of paint on this situation. Recalibrate it in her mind as a continuation of her trip. An extended stop in a city she'd already been intrigued by. The unsettling reality that she wasn't allowed to leave could remain stowed in a nice, dark, unacknowledged corner of her brain.

Sophia let out a short squeak when the doors of the chamber flew open and flooded the hallway with noise. She didn't miss the satisfied smirk her guard tossed her way. She pressed against the wall, making room for everyone to leave, but the king strode out first.

His helmet was back in place, and the only indication he'd acknowledged her presence at all was the bright flash of his silver eyes darting across her face. His tail flicked at her guard like a beckoning finger. A silent command. And just like that, she was dragged back along in the king's wake. Irritation made her fists clench as she realized he was leading her back to her rooms.

This was why she'd had to wait? So he could walk her home like a disobedient toddler.

When they approached the doors to the palatial wing her rooms were in, the guard stopped and positioned himself against the wall like a decorative suit of armor. The king himself unlocked the doors. Was he the only one with a key?

With an air of impatience, he held the door open, bright gaze unmoving. Her throat was tight as she passed through the threshold, inching away from his towering frame until he locked the door behind them.

"Your attendant is waiting in your rooms," he rumbled, extending an arm toward her door at the end of the corridor. "He'll see to any needs you have."

Sophia wanted to argue, pester him with questions, but the air felt different than it had a moment ago. There weren't other people around. No witnesses. Something about being in front of others made her situation less real. She could slip on a mask of bravery more easily when it felt like a performance, but not here. She was in a dark, locked hall with a massive warrior king who very clearly didn't care for her.

He turned on his heel and stalked away. "Wait," Sophia blurted.

The king stilled. His boots scraped as he swiveled in place slowly. She didn't know what to say, though. She had a million questions, but what overtook her in that moment was the uncertainty. She wasn't in imminent danger, but she wasn't clear of danger either. She had no home, no friends, no one else of her species within a hundred-mile radius, and the man in front of her held her life in his hands yet seemed altogether unconcerned with her existence.

"What do I do?"

His angled body turned toward her more, one horn of his helmet glinting with the tilt of his head.

"I mean," she tried to recover, to make sure the question didn't sound as vulnerable as it was. "Am I confined here? Do I get a key?" Her eyes darted up to the aggressive points and arches of the ceiling. "Should I just wait in my room until you and your Guild have decided whether I fetch a good enough price?"

Faint activity from her room buzzed through the silence between them. "Your chaperone has a key, and I care not what you do," he finally said. "Stay out of trouble, don't try to contact anyone outside the city without supervision, and mind the boundaries you've been given. Know that there will *always* be eyes on you. If I hear you've dashed out into the desert in the night, understand that *I* will be the one to hunt you."

She didn't know what came over her, but before she could hold it back, she sneered. "Before you go making threats, remember that I'm a pretty delicate bargaining chip."

The king straightened. "Watch your fangs, little human. Or they may be ripped out." A slow nails-on-chalkboard scrape of his tail across the floor set her teeth on edge, but she kept her jaw lifted. "A rider gains nothing by taunting their mount."

What the hell did that mean? Was she the rider or the mount in this scenario?

His blazing eyes lifted over her shoulder, breaking their seething glares. Her chaperone must be behind her, but she didn't look. Whoever was at her back was far less of a threat than the man in front of her. His gaze bore into hers for a fleeting moment before he turned and stomped down the hall.

What was down that way, anyway?

A high-pitched *tap tap tap* rang through the space from behind Sophia, but she kept her eyes trained on the king until the silver spike of his tail disappeared around a corner.

When she turned, she found a man, though his luminous golden skin and even brighter golden hood made him look more like Apollo in the dark glow of the hall.

"Hello. My name is Alno." He gave a quick bow. His warm honey eyes trailed over her. She couldn't decipher whether there was heat in his gaze, though. "I've been assigned as your attendant," he explained as she drew closer. He was tall too. Lean and beautifully built.

"You don't have to pretend," she sighed. "You're my chaperone. My babysitter."

He blinked, lip lifting to expose a white fang. "Baby *sitter*." He repeated in a mildly horrified tone. "I'll assume that term should not be translated literally. If you're implying I'm here to do more than assist you, you'd be correct. I'd rather not disappoint the king in this, so I hope you won't be too unwilling to allow me to keep close."

Sophia took in a deep breath. "I appreciate the honesty, Alno." A sense of dullness seeping into her bones, she trudged toward her room.

She stopped in her tracks. Had she walked into the wrong room?

What had been a dust and cobweb covered space only a few hours ago was now unrecognizable. No longer musty and thick, the air smelled fresh and lightly floral.

The floors gleamed. The domed metal sculpture surrounding the bed glimmered in the calming blue light flooding through the ceiling's stained glass and the newly revealed windows. Sophia noticed jewels inlaid in the malginash eyes that she hadn't seen before. Within the confines of the bed itself, the mattress was piled high with fluffy bedding.

"How...?" Had she been gone for hours?

"I oversaw a small army for the cleaning and stocking. Just let me know if you need anything else." Alno glanced around the room, the side of his mouth lifting in a satisfied smile.

"You're certainly good at your job. This is incredible."

Alno's shoulders pulled back proudly, but his brows raised in surprise. *Not used to receiving compliments?*

She trailed around the room as he stood near the door listing all the cleaning that had been done and describing what clothing they'd provided, in addition to what would be on its way as soon as he got her measurements. Alno had unearthed the space, and every inch screamed wealth. It was too nice. Truly a room meant for a queen. She wasn't worthy enough to set foot in a place like this, yet the king had insisted on it.

"Do you know who the king calls 'vermin'?" she asked. Unsurprisingly, Alno looked confused. She repeated what the king had said back in the chamber.

Her chaperone shrugged, but his gaze shifted nervously. He knew more than he let on. She'd have to chip away at that later. He showed her around, leading her through the three rooms that constituted the queen's quarters.

"What's behind that door?" Sophia pointed to the ornate door on the wall opposite her bed. Her rooms had two closets, a bathroom with an enormous bathing pool, and an adjoining study. What more could there be?

She was already across the room, fingers brushing the handle, when he rapped his tail against the floor twice in quick succession. "That leads to the king's quarters."

Sophia's swiped her hand back as if it had been burned, then spun to Alno, eyes wide. "What? Our rooms are…connected?"

Alno shrugged. "A queen may want to call upon her king from time to time." He joined her at the door, and she recoiled when he pulled it open, as if King Sikthand was waiting on the other side. But it was empty.

She was surprised to find not a room behind the door, but a long corridor. The ceiling wasn't as tall here, and the walls were covered in silvery-white metal lacework. Dim lighting lit the space just enough for her to see that the large door on the far side of the hall was black. Compared to the architecture of the rest of Vrulatica, with its imposing ceilings and angular metalwork, this area was strikingly…intimate.

"I'll never be able to sleep now," she whispered as she backed away.

Alno closed the door. "I wouldn't worry. You aren't his queen. And it's not as if you called for him." He gestured to a lever on the side of the door decorated to look like a flowering branch.

"What is that? Like a sex doorbell or something?" She eyed it warily.

Alno erupted into laughter, his hearty chuckle matching that of a man considerably rounder in the belly and redder in the face. "I heard humans were funny things." He grinned and slid a large bolt hidden beneath the detail work of the door into place. "I can't imagine he's ever used this passage, but if you're worried, just keep this bolted and don't ring any *sex bells.*"

She grumbled her thanks as Alno continued to chuckle. When she turned back to him, she caught him eyeing her. It wasn't the first time he'd done it either, but his looks were more confusing than anything else. There was interest in his lingering gaze, but his stares were also dispassionate. It was like he was admiring a statue...No, not admiring. Studying. Simply looking at something pretty. There was appreciation but no real draw beyond general approval.

Sophia didn't entirely mind. He seemed harmless enough, and she'd gotten used to odd stares from Clecanians during the tour. Her humanness was interesting to people, especially men, who outnumbered women to such a staggering degree. She took a pointed, yet polite step away, and pretended to be interested in the delicate blue leaves decorating the enormous dressing mirror's frame.

"Sophia of Earth," he began slowly from behind her. She groaned inwardly. Any other time she might've been interested in an innocent flirtation with the handsome golden alien, but in light of her current predicament, getting involved with Alno felt like it would not be worth the fun. He was gorgeous, but nothing in her stirred at his presence. Not even when she spotted his fangs, which usually made her insides tingle.

She raised her palm to stop him. "Sophia is fine."

"Sophia," he corrected. "May I smell you?"

She tried not to let her shoulders slump. This wasn't the first time someone had asked to smell her, and if she lived much more of her life on Clecania, she knew it wouldn't be the last.

"I don't know if that's a good idea." Sophia caught her reflection in the mirror, and quite a reflection it was. She hadn't bathed since fighting her way through a battle and rolling around on the dusty floor. Her hair was a knotted mess. She could feel the deep ache of bruises all over her body, and she was positive her brain must be shielding her from what she must smell like. Suddenly, the dark confines of the covered bed were the only place she wanted to be.

"Maybe tomorrow after I've cleaned up?"

Something in him snapped at that. His body went loose, his hands swinging from behind his back, and his tail swiping across the floor. "It's just… If we're going to be together day in and day out as I am assigned to be…" He let out an enormous sigh. "The truth is that if I'm going to recognize you, I'd rather it be over and done with."

She raised a brow at that. "More romantic words have never been spoken," she teased gently.

Sophia couldn't blame him for being impatient. For hundreds of years, Clecanians had lost the ability to recognize their mate, the other half of their soul. But with the arrival of humans came a resurgence of recognition. If her potential soulmate were standing in front of her and all she had to do to know for sure that they were the one was smell them? Well, she'd probably go around sniffing after folks too.

He shot her a grin, and although it was a nervous one, it was remarkably charming. "I don't mean to insult you. You're very appealing," he said, giving her another once-over.

It helped her ego that his gaze held more of a wolfish hunger when he looked her over this time.

"It's just"—his smile became something a bit gooier than she was expecting—"there's a female I'm taken with. I have hope that she'll return my interest one day." His brows furrowed in renewed determination as he refocused on Sophia. "So, if you are to be my mate by some miracle, I'd rather know now so as not to prolong my pain."

"What is she like?" Sophia asked. As expected, the golden glow of his skin seemed to burn brighter. It was contagious. Her chest warmed in time with his growing smile.

"She's..." His gaze went a little hazy as he searched for words to describe the woman he was so clearly enamored with. "Blinding," he finished with a sigh.

The last few days had been grueling. Nonstop adrenaline pulsing through her body had left her jittery, exhausted, and defeated. She didn't know what was coming or where she'd be in the next month, and yet she couldn't help the wide grin that split across her face.

Sophia swept her hair over her shoulder and tipped her chin up. "Come on, then. Have a sniff."

4

Sikthand's tail scraped against the floor of the small passageway. Any louder and she'd hear.

For days now, he'd watched her, Sophia. She was different from the other aliens in her party. Odd. He'd noticed it the first time he'd seen the humans together. Where they'd frowned at the malginash and hesitantly eyed the metal facewear many of his people enjoyed wearing, she'd looked on with fascination.

When that vile insect, Maxu, had crept through his city and freed the humans he'd been holding as leverage, her group had fled. But *this* female, Sophia, had fought. Or so he'd been told. Sikthand had shown up just in time to ensure no one else escaped and managed to sever the rope Sophia had been climbing, sending her plummeting to the ground.

He watched her now through the false mirror that opened into her room. She was a mess. Thoroughly tumbled from the events of the last day, but underneath the dirt and grime, he could make out her slender frame and delicate pale skin. Pleasant to look at, but weak.

The accounts of her fighting must have been exaggerated. His commander was more willing to believe she had hidden talents, but Sikthand couldn't see it.

He drew his gaze down her body, searching for the telltale musculature needed to wield a Vrulan blade properly, but found only supple flesh and soft skin perfect for a warrior's calloused palms to caress. He shook away the thought, curling his fingers inward.

Sikthand didn't like things he didn't understand, especially people he didn't understand. Over his many long years, assassinations, betrayals, and slimy politicians motivated by self-interest had turned him into what many deemed paranoid. He preferred observant.

If you watched anyone long enough, you could learn who they were. And if you learned *that*, loyalty was simple. Everyone had soft spots. Trust could be purchased by exploiting those spots.

Sophia turned toward the mirror. She was close, fiddling with something on the frame.

Where are your soft spots?

Her dark lashes shielded her eyes as Alno prattled on behind her. Sikthand tried to convince himself her hoodless, pale face was dull and unpleasant but couldn't. Hood or not, she'd be pretty in any city, on any planet. Her lack of hood made her appear open, like she could be trusted. A dangerous characteristic, in Sikthand's opinion.

Her chapped lips pulled to the side as if she were annoyed with whatever Alno had just said. Her dark eyes flashed upward, and she examined her own reflection. Some unknown emotion had her mouth thinning, but it was gone before he could decipher it.

She turned away from the mirror at Alno's words, and Sikthand swayed forward. He hadn't had time to examine that reaction when the chaperone's question hit his brain. The golden fuck had asked to smell her.

Sikthand stepped closer to the glass, fury rising under his skin like electricity. It wasn't that he cared if the human was recognized by some male, but if she was, she'd become less useful as a bargaining chip. In fact, she'd become *expensive*.

He'd have to pay some unknown price to keep her here, or risk the revolt that would surely ensue if a king sent away a mated female.

She faced Alno and declined. Sikthand hummed out his approval. She'd shown little warmth to any Vrulan since her capture. *Surely, she'll send Alno off now*, he argued silently.

But then...she smiled. Smiled at the pretty male as he opined over some female who likely didn't know he existed. Sikthand shouldn't care.

A growl froze in his throat as she flicked her hair over her shoulder, flashing the pale column of her neck. His fangs pulsed. Gods, he'd been too long without a female if this was his reaction to a glimpse of skin.

Alno crossed to her with a little too much enthusiasm for Sikthand's taste. He'd have the male sent to the mines at the earliest opportunity.

His golden nose dipped to Sophia's throat, brushing against her skin. Her lashes gave a little flutter as if she'd liked the touch. Sikthand bared his fangs. His tail flicked over the ground.

Step away, he silently commanded. Alno remained in place, breathing deeply against her neck. Sikthand inched closer to the mirror, his trapped growl reverberating in his throat.

The male lifted one hand to her bicep. Sikthand's toes hit the glass. He studied Alno's hand. No mating marks appeared on his skin. She wasn't his fated mate, yet he continued to leisurely breathe in her scent.

His mind played through all the ways he could punish the male. He'd start by learning which female Alno drooled over and bedding her.

When Sophia's brows drew together with uncertainty, as if she wanted to pull away, Sikthand's hand lifted to the latch that would swing the mirror open, revealing the passage he'd kept secret for all these years.

The reminder of his advantage stopped him in his tracks. Even before he'd detained the Tremantian group, he'd found his attention pulled toward Sophia at every opportunity. Something about her was dangerous. He didn't yet know why, but his instincts were telling him to take notice. To keep his guard up and study the human.

He'd only ever ignored those instincts once.

Ice slid into his gut. *Never again.*

This human was interesting to him. But just like all interesting things, the fascination would fade in time. All he had to do was wait and watch.

Sikthand would study her from the comfort of the shadows. She might seem harmless, but in his experience, those who seemed the most harmless had the most potent venom.

5

Sophia could think of few worse feelings than that of being excruciatingly tired yet too anxious to sleep. After Alno had said goodnight, hands free of any marks of recognition, and promised to be back early the next morning, she'd crawled into bed, dirty clothes and all.

She thought she'd drift directly to sleep, but no. The door that connected her room to Sikthand's taunted her. Through the opening to her enclosed bed, the door was still visible. In order to keep it in sight, she had to lie on her back, but lying on her back was just painful enough to keep her from sleeping.

After testing the bolt twice, she tried lying on her side. It was comfortable, but the door's out-of-sight existence made her skin crawl.

Finally, she decided that perhaps her grimy skin and knotted hair were getting in the way of her fully relaxing. She slipped into the bathroom, ran herself a bath, and came close to falling asleep in the tub. After much cursing, she dragged herself out of the warm water and nearly broke down in tears when she couldn't find a towel.

Her lids drooped as she dragged a comb through her slippery hair. The scrape against her scalp felt so good she shivered and moaned. Worries about what she should do kept creeping into her consciousness, but she shoved them down, burying them before her throat grew too tight.

There was no use in thinking about that right now. All she could do was plan one day at a time, and she already had her goal for tomorrow. She'd visit Heleax in the dungeons. He deserved to know what was going on. Apart from that, she also longed to see a familiar face.

She picked through the clothes Alno had left for her until she found a silky sleeping gown. Before putting it on, though, she decided it would be best to rip off the Band-Aid and see the damage she'd done to her body. One eye trained on the door, she padded over to the large mirror, stark naked.

There were some bruises marring her hips and legs. A bad one bloomed across her shoulder from when she'd fallen over in the chair. Two bands of red ringed her wrists. But all in all, the injuries looked manageable.

If portable healers worked here, she could use one of those, but if not, it wouldn't take too long for these to heal on their own. Before looking at her back, she took a long breath.

She turned, and her heart sank. Her back was black and blue. Battered and swollen, especially near her tailbone. "Shit," she hissed.

This was bad. She wondered if she might have bruised or broken something but was too nervous to confront that possibility. The idea of asking to be taken to a doctor made her insides rebel. Even thinking of the unnaturally powerful healing tube induced a spike of anxiety.

Maybe it was just bad now. Perhaps the swelling would go down after she had a good night's rest. No one's body could heal under these conditions, after all.

Set on ignoring the problem unless it became worse, she forced herself to eat a bit more of the food Alno had left for her, then grabbed two glass bottles and carefully tilted them against each of the doors in her room. If anyone tried to open a door while she was asleep, the bottle would fall over.

She wouldn't be able to do much to stop whoever came in from hurting her if they wanted, but at least she'd have a warning. Content with her booby traps, she crawled back into bed and fell asleep almost instantly.

***

Shattering glass had Sophia bolting awake. It took her several moments to remember where she was, but when she did, her eyes zoomed to the ornate door across the room. The fiery orange bottle remained propped against the wood. She ripped her blankets off, scrambling forward on her knees to check the other bottle, and shrieked when Alno popped into view in front of the entrance to her bed.

"What the hell!" She clutched at her thundering heart, willing it to slow.

"I could say the same." Alno's eyes were wide and worried. "There was glass in front of your door. Why didn't you answer? I've been knocking for ages. I finally let myself in to make sure you hadn't thrown yourself out a window."

Sophia mumbled a reply as pain lanced through her back. She winced and gripped the bedding.

"What?" Alno questioned, clearly annoyed.

Sophia glared up at him. "They. Don't. Open." She whipped a hand toward the windows and shooed him away so she could climb out of bed. "I checked them last night. Not to *throw myself out*," she added, rolling her eyes. "Just…to see." Sophia didn't mention that in her sleep-deprived mind she'd wondered if she could fashion a rope out of her sheets. A brainless thought, considering they were thousands of feet in the air.

"Oh," he said. "Well, here. I brought you some food. Unless you'd like to go to a dining hall to—"

The smell of fresh bread hit her nose, and she made a grab for the tray.

"We could try eating with everyone during the evening meal?" he offered as Sophia shoved a hunk of sweet bread in her mouth.

When she was able to swallow, she said, "I'd prefer to eat in here if it's all the same."

Alno settled into a chair nearby and sipped from a cup of his own. "I think it would be good for you to mingle."

"Good for who?" She snorted. One look at his pursed lips gave her an answer. "Oh. I get it. It would be good for *you*. 'Cause you could see your girlfriend that way, right?"

Alno didn't answer, but his shoulders tensed. She grinned over the top of her bread.

"Tell you what—if you help me out and answer my questions, I'll go eat in the upper dining hall with you tonight. Deal?"

A smile broke over his face. "Deal." He rose from his seat, tail swinging behind him merrily. "My job is to do just that anyway. What shall I help you with today?"

"I want to go see Heleax."

Alno's face fell. Before he could backtrack, Sophia scrambled into the bathroom and started getting ready. Annoyed mutters floated to her from the other side of the door. When she was dressed, she pulled it open and left it ajar while rubbing the sleep from her eyes. "What can you tell me about the Guild? And where the hell are the towels?"

Alno casually depressed an area of the wall, and a cabinet opened, revealing piles of fluffy towels. Sophia frowned and griped mostly to herself, "Cabinetry so integrated you don't even know it exists. Cool, cool, cool."

She dug through the cosmetics he'd provided, surprised to find they were more similar to Earth makeup than the cosmetic stamping machines most Clecanians used. Perhaps, like a majority of electronics, those machines didn't work here. The magnetic askait ore Vrulatica had been built on ensured very few electronic devices worked within the city.

Alno leaned against the doorway of the bathroom as she experimented with the makeup. "What do you want to know?"

She frowned at her reflection. The pink she'd put on her cheeks had disappeared into nothing. *Not blush, then.* "I don't know." She shrugged. *Do any of the guildmembers have power, and can I get them to outvote the king and let me go?* "How is the Guild organized? Were they voted in, or did they inherit their positions? I know the king's role is inherited."

"They are elected. Each guildmember is the head of the sacred six: the people, the law, money, defense, trade, and the mines. Speaker Besith is the head of the people. He sees to their needs and to Vrulan infrastructure."

"He's the one who appointed you, correct? Black beard? Looks like he just drank sour milk?"

"That'll be him." Alno smothered a laugh. "Magistrate Yalmi oversees our legal system. She also manages the archives and works closely with Commander Roldroth, who is the head of our armies and our riders."

"Commander Copperhead," Sophia muttered while trying and failing to open a long silver tube. She gave up, tossing the object back into a drawer. "What about the guy who wore plain clothing?" Sophia eyed the metalwork crossing back and forth over Alno's chest and tail, along with the many pieces of jewelry he sported. "He...stood out."

"Ah, that's the head of finance, Master Bavo. It's tradition for the head of money to live a life of meager means. Those with a penchant for expensive things aren't usually elected to his position, though Master Bavo cares even less about his appearance than his predecessors." Alno leaned in, a conspiratorial glint in his warm golden eyes. "I've heard he has a penchant for fine food, though. Spends a fortune importing delicacies from Gulaid."

"Scandalous." Sophia grinned. She caught her altogether unaltered appearance in the mirror and grumbled, "Why did I bother?"

"Who am I missing?" Alno wondered aloud, stepping in front of Sophia and tipping her chin up. He swiped a product from the drawer and went to work, applying color to her face.

She'd never had anyone else do her makeup before. Her grandmother hadn't worn it, and once she'd learned on her own, she was too picky to let anyone else near her. She held in a grimace and kept still.

"Oh, lovely little Lady Lindri. That's right. She runs the mines and oversees the metalworkers, though she'd much rather be tinkering with machines. Madame Kalos can be heard complaining all the way to the sky when she has to hunt Lindri down in the mines. They work closely, you see, as metal is our main export and Madam Kalos is our head of trade. Might as well be the head of buttons with the amount of time Lady Lindri gives her."

"Doesn't like her or something?" Sophia closed her eyes as Alno brushed something on her temples, one tongue glued to a fang in concentration.

"She thinks the madam pushes the miners too hard, always wanting more. More goods. More prestige. More respect for our city. Neither is wrong, but their goals are not aligned, to say the least." His mouth curled to the side. "I've done what I can, but I've never applied makeup to someone without a hood before. I realize now the colors I chose for you are not quite right."

Her head tipped to the side when she peered at her reflection. The makeup was interesting. Not bad, just...interesting. Rather than accentuate her eyes and the apples of her cheeks like she normally did, deep color had been brushed over her features in such a way as to brighten the center of her face. The way one might for a hood, she realized.

"So does the king have final say over the Guild?" Sophia asked while slipping on some sturdy shoes. She ignored the throbbing pain in her back that was frustratingly *not* getting better.

"For the most part. If the Guild comes to a unanimous decision that opposes the king, they have the power to override him, but it's rare *that* group agrees on anything."

She slipped on another boot and found him openly ogling her ass. "Hey! Aren't you supposed to be in love with what's-her-name?"

Alno grinned, morphing into a damn ray of sunlight. "I'm in love but not blind."

"Yeah, yeah. Just save that charm for her, alright?"

"If only," he groaned as he followed her out of the bathroom and then her room, locking the door behind them as they made their way out of the royal wing. "I become a mute idiot whenever I think about talking to her. She's always surrounded by her damn squad. I'd need to tail whip my way through just to get to her."

"Squad?" A group of Vrulans eyed her curiously as they approached from the other direction. Their gazes turned critical as they took in the simple outfit she'd picked. Alno had given her buckets of metal accessories to deck herself out with the way everyone else did, but she hadn't cared enough to rummage through them. Getting to Heleax was her only concern.

"The group of cloud chasers she rides with," Alno explained.

As they meandered down through the city toward the dungeons, he clarified the differences between cloud chasers and warriors. As far as she could tell, all cloud chasers, also called riders, were warriors, but not all warriors were riders. Grueling years of specialized training separated the elite cloud chasers and earned them respect throughout the city.

At this time of year, there were no storms on the horizon and no incursions in the Choke. Clusters of cloud chasers mingled around Vrulatica, drinking and socializing. Sophia studied them as covertly as she could while Alno guided her down through the city. They were all decked out in armor and leather like the king.

Was it a fashion statement? Or were they always prepared to fly off into storms at a moment's notice? Either way, Sophia marveled at the artistry and detail of their outfits.

Chain draped through hair. Forged golden hand bones affixed to the tops of gloves.

As they moved farther groundward, she wondered if she could get away with wearing outfits like that here. She'd just be a weak human playing dress-up amid a city of warriors who actually protected Vrulatica. They'd probably laugh her into tears if her puny ass tried to copy their style. Too bad. Sophia loved dressing up.

To her surprise, the dungeons were not below ground like she'd imagined. They weren't even low in the city. Rather, they spanned almost seven floors and hung, suspended in the core of highcity. Lifts that traveled from the very top of Vrulatica to the ground flew right by the dungeon levels. Only one stopped. And it was heavily guarded.

When Sophia and Alno stepped into the dungeon entrance, they were greeted by ten guards armed to the teeth with blades. Sophia swallowed. She'd always imagined a dungeon to be cold and damp. Maybe with some rats scurrying around. But the dungeons of Vrulatica were much worse.

It was sweltering and dry, like a sauna. Curved metal walls devoid of the extravagant designs that graced every other surface in Vrulatica made the entry chamber resemble the inside of a large cauldron.

"We're here to visit the Tremantian prisoner," Alno explained.

Weren't they boiling in all that armor? Sophia eyed the covered guards and pulled at her thin fabric collar. If the air weren't so dry, she'd be covered in sweat. As it was, any moisture that rose on her skin evaporated almost immediately. Why the fuck had Alno not warned her? She'd picked a long-sleeved top and pants to hide the bruises marring her skin, but if she'd known this awaited her, she'd have said to hell with covering up.

"We weren't told of any visitors," a muffled voice croaked out from one of the guards, but she couldn't tell which one had spoken since they all wore helmets.

"You don't need prior notice to visit someone here," Alno challenged.

A dark iron-plated guard stepped forward, a blade clinking at his back. "Rules are different for detainees. He hasn't been tried. Not an official—"

The air in the room shifted. Cooled. As if the faintest breeze had rolled through. The hair on the back of her neck rose.

As one, the guards' postures straightened. Though she couldn't tell for sure, they seemed to be staring not at her, but behind her. She spun and stumbled back a step.

King Sikthand stood an arm's length away, menacing and silent. How had he gotten so close before anyone noticed? Where had he come from?

His blazing stare bore into her from beneath his slitted mask. "Come with me."

"What…I…" Sophia shook off the shock from his sudden appearance and lifted her chin. "I'm here to visit Heleax."

Tense silence stretched between them. Faint clinking behind her told her the soldiers fidgeted as much as she wanted to. "Come with me today, and I'll allow you to see him tomorrow."

"Couldn't I go now?" She glanced behind her helplessly. "I'm already here, and—"

"Tomorrow or not at all, human."

Sophia's jaw tensed at his dictatorial tone. From behind Sikthand, Alno gave a nearly imperceptible shake of his head. Swallowing her rising arguments was like gulping down a knot of bees, but she managed to hold her tongue and silently nod her assent. Without a word, he entered the lift, waited for her to step in behind him, then slid the door shut before Alno could join them.

She hadn't noticed on their way down, but the space in the lift was small. Too small. Perhaps it was the lingering effects of the dungeon, but breathing felt harder than normal. She flattened herself against the wall, trying to put some space between herself and the enormous man planted in the center of the lift like he owned the place.

He does *own the place,* she grumbled to herself. The reminder set her teeth on edge.

"Can I ask where we're going, Your Majesty?"

The antlers of his helmet glinted as he turned his head. He eyed her over his shoulder. "To see a medic."

A medic? Her back had been killing her all day, but she hadn't told anyone. She cleared her throat. "Uh, thank you, but I don't need to see a medic." The image of the tube popped into her head, and suddenly she didn't feel warm anymore.

"I'd like to ensure you're checked out anyway," he rumbled. "If reports of you fighting were true, you may have lingering injuries you're not aware of."

The lift stopped abruptly, and her back bumped against the wall, sending a bolt of pain through her. *Oh, I'm aware.*

Sophia followed the king, trying not to drag her feet. Would it be too obvious if she pretended to stop and tie her shoe? If she stalled long enough, maybe he'd be called away and she could avoid the awkward series of events that were sure to occur.

If he found out she'd hurt herself as badly as she had, he'd certainly question why she hadn't mentioned it sooner, and there was no part of her that wanted to dive into her irrational fear of healing tubes today. She especially didn't want to explore that particular trauma with the formidable king. He'd probably think she was pathetic. Hell, *she* thought she was pathetic.

Who in their right mind would be terrified of a tube that could heal almost anything in a matter of seconds? Not even the few humans she'd tried to explain her fears to had understood. They couldn't fathom why she was so scared of something she'd never experienced.

It was a fair point. Sophia hadn't been conscious during her healing. She hadn't even known it was happening. She'd fallen asleep on Earth and awoken altered.

If anyone was to blame, it was the people who'd abducted her and the specific doctor who'd healed an unconscious, non-consenting woman. But they were faceless shadows, and for want of someone specific to blame, her anxiety had latched on to the only solid thing it could. The device that had changed her. Violated her.

The power this irrational fear had over her was embarrassing, but what was even worse was that she'd have no way of hiding it. No way of putting on a brave face and tricking the king into believing she was fine. Clecanians had a sense of smell far surpassing humans, and fear was an emotion they could scent. The closer they got to this doctor, the more she'd stink.

Her shoulders slumped. This would be mortifying.

The king led her back to the wing they both inhabited, and then to the left instead of the right. Tingles raced down her scalp as she followed. This was *his* side of the wing. Though no one had told her so, the area felt forbidden.

This side looked the same as hers except for a set of stairs winding into the ceiling. She hesitated at the foot of the steps, watching the king climb upward and disappear from view. Whatever was up there was loud.

Be brave, be brave, be brave. She forced her feet to move.

When she reached the landing, she froze. A malginash, enormous and intimidating, sat in a cavernous space in front of a wide arched opening that led into the sky. The source of the roaring became clear, and her stomach dropped.

It was the wind.

Miles and miles in the air, the wind was brutal. If she stood too close to that opening, one powerful gust would be all it took to send her free-falling thousands of feet from the top of the Vertical City. Her focus zoomed to the malginash as it stretched its spotted wings.

She was afraid—terrified, really—yet she couldn't help but let out a breath of wonder. "You're so beautiful," she crooned, grinning at the malginash who blinked its wide, cloudy eyes at her. "Look at those wings and those horns." The malginash started making a low clicking sound. Did that mean it liked her, or was it a warning?

Sophia kept herself glued to the wall while venturing farther from the stairs. She scanned the space for Sikthand, and her mind blanked for a different reason.

He'd divested himself of his armor. All of it.

"What are you doing?" She tried to keep her voice even, but it was difficult. She was less shocked by his face this time, but no less enthralled. Seeing him without his mask was one thing, but seeing him without any protective gear made her brain short-circuit. How was it possible he looked *larger* without armor on?

Before, she could pretend he was a frail, flabby sack of flesh under piles of metal. She eyed the bulging muscles of his arms and chest, the truth of how perfectly he was built all but smacking her in the face.

"The infirmary is located across the desert. Far enough that the askait ore won't interfere with their machines. We'll need to fly."

When Sophia gave him a blank look, he motioned to her back. "I saw you fall during your escape attempt, and you've been walking stiffly. I'd be surprised if there was no damage to your back. You'll need to ride with me, and I'd rather not injure you further by forcing you to lean against my armor."

"Thank you. That…" Her voice died out. Was it thoughtful? Yes. Right? She couldn't quite put her finger on it, but there was something tugging at her brain, keeping her from believing he was only thinking of her safety and comfort. Was she so intent on disliking him that she couldn't even accept a kind gesture?

"You are a *delicate bargaining chip* after all." He repeated her words from the night before, and she frowned.

With a wave of his hand, the malginash followed the king as he strode toward her. The click-clack of its nails on the stone made goose bumps rise on her skin.

"It'll be cold." He handed her a blood red cloak, and she slipped it on. The malginash knelt, and before Sophia could stop him, Sikthand had swept her up and deposited her onto the wide, cushioned saddle. She braced for a belated slice of pain, but none came. He'd somehow managed to get her up here without touching her bruised lower back.

Her breath caught as he slid in behind her. She'd been wrong—he didn't smell like *nothing*. He smelled delicious. Bright yet complex. Like leather and mist. It was so distracting, she almost forgot what they were about to do.

The malginash rose, lifting them at least seven feet off the ground. "Wait, I..." Her gaze zoomed around frantically. What could she hold?

Sikthand's arms circled in front of her and gripped the malginash's reins. The animal clicked. "Does that mean it's excited or angry?" she shrieked over the mounting bellow of the wind. Her nails scraped over the smooth leather saddle, but she couldn't find a secure spot. *I'm about to plummet into the sky, and I have nothing to hold on to.*

"She," the king corrected in a bellow. The open sky bloomed before her as the malginash stalked forward.

Sophia and Sikthand weren't touching. There was enough room in the saddle for both to sit with a few inches separating them. But as the sight of the earth far below came into view, all notions of personal space evaporated. She plastered herself against the king's front, wrapping both arms up and around his biceps, and turned her face toward his chest.

Her breathing was panicked, her heart galloping. As the malginash took its first step out of the king's landing bay, her stomach bottomed out.

6

Sikthand allowed Ahea to fall slightly longer than he normally would before guiding her wings to spread. An unbidden purr had risen in his chest when the human pressed herself into him, gripping his arms with all her might. He'd been forced to concoct some distraction so she wouldn't notice his reaction.

Vrulan females weren't typically this panicky, or if they were, their pride kept it hidden. They'd sooner dive out of a tower window than cling to a male like this. He didn't know why the action sent electricity to his groin, only that it did. Perhaps it was a remnant of the heat that had coursed through him last night.

He hadn't meant to look at her body. He'd returned to his room after watching her crawl into bed. Unable to sleep, he lay there, his mind churning over whether she'd decide to do something stupid like sneak out of her room. Finally, he'd dragged himself out of bed. Just to make sure she was still there. But when he'd arrived at the mirror, she was gone.

He'd been a breath away from storming out, calling for guards, and tearing apart every inch of Vrulatica to find her, but then she'd emerged from the bathroom glistening and naked. Sikthand would like to think that if he hadn't been taken by surprise, he could've looked away. He wasn't some wretch who used the many passages throughout Vrulatica to spy on unsuspecting females at their most vulnerable.

But he'd been frozen.

A beam of silver moonlight had lit her curves, particles of glittering dust dancing around her, and the world had slowed.

Sikthand hadn't watched her. Suspended in time, he'd *beheld* her. A goddess carved from the moon itself.

Even if she left tomorrow and he never saw her face again, that vision of her would live with him until the day he joined the sky.

Then her eyes had connected with his, nearly leveling him. When he'd finally remembered where he was—and that she was not looking at him but at her own reflection in the mirror—his chest had constricted.

It'd ripped him out of his stupor, and he'd forced himself to take a step back. His body had rebelled, but he'd known if he could make himself move away one step, then two, he'd also be capable of tearing his gaze from her.

But then she'd swept her long hair, black as the night sky, over her shoulder, presenting him with her back. As if the gods themselves were testing him, he'd managed to keep the rising growl from escaping his throat.

It was as though someone had taken a hammer to her spine. Ugly bruises marred her perfect body. They were everywhere. Her arms. Her wrists. Her shoulder. Sikthand had been wounded many times over his long life. He knew what injuries like hers must feel like. Bad enough that the pain lived close, stayed in your mind at all hours of the day, but not bad enough to kill you.

Why hadn't she said anything? His anger had flared, his tail scraping loudly, and he'd fled down the passageway before she could hear him.

Now, as she held on to him for dear life, he found himself not thinking her weak, but reasonable. Humans were impossible creatures. So fucking beautiful, yet so easy to break. When he'd sliced that rope she'd been climbing, causing her to fall, he'd known it would leave a bruise, but he'd never imagined it would be *that* bad.

This distracting human needed to stay breathing until the new leader of Tremanta came to power and he could off-load her on them. Until then, he'd need to watch her to make sure she didn't kill herself while doing something innocuous, like tripping down the stairs.

Sikthand breathed in the bright air and tried to ignore the way her slender frame fit within his arms. Would her small nails also dig into his biceps if he buried himself in her pretty body?

He dashed the thought from his mind.

Ahea caught a smooth air current, pulling them into a gentle glide, and Sophia finally pulled her face away from his chest. Her knuckles grew white as she gazed at the sky around her. It was a clear day. The sun beat down on them, but the wind carried away its heat.

She peered back at him, her lips almost curling into a smile. In her eyes, he could see how badly she wanted to trust him. How badly she wanted to be able to enjoy flying without fearing he'd let her fall. His tail tightened around his saddle's aft-grip.

As if he'd let her fall.

Transferring the reins into one hand, he dragged his other arm out of her iron grip. She scratched at his wrist, a bitter spike of fear permeating the fresh air, but settled when he slipped his forearm around her waist, cementing her against his front.

Her head dipped in the direction of his hold. Would she ask him to remove his arm? After a moment, her shaking fingers inched upward. Her whole body vibrated with fear, but she lifted her hand into the air, trying to hold it steady against the wind. When she reached as high as her arm would allow, she spread her fingers and beamed.

Ahea could have flown faster, but Sikthand found himself taking his time. She dipped out of a wind current a little too quickly, making them drop a few feet before gliding smoothly again. Sophia shrieked at the drop, then burst out with adrenaline-spiked laughter. The sound was so joyful, so free. He found himself surreptitiously guiding his mount out of air currents less smoothly than he might have otherwise. It felt like no time at all had gone by when the infirmary came into view.

They landed with a slight lurch, Ahea's talons scraping over the rusty sandstone ground. Sikthand dismounted first, then grabbed Sophia, careful to lift her so as not to cause her pain.

She vibrated in his grasp. Windswept locks of hair frizzed around her temples, and a wide grin transformed her features.

With a shaking hand, she gently patted Ahea's flank. "Thank you for the flight. You were wonderful." A smile pulled at Sikthand's lips, but he held it back as she faced him again.

Her skin was red, chapped from the wind and sun. His joy faded. Damn her delicate human body.

"I have everything ready, sire." The head medic, Vezel, hurried out from a set of stairs that dipped underground where the majority of the infirmary was located.

The grin melted from Sophia's face, and a sour note of fear tinged the hot air. He'd smelled it before—every time he'd come near her, in fact—but he had the distinct impression he hadn't caused it this time.

A sinking dread suffused Sikthand as Sophia looked to him as if for comfort, and his chest warmed.

No. Not again.

He couldn't afford for this ember of curious affection to burn any brighter.

To care is to suffer.

This lesson had broken him many times over, and he refused to let it happen again. Hardening himself, he frowned. "My time is not infinite, human."

Her gaze dropped to the ground, but he refused to speculate as to why. Whether she was embarrassed or hurt or merely had a bit of sand in her eye, his tone had worked as he'd wanted. The trust from a few moments ago was gone, and when she met his eyes again, her expression was guarded. She nodded solemnly, then walked toward the building.

An emotion—not grief exactly, but something related—made his jaw clench. He followed her into the infirmary.

The scent of her fear intensified the farther into the cool building they ventured. Vezel's nose curled. The medic glanced back to Sikthand, brows raised in a silent question. He shook his head. Sikthand had no idea what was making her so terrified, and he didn't care.

"Don't like flying?" Vezel tried, speaking to Sophia with a practiced smile in place on his pale silver face.

"Don't like doctors," she replied stiffly. "No offense." She aimed an awkward smile toward Vezel as they reached an exam room. She pointed into the dimly lit room, gaze resolutely remaining forward. "And I especially don't like that." Vezel and Sikthand followed the line of her finger. She was pointing at a medical tube, the device used across the planet to keep the dwindling Clecanian species alive and healthy.

That machine was the reason the infirmary and the rest of the many outbuildings had to be built so far away from

Vrulatica. The magnetic charge of the ore Vrulatica had been built upon made using any electronics within city limits both dangerous and pointless.

Though confusion was clear in Vezel's bronze eyes, he didn't question her. "You may not need that level of healing," he assured instead.

Sophia's guilty gaze slipped to Sikthand. "I think I will," she muttered.

"How about we take a look?"

Eyes wide, lips thinned into nothing, she shuffled into the exam room behind the medic. Almost at once, the air clouded with her pungent fear.

His duty ended at keeping her alive and healthy. There was nothing to fear here. She was safe whether or not she believed it.

She's not for me to concern myself with.

"I'd like to be seen to first, Vezel." The words poured out of him without his permission. *Fuck.*

Sikthand didn't bother hiding his scowl as he stepped into the exam room. When the human released a relieved exhale, his irritation doubled.

***

The tips of her fingers were numb, every centimeter of skin tingling. Though the entitled behavior of the king should make her want to roll her eyes, she didn't mind his demand to be seen first. She was grateful for it.

"I'll just wait out here." Freedom was only a few steps away.

Before she could move, the king activated the door, shutting her in with both men and the tube from hell. The king pushed past her, ignoring her longing gaze fixed on the smooth metal door.

"I'll need some time in the tube," he commented mildly.

With a sigh, she lifted her chin. *Might as well warm up to seeing the healing tube in action.*

The king's glowing eyes were already locked on hers as she forced herself to face the room. A slice of his muscular torso flashed into view when the king pulled his shirt free from his pants, and Sophia swallowed.

Awkwardly, she cleared her throat and slipped her gaze to the ceiling. "Oh, sorry."

"Calm, female. It's only flesh," was his growled response.

She did roll her eyes at that. Luckily, they were still pointed toward the ceiling, so she doubted anyone noticed. It was like every little thing she did irritated him.

Have a fun time flying on the malginash? Childish. Hesitate to follow an alien doctor underground? Ridiculous. Try to give him some privacy while he undresses? Prudish. If she bothered him so much, why not just let her wait outside?

The doctor's gaze bounced between them, also seeming confused as to why she was there.

Wait. Was he… Sophia shook off the thought before it fully formed. No, he couldn't be forcing her to watch him get healed to ease her fears. That was preposterous.

And yet…

The memory of the strong band of his arm locking her in place as they flew popped into her head. At the time, she'd just assumed it was a precaution to keep her from falling, but... Had he done it to make her feel less frightened?

He pulled his shirt over his head, and she shuddered. An enormous, sickening bruise marred his right side. He kept his right arm lifted at shoulder height, allowing Vezel close. "Bruzuk landed a couple good hits a few days ago," he rumbled by way of explanation.

A few days ago? Why hadn't he come earlier? Sophia looked on in horror.

"Yes, he came to see us that day." The doctor glanced up at the king nervously for a split second. "Seems you got some good hits in yourself. Perhaps a few *too* many."

Sikthand lowered his arm, his expression shuttering. "He celebrated too long. Finally got one good kick in and dropped his guard. Better he learns to keep vigilant from me than end up dead while fighting a feral Tagion." His glowing gaze cut to Sophia. "The lesson only sticks if it hurts."

"Indeed." The doctor's lips thinned disapprovingly.

Sophia couldn't fault his logic, but a tendril of unease slipped down her spine hearing how interchangeable *lesson* and *beating* seemed to be to the king. She had to remember that even among Clecanian standards, Vrulatica was a harsh city.

She supposed having a healing machine that could fix a broken arm in a matter of minutes would make training warriors a more brutal endeavor. Why describe a consequence when you could experience it and be back in fighting shape the next day? That must be why the king didn't so much as wince when the doctor prodded his purple ribs. At what point did one grow *that* used to pain?

The glass dome of the healing tube slid open, and Sophia stumbled back a step. She tried to play it off as though she was finding a more comfortable spot to lean against the wall, but judging from the scrutinizing furrows of their brows, she'd fooled no one.

They can smell the fear, idiot. The back of her neck flamed in embarrassment.

She held her breath as Sikthand climbed into the healing tube and settled. His body was a work of art, literally. If she had to guess, she'd say the black geometric designs covering him were not birthmarks, as some other Clecanian races had, but tattoos drawn using the unique magnetic ink native to Vrulatica.

Thick bands, narrow stripes, and solidly inked sections of muscle covered his torso. It reminded her of some blackwork tattoos she'd seen back home, except more dramatic. The precision of every line, the level of saturation, and the severe contrast to his ghostly white skin created a striking image.

The fact that the tattoos covered a powerful body, heavy with muscle, made them that much more appealing. The symmetry was excellent as well. Either the artist who'd drawn them was incredibly talented, or the king had the proportional perfection of the Vitruvian man.

A scroll of Clecanian writing running down his left pec disrupted the symmetry, and she frowned at it.

Inching closer and squinting, she tried to read the word. She could make out a few letters, but she'd never been good with vowels. The first two symbols might sound like *Ja*, though she didn't trust her memory enough to be sure. She tried to burn the writing into her mind so she could look it up later.

The machine whirred to life. Her pulse spiked, but as she tried to temper her fear, she realized she'd ventured within a few feet of the healing tube and, up until a second ago, hadn't noticed its proximity. Forcing her feet to remain planted, she scrutinized the tube suspiciously, tensing as millions of minuscule beams of light scanned his body.

"It looks like a cracked rib," the doctor explained while peering into a screen with scrolling script. "Do I have your permission to mend the rib and the bruising?"

She breathed out a sigh of relief at hearing this.

"Fix the rib, not the bruising. I don't have time to rework my design."

"What does that mean?" Sophia whispered to the doctor.

"The machine wants to fix all damaged layers, and it registers the ink as an intrusion. He'd rather keep his design intact and live with the bruise." At his words, the nausea churning in her gut settled.

This conversation felt unremarkable. A discussion that patients and doctors had every day. There was no way for either man to know how much this was helping her. By the time it was Sophia's turn to get examined, the terror making her worry she'd either vomit on herself or faint had dulled to a simmering dread and become something manageable.

Without a word, the king pulled on his shirt, eyed her for a moment, then exited the exam room. She wished he hadn't, even if that meant he'd witness her get undressed and see the severity of the injury she'd been trying to hide.

Her knees wobbled and her heart beat in her throat when she crawled into the tube, but she was able to grind her teeth and breathe deeply through the worst of her panic. The doctor winced while explaining her tailbone had been bruised.

It took a few tries to force her consent to heal past her teeth. Apart from fixing her tailbone, they only needed to mend some scrapes. Before she knew it, she was out and feeling like a new woman.

She hadn't quite realized how furtively she'd been moving until she could walk without tension. Her spine was a bit straighter too. Not only because the machine had helped align it, but from pride.

She smiled to herself as she thanked the doctor and made her way outside into the desert heat. *I did it.*

And whether he'd done so purposefully or not, the king had helped her. She wondered at his motives once more, but couldn't make up her mind. Was he observant and kind? Cold and duty-bound?

Sikthand stood outside near his mount. He ran his elegant fingers down the malginash's forehead and used his tail to scratch behind the creature's ear. The monster's eyes drooped, and warmth bloomed in Sophia's chest.

He was confounding, this alien king.

7

A prison guard led Sophia and Alno down a cramped stairway that branched off through a maze of halls. She was back in the dungeon, wearing proper clothing this time. Alno had stocked her closet with traditional Vrulan garb, but he'd had to convince her to wear it. At first glance, the thick fabric and heavy metal ornamentation seemed like an unthinkable option for the sweltering dungeon. She was grateful she'd listened to him now.

The inner lining of Vrulan clothing reacted to body temperature, keeping its wearer cool or warm despite the temperature of the air outside. She could only imagine how helpful that would be when riders flew through frigid storms, then landed in the blazing desert just beyond the mountain range to the north.

Even her short flight the day before had been freezing, despite the cloak the king had given her.

She shook the memory away, something she'd had to do frequently over the last day. On their flight back from the medic, she'd wanted him to pull her in again. A curious part of her wanted to experience being clasped in his hold without the pain from her injury muddling the sensation of his body. After all, it wasn't every day a girl had a perfectly reasonable excuse to rub up to a muscular alien king.

He was handsome in a way that had snuck up on her. And he was captivating, drawing eyes in every room he occupied. Whenever he was around, she couldn't help but stare. Unfortunately, he'd been a ghost since they'd landed back in the royal wing, and she itched to see his face again.

Straightening her spine, she reminded herself why she was here. It was *not* to daydream about the man who was literally holding her hostage. She had bigger fish to fry.

The guard directed them to a glass section of wall, and as Sophia got her first look at Heleax, her dislike of the king roared back to life.

He wasn't completely naked, but nearly. His skin was flushed, and sweat coated him, making his hair stringy and damp.

"Sophia." He shot up from the cot he'd been sitting on.

"What are they doing to you?" she hissed, noting the way his breathing deepened as if he'd just done a round of push-ups rather than taken a few steps toward the glass.

His brows knit before he noticed her horrified stare running over his body, chapped lips, and pinkened skin. "Nothing. Nothing. I'm fine. They keep it warm to make sure we're dehydrated. Makes prisoners less inclined to try to run away, knowing we might pass out before making it up the stairs."

"It's cruel!" Sophia spat. "What about heat stroke? You could die." She craned her neck and glared at the guard, but he was lost in his own world, staring at the ground, gaze far away. Was this so common it bored him? She grimaced.

Heleax grinned, dragging a chair from the corner of the room over to the glass and slumping into it. "They monitor us," he said, waving his hand, which had a blinking bracelet attached to it. "Keep us hydrated and healthy enough. It's more of an annoyance than anything else."

This was intolerable. "But you didn't even do anything wrong! You shouldn't be treated like any other prisoner. Just wait. When the Queen..." Her voice died out. There was no Queen anymore. At least not the one Sophia had known. She watched for his reaction to her slip.

Please don't let me be the one to deliver the news.

His grin faded. "They told me." His voice came out in a whisper, brows drawing downward.

"I'm so sorry." Sophia shook her head, the swell of sympathy burying her outrage. However upset *she* might be about the Queen, was nothing compared to what Heleax must be feeling. "Are you okay?"

He expelled a humorless laugh. "No. Pretty fucking far from it. I need to get back to Tremanta. Have you heard anything from anyone? Daunet? Did our group make it home?"

Sophia shook her head. "I don't know. Either they didn't go back for some reason or they made it back and didn't bother to tell us. Maybe they're dealing with the fallout after the Queen's death and haven't had time."

"Or maybe that *king*"—he snarled the word—"is blocking communication."

Alno fidgeted behind her, clearly uncomfortable with the conversation's direction. But Sophia felt frozen. Why hadn't she wondered that earlier? She'd just assumed he and the Guild had been telling her the truth, but how could she be sure? What if they had gotten back to Tremanta and were trying to contact her even now?

"You think?" she asked.

"He's a devious bastard. I wouldn't put it past him." As he said this, he glared at Alno, who scowled right back. She'd gotten the impression that although Alno didn't exactly revere the king, he respected him. From her chaperone's stiff expression, it was clear Heleax's slander had raised his hackles.

"You know, he asked for humans to be sent over." Heleax's voice lowered. "I heard a few of the soldiers talking about it after they rounded us up. They bragged that Tremanta would be forced to send over their precious humans if they wanted another scrap of metal from Vrulatica." Bitterness swept over her tongue, a stone settling in her gut as he ranted on. "Disgusting. Trading humans for goods as if they were goods themselves."

Would the king really do that? She gnawed on her lip. She had no reason to think he wouldn't.

Only minutes ago, she'd been complacent. A lock that had been keeping closed a compartment of cynicism and suspicion clicked open. She needed to be more careful. More guarded.

Sophia knew the answer to her question before it left her lips, but she was at a loss. "Is there anything I can do?"

He shrugged helplessly. "Stay alert. With any luck, the next king or queen will see fit to bargain for our release."

"Not mine," she muttered. If the rumor Heleax had overheard was true, there was no reason for the city to send Sophia back to Tremanta. He wanted humans here, and she was a human. Was that why he'd been so concerned with taking her to be healed? So he had a group of *healthy* human women to present to his people? Did he merely want his political trophy polished? A prickle of hurt tightened her chest.

She was quiet after leaving the dungeon. She and Heleax had talked about the Queen's assassination. He'd explained that an interim ruler, named at a previous date by the old Queen, would step in and oversee things until a formal election of the council could be arranged. At that time the interim ruler would either be rejected or approved and, if approved, ascend to the throne officially. Normally this took months, but with the tensions across the planet being as high as they were, Heleax guessed everything would be expedited.

And Sophia was expected to wait. She had absolutely no control over her future and no inkling whether the king or the Guild thought of her as anything more than a chess piece.

Her head was pounding so badly once they emerged into the vastly cooler halls of Vrulatica that she only had the energy to nod absently when Alno suggested heading to the dining hall to get some food.

"Sophia," Alno whispered after several minutes of silence, "I know you and the soldier are close, but remember not to get too entrenched in his version of the truth."

She shot him a critical look. It was clear he was trying to be gentle with his words, which only made her more upset. "I'm not entrenched in anything. I have a brain of my own."

"My king may not be perfect, but I doubt he would have tried to trade for humans. It doesn't sound right."

"Not right? He's keeping me prisoner here, Alno. He's assigned a chaperone to watch me at all times. He has Heleax locked up in a damn pressure cooker, and for what? Did Heleax do anything wrong? Did he break any laws? Does he deserve to be in there? Kept weak and miserable because he had the misfortune of escorting me to a city that promised we'd be safe and welcome? I think maybe *you're* the one who needs to not be too entrenched in someone's version of the truth because honestly, I have no trouble believing a king who would do everything he's done up to now might also try to trade metal for humans." She finished with a snap, the throbbing in her head doubling with the emotion rising in her chest.

"Yes, but he isn't hurting either of you, is he? Our king is very…careful," Alno said, eyes darting around nervously. "It's better to neutralize a potential threat than be burdened by the possibility it could cause harm." His words were eager, but she had no idea what he was attempting to say. "*Remove the tail, and it cannot swipe your legs out from under you.*"

Sophia turned, her eyes narrowing. "That's a fucked-up adage, considering you all have tails."

Alno groaned impatiently. "It's good advice that's served our king well."

There was a tone in his voice… Something wasn't being said, and she was fucking tired of reading between the lines. "So he makes a habit of castrating folks before they become enemies? Is that it? How often does he do this sort of thing, Alno? I'm starting to think there might be a whole dungeon level full of people who did no more than look at him wrong one day."

"Like I said, the king is cautious. He's grown more careful over the years. If there's a chance someone might be intending to hurt him, it's not uncommon that he…*secures* them and takes time to learn their motives."

"Stop saying careful and cautious!" she all but screeched, her voice bouncing off the walls. "There's a difference between cautiousness and paranoia. Locking up innocent people before they've done anything wrong isn't careful, it's unhinged."

"Well, if you knew…" Alno's lips slammed shut, his tail whipping across the floor. "Never mind. It doesn't matter."

He tugged her along gently. "All the good food will be gone if we don't get to dinner."

"Tell me what you're not saying," Sophia demanded, yanking her arm out of his hold. "If I knew what?"

Alno scanned the space around him, checking they were alone. "Under any other circumstance I would agree that he's paranoid, but…" He stared down at her, lips tensed, brows creased, holding back whatever it was he wanted to say. Then, expelling a deep breath, he swooped forward and began whispering furiously. "His mother was assassinated. Ten years later, his father met the same fate. He had a brother he never got the chance to meet. Why? He, too, was murdered." At Sophia's horrified expression, he nodded smugly. "And those are just his direct relations. The further back you go, the bloodier it gets. They're cursed. My father used to say the royal line must have picheti on their breath."

Sophia shook her head. "Pi—what?"

"Picheti. It's a metal carried in some of the plants in our desert. If too much is ingested, it taints the brain. It seems all anyone from the royal line has to do to inspire hatred is open their mouth." Alno's voice dropped. "I haven't mentioned the worst of it yet." He inched closer. "Fifteen years ago, he recognized a mate."

Her hands flew to her mouth. "Oh my god. They killed his mate?"

His lips thinned. "Yes and no. She died, but she wasn't his mate."

"I thought you just said—"

He interrupted her with a wave. "It was fake. Another attempt on his life. The female had drugged him one night during a tryst. While he slept, she'd slipped a special substance made from tattoo ink and dye into his eyes. As you may know, our tattoo ink is controlled magnetically. She fixed it so it remained invisible for days, then, when she was ready, she used a control to activate the ink. To all the onlookers, it appeared as if his eyes had changed with initial recognition. Our king had found a *mate*. The first Vrulan to do so in hundreds of years. I still remember the celebrations being so loud, the walls shook from ground to sky.

"He changed then. Wore less armor around the city. Even smiled on occasion. He thought the fact that he'd been mated would protect him in the eyes of his citizens. But others were suspicious. They went behind his back and investigated the female. To the tower's horror, they discovered she'd planned to kill him after she'd been confirmed as queen. She would've ended his accursed line forever and been left to rule alone."

Emotions swam in Sophia's mind, making it difficult to hold on to any solid thought.

Alno nodded, likely seeing the pity she felt reflected in her eyes. "He was forced to send her away. She died not long after." His voice turned solemn. "There were many dark years after that. The king protects himself and he protects our people, but he trusts no one. I think he believes that locking someone up before they can do something unforgivable means he won't have to hurt them."

The words resonated in her heart, making her throat thick. She understood Alno's defense of the king. She could not in good conscience agree with Sikthand's decisions, but she could at least understand where they came from.

A thought struck her. "What was her name?" Sophia asked breathlessly.

A large group of men emerged around a corner, laughing together as they walked toward the dining hall. "Who?" She allowed Alno to usher her along once more.

"The woman who faked her recognition."

"Oh." He made sure the group of men were still far enough away before whispering, "Japeshi."

Her lungs collapsed, sadness swelling in her throat until it ached. She'd studied the Clecanian alphabet last night before falling asleep. Something about Sikthand's out-of-place tattoo had pulled at her, and she'd itched to learn what it said. Now she knew.

It was her name. Japeshi. The woman he'd thought was his mate.

But why? She'd betrayed him in such a vile way. The Vrulan tattoos could be changed from one moment to the next using magnetic pens. It wasn't a comfortable process, but it was common. If her name was still there, it had to be because he wanted it there. For what? A reminder? Because he loved her?

The question burned in her mind as they entered the dining hall and took seats at one of the long tables. A cacophony of sound filled the grand space, hundreds of bodies warming the cold metal and stone architecture of the room.

The dining hall located in this section of the tower was where most of the riders and warriors took their meals, as it was closest to their barracks. Enormous windows covered one side of the room, allowing shafts of fading sun to throw stripes of light across the space. Rather than chandeliers like one might expect, the vaults and arches of the room's intricate ceiling were lined with light, making the ceiling of the room emit a glow that would brighten as the sun set.

Though the walls were built from dark metal and stone, there was enough richly colored décor and warm light to soften the gothic edge of the space and make it feel inviting. It helped that many were drunk and joyful.

Alno had explained that the cloud chasers often overindulged during this time of year. Conversely, throughout the time of year known as the Season, riders became serious and single-minded. It was paramount to the survival of Vrulatica that each cloud be emptied of every drop of moisture so that the city had a full reservoir of water for the year and also so the barren wasteland to the north remained bone-dry. The pressure placed on cloud chasers was immense, and they rewarded themselves for their dogged focus during the Season by carousing the rest of the year.

Apparently the Season was drawing close and was marked by a heightened amount of partying. Sophia couldn't imagine the grinning, flushed-cheeked Vrulans turning severe, but if the new Tremantian ruler didn't negotiate her release, she supposed she might be here long enough to see the shift.

A chorus of clanging tails on the floor told her the king had arrived. As if in a trance, her eyes sought him. He strode up the steps of his elevated table and took his seat, looming over the rest of the hall. A shaft of orange sunlight illuminated the table, but the angle was steep enough that it only lit half of his helmeted face. The other half was shadowed.

He hadn't been here last night. She'd wondered which of the many halls located throughout the tower he'd deigned to dine in, almost craving the heady presence he carried into every room he entered.

Sophia couldn't decide how she felt seeing him now. Her mind was in turmoil, wanting to choose either hatred or admiration but settling somewhere in the murky gray middle. She only realized she was staring when he suddenly stared back.

Every instinct screamed to break the eye contact, but she couldn't. Who was he? Was he vicious, or a man desperate to avoid vicious acts? Did he bury himself under armor to intimidate, or was it really to protect himself?

"Stop staring," Alno hissed, setting a plate of food and drink in front of her. "Before he notices that pity in your eyes and figures out I helped put it there."

Her gaze snapped away. Instead, she focused on sliding pieces of food around her plate, an oncoming migraine making her too nauseous to eat, even though it'd likely help. She sipped some water instead.

"That's her," Alno breathed, a dreamy grin crossing his face.

Sophia turned to follow his line of sight and saw a beautiful silver woman crossing to a long table packed with cackling men. The woman was about as tall as the men and wearing more metal than any. Hooking into her braided hair and running along her chin was a skeletal gold jawbone. The piece of jewelry moved with her chin as she spoke, and gold chains draped over her sculpted shoulders swayed as she took her seat at the table.

What a kick-ass outfit. The spark of longing took her by surprise. She'd been on autopilot, picking her outfits based on what was practical. She wished she could've enjoyed Vrulatica more before everything had gone tits up. She'd been so excited about exploring the shops in midcity, picking up some cool silver jewelry, and finally getting her first tattoo. Well, her *second* first tattoo.

Her real first tattoo had been a star on her left shoulder. It'd been blotchy and crooked and she should've left the dingy shop she'd gotten it in with an infection, but she'd fallen head over heels in love with it. The only reason she hadn't made a beeline for the multi-level tattoo studio, affectionately known to locals as the Flesh Forge, was because she couldn't decide whether she wanted to recreate her star as a tribute or begin anew.

But now a part of her felt that even though she was technically *allowed* to explore the city, doing so would be a betrayal. To whom? She didn't know. The Queen? Her friends who'd barely escaped? Heleax?

If she walked around decked out in Vrulan garb, sporting Vrulan-designed tattoos, wouldn't she come off like a poster child for Stockholm Syndrome? She didn't want to give the king the satisfaction of seeing her enjoy something his city—her prison—had provided.

Alno's dream woman shoved one of the men in her group, and he stumbled back. Sophia grinned. "That's who you're in love with?"

If she could have drawn Alno's expression at that exact moment, she'd make sure to add little red hearts in place of pupils. "Isn't she magnificent? The best rider in the bunch...other than the king," he admitted.

"Huh." She nodded and turned back to sip her water.

"What?" Alno seemed annoyed by her mild surprise. "You don't think she's glorious? Are human eyes as weak as human bodies?"

"Whoa." Sophia chuckled, holding up her hands in surrender. "Cool it with the species bashing. I think she's just as incredible as you described. She's just a little different than I thought."

"How?"

"I don't know." Sophia shrugged, choosing her words carefully. "You're more of a lover than a fighter. I thought she'd be the same. The way you talked about her, I just imagined some kind of delicate star-shine woman. I didn't think she'd be so bad ass. That's all."

"You thought I'd be attracted to someone weak?" Alno grimaced.

"No…I didn't know what to expect, I suppose. Everything in this city is surprising to me." She snuck a glance over to the king as she said this and found he'd removed his helmet. He was deep in conversation with Commander Copperhead. As though he could feel her eyes on him, his silver gaze met hers. A muscle in his jaw pulsed.

The commander rose to his feet. He slammed the tip of his tail against a round metal plate on the spine of his chair. A loud clang rang through the room, and everyone grew silent, all eyes turning to the commander.

He let the tension of silence build in the room for many long seconds before lifting his cup and shouting, "The umbercree have been spotted!"

Sophia jumped an inch off her seat when the room erupted in raucous applause. Armored tails hitting stone and metal filled the room with enough clanging to make Sophia feel like her head was inside the well of a bell.

"We fly to the forest in two nights." The commander grinned before retaking his seat. No hint of a smile cracked the king's elegant lips. In lieu of whooping along with everyone else, he raised his cup resolutely, then downed the contents.

Alno was still grinning and slapping his tail against the table when Sophia leaned in. "What are the umbercree?"

"Birds." He smiled, all traces of annoyance with her gone. "The umbercree fly through once a year to lay their nests in our trees. The storms always follow. When the umbercree arrive, we fly to the forest and have a big party to celebrate the start of the Season."

"One last hurrah?"

"You'll love it. There's mounds of food and drink. When the umbercree finish—"

"Not to interrupt…" Sophia tipped her head and raised her brows. "Are you sure I'm invited to this party? The king said I couldn't leave the city. Is he going to let me fly to the ground and hang out around a bunch of drunk people?"

The look of pure horror on Alno's face was almost enough to make her chuckle. "You can't miss the umbercree. They're pivotal! That would be…" He shook his head, searching for strong enough words. His gaze grew far off. "And if you miss it, that means I'll have to miss it too." He bared his fangs in disgust. "You *must* be invited."

She shrugged and hooked a thumb toward the royal table. "Yeah, tell Mr. High and Mi—"

A pretty woman with a gunmetal hood and silver eyes was leaning forward with both hands planted on the arm of the king's chair. She grinned at him, subtly pushing her tits together.

Dread coursed through Sophia. Poor girl. The king was likely to shove her off the edge of the raised table for being so presumptuous. Sophia braced, barely holding back a wince as she waited for his reaction.

Her jaw dropped when Sikthand's tail flicked out, curled under the woman's chin, and tilted her head up further. In answer, she bit her lip with a fang and held eye contact.

They were *flirting*. Sophia had no idea why she was so outraged by this.

"I look forward to this party all year. Difila will be there. I was finally going to talk to her. Ask her for a walk," Alno mumbled in a defeated voice.

"Are you seeing this?" Sophia couldn't stop looking. The woman had perched herself on the arm of his chair now, and Sikthand wasn't doing a thing about it.

Her chaperone grumbled. Pouting like someone had just stolen his teddy bear, Alno glanced toward the spectacle unfolding before them. "What?" His voice didn't have the slightest hint of surprise.

"Is this normal, then?" She couldn't think of what else to say. Sophia had only ever seen the king scowl, glare, and command. The image of him suggestively running his gaze up and down a flirty woman like any other man, was...well it was weird, wasn't it?

Alno focused on the king again, and his lip half lifted in confusion. "Is what normal?"

"Him." She tossed her hand toward the king. "Flirting. After what happened with that woman, I'm surprised." She whispered her words since Alno had made it clear it wasn't something folks talked about loudly.

Alno snorted. "I said he doesn't trust anybody, not that he doesn't *fuck* anybody. A king has needs, same as anyone." His gaze slipped to a laughing Difila as if he was thinking about his own *needs*.

Irritation rose in her. Suddenly the bright faces of the tipsy warriors didn't make her feel as warm and fuzzy as they had before. Everyone, apart from Alno, was having a grand time. Flirting, drinking, laughing. Even the grim king was seeking out a little bit of *happy* for himself.

She was alone in her misery, not even sure she'd be allowed to go to the biggest celebration of the year.

"Hey." She aimed a gentle smile toward Alno. "If you take me to my room right now, you might be able to hurry back here before she leaves."

It took only a moment for Alno to hop up from his seat, his bright grin warming his golden face once more. As she followed his near run out of the dining hall, she snuck a last peek at the king and flushed to find him watching her.

When Alno had locked the door behind her, leaving her alone, she remained stuck in place. Her mind was too overloaded to sleep, but there wasn't much else to do in her room. She supposed she could use the scroll Alno had let her borrow to study the alphabet.

Reminded of why she'd asked to borrow an alphabet in the first place, her mind slipped back to the king. She exhaled a growl of frustration.

Sophia didn't know how to process the emotions bubbling inside. Determined not to mope, she searched the room, tearing out drawers and digging through cabinets. *No paper.*

Stomping to the bathroom, she grabbed an armful of makeup and a cup of water, then returned to the main room. She collapsed onto the floor underneath the beam of light shining down through the stained glass, then tore open a pot of gray powder and started rubbing it over the stone with a finger.

The makeup would wash away, but she almost wished it wouldn't. Not even this drawing would leave a lasting mark on this place.

Time passed—she didn't know how long, but when she sat back, the bomb of anxiety building in her chest had been diffused and she breathed a little easier. As her nervous energy settled, exhaustion slowly crept back in.

Yawning, she retrieved a wet towel from the bathroom and sank to her knees. Water dripped onto the edge of her drawing, making a small section of black dribble into a crack in the stone. She studied the floor, suddenly possessive of the piece she'd been about to wash away.

Sophia lowered the towel into her lap. Maybe she could leave it till morning. The hair on her nape lifted, as if someone was sneaking a peek at the drawing even now.

She studied it again. She should erase it. What if Alno came into her room unannounced again in the morning and spotted it? But something in her rebelled. She hadn't made anything this good in a while. It wasn't as if she could take a picture of it to look at later. What was the harm in giving herself a chance to admire her masterpiece under morning light before destroying it forever?

She tipped her head to the side and smiled proudly, lids growing heavy.

I got the lighting right.

8

Most of the day had been a success for Sikthand. The human had flitted through his mind as soon as his eyes had opened, but he'd forced all thoughts of her away. A meeting with his Guild, discussing the newly announced interim Queen, Vila, and what her intentions toward them might be, forced him to think of Sophia again, but this time it was for practical reasons.

He'd then spent a few hours sparring with Roldroth. After choosing to fight younger warriors in order to give them some controlled practice with a seasoned opponent, a well-matched tussle with his commander had been welcomed.

Feeling a bit calmer, they'd walked together to the spire and met with the skittish male who kept watch of the weather and the heavens, confirming the forecasted umbercree and the storm systems that would likely follow.

Now that the new cloud chasers had been promoted, they'd also had a lengthy conversation about finalizing squads. Commander Roldroth had argued heatedly that the young Mubet should fill the vacant spot in a front line squad. Sikthand disagreed, feeling the boy was still too soft when directing his mount, but he'd deferred to his commander's judgment in the end.

Then he'd held hours with Speaker Besith, who'd relayed the complaints of the people to him along with Besith's recommendations. Sikthand had approved or denied as he'd seen fit and earned a considerable amount of backlash from Besith, as always.

The day had dragged on. He'd spoken and listened and decreed until his eyes ached. And in all that busyness, he'd managed to only think of *her* a handful of times. And yet...

Here he was again, behind the beautiful human's mirror, unable to tear his gaze away.

Bitter defeat had coated his throat as soon as he'd spotted her in the dining hall. Though he'd tried to fight it, attempting to force a reaction to the lovely Vrulan female vying for his attention, a part of him he'd kept subdued rose through his defenses like smoke. As soon as Sophia had left, Sikthand knew he'd follow. He could no more fight the urge than he could keep the Season at bay.

So here he sat, hidden, watching her. His eyes traced every spatter and smudge covering her forearms.

Curiosity burned through his tense muscles. No matter how hard he squinted, he couldn't make out what she was drawing. Her fingers flew over the stone, bits of crumbling makeup and clouds of powder surrounding her as she worked. The tip of her long braid was covered in gold from dragging across the floor, and her brows were set in a permanent furrow.

She was fascinating. Constantly drawing, then erasing, then redrawing. Her determination to get it right permeated the room, and he found himself hoping she'd succeed. When she dug through the littered makeup, not finding what she wanted, he felt the disappointment in her expression rise in him too.

And when she crawled forward on her knees, her shapely ass raised in the air, hunger heated his blood. *No tail.* The unobstructed view he could have if he lifted her skirt while she bent forward like that...

His tail flicked behind him silently. Resigned to the knowledge he'd never be able to keep it still, he'd removed the metal armor from the tip before visiting her mirror.

Gradually, Sophia sat back on her heels. Her dark eyes ran over her work. At first, her inspection was critical, but her gaze grew approving the longer she stared until it was clear her work of art was complete and she was now taking the time to admire it.

Tipping her head to the side, she reached out and gently ran her fingers over some part of the image. He itched to know what she caressed with such care. Perhaps he could sneak in after she departed tomorrow morning and see.

The umbercree celebration, he grumbled to himself. The next two days would be long. The tower would be in a tizzy about the party, and he'd need to sit through the celebration with his people.

Sikthand would try to enjoy himself…within reason, but he'd need to keep his guard up. Those out there who wanted to do him harm always seemed to think celebrations such as this were the perfect moment to strike. As if he'd feel more at ease surrounded by jubilant partygoers. In reality, events like the umbercree festival only made him more vigilant.

Attempts on his life had settled over the past decade. He'd come to believe that Japeshi's failed plan had struck a nerve with his people. He supposed he could at least thank her for that. Conniving as she was, the ferocity of her betrayal was so vile that it seemed even the Vrulans who wanted to see him off the throne pitied him enough to quell their attempts on his life.

But the air had changed as of late. It had all started with the discovery of humans. Whispers were first. They'd begun as judgments of the Tremantian Queen and curiosity toward humans. *What were humans? Could they really be recognized? Was it true they shared Clecanian ancestors?*

Then, when no progress toward reaching out to the Intergalactic Alliance had been made, the whispers turned louder and demanding. They'd wanted him to get answers when none were forthcoming. The fact that the Queen was not responding to anyone didn't matter to them.

He'd known then that this would be a dangerous period for him. No matter what route he chose, there would be those who would critique his choice.

If he'd done nothing and continued to merely press the Queen for a response, they would've called him weak and tried to kill him so that a stronger leader could take charge. If he'd declared war unless the Queen responded, they would've called him capricious and prone to illogical choices based on emotion.

He'd thought they'd be happy, or at least distracted, by the news that a group of humans were coming to visit, but no. Rumors spreading across the planet had made them hungry for the Queen's blood, so he'd made a decision. He'd allied with a few neighboring cities and agreed to cut off trade.

Madam Kalos had been livid, but the majority of the Guild had supported the play. Choosing to hold the traveling party hostage had been a late-stage decision, but he still felt it had been the right move at the time.

If the Queen had lived, he was sure she would've been spurred to a response. Unfortunately for him, she'd died and most of the humans had escaped. He'd been left looking like an erratic king ruled by his unstable male temperament.

Even before the mutterings of dissatisfied citizens started floating to him from his spies throughout Vrulatica, he'd resolved to watch his back. Distraction would be his downfall. If he didn't always keep one eye open until this wave of upheaval passed, he'd be dead.

And yet, his mind itched to think only of this human. He peered down at his hands again and found them mark free. She wasn't his mate. Even if humans *were* capable of calling forth mating marks, Sikthand knew in his soul that he was not meant to find a mate in this life.

The intense urges he was having where Sophia was concerned were the same urges any male might have toward a female like her. She was interesting and mysterious and beautiful. And she was living in the queen's quarters. Obviously he'd grow an unnatural attachment to any female living *here* of all places. It couldn't be helped.

Once she was gone, his small obsession would fade.

Sophia's limbs relaxed and her movements grew sluggish as she rose and trudged to the bathroom. He stared hard at the unrecognizable smears of grays, golds, and black.

His fists tensed as he watched her walk out of the bathroom with a damp cloth.

Is she...

Sophia lifted the dripping towel above the drawing, and he nearly growled. She was going to wipe it away. The mystery of what she'd worked on so passionately would plague him for days. He reached out, silently willing her to stop.

In that instant, she looked up, peering around the room as if sensing him. Elbows lowering to his knees, he leaned toward the mirror. *Can you* feel *me, little human?*

Sikthand let out a low breath when she dropped the towel to the ground at her hip, leaving her work untouched. A smirk threatened to curl his lips as he watched her recheck the glass bottles she'd tipped against both entries into her room.

Clever thing. If she only knew there were *three* entrances, not two.

The thought lodged itself in his brain while he watched her slink into bed, and it refused to leave his mind as the night dragged on and her body relaxed into a deep sleep.

There was no tripwire bottle in front of his mirror. If he was very quiet, he could slip into her room without her noticing. Just a quick look at her drawing to satisfy his curiosity. If he didn't see it now, he might never get the chance. What if she changed her mind and wiped it away in the dead of night?

Sikthand needed no more convincing. As silent as vapor, he slid into her room. Her luscious scent hit him immediately. Sweet and dark, with the barest bite of spice.

He'd visited this room many times over the years. He'd stand in the doorway, always aware of the dust accumulating over every cold surface. It had remained vacant and desolate for so long that Sikthand had almost forgotten how beautiful the queen's quarters were underneath the filth. The last time he'd seen the metal sculpture surrounding the bed gleam that brightly had been…

Fractals of ice spread through his chest, but the human's sweet scent pulled him from his wretched memories. The smell of her changed the space, transforming the room that haunted him into someplace unfamiliar.

It was dangerous. A part of him wanted to despise the room. Keeping it cold and dirty served as an effective reminder. These quarters *should*—and always *would*—be empty.

The female currently occupying them was a *guest*. Nothing more. If there were any other rooms he felt completely sure were Maxu-proof, he would have stowed Sophia there instead. As it was, the male who'd helped the humans escape had at one time been a close friend and Sikthand's personal spy. Like a pishot, he'd revealed a portion of the secret passages and tunnels Vrulatica was riddled with to the accursed male.

Luckily, he hadn't shown Maxu *all* the tunnels. And especially not the one leading from Sikthand's room into the queen's quarters. This room was secure, and that was the *only* reason he'd pushed for Sophia to occupy it.

He kept his ears pricked as he approached the drawing, but she didn't stir. His steps faltered as he caught sight of the piece, and his gaze flew to her sleeping form, then back. There, sketched in three different poses, was…him.

The image on the bottom was of his masked face from the shoulders up. He was something from a nightmare. Harsh light fell from above in such a way as to throw his face and body into sinister shadow and amplify the sharpness of his helmet's horns. His eyes glowed from the dark mask like two flashing daggers.

Sikthand would've been satisfied with this depiction of him. At least she had the good sense to be afraid of him. But the other two sketches had his mind reeling.

In one, he was scratching Ahea's muzzle, his expression stiff but not menacing. It was the last image that struck him the most. It was the one he'd seen her touch and the simplest of the three.

A portrait from the chest up showed Sikthand unclothed and unmasked. His profile glowed in gentle light warmed with dabs of gold powder. He seemed to lift his cheek ever so slightly toward the sun's heat, but his eyes were downcast. A profound sense of loneliness clung to them, though he couldn't understand how she'd put it there. Especially not when the rest of him looked so…beautiful.

The contrast between his pale skin and black hood was as intense as ever, but rather than appear severe and unnerving the way he'd always believed them to be, the combination evoked a pleasing duality. Like the bright moons against a black sky.

Was this how she saw him? Her stare had always lingered on his face for far longer than anyone else dared to look, but he'd thought that was a signal of her apprehension, not her…interest.

She must have studied his body quite hard back in the medic's office because she'd recreated his tattoos perfectly. All except one.

She'd either forgotten or deliberately omitted Japeshi's name.

Sikthand's muscles went rigid, his fingers twitching in agitation. What did the omission mean?

Opposing feelings battled inside him as he tried to work out her intentions. Before she could hear the flick of his tail against the stone, he disappeared back through her mirror.

9

Vrulatica had been abuzz for the last two days. Out of her window, Sophia watched as malginash hauling buckets full of supplies soared past her room.

No one was more excited than Alno. He went on and on about the food and the umbercree, but mostly, he talked about the outfits. Some people spent all year planning what they'd wear. Artisans from midcity took months building complex costumes for well-paying patrons.

On the horrified realization that Sophia had nothing acceptable to wear, Alno had dragged her to midcity, towing her from one shop to the next in the hopes of finding a last-minute treasure in the picked-through stores.

She didn't mind that they hadn't found anything spectacular, still apprehensive about showing enthusiasm toward the city holding her hostage. She'd kept it to herself, but she was actually pretty excited about the dress she'd found.

Alno had given the dress a bemused smile. "Really? That?" he'd pressed while plucking at the diaphanous fabric. "This is what you wear *under* the real outfit. On its own, it's so...soft and boring."

With the promise she'd embellish the dress using a discounted bin of metal bits and bobs leftover from more extravagant creations, Alno had grudgingly mellowed his search and allowed her to explore a few non-outfit-related shops in peace.

She'd found a lovely store selling art supplies. Though most were intended for various types of metalworking, she'd been able to scrounge together enough illustration materials to keep her happy.

Honestly, she hadn't been doing too poorly using her makeup to draw, though. For the past two nights, she'd worked with the creams, powders, and gels to funnel her frustration and express her awe of the city privately.

Though she wouldn't mind drawing Sikthand again, she'd refrained, choosing instead to decorate her floor with soaring malginash. She'd even found a few new colors in with the makeup that she hadn't noticed before. When she'd thanked Alno for adding the new hues when he'd restocked her supply, he'd given her a blank look.

Every area of Vrulatica she'd visited was as compelling as the rest. Sculptures and interesting architecture could be found on every level, but she had a hard time fully enjoying it. A near constant feeling that she was being watched tickled her brain. The indefinable sensation made her turn her head and check around her every other minute while she explored.

It was a silly thing to focus on since she *was* always being watched. Every Vrulan who passed made a point of studying the odd, drearily dressed human. But she couldn't shake the impression that this was something else, *someone* else.

Alno had chalked it up to her "permanently clenched ass." His charming way of explaining that if she just relaxed and gave herself permission to enjoy Vrulatica, the paranoia would fade.

Her morning visits to Heleax ensured she would not be taking Alno's advice anytime soon. How could she enjoy herself when Heleax was left to boil in his cell? Not only that, but he must've been dying of boredom. At least she could explore, take walks, talk to Alno, draw. Heleax was locked in a sauna all day, and the only company he had, besides her short visits, were occasional passing guards. When she'd admitted right to his sweaty face that she was headed to a party that night, each guilty word had boomed through her.

Of the basket of gifts she'd brought for Heleax, the guards had only let him keep two items. A book. And a metal ring puzzle. Though Heleax was grateful, he was more interested in hearing what she'd learned than he was with her presents.

She'd relayed everything Alno had divulged to her concerning the goings on in Tremanta, which wasn't saying much. Vila, a female Sophia had never met, had been named interim Queen. The vote—to either approve or deny her ascension to Queen—was being held in two days, and if she *was* approved, she would give a speech the same day that would be broadcast across the world.

Because there was no way to watch the speech in Vrulatica, the king and Guild would fly to an outbuilding near the infirmary and watch the holograph footage from there. Sophia had already decided she'd demand to be taken along, but hadn't had the time to say as much before Heleax had shot forward, attempting to convince her of what she already knew.

Sophia had silently let him argue his case. It seemed to help his mood to put his mind to work and give her wise counsel. She didn't mind feigning guilelessness if that meant she could leave Heleax feeling like he'd been useful.

The next time the opportunity to speak with the king arose, she'd bring up her request. She gave herself fifty-fifty odds of him agreeing, and those odds were generous.

According to Alno, he'd barely given permission for her to attend the party tonight, and his eventual acquiescence had been with the stipulation that she and Alno would fly there with him and stay within his eyeline for the duration of the event. She couldn't bring herself to explain to a beaming Alno that his chances of socializing with Difila under those restrictions weren't great.

Her chaperone had dropped her in her room hours ago so he could get ready. Sophia hadn't missed the pitying smile he'd aimed toward her dress and pile of mismatched metal bits as she'd poured them onto a table. "It'll look good," she'd promised. "You'll only be mildly embarrassed to be seen with me, not mortified."

He'd shrugged, unconvinced.

The dress would not be as extravagant as what most of Vrulatica would be wearing, but for her, it was a good compromise between her itch to stretch her creative muscles and her pride as a prisoner. Hours passed as she glued and sewed bright bits of metal to the cloudy white gossamer dress in straight lines. She suspected Alno would find the plain pattern boring, but she didn't care.

The sun began to set as Sophia dressed. She applied some luminous makeup, pulled half her hair back, secured it with a silver filigree comb, and attached a piece of facial jewelry behind her ears. The interesting piece ran over her cheeks and nose and was delicate enough to complement her outfit.

Vrulans were known for their hardcore armored pieces, and she imagined the desert would be full of extravagant spikes and chains. *Her* outfit, on the other hand, was gentle and ludicrously pretty. Almost angelic.

Alno was unaware, but Sophia hadn't picked the soft translucent fabric on a whim. *Angelic* wasn't really her style. No, this choice had been deliberate. Walking into this event in an outfit like this would have the same effect as a death-metal enthusiast stepping foot in a pixie convention.

She'd stand out. And she hoped her purposeful choice of garb would send a message. She might be attending the party, and she might be a cooperative prisoner, but she was *not* assimilating.

It was a subtle statement. And many might chalk her choice up to an odd human style preference. But it made *her* feel better.

A knock sounded, and nervousness crept up her spine. Alno's reaction would tell her all she'd need to know about how she'd be received. Scanning the room to make sure she hadn't forgotten anything, she answered her door and gasped.

He'd morphed into some kind of golden monster covered in magma. A headpiece of gold molded against his skin and ran up the side of his face until it bubbled toward the sky. More globs of molten gold and bronze dripped over his torso and lifted off his arms. His skin under the metal was shaded and disguised expertly.

Though the metal appeared as if it was liquefying, it was completely solid, and Sophia stood frozen in awe of the artist. Whoever it was had made it so when she stood back, it looked as though Alno was melting in zero gravity, his body oozing apart in all directions.

She was still lost in her admiration of his outfit as he gave her a once-over. "Better than I thought," he exclaimed. "Still unimaginative, but I think most will realize you didn't have enough time for anything better. And," he added with a wolfish tilt of his ghastly melting golden head, "it's arousing enough to make it interesting." His eyes fixed on the area of nearly sheer fabric that draped over her breasts. It wasn't see-through, but it let enough color from her skin shine through to give the illusion it was.

She chuckled and nudged him out the door, tossing on the cloak Sikthand had given her as she did. "You won't see anything. Save your ogling for Difila."

He guided her down the hall toward the same landing bay Sikthand had brought her to when they'd flown to the medic. She focused back on Alno, ignoring the nervous fluttering in her belly. "But you. Wow, Alno. Just wow. You look like a tragic, hot, terrifying…" She couldn't even express how ingenious his outfit was. "You look like a statue that's just been dropped in a volcano."

Alno preened at the compliment. His grin widened, his voice rising in volume as they took the last few steps to the landing bay. "Just wait. I saw glimpses of some spectacular costumes on my way here."

A malginash with a rider already mounted waited for them. An unwanted stab of disappointment flitted through her before she could stop it. Commander Roldroth, not the king, sat atop the malginash. He gestured to a bucket near the malginash's claws and waited for them to climb in.

Sophia had ridden in one of the cauldron-shaped bowls the Vrulans called buckets only once before when she'd first arrived in Vrulatica. She'd thought she'd prefer this mode of travel. They were held securely from chains by the malginash while they relaxed in a cushioned container not dissimilar from the basket of a hot-air balloon. But a sneaking voice reminded her how wonderful it'd been to fly while astride the creature's back, tucked against a warm, protective chest.

They took to the sky, and she had to admit the ride was smoother while seated in the bucket. The sun was still in the process of setting, and it lit the red desert in glorious shades of fiery orange. Soon the electric-blue sky would fade to black. Even if she'd briefly considered an escape attempt, she knew she'd never make it far in the dark.

Whoops and cheers echoed from behind her, and she spun. At least a dozen malginash, all carrying buckets of people, soared along behind them. The occupants of the buckets wore elaborate metallic costumes and gleamed in the sunset. Streamers of richly patterned fabrics and clear line strung with shards of shattered mirror trailed over the sides of their buckets and floated behind them on the breeze.

The riders dipped and turned, tossing the gleeful passengers around, their garlands of colorful fabric and glittering glass flowing through the wind. She couldn't help but grin at the parade of malginash all the way to the forest.

Though she'd heard the area described as a forest before, the beauty of the oasis sprawling before her took her breath away. The Vrulan reservoirs were located here. When the cloud chasers seeded their clouds, they always did it so the majority of the rain would fall in this general vicinity and pool in the wide basins of water stepping down the slope of the desert canyon. Tall skinny trees with willowy, razor-thin leaves peppered the scenery, but the ground between their trunks was mostly bare.

A waterside block of land, more sparsely populated with trees than the rest, had been decorated for the party. Seating areas made of cushions, low tables, and blankets spotted the sand everywhere. Tall tents lined the perimeter of the blanketed area, and through their raised flaps, she could see people mingling inside.

Gauzy fabric covered tunnels that branched off from the main party area, winding into the forest in all directions. She could just make out a few couples walking side by side through some of the paths.

Alno saw the direction of her gaze and gently nudged her shoulder, flashing his white fangs in a grin. "I'm going to ask Difila to walk with me." He lifted a bag, and she knew it would contain a gift.

Her smile faltered. Should she ruin his good mood and remind him he wasn't allowed to leave her side?

Taking a walk was a Vrulan courting custom done during special events or gatherings. A path, usually partially covered, was set up, and people could present someone they were interested in with a gift, then ask them to take a walk. If accepted, the couple would then stroll through the length of the tunnel and talk, and when the path ended, they separated. It was a pressure-free way to get to know someone you might not have spoken to before. It allowed the meeting to be public, yet hidden enough to engage in a private conversation, and short enough to not let the conversation grow awkward.

As the men outnumbered the women so severely, a request for a walk was almost always issued by a man. It gave single men hoping to be married a chance to present themselves favorably enough that a woman might remember them when it came time for her to choose a husband during the marriage ceremony. It allowed women to quickly meet many suitors and not be expected to mingle with any single one of them for the rest of the night.

Speed dating aliens. She snorted.

Excitement must have been clouding Alno's mind since, unless he planned to go on a walk with Difila *and* Sophia, he'd been ordered to remain at her side. "Alno, you know—"

"Hang on," he said as their malginash set their bucket among a group of vacant ones.

Commander Roldroth dismounted, and his malginash sped away toward a group of malginash splashing in the water.

When the commander reached Sophia and Alno, he clapped his enormous hands together, eyes scanning the party hungrily. Metallic green leaves sprouted from small copper curls all over his head as if they were growing out of his skin, and a collection of glinting charcoal bugs nestled in his hair. A black animal that was a cross between a lizard and a snake coiled its thick body around his neck and disappeared into his ear. Four golden feet gripped his outer ear and hair as if trying to pull itself deeper inside his ear canal. Sophia shivered, reminding herself it was only a piece of metal and not a real creature.

Alno took her cloak for her, and Roldroth's eyes caught on her outfit. "Not bad, human."

"I could have done better." She eyed him pointedly. "But as you know, I hadn't planned on being in town for this little shindig."

The commander chuckled at that. "Fair point."

They walked through the party, light music pulsing from some of the tents, and Sophia could only imagine how wide her eyes must have grown. Costumes surpassing anything she could have imagined could be seen every few feet.

If Earth was ever opened to Clecania, this would be a mecca for special effects makeup artists, Halloween enthusiasts, and cosplayers alike. Hell, she couldn't think of *anyone* who wouldn't at least find this group jaw dropping. It was like a Venetian masquerade—but if the masquerade was also a rave for blacksmiths.

A woman walked by in an outfit made of geometrically placed reflective silver pieces. The shapes covered her entire body and face and created broken reflections all around her. Sophia imagined her as a creature born from the inside of a kaleidoscope.

They meandered through the party, but she couldn't tear her eyes away from the Vrulans long enough to pay attention to where they walked. When Alno guided her to lower into a cushioned seating area, she dutifully sank down without complaint.

Commander Copperhead crouched before her, drawing her focus. A handsome grin split his face. "I know you hadn't planned to be here, but I'm happy to see you're appreciating it, nevertheless. And"—he held a small bag out to her—"I'd wondered if you'd walk with me?"

Sophia blinked at the bag, her brain still too gob-smacked by the umbercree festival so far to comprehend what he was asking. "Oh," she murmured when her mind finally caught on.

He was asking her to walk.

"Oh," she said again, a little louder when she recognized what that meant. Commander Copperhe—Commander Roldroth was expressing *interest* in her. Did she want to take a walk with him? "I'm not sure I can agree one way or another." She tried handing the bag back, but the commander didn't take it. "I'm supposed to stay within eyesight of the king."

She stiffened and peered around, now realizing if this was their assigned spot, the king must not be too far away. Her breath caught in her throat when she found him sitting on a slightly raised platform under a canopy. Intricate webs of blood red metal covered his bare chest. The pieces were affixed to him so perfectly they might have been surgically planted along his muscles.

The density of his black tattoos made every spot covered by the red metalwork look like it was exposed tendon and muscle, as if someone had skinned him and found he'd been built from latticed red metal all along.

The ornamentation was so intricate as it traveled up his neck, snaked over his cheeks, and dipped down the bridge of his nose that his black hood was the only bit of his face visible.

In the dying sunlight, his silver eyes reflected the metal of his outfit and glowed red. And their fiery focus was entirely on her. She stifled a shiver.

"Oh, that's right. I'll go get his permission, then we can be off." The commander was entirely unfazed by the king's foreboding aura as he marched over to him.

Sikthand didn't take his eyes off her until the commander had halted in front of his dais, stood in silence for a few moments, then tapped his tail twice on the raised wooden floor to get the king's attention.

Was it just the red reflection in his eyes making his scowl more menacing than normal?

Alno poured her a glass of something, and she mindlessly sucked down a large gulp. Fire coated her throat. She coughed and wheezed, feeling her empty stomach rebel. "What—" *Cough.* "What—" She coughed more. She peered into the glass at the thick milky liquid. And pointed at it, wincing, and gripping her neck.

Silent laughter had dissolved Alno into a shaking ball. He clutched his stomach, and his laughter redoubled as he caught sight of her flaming face. She had half a mind to toss the rest of the fire milk at him.

"I'm sorry. I'm sorry. I didn't think you'd drink it without seeing what I'd handed you." He wiped at his eyes. "It's renwaeder. It's a spirit made from one of our desert plants. It's quite strong. I was going to ask whether you wanted it mixed with water or juice before you decided to drink it down plain. Following it with a swallow of brine helps as well."

"It's poison," Sophia hissed as she watched Alno easily swallow a glass full after pouring in some water.

She was still clutching at her throat when the commander appeared again, looking disgruntled. He gave her a warm smile. "Our king is in a mood today. Perhaps next time."

"Sounds good," she croaked, voice raspy.

She tried to hand back his gift again, but he held his palms up and backed away. "Keep it."

Sophia swatted at Alno when he pushed another cup of something at her, but he laughed. "Water. I promise." She sniffed it before gulping it down.

It took many reassurances from Alno before she tried renwaeder again. She had to agree—it wasn't that bad once mixed properly.

They reclined together, gawking at the magnificent works of art adorning everyone's body. Drink and warm, dry night air left her muscles relaxed, and for the first time in days, she allowed herself to find some enjoyment in Vrulatica.

Every so often, a man would approach, handing her a gift. She'd force herself not to accept the trinkets, directing the men to the king instead, and watching as he dashed their hopes.

Some suitors would simply walk away without a backward glance, while others would shoot her a disappointed smile or tail wave before slinking away. As the alcohol worked its magic, she found herself sulking more and more.

This was the coolest party she'd ever been to, and all she could do was sit on a cushion and watch. Sophia wasn't the best dressed here by any means, but she looked nice. Her defenses were lowered, and although she enjoyed hanging out with Alno, a pretty present and a short walk with a handsome man didn't sound like such a bad idea. Yet the glowering dragon behind her had done nothing but turn down anyone who asked. It irked.

She opened the small bag the commander had given her and grinned at the ring. It was made of twining copper wire that fit over two fingers and was topped with a vibrant green leaf. It didn't go with her outfit at all, but she slipped it on anyway.

"Look at this. Isn't it…" Sophia glanced up to find Alno crestfallen. His golden glow ebbed to a mere flicker. She followed his morose gaze toward the king and sucked in an appalled breath. He was standing, the ghost of a smile on his face as he ran his fingers over the lapis bone detailing on Difila's thigh.

To an innocent onlooker, it might appear as if he were just admiring the craftsmanship of her costume, but the flare of heat in Difila's eyes said it was more. "Oh. I'm so sorry, Alno."

Her friend shook his head, drinking down the rest of his glass. He put on a smile, but it was strained. "It's no matter. I'll have my chance one day."

Guilt had Sophia's shoulders curling. *She* was why he couldn't have his chance now. Because he had to babysit her all night.

No.

The renwaeder suddenly heated her veins. She glared in the king's direction. It was *his* fault.

Neither she nor Alno were allowed to go anywhere or talk to anyone who didn't approach them first because he'd commanded they stay under his watch. All either of them wanted to do was take a walk for five minutes like every other Vrulan here. But now poor Alno, who'd been so willing to take the punches as they came, was going to have to sit here and watch the king flirt with the girl of his dreams.

What if he made a display of it like he had the other day at dinner? Sophia didn't know if she could bear to watch Alno witness that.

An idea struck her.

"You'd better appreciate this, Alno," she growled as she ripped a line of chain off her dress and dropped it into the small bag the commander had given her.

"Wha—" Alno hadn't noticed she'd risen until she was a foot ahead of him. He cursed, stumbling after her. "Sophia," he hissed. "What are you doing? Stop."

"Shh. If this goes the way I want, I swear to God you'd better make your move."

Alno started to argue more, but the king had noticed her marching over. One of his brows arched loftily.

A quiver of doubt hollowed her stomach as she stared up at the looming king on his raised platform. "Hello, Your Majesty." She gave an awkward nod to Difila, who glanced between them, hands on hips. "I'm sorry for interrupting, but…" She swallowed, stomach a battleground and heart thundering.

I can't do it.

She watched Difila's eyes flit to Alno and linger for a moment. Sophia may have imagined the spark in her gaze, but it was all she needed to muster the last dregs of her courage.

She held out the bag to the king. "Would you walk with me?"

10

Surely an eternity had passed.

The king had been staring at her for hours at least, his expression maddeningly unreadable. Sophia wanted to melt into the sand. She was almost positive if he looked closely, he'd see her body pulse in time with her hammering heart.

It'd seemed like a perfect solution a minute ago. If he agreed to go on a walk with her, not only would she be able to give Alno some much needed time alone with Difila, she'd also be able to broach the subject of accompanying them on the trip to watch the new Queen's broadcast if it happened.

But now she wasn't so sure. What if he turned her down? How embarrassing.

Her skin went cold. What if he *didn't* turn her down? On some logical level, she'd known what that would mean. But…

Steps slow, the king prowled forward. Each thump of his foot on the three steps leading to the ground were thunderous to her ears. She just managed to keep herself from flinching when his boots crunched into the soft sand directly in front of her.

His gaze bore into hers as he slowly slipped the pouch from her lax fingers.

Sophia swallowed.

"Let us walk, then." His deep voice sent sparks skittering over her shoulders.

All she could do was nod and follow him toward a dim tunnel near the edge of the forest. Sophia peered back at Alno as the entrance to the tunnel neared and found him gazing stupidly after her. She gave a vicious head jab toward Difila, who was also staring at them, and he seemed to rouse, plastering on a hasty grin and saying something to Difila that Sophia couldn't hear.

The corner of the woman's mouth lifted, and she tilted her head down at him.

Even if this walk ended up being the worst mistake ever, at least she'd given Alno a shot with his dream warrior woman. Sophia let out a satisfied breath and snuck a glance at the king. Her heartbeat stumbled when she found him watching her.

They crossed the threshold of the tunnel, and sound from the party grew muffled. She could feel Sikthand's stare still hot and heavy on her, so she busied herself with examining every decorative stitch of silver in the azure fabric covering their intimate path. The drapes of the walls were dense, but the fabric of the ceiling was thin enough that she could see the treetops and stars through it as they walked.

The king's frame filled much more of the tunnel than she cared for, leaving her with two options. She could walk so close to his bicep that their bodies were in danger of brushing together with one swaying step or skim against the fabric walls and reveal how skittish she felt. She would *not* be doing that.

They walked in torturous silence. Wasn't he supposed to be talking her up? Or was that her job since she'd been the one to ask him to walk? She chewed on her lip as she thought of what to say to break the silence. *Lucky we had such good weather tonight. No. Stupid.*

The king kept his massive arms clasped behind his back. Sophia suddenly couldn't remember what she did with her hands while walking.

She plastered them to her sides, then groaned inwardly. *Not right.*

Pulling them in front of her only made her look like she was trying to imitate a speed-walking suburban housewife. His elbow brushed her arm, and she nearly squeaked.

God, he looked good tonight. His outfit might be a bit gruesome, but it highlighted the sexy bulges of his muscles perfectly. She breathed in, and her lids fluttered. He smelled good too.

"Why did you pull me away from that female?" His rumbled words had her shoulders tensing.

"What?" She knew perfectly well what he'd said and what the question had meant, but she needed time to think of an answer.

The king stopped and faced her, his wide chest seeming much wider in the close quarters of the covered tunnel. "You interrupted my conversation with Difila. Were you attempting to take her place in my bed tonight?"

Sparks of electricity exploded over her scalp. "N-No!" Sophia sputtered.

"There's no other reason to ask someone to walk," he reminded darkly.

"I...I thought if..." He let his silver gaze roam down her body, not bothering to hide his perusal. Heat pooled in her belly. He'd never looked at her like *that* before. *This isn't the plan.* "Your Majesty, I..."

A wicked smile lifted the corner of Sikthand's mouth, exposing one of his sharp fangs. She sucked a slow breath, lips parting. "Find me majestic, do you?" He inched closer, his smell enveloping her.

Her brows knit. "What?"

"You keep calling me majestic. It's not often my looks are so exalted. Tell me, human, which parts of me are most glorious?" Sophia jumped when something slithered around her back and forced her a step closer. She realized as the tip came up to rest on the underside of her chin that it was his tail twining around her back and lifting up her front.

He pressed the sharp point into her skin just enough to force her chin to lift and her gaze to meet his. "It's..." Sophia tried to organize her thoughts, but all she could think about was how close her body was to his. One more tug of his tail and she'd be flattened against him. The heat building inside her trickled to her core at the thought.

His silver eyes flashed, then darkened.

"It's just a title," she finally managed. "Something people on Earth say to royalty. Your Majesty. Your Highness. Your Eminence."

"Despite your…current interest," He peered down her body again pointedly. Her face blazed. He could smell that she was turned on. "We both know you didn't bring me here to service you. So, I ask again, what do you want?"

"I want…" *I want you to pull me in and put those fangs to use.* She internally shook herself. *No! Bad Sophia! That's just the fire milk talking.* She closed her eyes, not able to think straight while staring at his handsome face. Why had she thought this walk was a good idea again? *Oh yeah.*

"I want you to take me with you if there's a broadcast from Tremanta." The words spilled from her lips.

***

Sikthand should've never allowed himself to accept her invitation. They hadn't been walking for more than a few minutes and he'd already almost crushed her to his chest, catching himself just before.

He was enamored with the human. Though he'd forced himself to remain in the shadows for the past two days, he'd given up trying to keep away from her. He liked watching her. He craved it. It calmed something in him.

He'd followed her as she explored his city, slipping between every crack, peephole, and mirror built into the tower by his ancestors. He'd scowled when she'd picked her dress for the night, regretting he couldn't give her something better.

How wrong he'd been. Her outfit didn't fit in with the other Vrulan costumes. It was gauzy and delicate. And it displayed hints of her bare body underneath in such a tantalizing way. His eyes had nearly dried out in his skull as he'd watched her walk toward him, heart braced for the moment he'd see a clear hint of flesh, but it never came.

Yet the dress was more than just a pretty frock.

She showed no signs of embarrassment for how out of place her outfit was compared to the rest. Quite the opposite. As he watched her expression, he'd seen a glimpse of it—defiance.

The mouthwatering female was making a statement. It had almost brought a grin to his face. But then the suitors, unaware of her fascinating mind, had descended on her in droves.

He wanted to rip every one of them apart. None of them saw the sly outfit for what it was. They just saw a luscious body wrapped in fabric thin enough to tear with a wayward slice of their tail.

The faint scent of her arousal drifted to his nose. His cock ached knowing if he dropped his tail from her chin at just the right angle, her dress would split apart like tissue.

But that wasn't why she'd walked with him.

Her gesture had been selfless. One done to help her attendant, Alno.

He admitted he'd been jealous watching them lounge together, talking about one inane thing or another. Smiling.

He could never have that with her, and envy burned in him like molten lead. He'd been in the process of seducing Difila so the innocent male might feel some of the jealousy he felt.

Sikthand despised Alno. He hated the way he easily reclined, laughing and drinking, not a care in the world. He wasn't constantly aware of who walked behind his seat. He didn't have to ensure his drink was filled with liquor from his personal stores.

He could just...exist.

But what made him loathe the male more than anything else, was that Sophia could exist with him. If he wasn't positive it would hurt his little human, Sikthand would have had Alno resigned days ago.

No, not *his* human.

His tail slipped away from the gentle curve of her back. She shivered.

Sikthand straightened, forcing his demeanor to harden. In another life, he could've been the one to warm her.

He turned and continued his slow steps down the tunnel. "I had already planned to take you along if Vila were to ascend."

"Oh." She sped to catch up to him. Her gaze slipped to his, hope lifting her dark brows. "Maybe you could allow Heleax to come too?"

"No," he growled.

Sophia chewed on her delightfully pink lip but didn't appear too surprised. The end of the tunnel seemed to grow farther away with each step, the silence making the air heavy.

"Did you… Did you ask Vila to send humans in exchange for reopening trade?"

He snorted. "Is that the rumor these days? No. Trade is closed until I have a confirmed ruler to speak with about reopening it."

"Oh," she breathed.

Sikthand swelled, wanting to say more, though he never usually felt the need to explain himself. He was not the kind of ruler who made a habit of bartering with lives.

"I like your outfit," she tried, changing the subject. Her gaze caught on his chest where Japeshi's name was almost visible. The drawing she'd done of him in which she'd omitted the name flashed through his head and made his jaw clench.

Her eyes were narrowed on his pec now. She was nearly glaring at Japeshi's half-hidden name. Jealousy? Or pity?

"Do you have a problem with my tattoo?" He all but hissed.

Her gaze snapped to his, and she blanched. She shook her head, eyes falling to the ground.

They walked for a few more agonizing steps before he rumbled, "That pitying look in your eye tells me you've learned what it says and what it means. I suppose your attendant enlightened you?" Sikthand already knew he had.

Brief mentions of his past had been sprinkled through Sophia and Alno's conversations, as if they'd discussed Sikthand's tragedies many times over. His dislike for the male deepened.

"No." Sophia stared straight ahead. "I heard about it from someone at dinner."

Little liar.

"And who was that? I'd like to have a word with them." He held back his smirk when her eyes darted around the tunnel, scrambling to think of a lie.

Horns blared in the distance, catching their attention.

"The umbercree are arriving," Sikthand explained at Sophia's confused expression. He scanned the tunnel in both directions. They were far closer to the end than the beginning, and most people usually ventured into the dark forest to watch the umbercree anyway.

He could lead her back, drop her with Alno, and let her watch the creatures from a distance. But then he recalled how amazed he'd been the first time he'd seen them. If she felt even a fraction as enthralled as he'd been, the work of art she'd create would be enchanting. She should have the best vantage possible.

"Step quickly." He wanted to place a hand on her spine, but he kept his fingers crushed together at his back, the slight pain a tether to his control.

When they emerged from the end of the tunnel, the forest was dark and quiet. The sky above was a deep velvety blue, and the stars and moon emitted just enough glow to backlight the thin swaying leaves of the minata trees.

The party some ways behind them buzzed with excitement. Lights began blinking out, extinguished so they could better see the umbercree, but Sophia eased toward him, worry crinkling her forehead.

His chest swelled at her subtle movement. It was unlikely she even realized what she'd done, but Sikthand felt it in every fiber of his being. "Calm, female. We watch the umbercree in the dark."

Her attention lifted to him, then she scanned the trees, shoulders tensing as if the fact they were alone together in a dark forest made her nervous. He hated that his presence had this effect, even though he'd worked diligently to elicit this exact response. He wanted her wary of him, didn't he? Wary was safe. Wary meant she'd keep her distance.

"Maybe we should go back?" One by one, the lights in the tunnel blinked out, throwing them into darkness. "Or not," she breathed.

He knew human vision was weaker and wondered how much, if anything, she could still see. From the way she wrung her hands together and scanned the space around the tunnel entrance miserably, as if she could no longer find it, he guessed not very much.

Rustling built in the air, and an umbercree swooped by their legs, hitting them with a blast of wind. Sophia shrieked and stumbled back. He caught her before she tripped over a minata root.

Damn her fear, souring the air around them. He wanted her to enjoy this. Not be terrified.

Sikthand pulled her trembling body in front of his and kept his hands heavy on her shoulders. "They are soundless creatures," he whispered into her ear as more umbercree rustled the tree overhead, sending leaves floating down toward them. "But in a moment, they'll begin boring their way into the trees."

Droves of umbercree swooped past, making her hair fly. She startled each time, backing further against his chest, but her fear had ebbed, a tentative grin rising on her face. Sikthand wanted to groan in frustration. Keeping himself immune to her was impossible.

He exhaled against her ear, unable to stop himself, and watched as her breath hitched. It would take no effort at all to kiss the warm pulse point thrumming at her neck.

An umbercree flew by so close its long tail brushed her ear, and she laughed. He loved that sound, yet he hated hearing it—a taste of something he had to pretend he didn't want.

She'd be gone soon. She wasn't his to keep.

Her head turned from side to side when a low tapping echoed from the trees above. "They bore holes in the minata trunks and eat the sap," he explained as the rumble of pecking umbercree built to a steady drum, filling the quiet night with sound.

"This is incredible." Her gaze flew about overhead, searching for the birds who were nearly invisible except for a faint outline against the bright moon. "I wish I could see them. Are they sensitive to light or something?"

"Just watch."

She chuckled lightly. "I'd love to, but I can't see…a…damn…thing…" Her voice died out. The umbercree had pecked their way through, and now glowing green minata sap seeped down the trunks.

All around them the forest bled, the vivid bright syrup running down the trees in rivulets.

Sophia took in an awed breath as the world around them began to glow. She gazed at the towering trunks coated in luminous green liquid.

The umbercree were visible now, their black bellies and long stretched tails painted in the sap they were lapping up. "They'll soon be full and drunk, then they'll find a mate. By the time morning arrives, they'll begin to build their nests."

She lifted her hand to a tree nearby and dipped her fingers in the sap. "It's like glowstick goo," she said, rubbing the sticky substance between her fingers just before her nose. "How? Is it radioactive?" She stretched her hand away, eyes flying up to him from over her shoulder.

He couldn't contain a grin, and her dark eyes slipped to his mouth. "No. It's from the soil," he explained, using all his considerable control to ignore the way her gaze lingered hungrily. "The trees love the metal deposits. They're full of them, and it makes their sap glow." She peered up at him through thick lashes. His resolve waned.

Her smell was making his mind go fuzzy. He could let himself slip. Just this once.

Sikthand allowed his hands to trail down her shoulders and settle on her narrow waist. The metal design of her white dress glittered in the glow of the minata forest. He sucked an inhale through his tight chest.

Her gaze deepened, as if she were thinking hard about something. "Can I ask you a question?" she whispered, her breath ghosting across his cheek. He nodded his assent. "Why do you still have it?" She searched his eyes and said the next words so quietly he almost didn't hear them. "Her name?"

Dull pain rolled through him. Sikthand had thought about removing Japeshi's name many times. As he gazed down at Sophia, he knew he needed to speak the truth aloud, not just to give her an honest answer, but to ensure he reminded himself.

He inhaled deeply, loneliness creeping in. "Removing it would imply there is room for something else to take its place." His fingers slipped from her waist. "There isn't."

11

The Flesh Forge.

Sophia hadn't known what to expect exactly, but the floors of space dedicated to Vrulan tattooing called the Flesh Forge matched their name perfectly—from what she could see over the burly shoulders of the man barring their entrance. Around the perimeter of the top floor were enormous, elaborately sculpted hearths. Each contained glowing vats of molten metal and large ceramic stills that dripped gleaming black liquid into glass containers.

"This is a *human*," Alno argued once more, as if the man hadn't heard him right the first time. "And a female. She needs to be seen by the most knowledgeable among you. Don't you want the honor of being the first inkmaster to make your mark on a human?"

Khes, a barrel-chested man with every centimeter of skin covered in tattoos, was a master inksmith. Apparently he was always in high demand and picky about who he drew on, his most famous client being the king. Sophia had cringed with embarrassment when Alno had demanded Khes himself take the time to meet with her, but Alno would hear none of it.

"And what if her human body can't take it?" the male growled back, his narrowed eyes traveling over her pale skin. "What if she reacts poorly to the ink? Then I will have been the first inksmith to disfigure a human, and how would that look? Besides, I can't have a wailing alien disturbing clients when she can't handle the pain."

Those words sparked something inside her, and she stepped forward, chin lifted. "*I* can handle pain." She hadn't elaborated, choosing instead to hold his skeptical stare.

"I've already shown you the report from the doctor. Humans should have no adverse reactions to our ink." Alno brandished the scroll he'd brought once again, but Khes was still maintaining eye contact with her. Both silently challenged the other to look away.

"Why should I listen to you anyway? You haven't felt the pain. Who are you to tell her she can handle it?" Khes sneered at Alno.

"Why would I cover this up?" Alno shot him a dazzling grin, flexing one luminous golden bicep, which only made Khes' tail whip around in agitation.

"Is there a reason for all this squabbling?"

Sophia froze, goose bumps breaking out over her body. She rotated slowly on one heel and found the king standing close behind, his helmet tucked under his arm. She peered down the empty cobbled alley he must have arrived from.

Had they all been so immersed they hadn't heard him approach?

"Sire," Khes greeted, tapping his tail on the ground respectfully. "This human wants to be inked, but I don't believe there has been enough study for me to feel comfortable."

Alno silently shook the file again, eyes wide with irritation.

The king's silver gaze slid to her, and her treacherous heart beat faster. Something about him had shifted in her mind after the umbercee celebration, and now she couldn't help but replay the feeling of his tail pulling her in and the sensation of his warm breath against her ear. A dam keeping her interest in him innocent—objective, even—had burst. Now she couldn't stop the butterflies flapping around her stomach every time someone mentioned his name. She had a fucking crush on her alien abductor. How absurd.

"Can this wait until you've visited the doctor again?" he asked, arms clasped at his back like they'd been when he'd walked with her through the tunnel.

"Well." She clutched her sketchbook to her chest. "I don't want to get my hopes up or anything, but if Vila ascends to the throne tomorrow and you're able to get in contact with her..." A stupid nagging dread tugged at her. "It's possible I might be going home very soon, right? If your...demands are met, I mean." She studied his reaction but saw no emotion flash over his stony expression.

Sophia still didn't know if he'd actually *made* or planned to make any demands of the new Queen. Supposedly his original reason for taking them hostage had been a demand for resignation. But now that the old Queen was dead, she didn't know where that left Sikthand.

If the rumors Heleax pushed on her were true, he was set on bargaining for more humans, but the king had scoffed at that. Maybe it was just a side effect of her crush, but she believed him.

Thinking hard on the value of a trade like the one Heleax described also made her doubtful. What did a few extra humans in your city get you, anyway? Best-case scenario, a handful of citizens would recognize their mates.

That might be beneficial, but was it really worth blackmailing a new Queen? It wouldn't save their species from extinction in the long run, and she couldn't imagine any of the girls back at the Pearl Temple coming quietly. If they knew they'd been traded like livestock, the Vrulans should prepare to learn how explosive human women could be real quick.

"If there is even a slim chance I could be leaving tomorrow, I'd like to make sure I don't miss out on getting a tattoo." She reeled in a spike of sadness. "I used to have a lot of tattoos, and I don't know of many places on Clecania that do them."

The king's jaw tensed. "You realize it will be quite painful, and you accept the possibility of a negative reaction?"

The chance she might need to be airlifted to the doctor frightened her, but her charts already stated the ink would have no effect. The only Clecanian materials she was allergic to—as were all humans—were byproducts of the Ripsli tree. "Yes."

"I don't want to be responsible for—"

"You will tattoo her," Sikthand interrupted Khes. The rigid authority in his voice made a flush rise on her chest. His glowing gaze finally broke away from hers, and he focused on the master inksmith. "As a favor to me."

"Yes, sire," Khes grated through a scowl.

She tried to hold back her grin, but a hint of it broke through as she thanked the king. His brows furrowed. He said nothing, just strode away.

"Come on, then," Khes grumbled.

Sophia stared at Sikthand's retreating back for a beat too long. When she turned back, Alno was watching her, brows raised and a knowing smirk curling his lips.

"What?" She nudged past him, heat rising on her neck.

Voice lighter than air, he shook his head. "Nothing. Nothing."

"Here's where the ink is distilled." Khes gestured unenthusiastically to the room at large.

Sophia took a few steps closer to a man suited in thick, nonflammable material. He tipped a vat of molten orange metal into an empty still, then forced it closed. The man caught sight of her watching and straightened.

Khes stepped in front of her, blocking her view. "This is dangerous work. I don't need you distracting them."

"Sorry." She followed him to the center of the room, where a set of stairs spiraled downward.

"What are you looking to get anyway?" Khes grunted, lips fixed in a frown.

Sophia brightened. She cracked open her sketchbook, flipping through messy drawings until she found the design she'd settled on. She held out the book to Khes, and he snatched it.

With a sigh, he peered down at the drawing and his steps slowed, his glower softening. He glanced back at her with a raised brow. "This is…good, actually."

"Thanks." She grinned. "I designed all my own tattoos back on Earth."

He rotated toward her on the steps, looking her over with renewed interest. "You removed them rather than making edits?"

Her lips parted as she thought of how to explain. "Where I'm from, tattoos are permanent for the most part. You can't change them like you can here. But…" She looked away for a moment, a familiar grief tightening her chest. "When I was abducted, they were removed…healed. I didn't know till I woke up."

Khes' expression hardened.

He swung away and stomped down the steps. "Fucking dregs. And those fucking machines!" Sophia exchanged a look with Alno. They hurried to keep up with him but skidded to a halt when he swung his arm around, pointing at them angrily with her sketchbook still clutched in his palm. "And it's not just them," he boomed. "It's those damn cities that see our work as some kind of..." He blustered silently for a moment. "Defacement. Simple minded, the lot of them."

He grumbled to himself the whole way down the stairs while Sophia and Alno held in their bemused grins.

When they reached the lowest level of the Flesh Forge, only a few eyes turned to watch Khes ranting away to himself. They peered up from their wincing clients with boredom in their expressions.

"Don't worry, girl," he pointed to her again, then his eyes caught on her notebook. He unclenched his fist from the slightly crushed spine and handed it back to her with an apologetic grin. Before she could slip it away, he patted the back of her hand. "We'll get 'em back. I'll draw as many as you want."

"Sophia," she reminded.

"Sophia," he repeated, his cobalt-blue eyes crinkling within his iron hood. He eyed Alno, frown a little softer than it was before but still present. "You want him watching?"

"I'm staying. Unless you want to take it up with the king," Alno jeered.

She elbowed him lightly. "Yes, I'd like him here, please."

Khes grunted and waved them on. As they wound through stations, Sophia grew uneasy. Vrulatica was filled with hardy warriors, and yet their clenched teeth and rapidly flicking tails made it seem like even they had trouble handling the pain.

Sophia had had sessions that lasted for hours, getting work done in some of the most painful spots on the body. But suddenly her confidence wobbled.

They approached a station larger than any of the others in the corner. Breathing in through her nose and out through her mouth, she attempted to settle the nausea bubbling in her belly.

"You. Over there. Keep quiet and stay out of the way," Khes barked, pointing at a seat in the corner. Alno settled into it with a flashy, over-the-top smile.

When Khes turned away, sifting through drawers, she slapped Alno's arm with her sketchbook. "Cut it out."

"You know what this process is?" Khes patted the bench in front of him, and she took a seat.

Sophia eyed the items in his hand with a relieved breath. *Just the drawing stage.*

"I know what the process is on Earth." She handed over her sketchbook when he beckoned for it, flipping to the correct page first.

He studied it, scratching his black hair with a brush dipped in red ink. "Mmm, and what's that?"

"Well, after you know what you're getting and where you want it and all that, they prep the area, cleaning and shaving it, then they put the stencil on so they have a guide." Khes nodded along as she spoke. "They inject the ink into your skin with a needle. Line work, um, like the outline or the heavier lines in the design, I guess? That comes first. Then they might change needles for color and shading after all the linework is done."

"Color." Khes' eyes lit with interest. "Now that would be fun." His brows furrowed. "When you say needle, you mean they inject the ink once, then inject the color later with another needle?"

"No..." Sophia thought about what she knew of Vrulan tattooing. "So here you inject the ink first and then you use a magnetic pen to move it around under the skin, right? But all the ink is already there?" He nodded. "Well, on Earth they draw with a needle. It is constantly going in and out of your skin as they draw." When Khes still looked confused, she explained again. "The needle is in a machine, and it punctures the skin thousands of times per minute."

Alno and Khes expelled identical sounds of disgust. "Horrible," Khes spat. "Don't you bleed?"

His lip curled more and more as she answered. "Well, the needle is pretty small, but yeah. Some bleed more than others."

Resigned disbelief had him shaking his head. "I guess you *have* felt some pain, then."

He began to freehand paint the image on her bicep the way she'd shown in her sketch, peppering her with questions concerning everything to do with Earth tattoos, from their permanency to their popularity, and enlightening her on the history of Vrulan tattooing in return.

At some point, Alno had drifted to sleep, a gentle snore rising from the corner. Khes sat back, and she grinned at the nearly perfect reproduction. "Now I understand why Alno was so adamant I see you."

His pale gray cheeks flushed, almost deepening to the shade of his iron hood. He hiked a shoulder. "After a hundred years, I should be good at something, I suppose."

He didn't have time to see Sophia's jaw drop before he turned to his workbench. "A hundred?" she breathed. "Is it impolite to ask Vrulans how old they are?"

"The older I get, the more I understand that *polite* is just a longer path to get where you want." He chuckled. "You want to ask me something? Ask me."

"How old are you?" She grinned.

He slammed a large black button on the wall, then tipped his head, eyeing the ceiling. "I'd say nearing two hundred if I've got the year right, which I sometimes don't."

"Wow." Though Sophia was still wary of the healing tube, she had to admit it had its perks. She would have guessed Khes' age to be closer to midforties. "Well, you don't look a day over a hundred and sixty."

His gaze widened at her until he caught her teasing grin, then he let out a barking laugh that had Alno bolting awake and crashing off his chair.

"Good morning, sunshine." She smiled at a disgruntled Alno as he rubbed his head and picked himself off the floor.

A whoosh filled the air, and a tube of gleaming black liquid appeared in an alcove in the wall. It must have been sent down from the ink forge above.

"Alright." Khes stepped close and held the vial up to her eyes. "I need to inject this into your skin all at once. It won't feel pleasant. It won't look pleasant. Good news is you won't need to inject more in this area unless you get it surgically removed with a healer."

She eyed the gloopy black ink.

"What will it feel like?" She forced the words through a clenched jaw.

Khes attached a short plunger-like device to the top of the vial. "Cold. It will be so cold it burns. But the sensation of the ink in your skin is what sticks with folks." He pulled a silver bucket out from under the bench and dropped it between her knees. "Many vomit their first time."

"And you wonder why I never got tattooed," Alno groused from the corner, now wide awake.

Sophia dragged the bucket closer, already questioning whether this was a good idea. He suctioned the plunger to her upper arm, almost at her shoulder, and caught her eye. "Ready?"

Fingers tensing on the lip of her bucket, she nodded.

Khes dragged a dial on a cord connected to the plunger vial, and acid leaked into her shoulder. She inhaled a surprised gasp, then bared her teeth and squeezed her eyes shut. *In through the nose and out through the mouth.* She focused on the sensation, trying to force her brain to get used to the pain, but Khes hadn't been wrong. She could handle the pain. It hurt a little more than her worst tattoo, but the sensation...

It was as if someone had sliced open a pouch in her arm and was now stuffing her with thickened, frozen lemon juice, lifting her skin from her muscle as they forced the stinging juice deeper.

It was sickening. Her stomach bubbled, and she focused on her breathing.

"That's done. I'm gonna guide the pool of ink into position with my pen now." She gave a tight nod but didn't dare to look or speak. If her shoulder looked anything like it felt, it would definitely force her stomach to empty.

Sophia clutched the bucket tighter, barely holding back a heave when Khes began. Her mind worked to convince itself this was okay. As he guided the design, it felt like a barbed string was being dragged around under her skin. She'd rather get a full-rib-cage-plus-armpit tattoo twice over than feel this revolting crawl beneath her flesh.

How had Sikthand done it? She pictured the sections of his chest that were almost solid black. Khes had only needed to inject a small vial for her design. How much ink did Sikthand have under his skin? Her stomach calmed as she thought about this, so she focused harder. She imagined each line on his chest, and when she'd outlined them all, she busied herself with picturing what marks might cover his shins, his powerful thighs, his…

"All done. Just need to lock it in place now." Her brain snapped back to reality. Sophia had no idea how long she'd been sitting there grinding her jaw and daydreaming over Sikthand's naked body, but when she opened her eyes, about ten Vrulans floated about the perimeter of Khes' station, watching her with curious expressions.

A large pad was wrapped around her arm and molded to her shoulder. Khes flipped a switch, and Sophia released an embarrassing moan. Warmth slipped over her shoulder and arm, numbing the pain so completely her lids fluttered.

Her breaths were still evening out when Khes pounded her back with a solid thump that made her pitch forward over her bucket. "You weren't lying. You handled that better than most warriors I know." He beamed down at her, and she preened. In a city where so many considered her to be just a weak human, she'd succeeded in impressing someone. It was a small thing, but pride had her spine straightening.

When Khes removed the pad, she hopped off the bench and sped past the group of gawking Vrulans to a mirror. There on her bicep was a malginash. It climbed up her shoulder, wings pulled back against its spine. With her pale skin peeking through its black face, it looked as if its eyes were glowing. Surrounding the malginash were a few bold geometric shapes and lines. Two moons—one crescent, one full—completed the image.

Out of nowhere, tears started to burn in her eyes.

For months now, she'd felt as if someone had rung her like a gong and her soul had been left to perpetually reverberate. But this tattoo had stilled the vibration. Like a hand wrapping around a ringing bell, the tattoo stilled her, grounded her.

She looked at her reflection and could almost see herself again.

Khes joined her at the mirror. "What do you—"

He let out a grunt when she threw her arms around him, a few silent tears sliding onto the metal designs covering his shirt.

She could feel him turning his head this way and that, as if scanning for help to remove the human pest clinging to him. Finally he whispered, "Most cry while *getting* the tattoo. Don't believe I've ever seen it happen after."

Sophia pulled away with a sniff. "You should be happy that in your old age you can still be surprised."

Khes let out another booming laugh, earning him bewildered looks from every Vrulan in the room.

12

Sikthand's eyes followed Sophia around the loading bay as Madam Kalos and Speaker Besith jabbered away at him. The whole Guild had been in a frenzy since news that Vila had been confirmed as Queen had been delivered that morning.

Though he'd trudged to the Guild chamber as soon as reports of her confirmation had come in, it seemed a pointless endeavor. Until they had some new, solid information to discuss, arguing about what Vila *might* do was a waste of time.

Time he would much rather spend watching Sophia stretch and putter around her room the way she did every morning before Alno arrived. He'd had to miss the view of her rumpled hair and heavy lids just so he could listen to his Guild argue about things they'd been arguing about for the past few days.

"She's known to be a shrewd counselor within the Intergalactic Alliance." Madam Kalos stood at Ahea's feet and spoke seemingly to Sikthand but spat the words in Speaker Besith's direction.

"Her input is always too severe, though," Besith countered. "The king must be careful in his approach. She may want retribution for our actions as a demonstration of strength."

"Nonsense. We aligned with six other cities when we cut off trade. We didn't threaten war, we only asked that her predecessor break her silence. She has no grounds to retaliate."

Ahea turned her head, snorting at the two wailing near her ear. He covertly patted her flank. *I know. Leave the squabbling children be.* As if his mount could hear his inner thoughts, she huffed in irritation and angled her head away.

"None of the other cities kidnapped three buckets' worth of their citizens. *Humans* at that!" Speaker Besith's eyes bugged. "I said it was a bad idea when you suggested it, and it was."

"Guildmembers." Sikthand kept his voice even. His father had drilled into him from a young age how vital it was to keep the Guild happy. One wayward insult could sow seeds of resentment. The Guild held power over their domains, and a dissatisfied guildmember could easily transform into a bitter enemy if he wasn't careful. It was always a game to ensure he sided with each member throughout the year on one issue or another to give the illusion he respected them equally. In reality, he had his favorites, and neither of these two were them.

"She won't be in power long if she doesn't reopen trade with Vrulatica. She won't risk that. Not for a mere slight."

"You—"

"Guildmembers!" Sikthand boomed. Their attention flew to him. His *mother* had trained him to be forceful. *They won't follow you if they see weakness.* He had to walk a fine line between displaying objectiveness and ruthless authority. "The Guild chamber is being stocked and prepared even now. We will meet after the address, and you will voice your concerns then."

They tapped their tails respectfully on the ground, but a flash of disapproval crossed over Besith's face. Sikthand took notice.

Cold suspicion flooded him, hardening his muscles and clearing his mind. He'd been distracted by the human as of late, following her around the tower like a simpering animal. How many other veiled looks had he missed while he gazed stupidly at the female?

Sikthand stared down at his hands, clutching Ahea's reins. There were no marks under these gloves, though he often found himself checking.

His mind had churned since the announcement of the new Queen came through. There was a chance he'd be forced to send Sophia away.

It's better she leaves. He tried to convince himself of the fact yet again.

He watched her so often, he was surprised he hadn't been assassinated out of sheer obliviousness.

Unable to control himself, his eyes found her, and an ache settled in his chest.

"Ready yourselves. We need to leave," he called to the room. The Guild divided into two buckets. One that would be carried by Roldroth, and one by him. Sophia glanced between the two, uncertainty crinkling her nose. He welded his jaw shut and forced himself not to demand she climb into his bucket.

Though he wore his masked helmet, her eyes rose to meet his. When she caught him looking, her gaze shot away. A light blush bloomed on her cheeks.

He could howl in frustration. This fascination was easier when it had been wholly one-sided. How much longer could he keep away from her if she continued to grace him with soft smiles and fleeting glances?

The leather reins groaned under his clenching fists as Sophia clambered into *his* bucket behind Lady Lindri.

Put her out of your mind.

He spurred Ahea on, Commander Roldroth following close behind.

As they took off into the scorching afternoon sky, Sikthand buried his emotions. He'd need to be the king today. Not an infatuated male. His people and his city were his priority, and Sophia was a pretty tool to be used for their benefit. It did him no good to think of her as anything else.

He'd vowed a long time ago to never let anyone within striking distance again. As he imagined her flying away from his city, a deeper hurt than had existed before Sophia's arrival pulsed through him. It would ebb in time. It always did. But the fact that he'd let his guard down enough for this measure of grief to exist at all infuriated him.

Before too long, the outbuildings nestled around the infirmary came into view, and he pulled Ahea into a gentle descent. When he dismounted, he didn't wait to walk with the rest. He needed to put distance between himself and the human. No matter what the day brought, whether she stayed or left, he would be cutting himself off from her. She was a distraction he couldn't afford.

A messenger was already there, setting up the feed for them, and he gave a respectful tap of his tail when Sikthand walked in and took his seat against the wall. He kept his head facing forward, helmet in place, as the Guild trickled in, speaking amongst themselves.

Lady Lindri was squeaking excitedly to Sophia as they entered, though he couldn't tell about what. Likely smelting. He'd only ever seen Lindri speaking this avidly to non-mine workers or metalsmiths when she was talking about such things.

Sophia grinned and listened, almost appearing interested, though it was clear from the subtle furrow of her brows that she was confused. He sucked in a growl, annoyed by the human. Wherever she went, his people seemed to love her, almost like they were unable not to.

She'd even charmed Khes. Sikthand had been tattooed by the old male for as long as he could remember, as had his parents before him, and he couldn't recall hearing the male laugh more than a handful of times. After meeting with Sophia once, he'd morphed into someone who might've been mistaken for jolly.

Sikthand had watched in the Forge too. Of course he had. He'd been watching when she'd arrived and had been unable to keep himself from intervening when Khes had turned her away. He'd like to believe he'd only followed afterward to ensure the inkmaster behaved himself, but that would be a lie.

A person's first experience in the Forge was always foul. Painful and sickening. He'd wanted to be there in case she had a bad reaction and needed to be whisked to the infirmary.

Rather than scream and cry as many did—or throw up the way *he* had as a lad, she'd shown a level of control he'd never imagined from a body so seemingly fragile.

She'd impressed not just him, but the whole damn room.

Madam Kalos pulled an irritated Lady Lindri away, and Sophia held her grin for a moment longer before shaking her head as if to clear it. As though she could feel his eyes on her, she caught his gaze yet again and took a step toward him.

His helmet muffled his growl. He didn't want her to come speak to him because he so desperately wanted her to come speak to him.

Luckily the communicator set into the floor of the stone room illuminated, projecting an image of the new Queen of Tremanta, and Sophia's focus snapped to attention. She sped back to her seat and absently lowered into it.

"We've suffered a loss," the new Queen began. "Our Queen was tragically killed one week ago. No words can fill the void she's left."

Sikthand hadn't been surprised when he'd heard the news. As a ruler who'd had his life threatened often, he'd known it was only a matter of time before the attempts started. As the planet's representative and guardian to the largest assortment of humans in the world, Sikthand could not imagine the stress she must have been under. But her stubborn silence? Her refusal to hear any opinions from the rest of the cities on Clecania? Sikthand was surprised she hadn't been killed sooner.

"We won't rest until we find her killer, but at present, our world is in crisis. This is a time of change, and I know our Queen would understand the shift in focus. As named successor, I'm ready to take her place. For the first time in a hundred years, her name shall be spoken, and mine shall be locked away until I've either stepped down or moved to my next life. Nabiora Vilafina, you ruled with benevolence and grace, and you'll be missed."

Sikthand couldn't read Vila's expression. There was a theory circulating that the female was the old Queen's daughter, but to listen to her speak now, he couldn't believe it. He had to account for the differences in Tremantian customs, though. Whereas Vrulans inherited their royal titles—unless their line was wiped out entirely—Tremantian rulers were expected to give up all ties. They had no family, no mate, and they weren't even allowed to keep their name, instead taking on the moniker of Queen. Even if Vila was the Queen's daughter, it may just be a word to her. She might have been as much of a stranger as anyone else.

"Nabiora was fair and kind," Vila continued. "Perhaps to a fault. She sacrificed in a way that made sense in the moment. She kept the humans safe. She kept them happy. But she did so by awarding them freedoms that not even her own people possess."

The little sound that floated from his Guild quieted at that. Sikthand sat forward in his chair, an ominous dread sinking in. His gaze flicked to Sophia and found her eyes narrowed.

"The humans of Tremanta were not required to engage in marriage ceremonies. They weren't required even to socialize with the public, though it's been proven they spark recognition wherever they go. Through study, we've learned that humans come from Clecanian stock. Their ancestors are our ancestors. Yet we don't treat them as Clecanians. We don't hold them to the same standards. Is that not an insult to them? It's no wonder we've struggled to draft an argument strong enough to support the reclassification of Earth. How can we argue humans are equal to us in intellect and ability if we don't treat them as we treat each other? If we don't have them abide by the same laws we abide by?" The room seemed to hold its breath. "As my first action, I decree humans will be subject to our laws."

Disgust slithered under his ribs.

"Furthermore, I feel in this time of upheaval and transformation, our cities need to come together. Only united can we move forward with the heavy task that will be acclimating a Class Three planet to our existence. For that reason, I've decided to disperse the humans. Unmated Earthlings will be sent abroad to reside in cities across the planet. Not temporarily on a tour but permanently. There's no reason that Tremantians should have more of a chance to recognize a mate than anyone else."

The wood of Sikthand's chair splintered under his palms. *Sent abroad.* If he sent Sophia back, would she just be packaged and delivered to some new city against her will? This was morally reprehensible, and that was coming from someone who danced around the edges of morality more often than most.

"In the coming days, I will be meeting with representatives around the world to discuss their expectations and aid them in preparing for their human arrivals. I am determined to make this transition as simple as possible. The humans under my care are wise, and I'm positive they will see the benefit in this plan. Though they all deserve autonomy, they will understand that they are special, and special things must be handled with care."

Sophia's hand raised to her mouth, and her unblinking eyes were aimed at the ground.

"We not only lost our Queen, though, we have also lost our planet's representative," Vila said, shifting focus. "In light of this unexpected death, the Leaders' Summit will be postponed one month. In two months, we will meet. I urge you all to think hard on who you'd like to see represent us and keep in mind the tenacity our new representative must have. Earth must be opened. Humans must be made aware that their unknown brethren are in need of help. We won't survive without them. I hope you will choose a leader who is prepared to make sacrifices for the survival of our race, and not one who chooses to take the longest route."

Sikthand scanned the room, noticing some of his Guild wore appalled expressions, while others exchanged meaningful looks.

The new Queen was campaigning for herself. She was using this address to outline her stances so that all those listening would see her as some sort of wise leader who knew that sacrifice was sometimes necessary.

Sikthand hadn't known what to expect from the new Queen. One thing was now clear—Vila was not to be underestimated.

13

Heleax wore an expression of utter disbelief when Sophia finished relaying the Queen's speech. They were both silent for many long minutes. Even Alno threw her pitying glances.

"Do you think they knew?" Sophia asked, her voice hushed.

Vacant gaze sharpening on her, Heleax lifted a brow. "Who?"

"Meg. Daunet. Our group. Do you think somehow they knew what this new Queen was planning and chose not to return?"

"Perhaps. It would make sense. But how could they know before she made her speech? And call her *Vila*." Sharp anger cooled his voice. "She is *not* my Queen."

"I'm suddenly not so sure I should want to leave Vrulatica," she whispered. At least she'd settled in here. Met a few people she liked. And she was treated with a certain amount of respect. If Vila sent her away...

"You think it will be different here?" Heleax hissed. "She's set a precedent. Humans in Tremanta have to follow Tremantian laws. I'm sure Vrulatica will follow suit. Do you know what their laws concerning marriage are?"

"No. Do you?" she tossed back.

Heleax only scowled.

"What about those of us who have been on Clecania for a year? I think there are a few women closing in on that deadline. Isn't a Class Four species citizen allowed to leave the planet after a year, according to Intergalactic law?" she questioned.

"They *should* be." She bristled at Heleax's doubtful tone.

"The thing is..." Sophia chewed on her lip as she thought through the Queen's actions. "What does she have to gain by doing this? Does she think the whole world will be grateful? Herald her as a fair leader? I can't accept she actually believes a word she said about bringing the world together. There was something underneath it. I just can't figure out what it is."

"It's true. Many cities will be disgusted by this."

"*I'm* disgusted by this," Alno muttered. He leaned against the wall casually, but the cords of his throat were tight.

Heleax shot him an irritated frown.

"Right. I'm sure there are plenty who are going to accept a handful of humans with open arms." Sophia's stomach turned as she thought about it. "But they must realize that humans aren't going to be happy about this. And they *have* to know that there aren't nearly enough humans in Tremanta to send more than one or two to each city, if that. What good is one human for a whole city of people? A human can be recognized by one Clecanian. The odds of that Clecanian happening to be in their city are astronomical." Sophia mentally tallied the humans she'd seen wandering around the Pearl Temple. "And honestly, there aren't enough humans to send to every city, so what about the cities that don't get one? How is she going to pick?"

Heleax's scrunched brows lifted, his eyes widening in realization. "The Leaders' Summit."

"What?"

"The person who will have the *real* power if Earth is ever opened is the planetary representative. It used to be the old Queen, but now someone new has to be elected. All newly established Class Three planets are required to have a Steward, a species who guides them in adjusting to their expanded existence and, knowing our particular ties to your species, I don't doubt Clecania will be named Earth's Steward. If that happens, our planetary representative will oversee all things relating to Earth. They'll dictate which cities newly arrived humans may settle in and determine what rights they have."

"Yeah. She talked about that vote a lot near the end," Sophia agreed.

A dark laugh bubbled from Heleax. "I bet she did. Every Clecanian city's leader votes at the Leaders' Summit and decides who the planetary representative will be. The pool of candidates isn't that large. Only current members of the Intergalactic Alliance can be considered for the role."

Heleax stared at Sophia, and she felt she was missing something vital.

"*Vila* is a member of the Intergalactic Alliance."

Understanding crashed over her and jaw dropped. "She's going to buy votes."

***

It had been a long day and an even longer night. Sikthand was irritable from the hours of discussion and theory-bandying of his Guild. It didn't help that he hadn't seen Sophia.

He'd cut himself off from her and wouldn't be visiting her mirror again. But she'd been like a drug to him, and he was suffering from withdrawal.

At least he had a few moments of peace alone in the quiet outbuilding before his scheduled call with the Tremantian Queen came through. Her request for a call had been delivered last night while his Guild argued over the possible ramifications of her speech.

Sikthand had known it was only a matter of time before he'd be required to enter into this political dance with the new Queen, but he'd hoped he'd have longer to sort through his Guild's many hearty opinions before he'd have to engage. They'd all had theories considering what she might say, ranging from a simple declaration of war to a kindly request for her human to be returned to her.

Sikthand had no idea what to expect. So he'd decided he would let her lead. Alone in the fortified outbuilding, he let his head fall back against his chair. The silence was like a cooling cloth on his throbbing head.

A light ping echoed around the room and reverberated through his skull. He grimaced.

"Queen," he greeted, with a grudging *tap-tap* of his tail on the ground.

"King Sikthand." The voice that floated from the communication pad was light and conversational. It was as though she were talking to a pleasant acquaintance and not a rival leader who'd kidnapped her citizens and cut off trade to her city. "If I remember right, you were never one for hollow pleasantries. Shall we get right to it?"

"It would be appreciated." He kept his tone respectful but a bit bored. He didn't want her to know she'd left the world stewing with her little speech.

"Wonderful. I believe you have a group of humans that belong to me."

Sikthand's jaw clenched. "As we told your advisors before, we have *one* human and one soldier. The rest escaped. I have no idea where they are."

She released a little hum that sent his tail flicking across the floor. "I suppose I'll have to believe you."

"There's no reason for me to lie. My qualms were with your predecessor."

"Perhaps an exchange to renew our good relationship, then? Nabiora had her faults, as I've said, and I am not unsympathetic to your motives in taking my citizens hostage. I've been in contact with the other cities that banded together to take a stand, and my only goal as the new Queen of Tremanta is to start my rule with transparency and peace."

"What do you want?" Dread pulsed in his throat as he waited for her answer. She'd want Sophia.

"I want trade reopened and..." There was a charged pause on her end of the line before she said, "I want your assurance that I have your city's vote for planetary representative."

Sikthand wanted to bark out a laugh, but he held back. "Vrulatica will vote for who it feels is best suited to the position."

"Of course," she cooed. "I'm new. You don't know me very well. But you did kidnap my people, and who's to say they aren't dead? Five precious humans gone. Anyone else might see that as justifiable grounds for war."

Sikthand released a seething breath through his nose. He kept his mouth closed. She was ramping up to some point, and he refused to play a part in her dramatic delivery.

"But I'm a reasonable leader. I don't think it has to come to that. In fact, I'm in the process of deciding where the humans under my care will go. I could send you, say...five to replace the ones you lost, and you can keep the one you have now."

Clarity hit, and Sikthand sneered. She was attempting to bribe him with humans, and she was likely to pull the same stunt with leaders around the world. "How many humans are in Tremanta?"

The rumor spreading through the world had guessed at thousands, yet if reports were to be believed, it was closer to dozens. She could only bribe so many with a small number like that, but if there were more that had been hidden away?

"Hundreds," the Queen answered. He could almost hear the smile in her voice.

Fuck.

"That's a very generous offer," he lied.

"I'm a very generous Queen. And if you see fit to elect me, I'll be a very generous planetary representative."

Sikthand's mind worked, filtering through all the options he had, all the plays he could make. She was crafty, but her plan to buy her way into office was not without its flaws. The question was, did it serve his city best to be on her side or to oppose her? His personal opinions about her methods and morals were irrelevant.

"I'll need some time to bring this to my Guild," he answered finally.

"Of course. But don't take too long. The Leaders' Summit is in two months, and I'll be busy deciding which cities are most suitable for my humans before then."

As Sikthand flew back to the tower, he thought through a plan. The problem was, all his plans involved Sophia being harmed or used in some way, and he had to ignore that unpleasant reality.

When he darted through the Guild chamber doors, the guildmembers looked as tired as he felt. Madam Kalos' normally coiffed hair frizzed around her forehead, and she nibbled quietly on a bit of bread.

Master Bavo had fallen asleep in his chair and now bolted upright, releasing a surprised hiccup. Sikthand took his seat, waited for the guards to seal the doors, then removed his helmet. "I bestow my trust," he recited in a rush.

"And we ours," they all echoed in varying groans as they settled in for another long debate.

As was customary, Sikthand relayed the phone call, then sat back and let them discuss, hearing their opinions bounce back and forth while he surveyed and judged.

"I don't see a downside to accepting her offer," Speaker Besith argued. "We'll have more humans, which will lend us some hint of prestige, and if the goddess of fate smiles on us, each will be recognized by a citizen."

"Is Vrulatica a city that can be bought?" Roldroth all but bellowed, his stance on the topic clear from the beginning. "Our vote is our business. We'd be trading our honor for a handful of humans. As for prestige, you think anyone will look upon us with esteem when they realize we are just a tool for the Tremantian Queen?"

"But it isn't just a handful of humans, is it? If she becomes the planetary representative, she'll have the power to guide the flow of humans into Clecania. Do you really think she'll speak kindly of the cities that took a stand against her?" Besith countered.

Bavo yawned. "Only if she wins."

Magistrate Yalmi pored over the piles of books and scrolls in front of her, a few toppling off her small table. She caught them easily with her tail and plopped them on her lap. "In all likelihood, she will win. Every city she brings her offer to will be having the same argument we are. Some will want to agree just for the offer of humans in the interim. Others will not want to risk the chance she is voted in and their city suffers. There are not enough who will deny her out of honor." Yalmi peered at the king. "She *will* win."

Kalos nodded with red-veined eyes. "We have no choice. Trade needs to be reopened. It's already been closed for too long. The space elevator is in Tremanta. They make up a quarter of our exports planet wide."

"What of the humans?" Lindri asked, having remained quiet and solemn for most of the day. "Is it not fair to wonder what they will think of the Queen?"

The room fell silent.

"What do you mean, Lady Lindri?" Roldroth asked.

"Well, let us assume for argument's sake that Earth is reclassified and human representatives come to visit our planet. Surely, they'll speak to the other humans she's shepherded around the planet, presumably against their will. Will the Earthlings not be outraged? If they know our planet's representative has bought her way into the role by playing with human lives, I'd imagine newly arrived humans would avoid settling in those cities that supported her."

Sikthand considered this. It was a fair point.

"Up till now, we've been thinking of humans as pieces in a game—which, as unfortunate as it is, they are. But Lady Lindri is right. Once the whole planet is made aware of her plotting, they will certainly oppose her. And the humans she has used will not remain silent. If more choose to settle on our planet, does it not stand to reason they will do so in cities that spoke out against her cruel treatment? It is a *long* game we must play now." Commander Roldroth nodded along to his own words.

"But what *is* our play?" Madam Kalos rasped. "Cut off trade for good? We have no idea what the Queen will tell the humans when Earth opens. She was clever enough to lock in a victory for herself. What if she finds a way to convince them her actions were justified? I'm not sure we can risk it."

"She's right." Speaker Besith shook his head. Rarely, if ever, did he agree with the Kalos. "Unless we can be certain humans will come here of their own accord, we can't risk cutting our people off from Earth."

"What if they *wanted* to come here?" Yalmi had frozen, her hands splayed on a large tome laying open in front of her.

"How?"

She peered up at the room, eyes glittering but shuttered, as if she was about to say something silly. "What if there was a human here who made them feel as if this was a safe city to settle in?"

Sikthand sat up.

Commander Roldroth raised his chin thoughtfully. "Who? Sophia? Even if she stayed, why would her word count for any more than the other humans strewn across the world?"

"Because the human living in Vrulatica…would be queen." Yalmi grinned, growing more excited about her idea with each passing second.

Silence reigned in the chamber. Sikthand felt his heart hammering so loudly he was surprised hollow drumming didn't resound from his armor.

"A quee—our queen?" Bavo laughed. "You want the human female to become our queen?"

Lindri laughed along, but dread turned Sikthand's hands cold. The Guild might not have realized it yet, but it was a perfect solution. One he would never agree to. Luckily he wouldn't have to. His Guild would never come to a consensus on this. It was too wild of a proposition.

"Is that even legal?" Lindri craned forward to peer at Magistrate Yalmi.

"Yes." Yalmi tapped her tail on the book before her. "Nowhere in our laws does it state that an alien cannot be queen. Just think of it. A *human* queen. When Earth opens and they are told of Clecania and all its rulers, where do you think timid humans looking to live on our planet would go? One where their kind exist under a fragile concept of freedom, or one where an actual human is in charge?"

Fury was rising hot and white, licking at his neck. He would not be forced into a marriage. Not again.

"What do you estimate the response of our people will be?" Lindri asked Besith.

Besith glanced at the king warily. "The feeling for a long while now has been unease that a male rules alone. They've wanted a queen for quite some time. I think, like us, they'll be surprised, but I also imagine they'd see the potential of putting her in power."

The memory of Japeshi kneeling in the center of this very room, spitting blood and cursing his name, flew back into his mind. He'd managed to keep the memory at bay for so long, and the unexpected reminder was a knife to his gut.

"No," Sikthand growled.

It was a break in tradition. The king had the power, but when in the Guild chamber, he was meant to listen. To keep silent and be counseled. But he had to stop this insanity.

Lindri stared, her wide eyes filled with sympathy. "Sire—"

"I will *not* marry the human." He barked, tail thrashing so hard the metal tip embedded into the stone of his throne.

The chamber fell silent once again.

"I believe your Guild is in agreement, sire," Madam Kalos whispered. "But you may call for a formal vote if you'd like to be sure."

Sikthand gazed around the room, each face set, no one opposing Kalos' statement. He reeled in his emotion. An image of Sophia danced in his mind, and his chest seized.

All the danger he'd been shielding himself from would be multiplied infinitely if he did this. Unlike typical marriages that only lasted three months, a royal marriage like this would be permanent. She wouldn't just be a tempting female, she'd be his *wife*. To him, a more dangerous person did not exist.

The world would whisper in Sophia's ear, injecting venom. What if one of the Guild decided he was no longer needed when a precious human queen took the throne? What if *she* decided he was no longer needed?

This marriage would make him worse. His paranoia was flourishing even now. He'd see danger around every corner. He'd be faced with the female who haunted his every waking thought for the rest of his life. How was he supposed to live?

But if his Guild was single minded, he couldn't refuse. He could call for a formal vote to ensure they were in agreement, but the lack of objection in their hopeful expressions made it clear they were.

Sikthand had all the power in the world. He could wage wars and control the storms themselves, but in this moment, he was powerless. Rationally, he knew this was the smartest choice. The knowledge made the sting harsher.

The Queen would not go to war if they refused to return one human. She couldn't afford it, and she didn't have the time to spin her decision as something honorable. Vrulatica would be an easy choice for any human looking to settle on their planet. They'd flock here. Vrulatica would remain the powerful, independent city it had always been, and his people might, for once in his life, accept him.

Marrying Sophia was the best choice for his people. All he had to do was consign himself to a life of longing and suffering.

His eyes stung, a ghostly sensation that often haunted him. It was how they'd felt when Japeshi had activated the ink she'd injected. At the time, Sikthand had reveled in the pain, thinking it was normal when recognizing a true mate. He was a male covered in tattoos, one well versed with what askait ink felt like under the skin. And yet he'd been utterly blind.

He couldn't be blind again. Even if he managed to live through another betrayal, he wouldn't *survive* it. Not if it was *her*. Not if it was Sophia.

But he had no choice.

"She must agree," Sikthand growled.

Some relieved breaths circulated through the room. "And she will, sire. Who would not want to be queen?"

He scoffed at that. How oblivious the world was to the life of a ruler.

"Speaker Besith, send one of your males outside to fetch her," Madam Kalos chirped, smoothing her hair away from her hood.

"No," Sikthand boomed again. He glared around the room, rising from his chair. Before they could argue, he made his way toward the door. "If I am to wed a stranger, I will at least be the one to ask her."

And he would ask in such a way that she would be stupid to agree.

14

Sophia trudged back to her room, thoughts swirling. Alno had tried to get her to eat a little at dinner, but she was too distracted. What did this mean for her? What did it mean for the humans in Tremanta?

Did she even want to go back there now? There was nothing stopping the Queen from sending her right back out into the world.

"I'm sure the king will allow you to stay," Alno whispered.

Her attention drifted to him. "I don't want to stay."

The corner of his mouth curled down. "You…you want to go back?"

"No," Sophia breathed. At least she knew that much. "I want to know what happened to my group. I want to go somewhere I'm safe and free." Rage suddenly flared in her, and she hurled her napkin-wrapped leftovers down the hall. "Is that really so much to ask? I want to choose for my fucking self. Not be bounced around like a damn pinball."

Alno fell silent again, and Sophia didn't have the energy to restart the conversation. By the time they reached her room, she was boiling. She hated every last Clecanian at this moment, including Alno, and she didn't care how irrational that was.

He walked into her room ahead of her but halted abruptly, making her collide with his back. "Ow. Your fucking tail...scraped..." Her voice died out. "Me."

Sikthand was in her room, spread out in a chair by a roaring fire in the hearth she'd never even tried to light. He was flipping through the pages of... *My sketchbook!*

"Hey!" she blurted, rushing toward him with the intention of snatching it away.

Before she could reach him, he'd stood, tossed the sketchbook onto a low table with a heavy thump, and aimed a stony stare at Alno. "Go."

She wanted to throw out a mean-spirited comment as Alno fled, something about him running with his tail between his legs, but she couldn't form anything coherent before he was gone. Probably better that way. He didn't deserve it.

She snatched the book from the table and chewed on the inside of her cheek, forcing her attention toward the king. Sikthand's skin was paler than usual, his hood a slightly less intense shade of oblivion black than normal, and his hair was loose and wavy around his spike-tipped shoulders. Flickering fire reflected in his armor, making the metal glow.

This room was large—massive, even. And yet he seemed to take up all the air.

"What are you doing in my room?" she asked, clutching her book to her stomach. He'd only ever been in here once, and the room had looked very different then. The fire popped, making her flinch. She knew he must have access, but his intimidating presence only a few feet from where she slept every night was both unsettling and far too intimate.

"If you prefer I *not* enlighten you as to what my Guild and I discussed, I can leave." His voice was colder today. It contained no hint of that smooth heat that made her breath hitch.

He was a stranger again, and the small crush she'd been harboring cowered behind a healthy spike wariness. She should chastise him for being in her room, for looking through her things, but if today had reminded her of anything, it was that she was not a guest in this city. And *King* Sikthand could do whatever he wanted. "No, I'd like to know. Sorry."

He stared, something like fury glinting behind his eyes. A muscle twitched in his jaw.

Sophia forced herself to hold her ground and keep her breathing even.

"The Guild, in its infinite wisdom, has decided that you and I shall be married."

The words echoed in her mind. A buzzing warmed her ears, and her arms went numb. The loud crack of her book hitting the ground made her jolt in place. She looked down at it, unseeing.

Her gaze met his bright silver stare, and reality snapped back into place. She swept the book off the floor. "That's…"

She shook her head, studying his expression. Had he agreed? Did he assume she'd be marrying him? Or was he telling her so they could share a joke? So they could laugh at the silliness of his Guild together.

"It's ludicrous," he growled, answering her unasked questions.

She blew out a short chuckle. "Yeah. Okay, for a second I thought…" Her relief was short-lived when he didn't laugh with her. "You said no, right?"

The muscle in his jaw jumped again, and he turned toward the fire. "I made my objections known. Unfortunately, they are in agreement on this particular issue."

Sophia's pulse thundered through her veins. "Does that mean I—"

"While *I* am forced to go along with their whims"—his gaze speared through her—"*you* are not. If you tell them no when they ask, this will be through, and you can go on with your life."

Sophia stilled. "What does that mean? Go on with my life?"

He shrugged, firelight dancing in his eyes. "You'll be free to return to Tremanta."

She scrunched her brows, staring at the floor and pacing. Her gaze flicked toward him as she walked, keeping him in her sights. Something was nagging at her, but she couldn't focus through the cacophony of feelings swirling inside. If he freed her, she could go back to Tremanta or somewhere else. But where?

Though just because she didn't know where to go next didn't mean she should stay here. And certainly not if that meant she'd be forced into a marriage. She eyed Sikthand and noted the scowl darkening his expression. Clearly she'd be forcing *him* into a marriage if she agreed as well.

Her head snapped up, her body going still. "Wait, would this marriage be temporary?"

"No," he growled.

"Does that mean…" The ground seemed to shift under her. She spun toward the king. "Would that make me…" Sophia couldn't seem to push the word past the disbelief knotting her throat.

"Queen." He spat the word. "That *is* how it works," he sneered.

Sophia laughed at that. A high, delirious laugh that had not an ounce of humor in it. "What?" she all but shrieked. "That's just…" She shook her head and licked her dry lips. "Why? Who the hell would want me as queen? I'm not Vrulan." She let out another panicked laugh. "I'm not even *Clecanian.*"

"I think it's as preposterous as you do." Sikthand strode toward her large dressing mirror. His steps were smooth, but she could almost see the rigidity of his muscles beneath his armor. "They believe having a human queen will make other humans more likely to want to settle here."

A light bulb crackled to life in Sophia's mind. How many out there felt the way she did on some level? How many were stuck, not wanting to remain in Tremanta, but not knowing where else to go? If she *were* the queen of this city, could she provide a safe place? Could she help?

As if he could see the wheels turning and her interest shifting, Sikthand's tail scraped across the stone, drawing her eyes. "You do not want this. Do you think my people will take kindly to a human queen? They'll disembowel you." He stepped closer, and she backed away at the brutal hatred oozing from his gaze. "*I* don't want this. I don't want *you*."

Sophia stumbled back another step. The venom coating his statement stung more than she thought it would.

"Our marriage would be a cold one. No affection. And how do you expect to rule Vrulans? You're weak." He surveyed her from head to toe and grimaced. "My people don't abide weakness. Not in their leaders, and not in their *beds*." He was within a few feet now, and tears were burning at the edges of Sophia's eyes. "You can't be their queen, and you will *never* be *my* queen."

A tear broke, slipping down her cheek. Sikthand eyed it disdainfully. But the hot track of the tear made fury bubble up inside her. "And you think I want *you*?" she hissed. "You're cruel and cold, and you lock up anyone who looks at you wrong. You're just a scared boy. I might be weak, but at least I don't pretend not to be."

His hand shot out and sealed around her throat, forcing her feet back until her spine slammed against the cold stone wall. She regained her breath with a gasp.

"Careful, female." His growl was deadly.

The chilled metal of his gauntlet and her spike of adrenaline had her shivering within his firm hold, but fire still coursed through her veins. "And you certainly stare at me a lot for someone who finds me so repulsively weak."

The corner of his mouth curled in a cruel smile. "Have you mistaken my curiosity to fuck an alien as genuine interest?"

She bit the inside of her lip to keep her chin from wobbling.

He dropped his face so their eyes were level and their mouths only a breath apart. His hand caging her neck, squeezed gently. "You'll visit the Guild tomorrow night. I pray your underdeveloped human brain is capable of seeing sense before then."

***

Sikthand bared his fangs. He was letting all his self-loathing show on his face and allowing her to believe she was the cause. He'd anticipated making her angry, but he hadn't prepared himself for making her cry.

He stepped away, pulling his hand from her neck, and forced himself to watch as another silent tear dripped from her lashes. His chest cracked open at the sight.

It was better this way.

He stalked out of her room and down the hall, not bothering to close the door behind him. When he was safely in his room once more, he heaved in thundering breaths.

Don't.

His eyes lifted to his mirror.

Don't go.

He flung his gloves off, then pulled at the armor on his neck, suddenly unable to breathe. The battered pieces crashed to the floor, teeth-grinding clanging filling the room. When it was all off, even the bits on his tail, he snatched a chest plate from the ground and pounded the metal in with a fist until it bowed.

Sikthand stood, knuckles bloody and stomach lurching. He stared at the mirror. Then, unable to hold himself back any longer, he walked through and crept down the passage to her mirror. Sweat poured down his spine as he sat in the chair he'd dragged here days ago. He kept his eyes shut, licking his lips and mentally preparing to see what damage he'd left behind.

He let out a deep breath through his nose, then looked. What he saw made him want to rip his own tongue out. She was sitting on the ground, her book of drawings propped open on her lap, and she was crying. Not the contained, silent tears from before, but deep sobs that shredded his insides.

Watch, coward, he hissed to himself.

She peered down at the book in her lap again, then let out a fury-filled shriek and hurled it into the fire.

He flinched. There had been more than a few drawings of him in there.

Her features, tight with anger, fell when the flames flared, consuming the little book in a flash. Her lips parted as though she couldn't believe what she'd done. Then her shock turned to misery again, and she buried her face in her hands.

To keep himself from crashing through the mirror and pulling her into his arms, Sikthand retreated back down the passageway. He didn't stop at his room. He flew through the wing until the violent wind howling through the landing bay forced his steps to slow, and called for Ahea.

Only when he was in the most deserted area of the Choke would he let himself explode.

The human has to go.

A little evil thing inside him whispered, *Why, though?*

He shook his head. Sikthand would *not* listen to that voice again. The one that tried to convince him he could lower his guard. He'd listened to it before, many times, and he'd only ever been proven a fool.

Once she was gone, things would get better. His mind would return, and he could go on with his life.

He stared at the hazy halo around the nearest moon, a sure sign a storm was on the horizon. The silhouette of Ahea's enormous spread wings flashed by. Soon, he'd bury himself in a storm. Surely bolts of electricity sizzling by his ears would banish the memory of her tear-stained cheeks.

Even as he had the thought, he knew it wasn't true.

15

Sophia wrung her hands together as covertly as she could. All but one member of the Guild sat before her. Lady Lindri had apparently been called away due to an emergency in the mines and was just now on her way back.

She'd purposefully gone without food today, knowing that her already queasy stomach would not be able to hold anything down during this meeting. A wave of lightheadedness hit her, and she regretted her decision.

She peered up at each guildmember eyeing her with burning curiosity and tried to hold their stares. There was only one set of eyes she avoided, and they belonged to the black and white demon sitting higher than the rest.

After Sikthand had eviscerated her confidence and left, Sophia had devolved into a weeping puddle. She'd cried for so long her throat burned and her head throbbed. She'd cried until there'd been no tears left, and then she'd reflected.

Every path she could imagine had been examined that night, and all roads led to one terrifying conclusion.

Lindri burst through the doors, wiping soot off her cheek, her curly hair still smoking slightly, and stumbled into her seat with the rest.

Sophia's shoulders tensed when the heavy doors slammed closed behind her.

"I bestow my trust." His voice sent a pulse of heat through her. But this time, it was the heat of anger.

"And we ours," she grated, eyes dutifully on the ground.

"Sophia, you've come to respond to the Guild's request for us to be wed. What do you have to say?" The king's voice was tight but also a little bored, as if he knew what she was going to say already.

This is what I practiced. Just look up. Be strong.

After a moment more of internal arguing, she gathered her courage, lifted her chin, and took her time looking each member of the Guild in the eye. "The king told me what you all decided." She swallowed. The words weren't quite ready to leave her throat. "I've taken some time to think it over." God, she hoped she wasn't making the wrong decision. She finally forced her eyes to connect with the king's narrowed gaze. His distaste helped lock in her courage. "I agree to be your queen," she declared, spine straight and head held high.

Relieved breaths echoed around the room, but she kept her gaze on the king. His chin dipped forward, his fangs peeking out under his upper lip. Sophia glared back. She might be physically weaker than the Clecanians, but that didn't make her weak of will. It didn't make her any less smart or any less capable. In all likelihood, she'd turn out to be a truly shitty queen. *Underqualified* was an understatement. But if there was even the barest possibility she could help her people, she wouldn't let this asshole's dislike of her keep her from doing just that.

"I'll make all the arrangements," Besith called. "Master Bavo, I'll need that budget you drew—"

"But"—she lifted her brows, heated gaze still locked with the king's seething one—"I have a few conditions."

The room fell silent. "Conditions?" Madam Kalos asked blankly.

"You realize you'll be queen, girl? You should be thanking us." Commander Copperhead chuckled.

She pursed her lips and sliced her gaze toward Roldroth. "Sophia. Not *girl*," she chastised with a confidence she didn't feel.

This was the moment she'd been waiting for. The one she'd been practicing for all night. She'd gone over absolutely everything she'd learned about this city and its people. She'd replayed every bit of information she'd learned about the king. And most importantly, she'd recounted what she knew about the humans and the politics that would shape the world in the next few months.

Her conclusions had been clear and exhausting. From the moment she agreed to become queen, Sophia would need to change. She'd replayed the Tremantian Queen's first public speech in her mind and had taken notes. *Be strong. Be confident. Bullshit your way through.*

Sikthand's words from last night rang in her ears, and she knew the Vrulans thought the same. They believed she was weak. The first time she spoke to them, she'd need to make a statement. She'd need to show that she no longer considered herself a prisoner. She was a future *queen*, and she would be taken seriously.

She raised a brow toward the commander. "I believe you asked me to be queen because you know you *need* me. Isn't that right?"

The commander's mouth shut.

"I'm the one who knows what to say to make humans want to come here. And I'm also very likely to get my head chopped off for my efforts, if some are to be believed." She shot a glance toward the king, who gave her a cold smile in return. "So, I have conditions."

"And what would they be?" the king all but hissed.

"One, you will let Heleax go. There's no reason he needs to be kept locked up here." She spoke over the murmuring guildmembers. "Two, I will be allowed to go wherever I want, whenever I want, and speak to whomever I want, without an attendant. I'll get a communication code so I can receive private messages from outside the city. In short, I am not a prisoner here anymore. I am a future queen, and I expect to be treated as such." Sikthand sat back on his throne, looking down his nose at Sophia. "And three..." She licked her lips again, knowing this demand might be the one that broke the camel's back. "Our city votes for the planetary representative of *my* choice."

Angry muttering broke out around the room now.

"Surely you can have a say, but we'll need to choose who we think is best."

"You're too new to all this. What if you choose someone terrible?"

"Hey!" She clapped twice, her breathing quick and shallow. When they eyed her hands, she hiked her shoulders. "I don't have a tail." She said matter-of-factly to explain why she hadn't tapped twice as was customary when asking to speak.

Sophia feared the action only further highlighted her differences, so she launched back in before they could think too hard on her tail-less-ness. "I will *not* be a queen in name only. If I am your queen, I ask for the same respect, responsibility, and authority that King Sikthand holds. And in return, I will give you an advantage that no other city on this planet can claim. Having a human queen will not only make Vrulatica more attractive to the humans on Earth, but I can offer the Guild and our people a perspective only an Earthling can provide. I'll be able to tell which candidate will be best received by my government, and I know which will have them pointing their rockets into the sky. Respectfully, you are only able to see things from one side. I can tell you Vila will not do as well as she thinks. She's too cocky, and unfortunately many of the leaders on our planet still have issues with women in leadership being competent at their jobs and saying so out loud. She *isn't* the smartest choice."

The guildmembers eyed each other with raised brows, clearly surprised by this. Sophia's chest bowed. She'd had to convince herself all night and all day that she actually had something to offer as queen. And now she saw a glimpse of what she'd been trying to convince herself of reflected in their exchanged glances.

She could do this. Her eyes met Sikthand's again, and goose bumps rose on her neck. That was, if he didn't kill her first.

"That's why my third condition is so important. And it's also why I won't be marrying anyone until my vote is cast at the Leaders' Summit."

16

A hammering knock sounded at Sikthand's bedroom door, and he swung it open.

"Can you explain to me why I had to cancel my appointments and rush up here when…" Khes caught sight of Sikthand's upturned room and hummed out a disgruntled sound.

"I appreciate the rush," Sikthand commented blankly. It had been days since he'd slept. And the thing that dominated every spare cell of his brain lay a handful of strides away. He needed a distraction, and pain seemed like the perfect way to blind himself for a few blissful moments.

Khes set his travel case down at the bench they always used for his tattoos. Sikthand had stopped visiting the Flesh Forge over a decade ago when a bottle of ink containing poison had been sent down to Khes after his arrival. He'd locked up the old man for a month while he'd rooted out who the real attempted murderer had been, and to his surprise, Khes had never held it against him.

The inkmaster might be the only person in the tower he trusted.

With one hand, Sikthand ripped his rumpled shirt off his back and gestured to two lightly striped areas encompassing his shoulders and scapula. "I want them filled."

Khes' hands stilled at the clasp of his bag. "Filled? That'll take two whole vials at least."

"If not more," Sikthand grated.

Pulling his chair up to the bench and prepping his vials on a thin expandable table he'd retrieved from his bag, he openly studied Sikthand. "You tell me why you're looking to put yourself through this, and I'll fill you full of acid."

Though he should guard his words, he couldn't hold them back. Besides, the city would know soon enough. "Soon you'll hear the joyous news," he started, feeling one vial suction onto his shoulder blade. "The king is engaged."

Khes' hands stilled while suctioning on the second vial. His chair scraped as he scooted sideways until he could look into Sikthand's eyes. When he saw the truth in them, he swore. His gaze zoomed around the broken glass and warped metal littering his room with new understanding.

He moved back to his work without a sound. It was a quality Sikthand loved about the male. He didn't speak unless he had something to say. No blathering apologies or asking him how he felt or making empty promises about things getting better.

"Ready?" he asked when both vials were placed on Sikthand's back.

Sikthand's mind raced back to Sophia in the Guild chamber. So confident, and brave, and beautiful, staring him down with fire in her eyes just like every queen he'd ever met. "Yes."

Burning, ripping pain coursed down his back, and all vision was wiped away. He breathed through it, nearly sighing from the black oblivion. But he'd done this so often that he grew numb to it far too quickly.

"Who's the female, and what death have they threatened you with?" Khes asked as he dragged his pen along Sikthand's back.

Sikthand thought her name before he said it aloud, and a rush of warmth raced over his skin, dulling the pain even more. "The human." The drag of metal paused. "It was the Guild's decision, and the little cricksan agreed. She even made demands."

The pen moved again, but Khes made no sound. Suddenly, though he'd never craved it before, Sikthand wanted to hear what the inkmaster had to say.

He ground his teeth, waiting for Khes to say something, anything.

"What do you think of that?" Sikthand prompted when the man said nothing.

"You've had worse wives." Sikthand wanted to bark out a laugh at that understatement. He'd had *no* wives. He'd had plenty of almost-wives, though.

Two had been openly covetous of his throne and had been turned down by his father. One had been clumsily bragging about his interest in her at a bar while cozying up to a handsome copper male, and the last had been Japeshi, who'd broken down his defenses only to be caught nights before her assassination attempt.

Sikthand wasn't a male that *could* be loved. His position always got in the way. And aside from his royal blood, his looks didn't win him many points. Females chose him for other reasons, not because he lit up a room like Sophia's errand boy Alno.

His mind wandered back to Sophia's drawings, and his chest expanded. She didn't draw him like she thought he was ugly.

"You know how to watch yourself now, boy. You won't be caught unawares. So, what has your mind so fucked that you destroyed all this good metal?" Khes said, rousing him from his musings.

Pain hit him again, and he held in a gasp. How had thinking about her made it all disappear? How was the human more powerful than the lines of liquid metal boring paths under his skin?

"Is it these demands?" Khes dragged his pen over Sikthand's back muscles hard enough to make him wince. "Because let me tell you something, you are Sikthand, son of Queen Sesei and King Thedvar. You are stronger than forged askait, and you bend to no one."

"No. I don't bend." Sikthand's eyes drifted to the mirror. Truth rose like acid in his throat. "But I could break for her."

Khes stilled. "Look at me."

Sikthand didn't. He knew weakness shone from behind his eyes at the moment, and he couldn't show that to anyone.

The inksmith dragged his chair in front of where Sikthand sat and forced their gazes to meet. "Would it be so terrible? Not everyone is untrustworthy."

"No, not everyone." Sikthand let out a tired exhale. "But people don't have to be bad to do bad things. All they need is a good enough incentive. I may trust that her soul isn't rotten like Japeshi's, but I don't believe she could ever care for me more than she does for humans, and I wouldn't expect her to. If she knew she could help her people by betraying me, she would. A noble incentive, but still one that poses a threat to me and to *our* people." His eyes flitted to the mirror.

Khes grumbled in thought at that, but got back to work.

I can't let my guard down.

His mother's oft-repeated words rang through his ears, icing over his thawing heart. *It's when you take your hands from the reins that a gust can rip you off your mount.*

17

Sophia squinted through sore eyes at a twirly symbol with a dot in the center. She'd looked this one up about five hundred times, and she still could not remember the sound it made.

"Need help, *Your Highness*?" Alno crooned.

She glanced up at him with a frown. Oh, how she'd regretted revealing the different ways in which humans addressed royalty. "No," she lied.

If she'd thought that Alno's temporary shock at her revelation that she would become his queen would earn her a little more formal respect from him, she'd been wrong. It was a relief, really. She didn't know how she'd managed to keep it together without his annoying yet welcome teasing.

He shrugged and continued to pick at his nails, his feet propped on the gleaming table of the quiet archives.

"You know you don't have to follow me around anymore." She focused on the symbol again. It was one of the characters that indicated a sound combo. *Rp* like in *harp*? *No.*

"Thanks to you I've been upgraded to *queen's* attendant, but since no one is supposed to know about the engagement yet, Besith thought it would be best to carry on as normal. Besides, you *do* need my help, even if you're being prickly about it." He hid the sound she was racking her brain to find within a cough, then grinned widely at her.

Ks. As in *smacks*. As in what she wanted to do to that smug expression.

She sighed. "Thank you."

Over the past week, Alno had been very helpful. She just hadn't gotten over her shitty mood that Sikthand and the pressure of becoming a queen had instilled in her.

She read some of the Clecanian words out loud so her translator could recite them in her ear and confirm she'd understood the paragraph correctly. She hadn't.

Sophia slumped back in her chair, rubbing her eyes.

"You know…" He held up a small clear rectangle and waved it through the air.

"I don't want a reading glass. Stop asking," she interrupted, holding up her hand. The small technology that translated written words was one of the few electronics that worked in this city. It was such a temptation, but she was going to be a Clecanian queen. It would be ridiculous for her not to understand their writing.

Her words echoed through the cavernous space, and she hunched back down over her text.

Alno grimaced. "Why do you keep wincing like that when you speak? I told you this isn't like that quiet place on Earth."

"A library," Sophia corrected.

Though the public was allowed into the archives, they had to get written permission first, and visitors were kept sparse in order to ensure nothing was stolen or damaged. Yet it reminded Sophia so much of a library with its rows of scrolls and stacks of books, that she couldn't help but flinch every time Alno raised his voice to a normal volume. Magistrate Yalmi had been overjoyed when Sophia had requested access, and she didn't want the guildmember to think badly of her.

As if the world were trying to help her express her swirling emotions, the Season had arrived, bringing a vicious storm with it. Moody clouds lit from within by green dye, dimmed the light through the windows, making the tower a little sleepier than usual.

Sikthand had made himself scarce, only appearing for dinners or flying past her in the halls flanked by guards. She couldn't figure out if that was a good thing or not.

In the Guild chamber, she'd delighted in defying his wishes to his face. It was less than he deserved after being such a royal dick to her. But now reality was setting in.

They may not have the kind of relationship a married couple normally did, but he was still going to be her husband. According to the scrolls Yalmi had pulled for her to read,

Sikthand and Sophia would be required to make decisions together, neither outranking the other.

As distasteful as it might be to the stuck-up king, at some point they'd need to actually *talk* to each other. They couldn't rule with guildmembers as their mediators forever. The Guild was very nice and all, but they were overwhelming.

Still, she'd avoided meeting Sikthand's gaze for days now. When she accidentally did, she couldn't decipher anything.

Anger? Regret? It was all a mystery. He was gone most of the time, volunteering for cloud seeding *"more than a king should,"* if Madam Kalos was to be believed.

She'd been visited by almost every member of the Guild many times over. Some, like Yalmi and Lindri, had seemed genuinely concerned, and took time to answer all her questions while subtly listing off the many concerns they had within their departments.

Others, like Kalos and Bavo, had only seemed interested in coaching her. They'd given her overviews of each planetary representative candidate, saying very little about some, and a great deal about others. The rest of the time, they listed the things she'd need to do once she was enthroned. Only later, when Sophia had examined their lists, had she realized the tasks were not things she *had* to do, but things they *wanted* her to do. They'd simply explained them as if she had no other option. It was manipulative. They were using her inexperience and lack of knowledge against her, and she didn't appreciate it.

Sophia kept what she'd witnessed of Sikthand's behavior in mind as she dealt with the Guild. He never cut them off or hinted that he was uninterested in their opinion, and so she behaved the same, though she now understood why Lady Lindri tended to hide in the mines.

Madam Kalos was relentless. She critiqued Sophia's clothing, her makeup, her manner of speaking, and *always always always*, her weak human frame.

She couldn't tell whether she preferred Madam Kalos' overabundance of advice to Besith and Roldroth's silence. They hadn't said two words to her since she'd accepted the role, and she couldn't decipher what that meant.

They'd pushed for her to be named queen, so why did they suddenly want to pretend like she didn't exist? Or did they believe she should be left alone?

She'd have to seek them out and win them over. She shuddered at the thought, but she supposed she'd have to get used to political ass-kissing like that now.

She still couldn't quite wrap her mind around it. Her. Queen.

What the fuck was she thinking?

She couldn't be queen. And definitely not to a city of warrior aliens who measured worth in strength and who had a penchant for assassination attempts whenever they found their monarch lacking. Doubt lived inside her like a coiling snake, and all she could do was pretend like it didn't exist.

Sophia sat up and focused on reading the next section.

Queen Yiphrie, first of her line, was…something…the throne after…something…and blood…something.

She let out an exaggerated groan, and Alno slapped a palm over the text. "Let's go get some dinner."

Sophia couldn't find the strength to argue. Alno helped explain what she had read as they walked to the dining hall. Apparently Sikthand was the seventh ruler of his family to take the throne. One of the reasons there was still a vendetta against him was because his ancestor, Queen Yiphrie, had overthrown the queen of the time by killing her in her sleep, or so the story went.

Just as Alno had hinted previously, the blood-splattered history of Sikthand's ancestors was gruesome. Stabbings, mysterious falls from landing bays, poisonings, and in one instance, mauling by the king's own half-starved malginash.

She couldn't imagine growing up learning about the many ways in which your predecessors were murdered, knowing you were very likely going to meet a similar fate. And what killed her about the whole thing was despite her dislike of Sikthand, he honestly seemed like a good king.

He wasn't like his great-great-grandmother who abolished cloud seeding, unwittingly causing a drought and allowing an alien army to congregate in the Choke. And he wasn't like his great great-great-uncle who became so obsessed with the idea that an undiscovered, more powerful metal lay in a layer underneath the askait ore that he dug the mine until it collapsed, taking a section of the tower with it.

Ruling Sikthand

Sikthand ruled fairly, for the most part. When she'd brought this up to Alno and asked what he'd done to make his enemies hate him so much, Alno had just shrugged and said, "There are always those who think they could do better. Hating him for his ancestors' mistakes is just a convenient excuse."

The only Vrulan rulers she'd read about who had enjoyed a relative amount of safety were the mated monarchs. It seemed that matehood was held in such high regard, even centuries ago when it was common, that mated rulers were nearly untouchable.

Her mind wandered to Japeshi again, and hatred simmered in her gut. Despite the hurt the king had caused with his callous words, there was an unguarded soft place in her heart for him, and the loathsomeness of that woman's plan made her blood boil.

Nobody who'd grown up looking over their shoulder deserved to have safety and love dangled in front of their nose like that. It was beyond cruel.

The more Sophia read about the king and his family, the harder it was to hate him. If anybody had the right to be calculating and cold, she supposed it was him. Maybe in time, when he finally realized she had no intention of offing him or asking him for more trust than he was willing to give, he would warm to her.

She adjusted the knife she kept hidden on her thigh. It hadn't passed her notice that as soon as she was announced as the next queen her life would become much less safe, much more quickly. Her human status would probably help keep her alive, but it could only protect her for so long.

Lightning flashed outside the arched windows as Alno described each section of the tower in more detail, and she couldn't help but wonder if the king was out there. Rain pounded against the glass, so thick the desert and mountains beyond were hidden from view. Bright green explosions lit the sky in the distance, but there weren't as many as there had been a few hours ago. The riders must be reaching the end of the storm.

Though she'd known the feeling of the hall would be different after the Season officially began, she still marveled at the change. The riders weren't somber or anything. Light laughter could still be heard around the room, but it was much quieter these days. Haggard, wet cloud chasers with waxen faces and drooping lids shuffled in off their long shifts and sipped imported mott. Others shoveled thick cuts of roasted meat into their mouths to fuel themselves for the storms ahead.

As she took her seat and Alno left her to go speak to a few of his friends, she stared at the high table. Sikthand's chair was empty. She glanced at the space around the chair. Would they scoot his to the side and put a seat for her next to his? Her skin crawled, her neck already heating when she imagined sitting there raised above everyone else as though she thought highly of herself.

Sophia picked at the tender meat on her plate. She'd need to pretend like she belonged. But how the fuck was she going to accomplish that?

She thought of how Delia, the resident queen in some of her LARP events, acted to get ideas but discarded them all. Delia always used a funny British accent and spoke as if her stomach was filled with air. It was entertaining but would hardly work on this group. Sophia hadn't participated in any events for over a year now, and even her hardened warrior-maiden character, Skaja, was hard to call back to the surface.

Sophia would have to create a new alter ego, one hard like Skaja but queenly. Her head throbbed, and she made a deal with herself to think about it later. She needed a damn break from thinking right now.

The hair on her neck prickled, and she froze with a slice of meat halfway to her lips. She swiveled and found the king's eyes glued to her as he stomped into the dining hall, helmet tucked under his arm.

Have you mistaken my curiosity to fuck an alien as genuine interest?

She tried not to wince as his words replayed in her mind. Sophia *had* mistaken him. Stupidly, she'd thought his lingering stares had meant something more. She peered up at him and the other dripping cloud chasers trailing in behind him, leaving a sopping mess on the floor that a gangly male rushed to mop up.

She frowned to find him still watching her. It irritated the fuck out of her that his cruel words hadn't completely smothered her crush. He was still beautiful and damaged, and the moments of fleeting tenderness had felt too real to be written off. Her heart ached to think how much easier this would all be if he liked her, even a little.

Some cloud chasers plopped down near her and gave her courteous nods. She had to remind her tensing shoulders that they couldn't possibly know she was to be queen yet and, therefore, had no reason to want to kill her.

The guy across from her, sitting in Alno's vacant seat, lifted his helmet, which resembled some kind of pointy-faced animal skull, and clunked it down onto the bench next to him. He had a deep bronze hood with rose-gold skin and molten gold eyes. His wavy hair matched his hood and hung around his ears. Sophia glanced down at her plate when he caught her openly appreciating his features.

"Hello, human." He aimed a brilliant lopsided grin at her, and her heart picked up speed. It was nice to be smiled at.

"Hi." She grinned back. Maybe this was what she needed as a free woman, before she'd have to spend all her meals stuck to the grumpy king's side. Some nice flirting with a man who gazed at her body hungrily rather than with derision. "It's Sophia, not *human*," she said with a raised brow, giving him a bit of the flirty sass that seemed to work on Earth men and Clecanian men alike.

He lifted his brows, and his grin widened. "My apologies, *Sophia*."

She liked the way her name slid off his tongue. "How was cloud seeding?" she asked, eyeing his dripping armor.

"Oh, wonderful! My mount nearly bucked me off from excitement when the first bolts struck. She's been cooped up too long since having a litter." He cut his meat up into small chunks as he spoke, but waited to eat until he was done speaking. She found it charming.

As they talked, Sophia relaxed deeper and deeper into the conversation. The male, Drabik, was easy to like. He was large, with a chiseled jaw and the kind of eyes that made women sigh. And he was smart and funny, regaling her with stories from his cloud-hunting adventures. He knew how to work a conversation, slipping effortlessly from polite chatting to flirty banter to thinly veiled innuendo. It was all so *easy*.

Her head didn't throb. She didn't feel like she had to act any particular way. He didn't scare her or confuse her. He also didn't send her stomach swooping like a certain tactless king, but that was okay.

Pricks of awareness alerting her that said king was watching kept invading her happiness, but she ignored them, refusing to give him the time of day. Like he'd said, they would have a cold marriage.

She'd looked up the term, and apparently, it wasn't uncommon. Many ruling couples throughout Clecania had what was called a *cold marriage*. It just meant they ruled together but didn't mingle in a romantic way. They were business partners.

Sophia could live with that. Especially if she was able to find someone else to fall in love with. It was far too soon to say if that person would be Drabik, but he was pleasant enough to talk to. It was nice to think that though she felt utterly alone right now, she might not always feel that way.

The diners in the hall came and went as they chatted, empty plates pushed aside. "When is your next shift?" she asked.

"Not until the next front moves in." He tipped his head back and forth. "A few days, maybe."

The side of her face felt like it was burning, and she couldn't hold back any longer. She masked her actions by aiming her head to the side to take a drink, while peering at the high table as if bored. Cold fury seemed to puff from Sikthand's nostrils, his gaze seeping into her bones and chilling her to the core.

It only spurred her on. He had no right to look at her like that. What the fuck was she supposed to do with that stare? What did it mean?

She turned back to Drabik. "And what do you normally do in the meantime?" Sophia smiled, flicking the hair off her shoulder to expose her neck. She'd found that most fanged species liked the move, and as Drabik's gaze zoomed to the column of her throat, she knew she'd guessed right.

He sipped his water and hiked a brow. "Rest. Exercise. Find some distraction."

The words were innocent enough, but she gasped when his tail wrapped around her calf under the table. This would be fun. This would be easy. She wouldn't have to agonize over every word. He was sweet and sexy and direct.

A part of her she didn't want to focus on, whispered that he might also be the way she smothered her little infatuation with the king for good. But was that a good reason to start seeing someone? To get herself to stop thinking about someone else?

He grinned at her, his tail slipping along her calf under her dress. She waited for fluttering to erupt in her belly, but nothing happened.

A loud clanging reverberated through the room, jarring her bones. All heads zoomed toward the high table where Sikthand was now standing, feet planted wide. Darkness oozed off him. The dining hall remained silent, waiting for whatever his announcement was, but Sophia's throat felt like it was closing.

He was staring straight at her, and she had a sinking feeling she was about to be embarrassed.

"The human"—his venomous glare landed on Drabik—"is mine."

Sophia's jaw dropped. Drabik's beautiful warm eyes met hers, and a moment of sadness passed between them. His tail slipped from her leg. "I just made my way back into the king's good graces." It felt like a hollow apology, but Sophia understood. Drabik inclined his head toward her before solemnly trudging away.

Murmurs around the room floated to her ears as Sikthand retook his seat. The Vrulans shot her curious glances and exchanged gossiping whispers. Sophia's veins lit with fire. She glared toward the king, who was sitting back in his chair smugly. Roldroth leaned in at his side and whispered something in his ear.

Sikthand's silver gaze met hers, and he lifted a hand, beckoning her. He'd just publicly declared her off-limits, and now he was calling her over like a pet.

Fuck. Him.

Eyes already burning with unshed tears of frustration, she slapped her napkin down on the table, shot out of her seat, and, ignoring the stares of everyone in the room, charged in the opposite direction of the king.

18

Flushed and fuming, Sophia flew through the halls, not quite sure where she was going. He'd be coming after her. She didn't know how she knew, but she did. She pivoted, heading in a direction she hadn't gone before. He'd find her eventually, but maybe she could get a few minutes to herself to calm down before she had to look at his infuriating face again.

Fucking confusing asshole king.

She hit a shadowy dead end decorated with a sculpted armored woman appearing to be in freefall, and spun in place.

Sikthand stood silently at the other end of the corridor. Sophia just about hissed.

She charged forward, intent on barreling right past him, but of course he stopped her with an arm barring her path.

"Who the fuck do you think you are?" she spat, shooting daggers from her eyes.

"The king," he drawled.

She crossed her arms over her chest and took in a steadying breath.

Before she could get her string of insults wisely buried, he hauled her forward down the hall. "What the fuck? Why did you do that? I researched cold marriages, you know. They all have outside partners. It's an established thing. I can *flirt* with whoever I want."

His face was stony, and his mouth remained locked. She tried to wrench out of his hold. If he wasn't going to even acknowledge her, then she refused to be dragged around any longer.

With a growl, he scooped her over his shoulder as if she weighed nothing and continued down the corridor. Her face flamed. What if someone saw her like this? It would not only be embarrassing, but when she was named queen, people would remember. They'd talk about how the king had tromped through the halls with his weak human queen bent over his shoulder.

"Put me down," she growled. She wriggled, her hands slipping off his slick armor. His cold metal-clad hand came to squeeze the back of her upper thigh, sending a bolt of electricity sizzling down her leg. She froze. "Take your hand off my thigh."

He adjusted her on his shoulder so he could open the doors to their wing but made no move to alter the position of his hand. She held back the fury threatening to leak from her eyes in the form of tears. "Why are you doing this?" she moaned miserably as he took the steps to the landing bay two at a time.

His jaw seemed to be wired shut as he plopped her onto Ahea's waiting saddle and wrapped a cloak around her shoulders. She tried to slide off the other side, but he leapt into the saddle behind her and spurred Ahea on so violently that Sophia had to grip his knees to keep from tipping off.

"I'm giving you what you want," he growled at her ear just before he guided Ahea to dive headlong into the blistering rain. The wind blew the storm in every direction, her cloak doing little to guard her dress. She was soaked through within a minute.

Lightning flashed across the sky to her right, and acid-green explosions illuminated the clouds. Thunder rattled through her bones not a second later, wiping away her anger in an instant. They flew just beneath the storm, and it was horrifying. She couldn't imagine how much worse it would be flying through the clouds.

A gust of wind jostled Ahea and Sophia screamed as her ass lifted, hovering off the saddle for terrifying seconds before Sikthand's arm came around her hips, wrenching her back down. The rain pelted her eyes so furiously she couldn't guess which direction they were heading. She pulled her cloak tight over her face to keep out the sting of zooming horizontal drops and attempted not to jump every time a clap of thunder quaked through her stomach.

She peeked out as the rain gentled just in time for Ahea to crunch into the muddy ground.

It took her a moment to get her bearings. The city was behind them, and in front of her was a man and a...cruiser.

It was Heleax. Back in his uniform and looking a bit more deflated than he had when they'd first arrived in Vrulatica. Sikthand slid off Ahea, then dragged her down too. She blinked through the rain at him.

"You're releasing him now?" Sophia asked. She hadn't known why this was so surprising to her. So simple with no pomp and circumstance. She'd half imagined a public pardon in which Heleax would be proclaimed free, but this was so quiet. Like he was being kicked out the back door with a garbage bag of his stuff.

"I'm releasing you both."

She froze, eyes narrowing.

"You never wanted to be queen, only freedom for you and your friend. I'm granting that. Go."

Sophia glanced over to Heleax, heart thundering. Her guard glowered murderously at Sikthand but made no move to attack, his gaze warily sliding to Ahea every few seconds.

"What? But what about the Guild?"

"I'll deal with them."

I could leave.

The weight of the world seemed to lift from her shoulders. Sophia didn't want to be queen, but if there was even the barest possibility that she could make a difference, didn't she have to try?

But what was she conscripting herself to? A life of constant judgment and scrutiny? A cold marriage to a man who despised her? "Why did you just claim me if you were planning to let me go?"

Movement caught her eye, and she spotted him clenching his hands into tight fists. They relaxed as soon as she glanced at them, but in an awkward way, like someone trying to make their hands appear relaxed. "I misspoke."

Sophia's mind worked, trying to come up with any reason for his actions, but none of them accounted for the intensity she'd seen in his eyes. He hadn't claimed her in an aloof way. It'd been a possessive *piss on what's mine so no one else touches it* kind of way. But that didn't make sense.

"Take off your helmet." She tipped up her chin, lashes fluttering in the falling rain. When he made no move to do as she asked, she explained, "I want to ask you something, and I want to see your face when I do."

At length, he unclasped his helmet and lifted it off. His jaw was tight, his eyes narrowed against the rain. Wide shoulders clad in deadly armor were outlined against a flashing sky.

"Do you *want* me to leave?" She held her breath, watching for any hint of emotion.

The barest flash of a wince passed over his cheeks, his brows twitching. "Yes," he said, but she couldn't unsee the split-second reaction.

There was something within his expression when he spoke to her. Even when he looked at her. It was confusing since it clashed so heavily with his icy words, but if he were any other person, Sophia would think he was lying.

"Don't go anywhere," she whispered.

Sikthand's chest rose in a deep inhale. He stepped away. Sophia kept peeking over her shoulder as she made her way to Heleax.

"Are you alright? What's going on?" the guard hissed when she was within a few feet.

Heleax knew what had happened the past few days. She'd made sure to keep him in the loop. Suffice to say he had not been as keen on the idea of her as queen. If anything, he seemed to hate the idea more than the king himself.

"He said he'll let me go with you."

Heleax's eyes widened. He grabbed her by the wrist and attempted to drag her toward the cruiser, but a clicking growl had them both freezing. Ahea's white cloudy eyes seemed to glow. Sikthand was already astride, helmet in place. Was he so sure she'd take the easy way out?

"Wait, Heleax." She tugged her wrist from his hold. "I think I have to stay."

"Are you insane?" he barked. "You won't survive here. That male is a monster. One wrong word and he'll throw you in my empty cell and pretend like you ran away. Have you thought of that? What if that's what happened to the others? What if they were shot down as they escaped and he's just telling you they got away? Why else wouldn't they have sent word?"

Sophia was getting more and more tired of Heleax. His conspiracy theories had seemed reasonable at the start, but the more she'd learned about Vrulatica, the Guild, and the current political climate surrounding Tremanta, the less his accusations made sense. The ugly truth was that on some pouty irritating level, she could see the intelligence behind her kidnapping, and she couldn't help but wonder if it hadn't been Vrulatica, how much longer would they have toured before a different city took it upon themselves to do the same?

"Perhaps they got word that the interim Queen was planning to disperse them like gifts to cities across the world and decided not to go back. Honestly, I'm surprised you want to go back. Do you really agree with what she's doing? Does your loyalty to Tremanta mean you're going to go back and serve her? Are you going to drag humans from the temple so they can be shipped off when the time comes?" Sophia accused, not bothering to hold back her annoyance.

A flash of hurt crossed over his face, and his head snapped back. "I…" He placed a palm on her shoulder. "Of course not. But we can't stay here."

"*Here* is where I have the best shot of making a difference. The Vrulans might be picky about their leaders, but they don't dislike humans. Like any other city, they want them to come here. What if I could make this a haven for all the humans worried about being displaced? A human-friendly city. I told you not one member of the Guild was pleased with the Queen's decision."

Heleax crossed his arms over his chest. "They didn't object for moral reasons, Sophia. Don't see kindness where there isn't."

Sophia mimicked his stance. "That's true, but they didn't all jump at the opportunity either. Just because they don't allow their personal morals to guide their decision making doesn't mean they don't have any. I think they're reasonable, and I don't think they're as heartless as you do."

"You think you could make Vrulatica friendly?" he scoffed.

She almost wanted to laugh. "I honestly don't know. But I do know there's a possibility I could have some power here. If I leave, I have absolutely none."

Heleax considered that. "Okay. You stay for now, but I promise you, I'll figure something out." His gaze flashed behind her. "How long until you have to get married?"

"Less than two months. Sometime after I confirm he voted for my choice at the Leaders' Summit."

"I'll figure something out," he urged again, gripping her hands. Sophia didn't have the energy to argue.

She thought back to her years of LARPing before saying, "I can pretend to be a queen. Don't worry." A flash of concern speared through her. Would it be a life of pretending? Was it possible for her to ever think of herself as a queen? Or would she always be a girl playing dress-up?

They exchanged unsteady goodbyes before Heleax crawled into the cruiser and sped away.

She faced Sikthand and took a deep breath.

Lightning flashed across his armor and glinted off Ahea's antlers. He looked so powerful sitting astride the enormous creature, backlit against the spectacular tower of Vrulatica as it disappeared ominously among a blanket of glowing green clouds. This terrifying warrior king would be her husband, and she was going to figure out a way to make it work.

She straightened her spine.

"I'm staying."

***

Sikthand stared after the cruiser disappearing in the distance, his stomach a confusing tangle of relief and regret. So close. He'd been so close to getting rid of her for good. So close to losing her forever.

He could smell her heady scent lingering between the warm raindrops as she walked toward him and couldn't keep his chest from tightening. It meant nothing.

Her demand to stay was in no part related to him. She was doing it to help her people. Not because she wanted to be his queen. How could he blame her after the vitriol he'd spewed at her? Yet he couldn't keep his arm from slipping around her possessively as she climbed up and took her seat in front of him.

They lifted into the sky, and the incline had her sliding back to firmly plaster against his chest. Her cloak tangled around his forearm, and he lifted his hand from her waist to shake it out. When he replaced it, he slipped his palm beneath her cloak and across her ribcage so that his fingers wrapped around her ribs.

He wished he could feel more of her. His gloves masked it, but he could just imagine how hot and slippery her rain-soaked skin would be against his palm. A gust had his fingers curling into giving flesh to hold her steady. He ached to know how it would feel to dip the pads of his fingers into her skin, to stroke and knead. He squeezed a little tighter, and she stiffened in his grip.

May lightning strike me, he silently cursed. This female was dangerous. He couldn't seem to control himself around her. First, he'd claimed her in front of the whole damn dining hall without any right. She wasn't his, and he'd made damn sure she knew he didn't want her to be his. Now he couldn't keep his touch cold.

She even made him mindless enough to want to shed his armor. His only protection. It had saved him countless times, and yet he wanted to fly through this storm in the thinnest clothing possible so he could feel the curve of her spine melt against his chest and know the rhythm of her heartbeat as it pulsed against his palm.

He worked with Ahea to guide them through the storm, his malginash a mistress of sensing building electricity and steering her unprotected human passenger far from the gathering bolts. When they returned to the landing bay and he helped Sophia down, her cloak, heavy with rain, slapped to the ground, almost making her knees buckle.

She threw it off, coughing where the tie had dug into her neck.

He ignored the urge to pull her head back and examine her throat for damage by slipping his helmet and gloves off, and unstrapping Ahea's saddle. He'd worked her hard the last few days, keeping his mind occupied with cloud seeding, and Ahea deserved some time off.

"Hey. We're not done," Sophia called from behind him.

"I don't need you for anything else." He kept his voice emotionless, not bothering to turn around.

A small gurgle of exasperation bubbled from her. "Why did you put a verbal brand on my ass back at dinner? Huh?"

He sighed. He hadn't intended to. Something in him had just snapped. He had no answer for her. Not one that wouldn't clue her in to his real feelings. He'd wanted to rip off that male's tail right there in front of everyone.

"Don't ignore me, you fucking tin man!" His shoulder dipped forward an inch as something bumped into it, and he froze. Had she…?

Now on high alert, he sensed when her hand shot out to shove him again. He spun, catching her wrist and forcing her back from Ahea a few steps as his mount clicked a warning growl.

Sophia's pupils were dilated in anger. "Stay out of this, Ahea," she barked.

His mount fluttered her wings indignantly but surprisingly did quiet her growling.

"Did you strike the king, human?"

A smile threatened to tug at his mouth as the little female actually rolled her eyes. "Calm down. I shoved your shoulder. You barely even noticed it. Explain yourself," she grated. "Why did you do that? I am trying my best to not take anything you say or do too personally. I'm working my ass off to learn everything I can so I can be a good leader. I'm devoting myself to being queen, and you have told me that we won't be together romantically and that's fine, but are you expecting me to be celibate for the rest of my life? What's with the *mine* bullshit?"

Sikthand's lips tightened. He dropped her wrist, and she stumbled away. His heart thundered to life as he caught sight of the dress she was wearing, now wet and clinging to her curves. His jaw slackened, his fingers curling in as he itched to reach out and trace the delicate folds of fabric.

Sophia noticed.

She studied him, her gaze flicking over his face. Her brows softened. "You *are* interested in me, aren't you?" she breathed.

He spun away, returning to kneel at Ahea's side. "Incorrect."

"You want me, and you hate it, don't you?"

His neck burned, his skin sparking with awareness of her proximity to his back.

"You don't want to get married, so you've been trying to scare me off with your huffing and puffing. But really, you *like* me."

"No," he all but shouted, rising to his full height. He whirled on her to get her to back away, but as soon as he turned, her fingers curled around his neck and her mouth lifted to his.

The howling wind settled into a distant whisper, and the rain sizzled off his heated skin as soon as it hit.

He didn't understand this. Didn't know what she was doing, but her soft lips kneading his was the loveliest paralytic.

Her mouth was warm and giving, her fingers gentle where they dug into the hair at his nape. His heart was stuck mid-beat, breath no longer necessary. He could nearly taste her, and then her lips parted, and her tongue swept across the seam of his mouth.

Sikthand, the king harder than askait, trembled.

The blade he'd retrieved at lightning speed when she'd lunged for him slipped from his fingers. The clang as it hit the stone ground was a distant tinkling in his ears.

He matched her mouth's movements, clutching her upturned face with both hands and tasting her. Each slide of her hot tongue against his sent fire coursing through his belly and electricity exploding over his skin. Her mouth was sweet, her tongue scalding, and he angled his head to drink her in deeper.

He'd eat her pretty cunt this way, delving his tongue in as deep as it would go, licking every curve until she quivered and broke. She let out a desperate moan, her nails digging into his neck, and he growled in response.

But then she yelped in pain, and he jerked away.

A bead of blood dripped from her flushed lower lip. "I'm okay," she breathed, her lids heavy and the heady scent of arousal rising in the air between them. "It was just your fangs."

His fangs? His thumb moved from her cheek, where he was holding her upturned face, down to swipe over her bloodied lip. The tang of metal hit his nose.

Sikthand's mind returned to him slowly. He took stock of where they were.

She was smashed against his chest, his tail wrapped around her back to hold her securely in place. How hard had he been crushing her against him? With his armor shielding the feel of her body, he worried it had been too hard.

He'd hurt her. He'd been mindless. This wasn't right.

Slowly her brows furrowed in worry, and she lowered a few inches. Down from her tiptoes, he now realized.

It took exceptionally more willpower to get his tail to remove itself from her back, but when he did, it was as if his thundering heart finally registered in his ears.

He turned away, needing distance from her scent, her body, her divine mouth before he lost himself completely.

"Leave," he growled, his lungs heaving in all the air he'd deprived himself of at once. Under his armor he was shaking, panicked.

"I...I don't understand. We could have a *real* marriage. It wouldn't be easy, but—"

"I shouldn't have claimed you." He faced her, his heart constricting at the mere sight of her heartbreakingly beautiful face. "It was a moment of jealousy, I admit. Nothing more."

"I don't believe you." A change in the wind brought rain slashing in at a harsh angle. Lightning flashed over her face and highlighted the smeared blood on her chin, a gruesome display.

The sight helped ground him. Sikthand stepped close, hardening his heart and blinding his senses. He gripped her chin in a cruel hold.

"This is a temporary fascination, human," he hissed. "You are but a Season. Calamitous, powerful, *consuming*. But like the rains, you too will pass." He dropped her chin and straightened to his full height, towering over her, not revealing the crippling ache constricting his stomach. "I need only weather you."

19

A week had gone by, and Sophia still couldn't get ahold of her feelings. The king claimed to not want her, but…that kiss.

She'd impulsively kissed him to see how he'd react and prove to them both that his feelings about her weren't as cold as he let on. Realizing her plan was already a failure when she'd remembered Clecanians didn't kiss on the mouth like humans, she'd been about to pull away, but then he'd reacted.

The way he'd held her, the way he'd gripped her face, the pained furrow of his brow, and the rumbling purr that had vibrated from her lips all the way to her lower back where his tail crushed her against his armor. Intensity like that couldn't be faked. She didn't think he knew what a kiss was, and yet it had been the best of her life.

It hadn't been smooth or suave or gentle. It'd been scorching and rough, like he'd been trying to lay claim, and damn if it wasn't seared into her memory. She'd laid in bed staring at the door that led to his room and swiping her tongue across her cut lip long into the night.

Sophia winced as askait ink pooled underneath her skin, tearing her mind away from the memory of that night. A wave of nausea rose in her throat, but she swallowed it down.

"You're back soon," Khes commented. He hadn't said much to her since she'd arrived at the Flesh Forge asking for him.

She needed something to keep her mind occupied, and luckily Alno had taken it upon himself to get her a new sketchbook, so she had a few pages of tattoo designs to keep her busy. She hadn't had the opportunity to thank him yet for the thoughtful gesture because she hadn't seen him much in the last week. He'd been with Difila.

Since the umbercree celebration, the two had spent more and more time together. Sophia now had Difila's cloud-chasing schedule memorized since Alno all but disappeared when she came off shift.

Sophia couldn't be too annoyed by his absence, though. She'd pushed for him to take time off, arguing that they were in a weirdly calm period right now and that he'd be stupid not to run when his dream girl called.

Once she was announced as the future queen, she'd need Alno to keep close and help her navigate her new life. It made sense for him to take all the time he could to enjoy himself before that happened.

Even though she'd practically kicked Alno toward Difila, Sophia tried not to let jealousy grip her too tightly. Alno was just a friend, and she knew how utterly obsessed he was with Difila. But the truth was, he was her *only* friend. Without him following her around and reminding her to eat, she had no one. Even Heleax was gone.

Her days had become increasingly isolated over the past week. She'd wake up, grab breakfast on her way to the archives in midcity. Stay there until the red glow from one of the windows turned blue, an effect she'd learned tracked the time of day. Then, when her stomach gnawed at her hard enough, she would go to dinner. Sometimes Sikthand would be there, sometimes not, and she couldn't decide which she preferred. Both seeing him and not seeing him left a funny feeling in her stomach.

Nights were spent drawing or studying in her adjoining office. Her massive polished table was piled high with scrolls and papers she'd taken back to her room. She'd study until her head was swirling with historical facts, dates, and laws, then she'd crawl into bed.

It was lonely.

There was an ever-present sense of accomplishment bolstering her. Her reading was improving, she recognized more and more folks throughout this section of the tower, and she'd even come up with a few viable ideas on how they could make Vrulatica more human friendly, but she'd never felt quite this isolated before.

The only other people she could talk to were the Guild, and they weren't exactly an open bunch. She had to watch her words around them, be guarded.

Maybe that was why she'd decided to change it up and get tattooed today. She had to find a way to inject herself with some happiness, and seeing more of her designs come to life felt like a perfect way to accomplish that.

"I'd like to get most of the sleeve done before...too long," she said, quelling the urge to explain that she didn't think she'd have time to come down and get tattooed after she was announced as the next queen.

Khes held her gaze for a few beats too long, and she narrowed her eyes.

He knew something.

She tipped her head toward him. "I think I'll be busy in the coming months," she added slowly. Khes' expression was unchanged at hearing her seemingly innocent explanation. She was probably just seeing things that weren't there in the hope she could find somebody else to talk to. Sophia turned away.

"If you end up being too busy to visit, I can always go up to your room and work on you there," Khes grumbled.

"That's nice of you," Sophia said through a wince as the pen began to move over her forearm, drawing a base of stylized clouds that would climb up from her wrist and flow into the malginash's tail on her upper arm.

A moment of silence passed. "It's what I do for the *king*. It only makes sense I do the same for you," Khes nearly whispered.

Sophia whipped toward him, eyes wide.

"Ach!" He threw his hands up, brows slicing down angrily. "Hold still," he barked, wrenching her arm back into position.

"Y-You know?" she whispered.

He glanced up from his work, holding her gaze as if confirming with just his annoyed stare. "The king's been getting a lot of work done recently in that torn-up room of his. He revealed the reason behind his dark mood one day." Khes' mouth thinned. "A bit dramatic, if you ask me."

Sophia grinned. Those few sentences made her feel better than she had in days. "A bit dramatic," she whispered to herself, chuckling.

"Though I suppose the circumstances call for it," Khes admitted. He dragged his pen over the bones in her elbow, and her mouth filled with saliva. Sophia slammed her eyes shut and breathed in and out through her nose to keep her nausea at bay.

In her hazy, pain-filled mind she couldn't keep the question she wanted to ask from spewing out of her mouth. "Are you disappointed?"

She had to know. Alno had been ambivalent. The Guild had been excited, but not because they thought she would make a good queen. And Sikthand thought she would fail. But what would the people—soon to be *her* people—think? Being hated by a whole city would be a miserable existence.

He tipped his head to the side, squinting at his work. "I think it's coming out nicely."

"No." She wiggled her arm until he peered up at her. "Are you *disappointed*?"

Understanding had him leaning back in his seat. "I can't say I'm disappointed. I can't say I'm approving. I don't have opinions like that about things that haven't happened yet. You show me what you can do, and then I'll tell you if I'm disappointed."

The knot in her throat loosened a fraction. "Fair enough." He was right. There was no reason to fret over people's initial reactions. She'd worry just the same, but she had to remember that what she really needed to focus on was working as hard as she could to prove herself. *Earn their respect. Don't expect it.*

She sucked in a breath as he resumed work on her tattoo.

"Our king has been through a lot." The words seemed to be pulled out of him against his will. "You planning to disappoint him?"

She peeked at Khes through squinted eyes, still trying to breathe through the pain. His voice had sounded tight, almost...protective.

"How long have you known the king?" she asked.

"You know how old I am. I've known him his whole life. Many people have." She studied the frown cemented in place on his face.

"No. You *know* him. I can hear it in your voice."

His eyes flashed to her, then back to his work. "I'm the inkmaster for the royal family. I gave him his first tattoo, tattooed his parents before him and his grandparents before them. This marriage..." Khes grunted, his voice raspy, as if he'd said more than he normally did in a week and was pissed about it. "I'd be unhappy to see this marriage..." He cleared his throat and lifted his pen. Khes met her stare, a stern set to his eyes. "It'd be a shame for him to find any more cause to hate the world."

She smiled at him. "Just an ancient softie, aren't you?"

He growled and slipped the pen around the tender skin near her wrist hard enough to make her squeak.

"Ay! Okay." Her fingers curled into a fist from the pain, but she kept her expression sincere. "Khes, I don't plan to give him cause to hate the world," she assured quietly. "I don't think I can do this without him," she whispered, some insecurity leaking into her voice.

He studied her closely, searching her face for the truth. He must have been happy with what he saw because he nodded. "Then don't try to do it without him."

"Kinda hard when he won't talk to me." She sighed, resting her chin on the back of her chair.

"You're his queen. Make him talk."

She rolled her eyes so he couldn't see. "And when he hops on Ahea and flies away? Should I scream after him?" she whined.

Khes grunted. "Can't solve a simple problem like this, then I suppose you *will* disappoint me."

Sophia laughed and winced. "Jesus, Khes, don't hold back on account of my feelings or anything." But she didn't mind.

Khes wasn't wrong. Sitting around moping, waiting for Sikthand to approach her wasn't going to work.

20

Sophia didn't leave the Flesh Forge until late. The dining hall contained only scraps of stale food from dinner hours before. She brought a plate to her room and ate it in her study, the *queen's* study, while staring at the cold hearth. One day, she'd need to learn how to build a fire.

She glanced around the area in front of the hearth, scanning again for wood or matches or anything. But there were only unfamiliar canisters. Fires here weren't built like they were back on Earth, and she was too cautious to guess at it. She'd likely end up setting the whole wing ablaze. If she ever saw Alno again, she'd make sure to get him to teach her.

Her quarters felt different to her now. More imposing. Her rooms weren't just a temporary residence anymore. This was her home, her space forever. The study, which she'd rarely set foot in before, wasn't just a fun bonus library. It was where she'd anguish over decisions that had the power to change the world.

Again, what the fuck am I doing?

To soothe her panic, she smoothed her fingertips over the new design inching up her forearm. She traced over a small spot on her inner wrist where she'd hidden an umbercree within billowing clouds. Mind veering toward Sikthand again, she shook her head to clear it.

She had their whole marriage to agonize over that knee-weakening kiss, but she only had a month and a half until the Leaders' Summit. That was where her mind had to be.

Pushing her food aside, she crossed to the mostly empty shelves she was slowly filling with collected scrolls and reference books. She pulled all the candidate files Yalmi had provided her with and felt a familiar sense of overwhelm set in when she opened the first one.

Dates with years she didn't understand were paired with service to places she didn't recognize.

Agers Kutaf. Toki 14 to Uranid 67, 400th Gui cycle. Title: Attaché to Grempling Studia Volux. Earned forty thesklines for his service.

"What the fuck does that mean?" she groaned.

For all Sophia knew, the person that this file belonged to could have served ten years in the military or two months in a candy factory. *Studia* made her think his role was somehow academic, but *thesklines earned for service?*

She shoved the file away and collapsed back into her chair with folded arms. This was useless. Her leg bounced as she glared at the papers on her desk.

You know what? Fuck it.

Shoving files into a haphazard pile, she scooped them into her arms, then threw a dozen or so scrolls and a heavy book into the mix for good measure.

She stormed into her bedroom and checked her reflection in the mirror. A few scrolls toppled out of her arms when she tried to use one hand to smooth her hair and wipe the dark makeup smudges away from under her eyes.

Ignoring the embarrassing reflection of her failed efforts to pick the scrolls up off the ground without allowing more to spill from her arms, she lifted her chin and breezed out of her room. In less than two minutes, she was standing in front of Sikthand's door, breath unsteady. She ground her teeth, clenching and unclenching her jaw while staring at the dark wood.

Just knock. Be confident. Don't take no for an answer.

She pooled her pile into the crook of her right arm, curling her shoulder to keep a few precarious scrolls in place while she lifted her fist to knock, but before her knuckles grazed the door, it flew open and Sikthand barreled out, almost running right into her before freezing.

Hand still raised in mid-knock, they stared at each other, both startled into silence. He didn't look surprised to see her, though, more confused.

In slow motion, one of the scrolls wedged under a file began slipping free, making a deafening scrape in the utter silence of the corridor that would have been hilarious if it didn't mean Sophia was about to have to make a fool of herself trying to pick it up.

The uncovered tip of Sikthand's tail flashed out before the scroll fell, and without breaking eye contact, he slowly forced it back into place.

"Uh, hi." She cleared her throat and finally lowered her hand. Her brain registered his armorless frame, and she forced her eyes to stay trained on his face, or the ground, or the wall. Anywhere except at his defined chest visible through the loosely laced front of his long-sleeved navy shirt. His hair was unbound but combed back from his forehead as though he'd run his hand through it in frustration a hundred times and the strands had given up trying to fall forward. "Can I come in?"

It was obvious he'd been going somewhere in a hurry, but she didn't want to acknowledge that. Asking where he was headed would just give him an excuse to leave. She'd be the queen, and she needed to start acting high and mighty.

Her question registered, and his brows creased. He looked over his shoulder at his room as if inspecting it. She took his distraction as an opportunity, slipping under his elbow and striding inside.

Khes had mentioned it was messy, and boy, he hadn't been lying. Scrap bits of metal lay all over the place. A corner of the room with an array of weapons, tools, an enormous blazing hearth, and a grinding stone contained the most scraps. The king must have a metalworking hobby. Interesting.

"Is there somewhere I can put these?"

His shock was finally wearing off, and a cold mask slipped into place. "What are you doing here, Sophia?" he asked sharply.

"An impromptu meeting. I have some stuff I need to go over with you," she commented mildly, as if they both weren't hyper-aware that the last time they'd spoken had ended in a scorching kiss.

He peered around his room, eyes falling on piles of clutter here and there. His shoulders lifted with tension, almost like he was embarrassed.

He stepped over to his door, opening it again. "I don't have time for that. We can meet some other day."

She huffed out a breath of frustration but kept herself rooted in place. "No."

"No?" he parroted, brows lifting.

"I don't have anyone else that I can talk to. I'm going to be queen, and you're going to be my king. We need to discuss things *together*. I have an armful of information that I don't know how to decipher. I can't go to the Guild because I can't trust they'll tell me everything and not cherry-pick their information based on who they want me to vote for. I don't know anyone else in the city who cares about politics. Like it or not, we *have* to talk." She let a little bit of desperation leak into her voice. "I need your help."

His hand gripped the door, his knuckles white, and he stared at her, a muscle twitching in his jaw. He looked out into the empty hallway for a few silent moments before finally letting out a growl of irritation and throwing the door closed.

Sophia didn't even flinch at the *crack* of it slamming shut. She'd won.

He faced her again, resigned but clearly unhappy about it. "In there," he growled, pointing to an open door. She made her way through without complaint, though her insides begged her to stay in his bedroom and peek at every corner of his private space.

His rooms were a mirror of hers. Even before walking through the door he'd gestured toward, she knew she'd walk into a study.

The layout was identical. Bookshelves lining one curved wall, a twin desk in a glossy black finish, and metal branches tipped with glowing orbs spreading across the ceiling like hanging constellations.

Yet his study looked more…kingly.

Maps were stuck to the walls, the bookcases were overflowing with all manner of written work. The rug covering the stone floor was compressed in certain areas, as though giving her insight into where her soon-to-be husband liked to pace. She ignored the trickle of warmth that bloomed in her at knowing something personal like that about him. Cups were piled on the table, some still containing white liquid.

Her arms ached, so she dropped the load she was carrying onto the desk, lunging to keep a few things from slipping off the corner.

Her stomach dipped when she turned and saw him leaning against the doorframe, arms crossed over his chest, hair brushing his strong shoulders. She knew his silence was a challenge. He was waiting for her to spit out whatever it was she needed to say, but she couldn't bring herself to be annoyed. This was good. This was progress.

She picked up one stack of papers off the table at random and flipped through the candidate file. "Thania Seeker from Caelestis," she announced. As good a place as any to start.

Sophia made her way to the chair behind the desk, now suddenly very self-conscious about reading aloud. She scanned the first line. "What is Dydall?"

With a sigh, he lifted off the door frame and sauntered into the room, stopping at a corner laden with glassware and a large jug of liquid she hadn't noticed before. "It's not a *what*. It's a where. A religious temple of the Caeles. Thania was a high priestess for about fifty years before she turned her eye to politics."

Sophia kept her focus on the file as if reading silently, but all her mind could concentrate on was how Sikthand had slipped behind her chair and now loomed at her back. A glass came into view in front of her, and he set it down with a light thump.

She peeked at his thick forearm, roped with muscle. Heavy black bands traveled down from under the folded cuff of his shirt and connected with the stripes running over his fingers like black angular bones.

Sophia swallowed and averted her eyes. It should be illegal for a man with forearms like that to push up his sleeves. She fidgeted when he didn't move away, flicking her thumb over the decorative metal corner piece holding the papers together.

He smelled so good without armor on.

"Okay," she finally replied, scrunching her brows and forcing her eyes to move back to the file. "She... So what does it mean when it says 'was in rotation for *merps-oh-ree*—'" Sophia stumbled over the word, heat rising on her neck.

"Menkscreen," he corrected, his rumbling voice near her ear sent shivers down her spine.

Fuck. She'd forgotten that damn *ks* symbol again.

He plucked the file from her fingers and crossed to a well-worn chair in the corner of the room. "If you ask me about each of these terms one by one, we'll be here for years," he grumbled. "I'll read this to you and explain as I go. You listen."

She tamped down her annoyance with his imperious tone and nabbed her glass from the table before joining him. She plopped down into an almost identical chair across from him.

The fabric on the arms of his chair was worn and faded compared to the bright clear pattern on hers. Even alien kings had funny little habits. Each day, he must come in and choose to sit in that chair rather than this one.

It was another small insight into the king, trivial as it may be—yet she liked knowing. These bits of information felt forbidden. They didn't matter at all, but she bet she was one of the only people in the world who knew which chair the king preferred to sit in. The only one who knew which side of the desk he paced on and what type of beverage he drank while working.

She smothered a stupid grin and took a sip of her drink. It was a watered-down version of renwaeder. Her throat burned to let out a cough, her eyes watering. She managed to keep it down and save some dignity. He eyed her, his long strong fingers brushing against the top corner of the paper held upright in his lap.

"Seeker from Caelestis is a title given to officials from Caelestis who travel to cities around the world, learning from other rulers and immersing themselves in different cultures. They use what they learn to better their city and, in Thania's case, improve our relations with Alliance species."

Sikthand continued to read and explain, and Sophia tried to concentrate rather than let her mind wander to how delicious his voice sounded. It was hard work.

As it turned out, Thania seemed like a pretty good candidate. Though she'd spent a near lifetime dedicated to her temple in her home city and another lifetime wandering the world as a Seeker, she'd taken her experience and approached her role as intergalactic council representative with wisdom and compassion.

One of her more memorable accomplishments, in Sophia's opinion, was her hard-fought battle for leniency in dreg offenses. Dregs, meaning citizens of planets not belonging to the Alliance for one reason or another, who unlawfully traveled through the galaxy for things like supplies or trade, had been dealt with harshly to make a statement.

Thania had fought for dreg crimes to be judged individually rather than continuing to dole out blanket sentences regardless of whether the crime was illegal purchase of building materials or space piracy.

However, Sophia didn't like rumors of favoritism toward Thania's home city. That could be a problem. Then again, she supposed it would be difficult to find a truly objective representative when they were all from one city or another.

Just like on Earth, the country you were from was a part of you, and unless you found somebody with no country to speak of, there would be some sense of allegiance that had to be looked over. Sophia herself wasn't objective by any stretch.

Sikthand answered her endless questions clearly but seldom elaborated. He rarely even looked at her, so she made sure to stare at him extra hard. She couldn't decide why. Perhaps this was her way of chastising him for not looking at someone when talking to them.

Or maybe the renwaeder had worked its way into her bloodstream, making her a little more relaxed than she should've been.

It'd been a couple hours, and they'd only made it through one file. Every other word was foreign to her and needed explanation. Every proper noun, many phrases, any mention of foods or plants or animals. It was vindicating to have someone else acknowledge that being able to read wasn't the same thing as being able to understand.

Sophia wasn't stupid. She was from a different planet, and watching him arrive at the same conclusion had relief spreading through her, especially when his cruel words about her *underdeveloped human brain* played through her head at regular intervals.

When she'd interrupted him starting to clarify the difference between the Brudelerion and Brudelure Alliance species, explaining the difference herself in simple terms since she'd already looked it up days ago, he'd appeared impressed. Her chest had bowed, and a smug smile stayed glued to her lips.

It felt nice for someone to finally realize how out of her depth she was and how hard she had to work to know even as much as a Clecanian child.

He slapped the file down on a low table between them and ran his hand through his hair in exactly the way she'd imagined he had. Her grin widened, and she tried to hide it when he peered at her. One more private habit she knew about the king that not many others did.

He frowned, not understanding what her smothered smile was about, yet suspicious of it all the same. "We can go over the others another time."

She nodded. It was late, and she was tired. "One per day should do it." She had the choice to phrase it as a question, but she didn't. This was a demand.

He raised a brow at her and sipped his drink. "One per day seems excessive."

She shrugged, her movements a little sluggish. "That schedule actually feels a little too relaxed considering the Leaders' Summit is in six weeks and that was one of the thin files." Her drink was empty, so she rose from her seat to refill it. Heat from his gaze warmed her back as she strolled by his bookshelves, examining the items with interest on her way to the jug of renwaeder. Would he tell her to stop? Make her leave?

"Who do you want to vote for?" she asked.

"Your demand doesn't give me a say, remember?" he sneered.

She peered over her shoulder at him. "It doesn't mean I don't wanna know. I'd like to hear your opinion."

"I don't know. I haven't decided."

She stopped in front of a wide map and rolled her eyes. Something that was becoming a new habit in this city. "Well, who are your favorites, then? What are your thoughts on the candidates?"

"I don't know whether Vila still isn't the best option."

Sophia was searching the map, trying to pinpoint Tremanta, when his words caught up with her. She spun around. "Are you kidding? Vila?"

He shrugged, the pad of his thumb tracing over the lip of his glass. "She's clearly smart, resourceful, cunning, and as far as I can tell, her main objective is to get Earth opened. I want that too. Our planet needs that. Our *people* need that. It might be better for our world to have someone ruthless in charge."

"But…" Sophia argued. "But the *way* she's doing it. It's deplorable. How can you support a ruler like that? She's as bad as the Insurgents."

He grinned, exposing a fang, but it wasn't a grin of happiness, it was one of disdain. "What I *personally* support doesn't matter. My morals hold no weight. My duty is to my people, as is yours. And as for the Insurgents"—he lifted a thoughtful brow—"they did find a species capable of preventing our extinction. Did they not?"

Sophia's mouth slammed shut for a moment. "That doesn't justify *how* they did it. It wasn't right."

"*Right* doesn't exist as a ruler. I can't make decisions based on what's right or wrong or good or evil. Whoever put it in your head that being a queen meant you could lead ethically lied. Being a ruler is being strong enough to make terrible horrible decisions so that your people can lead lives free from pain and fear."

Sophia studied him, frowning. "I don't agree. The *how* matters."

He shook his head and let out a humorless laugh. "You don't have to agree. If you last long enough, you'll see it for yourself. As a queen, you'll have to choose what our city stands for. What's worth fighting for and what isn't, not based on what's *right* or *wrong*, but based on what allows your people to live unconcerned lives. And despite the fact that every intention you have is pure, they'll hate you. They can't help it. There is no decision you will make, *ever*, that everyone will support. You either don't do enough, or you do it the wrong way, or you're too soft, or you're too vicious."

Sikthand grew more animated as he spoke, pouring out decades of pent-up bitterness and anger into his growling voice. He ground to a sudden halt and blinked at her as if just realizing she was still there. He glanced away, taking in a deep, exhausted breath that gave her the impression he hadn't truly rested in a very long time.

"People need something to be upset about for their happiness to be real," he explained, voice emotionless. "We only notice the day because there is night. We're only truly quenched by water after thirst sets in. They need the negative, even if they manufacture it. It's the only way they understand the value of the positive. As their queen, you're an easy target. They'll look for any crack, any blemish and scream about it. But the fact that they're screaming about you and not perishing in wars or starving in the mines will show you you've done your job well. And when you die, they'll visit your statue in the Heroes Hall and wail over what a wonderful leader you were, though you won't be around to hear it."

He met her wide-eyed stare, a harsh severity to his gaze. "Our people are afraid. Though the world has fought for hundreds of years to keep it at bay, extinction is coming. If Vila is our best chance of getting Earth opened and giving our people a glimmer of hope, then her effectiveness outweighs her vile methods. It's not right. But that never matters."

Sophia stared at him silently for a long time, trying to process the magnitude of Sikthand's worldview. Was he right? Or was he just jaded?

She grabbed the jug of alcohol and settled back into her seat across from him. "You're the bleakest person I've ever met." She took a long breath. "But I'm determined to prove you wrong."

Sikthand was sprawled back, knees spread wide, the floral-patterned chair looking as much a throne as any other seat he occupied. There was a frown permanently etched on his face, but there was something about his relaxed posture, and the glint of interest in his eyes that made Sophia wonder whether he wasn't enjoying this conversation, wasn't enjoying dumping out all his deepest darkest woes onto another person.

Sophia had been feeling so alone for the last week, but that isolation must be just a drop in the ocean compared to what Sikthand must have felt his whole life.

"The old Queen wasn't as cynical as you," she commented, wondering if his inherited title is what had made him such a defeatist.

"I bet she was more cynical than you think. She was just better at hiding it." He leaned forward, his elbows coming to rest on his knees. "That rumor about her stashing thousands of humans away—"

"Turned out to be just a rumor," Sophia shot back.

"But she had *hundreds*," he countered. He tipped his brows up, waiting for her response, already knowing he'd won the point.

Sophia chewed on her lip. She still couldn't account for that. Where had they all come from? The Guild had explained that the queen had hundreds of humans still asleep in pods.

Had the old Queen really hidden them away? It made her question everything.

"So, what should I prepare myself to deal with? What do our people blame you for?" She poured him a glass before pouring her own. He stared at it suspiciously for a few seconds. "What?" she asked. Had a bug fallen in his cup or something?

"I usually pour my own drinks," he muttered. His eyes were still narrowed at the innocent white liquid.

"Worried I slipped you something?" she joked, but his silver gaze flashed to her.

"You wouldn't be the first." The absence of any emotion in his voice as he admitted he'd been poisoned before had dread racing down her spine.

Her heart hurt for him and for the effort it had to take to live so cautiously. It must be exhausting and awfully lonely. "I'm not going to do that, Sikthand. I'd never do that to you," she urged softly.

His brows furrowed, his bright eyes scanning her face as if he desperately wanted to believe her but just couldn't. He held her gaze for a moment longer, then took a sip. A muscle in his jaw ticked as he gulped down the liquid and sat back.

"My people," he began, "feel we do too much. We seed the clouds, which takes months of time and effort. It's dangerous, but it needs to be done. The blind spot in the Choke is our planet's greatest weak point and is often exploited by neighboring dreg planets. So, we also make sure to send out scouts often and then warriors to smother any invaders we find. Vrulatica also supplies the world with the askait used in electronics, and we do it without being able to use any electronics ourselves."

"That *is* a lot." She nodded. "So, they think we should stop one thing or another?"

He chuckled again, a lopsided grin exposing one glorious fang. Sophia tried to imagine how a smile of actual happiness would look on him, and her heart picked up speed. Was it even possible to make him laugh?

"No. We've tried that. About one hundred and sixty years ago we demanded to share scouting duties with Emek, a city to the north of the Choke."

"The Great Fouling." Sophia nodded, recalling the unfortunate event from the history she'd been learning.

His black brows raised as if impressed, and he nodded. "Yes. Our forces squabbled, both armies used to being in charge. The Tagion watched and exploited that weakness. They set up a fake incursion close to Emek, knowing it was our time to defend but understanding that squads from Emek would be sent out as well since they were territorial and untrusting of our abilities. They took the distraction as an opportunity to sneak into Vrulan borders and poison the reserve."

He sighed as if it were a regrettable event and not as horrific as the book she'd read made it out to be. "Many Vrulans were lost before we discovered our water had been tainted. My ancestor, Queen Slesain, mysteriously slipped and fell into a vat of molten metal, and we went back to guarding the Choke on our own after that. Every few decades our people seem to forget about that period of history, and we have to remind them."

Sophia shuddered. Out of all the ways to die, boiling metal sounded like one of the worst. "How do you deal with it?"

He waved a hand dismissively. "We listen. Hold public forums, hear complaints and—"

"No," Sophia interrupted. "How do *you* deal with it? You basically just outlined a miserable existence in which you are constantly judged and criticized. Nothing you do makes them happy. In fact, you've almost been assassinated a bunch of times. But you're still here. You're still trying to be a good king. What keeps you trying? There must be something worth fighting for."

His face twitched, and his eyes flicked around the room. The king shifted in his chair as though he'd never been asked something like that before. He considered it, remaining silent, brows drawn in concentration.

"I watch my people. I see them cooking meals and hugging their children and creating beautiful works of art, and it brings my life meaning. I might suffer, but I'm a king. I was born to bear that particular kind of pain, and so I do. We all have roles to play. And mine—" He caught her rapt gaze. "*Ours* is important. Extraordinarily so."

How could a man so jaded also be so full of purpose and…goodness? She saw it now, though she hadn't fully before. Sikthand was a good king. He was quiet and strict, but he cared. She could see his desperation to be accepted by his people practically oozing from his pores, but he didn't let their lack of warmth affect his bone-deep belief that they deserved happy lives.

"That's a really beautiful answer," she breathed, pouring all the sincerity she could muster into her voice. The compliment seemed to make him even more uncomfortable than the question had. "For the record, I think you deserve to find some joy in your life too. You're a king, but you're also a man. You weren't *only* born to bear pain."

"That's quite an idealistic view. Too bad it's a fantasy. You'll see." Sophia couldn't decide if his firm tone was there to convince her of his words or himself. He downed the rest of his drink and rose from his chair. "It's late. I've told you what I know, now we're done."

"Sir, yes, sir," she recited, bolting out of her seat and bowing overenthusiastically. She could swear his lip nearly twitched into a smile.

"Take your mess with you," he commanded, gesturing toward the pile of scrolls and files she'd dropped on his desk.

Sophia scratched her head, uneager to haul it all back to her room. "I'll be back tomorrow. Does it matter?" She piled a few things together. "Can I use the shortcut door to my room?"

The swish of his tail against the floor and the barest hint of a growl sent electricity skittering over her scalp. She turned to look at him and found him stiff. The only bit of him moving was his tail. "That passage is not a *shortcut*. It's used for a very different purpose, and unless you'd like me to find that *joy* you were referencing tonight, you'll stay out of it."

Sophia gulped. His gaze flashed to her mouth, and his silver eyes turned molten. Heat slipped down her insides and pooled in her low belly.

He tore his attention away. "Just leave the mess."

She was leaning over slightly, the papers bundled in her hands, her knuckles resting on the desk. The edge of the table hit right at the crease in her hips. It would be the perfect height for…

She pulled her hands back, jerking her head in a nod before speeding out to the non-sex-passage exit of his bedroom.

When she was through the door and in the hall, she turned and extended her fingers for a handshake. "We got a lot accomplished tonight," she croaked, feeling like she was wrapping up an awkward business meeting. "We can definitely make this a good partnership." He stared at her hand, mystified, and she finally dropped it. "O-Okay, then," she stammered, before speed walking away. Halfway down the hall, she buried her flaming face in her hands.

Unless you'd like me to find that joy *you were referencing…* Sophia shivered.

Later that night, when she was wrapped in the protective metal nest of her sheltered malginash bed, she smiled to herself. They hadn't said any ugly words to each other all night. In fact, she'd just had a surprisingly deep conversation. Sophia had succeeded in wearing him down a little, and she'd had the added bonus of seeing his private space, which felt terribly inappropriate in the best way.

As her eyes drifted closed, she recalled how he'd almost knocked her over trying to leave his room. Where had he been going?

21

He wasn't ready for this.

Sophia was being announced today, and every cell in Sikthand's body was tied in knots. Usually he felt prepared for difficult situations. Flying into a deadly storm or battle didn't faze him. It was easy to keep his wits when he knew danger was coming from all sides.

But this was different. It wasn't only himself he had to worry about anymore, and as much as he wished he could split himself in two, he couldn't. He strapped his metal on extra thick, his shoulders already aching from the weight of it, and prepared to parade himself through Vrulatica on his way to the throne room in lowcity.

He had no idea what reaction his people would have to the engagement announcement disseminated early this morning. The Guild had pushed to hold a public forum so citizens could come and voice their support or their complaints, and he had, without question, refused to allow Sophia to attend.

She would remain safe in the queen's quarters until he'd taken the temperature of his city.

Not only did he have his own citizens to worry about, but the world. Some cities would be jealous, some appalled if they deemed a Class Four planet species unfit to rule, and Tremanta…well, he had no idea what the new Queen would do. He and the Guild had decided to let the announcement stand on its own as a statement rather than reaching out to formally accept or decline her offer of humans in exchange for their vote.

They'd reopened trade to Tremanta as if it had merely been paused. This morning, the Queen should have awoken to shipments of askait and news that Sophia would become queen of Vrulatica.

It was a dangerous move. She could very likely take offense. After all, they were making a hostage human their queen. Though it would be idiotic, especially considering this marriage was consensual, the Queen had grounds to call for war if she so wished. He hoped it wouldn't come to that. Their askait deposits alone should keep her quiet, but he couldn't be sure.

It was paramount that he remain vigilant, but that was proving more than a little difficult. He'd thought their nightly visits would subdue the irritating temptation to follow Sophia, to have her in his sight always, but the urge had only grown stronger. He found himself loitering in his study long after she'd left and inhaling her lingering scent.

His duties had become more demanding the past week, requiring him to be called away often as they discussed strategy for the building storm system moving in. But Sikthand had found himself rushing back to his rooms every night and sitting on his bed, unable to focus on anything as he waited for her to knock. Always three gentle raps high on the door.

Whenever she glided through his room, smiling gently in that way that made his gut tighten, all his worries ebbed. They were still there, bubbling at the corners of his mind, but she blurred them somehow.

Her presence was as glorious as it was dangerous. The leery voices inside that hissed warnings about who he needed to spy on weren't as pressing as they used to be. When she was away, though, the voices returned with a vengeance.

She knows your habits now. All she'd have to do to betray you is slip something into your wine.

The Guild has seen how distracted you are. This is the perfect time for someone to strike.

You haven't trained in weeks. You're growing soft.

The whispers were true, but he didn't know what to do about them. He couldn't keep himself away, and he didn't want to. What she'd said had stuck with him, gnawing at his chest as he actively tried to ignore it. He deserved to find some joy too. Well, his joy was watching her, and it was the only joy he'd permit himself.

Being in the same room as her and allowing himself to sink into the peace that she brought, even if all she did was silently go about her life within his line of vision, made his mind buzz with warmth.

During their meetings, he loved to watch her read the most. He'd study her nose, waiting for the moment it scrunched. A question wouldn't be far behind, and he looked forward to the instant her beautiful eyes connected with his as she asked it.

He'd even begun playing a sick game with himself. He'd altered the tattoos on his forearms every couple of days. Then, when he knew she was gone, he'd sneak into her room and flip through her drawing book. The pleasure he got every time a new sketch appeared with his updated tattoos was indescribable, and well worth the pain of getting them altered.

She watched him too. The notion should terrify him. Someone who paid that much attention would be sure to see cracks in his armor, but it was also thrilling to know she studied him so closely when he wasn't looking.

Yes, Sikthand had allowed himself a bit of joy, but he didn't let himself have anything more, though his body ached for her. He kept his expression stony whenever she was around, not allowing any of his internal mooning to show on his face. He never permitted her to linger in his bedroom. Her smell needed to be contained to the study, or he'd never get any sleep. And never, under any circumstances, did he allow himself to touch her.

Memories of their kiss still plagued his dreams. He thought the only reason he hadn't fallen into total madness at the memory was because, thankfully, his armor had shielded him from experiencing the sensation of her body crushed against his.

Sikthand was in control again. It was a control based on vicious internal negotiating and compromise, but it was something he could cling to.

He left his room and stomped through the halls, flashing his formal armor, a contingent of soldiers following behind.

The Guild was waiting for him when he arrived in lowcity. Madame Kalos looked overjoyed, which allowed him to relax a fraction. If there were whispers of her trade being affected, she would have worn a very different expression. There must not have been any negative news from Tremanta in that regard.

Lady Lindri had tried dressing in a slightly cleaner pair of pants than normal but still looked like she'd rather be anywhere else. He often felt that if he didn't need to keep a healthy social distance between himself and the Guild, that he might've been friends with Lindri. She'd taken the Guild role at the urging of his parents, and she'd never hidden the fact that she hated it.

She did a good job because it benefited the people she cared about, the miners and the metalsmiths, not because she had any great interest in power. Her situation felt similar to his in that way. Taking the responsibility because it was expected, not because it was wanted.

The massive throne room was at the edge of the tower in the most skyward section of lowcity. The room was divided into four segments. Two on opposite sides of the room were tiered stands lined with benches. Between them was an open standing area where people could stream in if they were unable to find a seat or wished to speak. And at the head of the room was the royal throne and the Guild's section.

Behind their seats, the curved wall was decorated with enormous slabs of glass, giving the visitors an unmatched view of the desert, minata forest, and mountains beyond.

His throne, isolated and monstrous, was in the center of this section, with the guildmembers' seats fanning out on either side below. The late afternoon sun had broken through the dissipating storm and backlit the throne. From this angle, the view was as beautiful as it was grandiose.

Sikthand only ever got to see it this way before taking his place as king. He wondered how many of his citizens considered the fact that his throne faced *away* from the beauty of the room, that the architect hadn't inlaid the walls with askait tiles or created the organic windowpane design for his enjoyment.

He eyed the throne that had been specially built upon his ascension. Would they demolish it when they built Sophia's throne? Or merely construct hers to the side of his? It would throw off the balance of the room.

He didn't care one way or another. A wooden chair would have been sufficient for him. But who would respect a king in a wooden chair?

The room was already filled with citizens. Those who had arrived early sat in the stands, while the rest filed into the standing area. Inhaling a steadying breath, Sikthand marched toward his seat, using an elevated platform that led directly to his throne.

He pricked his ears up as he walked, hand resting on his axe just in case the whizz of a flying weapon caught his attention. The murmurs in the crowd nearly vibrated the stone underfoot. Whether the undertone of the buzz was excitement or anger, he couldn't tell. He eyed the crowds, trying to isolate faces and expressions. He spotted crossed arms and shaking heads but also grinning and enthusiastic wide eyes. It had been too much to hope that the majority would be happy, yet he'd naively hoped anyway.

Sikthand took his seat, spine straight and chin lifted. For good measure, he slipped the axe out of his belt and held it casually in one hand. The Guild took their seats on the platform below him. He slammed his tail against the hollow metal base of his throne, sending a booming clang around the room. The citizens fell silent, and his Guild opened the tedious session.

He watched on as Speaker Besith, the voice of the people, made his declarations and announcements. Sikthand was impressed with the male as he listened to him outline the positives of having a human queen. A few closed-off soldiers in the stands to his left considered the Speaker's words, nodding slowly with raised brows and tucked chins as though Besith was changing their minds for the better. Sikthand made a mental note to approve one of the projects Besith had been fighting with Master Bavo to fund.

The rest of the Guild stood when Besith was done and contributed their opinions on the matter, each describing how the instituting of a human queen benefited their particular branch of government.

Master Bavo's words had a scowl rising on Sikthand's face. He chose to focus on the many *distressing decades* Vrulatica had remained queenless. The prejudice that many had against male leaders ruling alone had been a constant source of irritation for Sikthand. A queen ruling on her own would not earn nearly as much scrutiny.

As frustrating as it was, he saw many Vrulans in the audience nodding along approvingly with Bavo's words and knew that whether or not he liked it, the point would win over many disapproving citizens, so he couldn't complain.

Commander Roldroth had the least to say, though he strongly voiced his support, and though Magistrate Yalmi had the most to say, Sikthand felt her speech had the least impact as it was intellectual and dry and brimming with statistics. When the Guild was through, they took comments, each fielding questions pertinent to their domain.

The worry in his heart lifted whenever his citizens asked about the ways in which Sophia might entice humans to live here or what programs would be put into place throughout the city to aid human integration. The Guild explained that over the coming weeks, Sophia herself would be touring the city, meeting with businesses and government facilities, but that she wouldn't formally announce any plans until she was enthroned.

Impatience was clear on their faces, but it seemed to be an understanding impatience, which was a thundering victory in his experience.

Yet even through all the hints of hope, darkness crept into his chest. There were those Vrulans who objected on the simple grounds that Sophia was not Clecanian and therefore had no right to rule. They likened it to appointing a malginash pup as queen, which had made Sikthand's grip on his axe tighten.

He knew this bias would exist. If he didn't know Sophia as well as he did, he might've had the same objections. Despite the benefits, despite the potential for them to meet humans and recognize mates, the mere notion of an alien ruling the proud Vrulans would be a nearly insurmountable obstacle to some.

There were other questions that, though respectfully asked, had his mind sparking with warning.

What changes will she make, and will they unfairly favor humans?

What will happen to the marriage ceremonies considering humans do not believe in dutiful marriage wherein reproduction is the goal?

After Roldroth had explained that even the human males would not likely become warriors or cloud chasers since they didn't have a tail to keep them locked on their mount, some Vrulans had questioned how a weak species like that could fit into their society and whether male humans should be allowed to relocate to Vrulatica at all.

But the people Sikthand made a mental note to investigate were those who brought up Vila. He didn't know how, but it was clear some of the citizens were aware of Vila's offer of humans in exchange for their vote. Perhaps Vila herself had found a way to disseminate the information or, as unfortunate as the thought was, one of his Guild or one of their advisors might have leaked the news.

One male with a rose-gold hood and silver skin asked about it directly, causing a rush of murmurs to spread through the hall. "Why not support the new Tremantian Queen as planetary representative? She'd have more power than a human queen would in funneling humans here." He topped off his arguments with examples of the ways in which humans were less physically developed, hinting that Sophia wouldn't be capable of fulfilling a queen's duties.

It was ridiculous, and thankfully Magistrate Yalmi jumped in to explain with hard facts how his understanding was flawed. Though humans were less evolved in terms of their physicality, they were no different mentally. Sophia was smart—smarter than most Clecanians he'd met, and she was damn perceptive. Whatever she might lack in muscle, she made up for tenfold.

Though Sikthand knew this, he also knew bias and rumors would hurt her in the short term. She'd need to prove herself on her tour through the tower.

Later, while the Guild celebrated how positive the feeling of the forum had been, Sikthand remained unsatisfied. Sophia had officially become a target. A single-minded determination settled in him, overpowering his urge to shadow her.

He'd return to the tunnels, employ his best spies, and fill the dungeons if that's what it took. Sikthand would not allow his queen to be hurt.

22

"Is this really necessary?" Sophia grunted, almost collapsing under the weight of another piece of metal as Alno strapped it to her shoulder.

"The king has decreed it so," her friend declared, sarcasm heavy in his voice.

"I know it's for my own protection, but it's so freaking heavy. If I fall over, there's a good chance I won't be able to get up again. I'd be a sitting duck," she groaned, lifting her arm to test the weight of the metal plating on her body. It wasn't exactly armor, not fully. But it was just shy of it.

"Sitting duck," Alno whispered to himself, smiling. He did that often whenever he found one of her human sayings funny. "I'll have to tell that one to Difila. She loves hearing all your human phrases. They're adorable."

Sophia frowned under a mountain of metal, feeling like a gangly teenager swimming in their father's armor.

From what Alno had told her, the mood of the city was pretty positive. Though they didn't like *her* specifically, they enjoyed the idea of what perks a human queen might bring Vrulatica. Currently she was more a prop than anything else, but for now that was fine. She could prove herself over time.

Maybe.

Or maybe she was being colossally delusional to imagine a graphic designer from Seattle who desperately missed her outdoor movie nights and disgustingly sugary coffee concoctions would make a good alien queen. But whenever that thought arose, she dutifully bashed it into pulp and skipped right over it. Delusion, for now, was fine.

The fact that Sikthand had built up the security surrounding her was not unwelcome exactly. Now, whenever she left her room, she was escorted by at least two armed soldiers. She supposed they made her feel a bit safer, but they also erased any sense of privacy.

She had to remind herself not to be upset about it, though. If she was going to be a queen, then this was her new normal. Better to stay alive than hang on to some imaginary sense of normalcy that regular folks had.

It also produced an unreasonably fluttery swarm of butterflies in her stomach when she thought about Sikthand brooding over her safety. When he'd dropped off this metric-fuck-ton of armor for her to wear, grumbling that it would keep her shielded during her tours, she'd nearly tossed him her panties as a token of thanks.

She could chalk up his protectiveness to a simple political play. It wouldn't do to have his future queen murdered after all—a human queen, at that—but she liked to imagine that he fretted over her for other reasons too.

"So things are going well with Difila?" Sophia asked. On cue, Alno beamed, lighting up the whole room in glowing gold.

"She's more wonderful than I imagined," he sighed, strapping some shin guards to her legs.

"That's good." Sophia wobbled as he pulled them tight. She tried to be glad for Alno. He was so damn happy. But if things worked out for him, it meant he'd go off and get married and devote all his time to his new wife.

She could still visit him as a friend, but if marriages here were anything like they were in Tremanta, her visits would be more of an imposition than not. It was like an alien version of her friend getting a boyfriend and vanishing from the face of the earth. Except in Vrulatica, she didn't have any other friends.

Sophia would have to start over with another attendant, and what if she didn't like them? The thought was exhausting.

"Don't worry," he said, seeming to read her mind. "She doesn't want to try for another child yet since she was just made a cloud chaser last year. No marriage in my future until my love has a statue in the Heroes Hall."

Sophia caught the tightness around his mouth as he explained.

"I'm sorry. You could always get married without trying for children," she offered, even knowing it was very unlikely by Clecanian standards.

He laughed. "What, like you? No, thank you. That's a human thing. Difila has far too much honor to engage in frivolous marriages."

She frowned but tamped down her annoyance. When Clecanian women entered into marriages knowing full well they did not want to try for a child, it was deemed *frivolous* and cruel. They'd essentially be signing up for a few months of pampering without giving the male in question a fair shot at the honor of offspring.

Sophia let her mind wander to that problem. She still hadn't figured out how she was going to reconcile human concepts of marriage and Clecanian ones when the time came. She was sure there were plenty of humans that would be willing to enter into a temporary marriage, but then to have children and move on to a new marriage without them? That would be a bigger issue.

She'd need to introduce human relationship customs to the Vrulans so they were prepared. They'd be open to it. She felt confident in that estimation. After all, the only reason temporary marriages were prominent these days was because males outnumbered females so ridiculously and repopulation had overtaken romantic attachment in terms of importance. Once Earth opened and Clecanians didn't feel quite so threatened by extinction, she was sure long-term relationships would become more popular. Right?

She wheezed out a breath as Alno slammed a solid metal plate against her back. *They'll be as flexible as steel,* she thought, letting her pessimism win for a moment.

Alno shoved a helmet down over her head before giving her a supportive shove out the door. She clattered through the halls, legs spread as if she'd just gotten off a horse. "I look like an idiot," she griped as her soldiers for the day surveyed her with twitching mouths.

"A very safe idiot, though." Alno grinned. "Come on. You're gonna have to get used to this sooner or later. It's what a queen wears."

She frowned at that. "Shouldn't the queen wear whatever the hell a queen wants?" she grumbled.

When she'd first started her Tremantian tour around the planet with her human group, she'd gotten used to the constant staring and whispers surrounding them. The fact that she was an alien was not something the Clecanians let her forget.

Over the past month, the Vrulans had become more comfortable with her. They hadn't been staring as much, and she'd fallen into a rather pleasant pattern of polite nods and familiar tail waves with a few faces she saw on her way to the archives every day.

That was all over with now.

She was an alien queen crashing through the tower in metal that was too heavy for her. Her neck ached from the helmet she was forced to wear, and she kept clanking loudly, her head on a constant swivel.

How had Sikthand survived into adulthood with his peripheral vision always so blocked? Though the suit she wore under the armor was made from the specialty cooling fabric, her skin *wanted* to sweat. It felt gross not to be able to. Like her body was disagreeing with itself over whether she was actually working hard.

As it turned out, the bumpy start to the day only grew bumpier. They toured the mines, accompanied by Lady Lindri. The mazes of old mines and active ones were incredibly fascinating, but Sophia only managed to think so after she was free of them.

The tour had been, in a word, claustrophobic. Between the knowledge that she was in tunnels underground and the restrictive weight of her armor, Sophia had been close to hyperventilating.

She hadn't known tunnels would be an issue for her until she was a mile underground in the dark, trying to breathe through a panic attack. They'd turned up the light for her, finally realizing that her human eyes were too weak to see in the dim light. But perceiving more detail in the rock that surrounded her on all sides like a grave had definitely not helped.

She'd managed to bite down on her fear and breathe through the tour, her masked helmet hiding a face surely drained of all color. On Earth, she would have probably gotten through the experience with everyone thinking she'd been temporarily fearful, then pulled through. But this wasn't Earth, and the worst part of the whole day was understanding that each and every Clecanian within sniffing distance knew exactly how terrified she'd been.

Their much-heralded queen, petrified of the mines that supported their whole city. She was an absolute and utter failure.

Sophia had shambled back to her room, pleading with Alno to bring her food so she wouldn't have to face the dining hall. She hadn't worked up the nerve to eat there yet, knowing she'd be expected to sit at the raised table. Her embarrassing display today confirmed that tonight would *not* be the night she braved it.

Though they'd quickly hidden it, she'd caught more than a few looks of derision from the miners as well as her guards. She didn't doubt that before breakfast tomorrow, the whole tower would have heard about her embarrassing day.

Alno tried to cheer her up as he helped remove her armor, but everything he said just forced her throat to tighten even more. She kept quiet until he was gone, then crawled to the bathroom and disappeared under the scalding water of a bath.

She let out a shriek under the surface, misery making her want to stay down there forever. Slipping her head up, just until her nose could take in air, she sulked and waited for the heat to soothe her cramping muscles.

She'd tried *so* hard, yet at the first opportunity she'd proved herself to be just a scared little human.

The water of her bath turned cold around her before she forced herself out, dragged on a nightgown, wrapped up her knotted wet hair in a sloppy bun, and crawled into the dark confines of her bed.

Humiliated, she'd decided not to go to Sikthand's room. Her eyes remained wide, replaying her day and cringing. A small, pouty part of her wondered whether Sikthand would come to check on her when she didn't show up to their nightly meeting.

He didn't.

Her throat clogged painfully. He'd probably heard what happened and wanted to make sure to give her the space to lick her wounds privately. She sniffed, pulling her covers up to her chin. That's what a Vrulan queen would do, right?

It was just a bad day. A *really* bad day.

23

The next morning Sophia awoke feeling better. Sometimes a night of sulking was all it took. Just a few hours of self-approved wallowing and her determination returned. *Today will be better.*

Luckily, she was heading to the farming floors, and she was convinced she could at least keep herself from being terrified—unless, of course, they chose to slaughter an animal in front of her or something. Her stomach turned. *Oh shit.* What if they slaughtered an animal in front of her? She quickly shook off her groan, deciding to remain optimistic.

Her body crumpled when she tried to crawl out of bed, and she ended up curled awkwardly on the floor as she waited for her legs to stop cramping. She stretched, loosening her muscles before attempting to stand again.

When Alno arrived with some food, she was still moaning and groaning, dragging herself to the bathroom and wincing at every little movement.

She almost cried when he started strapping the armor back on, but she sucked her tears down. This wouldn't *kill* her, it would just suck.

She had one arm sheathed in metal when a knock sounded from the bottom of the door. Though she knew it was a tapping tail, the sound echoing from the unexpected area of the door continued to surprise her, and she constantly had to remind herself that the Vrulans weren't going around kicking doors.

Alno went to open it, and Sophia let her arm plop down onto the table so she wouldn't have to support it any longer.

Her pain was forgotten as she spotted the king towering in the doorway. "I'll be joining you today," he said without preamble. "You don't need to wear that if you don't wish to." He nodded toward her armor, and she almost dove to kiss him. If her body wasn't so sore, she might have.

She moaned when the last of the metal slipped off her arm and hustled to peel herself out of the cooling fabric suit before he changed his mind. A billowy purple top, the lightest fabric she could find, was paired with thick flexible pants made from a buttery-soft fabric similar to leather. Peering in the mirror, she frowned at her reflection. She could just hear Madam Kalos' voice in her mind complaining about her simple human preferences.

She thought she looked fine, but she knew her attire wasn't *proper*. She had no metal adornments at all. Her outfit was the equivalent of throwing on a pair of sweatpants for an important business meeting. Definitely not queenly.

Oh fuck. Am I never going to be able to wear sweatpants again? She zoned out for a second, mulling over the distracting thought. Her eyes slipped closed, and she clicked her tongue, grieving the drawer full of cozy lounge sets likely dropped at Goodwill after she'd gone missing from Earth.

She glowered at her piles of metal accessories. The idea of adding weight to her outfit had an ache pulsing through her shoulders already.

Suck it up. You're gonna be a queen, she barked at herself before slipping a netted chain mail–esque garment over the top of her flowy shirt. It added a negligible amount of weight and looked cool in Sophia's opinion. Like a fashionable way to bring chain mail into the future.

On her hands she wore sheer black gloves decorated with silver bars and tipped with metal claws. She then piled her hair into an elaborate headpiece, not quite a crown since they didn't wear those here, but close enough to give her a royal boost. She threw on her favorite piece of face jewelry that traveled from her ears over her cheeks and the bridge of her nose. It was pretty, but it also comforted her since it reminded her of her glasses.

The only thing she didn't like about the outfit was that her tattooed arm wasn't exposed, but until she had time to shop with intention, rather than just wearing the clothes Alno had provided for her, she'd have to make do.

She thought she looked pretty damn cool, but when she walked out of her bathroom, both Alno and the king surveyed her with disapproving frowns.

"It's a bit flimsy," Alno remarked.

The king shot him a cold look as if he didn't like Alno commenting on her outfit, even though he'd seemed to agree.

She'd argued with Alno about this before and wasn't in the mood to defend her human style. "Look, even if I wore full armor, it's not like I have a chance in hell if somebody is out to kill me," she argued. "I can't fight back, and if I have to carry around all that metal, it won't be any Vrulan who kills me, it'll be my own failing body."

"But you can fight a *little*," Sikthand said, rising and staring at her as though waiting for her to confirm his statement. "You said you 'can't fight back,' but that's not entirely true, right?"

Shit. She'd hoped this embarrassing day would never arrive.

When she didn't say anything, Sikthand glanced from Alno to her. "There were reports of you fighting during the escape. You might not be a warrior, but you know the basics of defending yourself. Right?" He glared toward Alno. "Right?"

Alno lifted his hands as Sikthand's tail began to scrape over the ground.

Sophia cringed and sucked her lip in to chew on it. "So, about that..." How the hell was she supposed to explain this without dying of mortification? "Back on Earth, I was in a LARP group." At his blank look, she explained, "Live action role playing. We dressed up sometimes for long weekends, and we...well, we created characters and pretended to be them. Fighters, witches...bards." Sophia swallowed at

Sikthand's widening eyes. "I had a warrior character I liked, so I learned some moves, but the weapons we used were all…foam," she added, wincing. "During the escape, I knew the soldiers weren't allowed to harm any humans, so I picked up a weapon and swung it around like I do my prop sword, and I guess I was convincing enough to make them back off."

Sikthand blinked at her. His mouth opened to speak, but then he closed it again. Anger filled his expression. "You don't know how to fight?" he boomed.

She hiked her shoulders.

He whirled on Alno. "Strap her armor back on."

"No!" she screeched, flying toward him and gripping his hand on instinct. "Please, I need a recovery day. It's *so* heavy. And you won't let anything happen to me, right?" She batted her lashes up at his scowling face. His gloved finger twitched under her hand as if he wanted to squeeze her back. Her belly swooped.

After a few tense moments, he growled, "You stay at my side."

Before they left, Sikthand retrieved a small arsenal of light blades from his room and strapped them across her body. She didn't know how to properly wield any of them, but at least she wouldn't walk around looking completely unarmed.

Sophia tried not to be annoyed that Sikthand hadn't asked after her last night. He seemed mighty concerned with her physical well-being, but had he cared about her mental spiral the night before? Apparently not.

Maybe he'd decided to accompany her today because he'd heard how hard yesterday had been for her. Her chest warmed at the thought.

Or maybe he decided to come to make sure I don't royally fuck up again.

"I won't let anything happen to you," he said. His gaze was protective and riveted on her eyes before it dipped to her mouth. She shivered, and all her annoyance trickled away.

The farming floors were worlds in and of themselves. Each floor spanned the width of the whole tower. Livestock grazed throughout. Big beefy creatures with antlers that looked like a cross between a hippopotamus and a moose ambled among the grass between rocky outcroppings, mingling harmlessly with the hordes of other smaller animals that speckled the expansive indoor bio environment.

Their guide, Ezros, was the closest thing Sophia had seen to a Vrulan geek, and she liked him immensely. He grinned while explaining the ways in which they filtered in sunlight and imitated rain. Rapt, he took notes as she listed the most common types of livestock on Earth and tried to guess at their size.

How much did a cow weigh? Estimations like that had never been her strong suit. Someone could tell her they weighed five hundred pounds or five thousand pounds, and she'd believe either. Neither Ezros nor Sikthand seemed disappointed with her uncertainty, though, and she breathed a sigh of relief.

Many stories high, the vertical gardens where the fruit and vegetables were hydroponically grown were astonishing. Enormous mechanical scaffoldings raised and lowered throughout the rows of produce, farmers gathering orders as they came in.

Sophia spent hours listing foods she thought should be grown here and describing Clecanian produce humans had already found they preferred.

The human database her friends back in Tremanta had been working hard to build had contained food substitutions. Data from scans that reacted to brain activity and identified favored smells and flavors among humans was combined with chemical compositions and flavor profiles of Clecanian foods. Back in Tremanta, Sophia had devoted a day or two to tasting a variety of foods and describing the closest Earth counterparts she could think of.

It was an odd process. Some Clecanian foods tasted like one thing, had the exact texture of another, but couldn't be used like either. She'd given up trying to help classify foods in Tremanta after realizing a background in cooking was enormously valuable, and the only cooking she liked to do involved a microwave.

But descriptions of the time she *had* devoted seemed to help Ezros immensely, and she gave herself a mental pat on the back. "Maybe we could fly to the outbuildings when the storms clear and I can copy some information from the human database we were building in Tremanta. I think I still know how to log into it," she whispered to Sikthand as Ezros went off to retrieve a rare spliced fruit he'd been experimenting with.

Sikthand hovered close, remaining glued to her side all day. "Do you mean the species information listed in the Intergalactic Alliance database?"

Sophia had to work very hard not to acknowledge the way his gaze strayed to her mouth whenever she spoke.

"Yeah," she breathed, then shook her head. "Wait, I mean no. This is different. The humans staying at the Pearl Temple had gotten together and were starting to build a database of our own. We were filling it with everything we knew so that Clecanians could learn about us from us. We have historians and cooks and scientists all contributing to it. It's taking forever since there's so much to say, but I think it'll be really helpful for it to be included in the Vrulan schools once it's completed." Her brows furrowed. "I thought all the cities on our tour were given access to it. Weren't you?"

Ezros reemerged, holding a giant purple leaf and capturing her attention. It was thick, like an aloe plant, but had curly edges. "Here—I wonder if this fruit tastes like any of your Earth foods."

Instinctually, Sophia reached for the leaf fruit, thinking a snack sounded like a great idea, but Sikthand grabbed her wrist. Ezros' gaze flicked back and forth between them, his smile dimming, gray eyes widening. He rushed to break off a piece of the leaf. "Oh, it's not dangerous. I checked the chemical composition myself, and there is nothing harmful to humans." He popped the bit of leaf into his mouth and chewed.

Sophia glanced up at Sikthand, realization dawning. Either intentionally or unintentionally, he was worried the new food might harm her. She supposed it was fair that she be slightly more cautious when trying random foods people offered her, but she couldn't live her life in a panic.

When Ezros didn't start foaming at the mouth, she reached out for a piece to taste herself. Sikthand beat her to it, breaking off the tip of the leaf and chewing angrily.

Sophia had no idea what she should feel in this moment. The king was literally testing her food for poison. She had to contain her swoon.

He gave her a short nod when a few minutes passed without anyone dying, and she popped some of the leaf in her mouth. Her head snapped back as the luscious taste hit her tongue. It was tropical and sweet and reminded her of a creamy vanilla pineapple.

Ezros beamed when she asked to have the rest so she could munch on it while finishing their tour. Her awareness kept flitting back to Sikthand, who remained close to her side. She offered him another piece of fruit and made sure he saw her casually lick her fingers after he'd accepted it.

His eyes darkened, and his great armored chest expanded and emptied with what looked like a pained sigh. Though she wanted to do it again, she held herself back.

The day had bolstered her confidence. She felt she'd made a good impression. She'd asked pertinent questions that seemed to surprise and delight Ezros. He'd even taken them on a small unplanned excursion to the fungi habitat after she'd asked where they grew the salty mushrooms she always piled on her plate at dinner.

Though the artificially forested area was dark and humid and smelled horribly of rotting plant matter, she loved it. Plugging her nose and grinning, she'd let him lead her around and point out all the species they were cultivating, a majority of which were used for medicines that Vrulans took when their ailments were too mild for a medic visit.

Electric-blue fungi spread over the mossy ground in a pulsing network, while mushroom caps the size of umbrellas stretched high above her head.

Maybe she should design a fungus sleeve. The impermanence of her tattoos opened a ton of creative doors that were starting to excite her. She could cover her body in mushrooms one day, then have a horror theme the next as long as she could stand the pain of getting them changed.

One pale mushroom that crawled up the side of a decaying tree and seemed to drip black tar off the lip of its head caught her eye. When she commented on how she might want to incorporate it into a new tattoo design, Ezros had been overjoyed. He practically squealed as he explained that it was also one of his inventions. "My queen will mark herself with something I created? It would truly be an honor."

She beamed at Sikthand, seeing if he'd also heard the male say *my* queen. She'd won someone over. A flicker of warmth softened the king's mouth as he took in her smile, and she felt like she'd had two victories today.

She'd practically skipped to Sikthand's room later that night, but when he let her in, her face fell at the sight awaiting her.

The center of his room was clean—not because he'd tidied up the clutter, but because he'd cleared it in order to set up a mini training area.

"I'm gonna learn to fight, aren't I?" she groaned, rolling her still-stiff shoulders.

24

"I'm not going to hit you," Sophia argued, her slim arms crossed over her chest.

"Correct. You won't be *capable* of hitting me. Try anyway. It's the quickest way for me to see how you move." Sikthand scowled. He could not believe he hadn't asked about this sooner. The human didn't know how to fight. He wanted to roar in frustration.

All the times she'd been out on her own… He'd known she wouldn't be likely to best one of his soldiers if they chose to attack, but he'd assumed she was proficient enough to hold her ground for the few minutes it would take for her guards to intervene.

She clicked her tongue, offended. "I could land a hit if I really tried," she argued weakly. He lifted his brows, which made her lips purse. "Okay, fine. There's no chance in hell I hit you, but it feels weird to try. I've never attempted to hurt anyone before."

Her soft admission should've irritated him. There was not a Vrulan alive who hadn't learned the basics of self-defense, and this human wanted to be their queen. Yet her unwillingness to show him even an ounce of aggression did funny things to his chest. He tamped down the urge to rub the heel of his hand over his sternum and continued to aim a frown at her until she let out a defeated groan.

Dread coiled in his gut as she began to throw sloppy punches and kicks in his direction. He dodged them all, guessing her move by where her determined gaze landed before she'd even tensed to attack.

It would be a miracle if he managed to keep them both alive.

Before long, she was out of breath, her cheeks flushed and her movements sluggish. She put a bit too much power behind one punch, and when he dodged, she went sailing past him. He caught her by the hips before she face-planted into the mat.

The flesh under his palms was soft, and his fingers sunk in as he pulled her upright. This grip would be heavenly if he needed purchase while fucking her from behind.

He had to mentally peel each digit back to get his hands to leave her hips. They felt so much softer than they looked, and he burned to know which other parts of her body were supple and giving.

By the Goddess, he might need to let her fall next time if he was to keep up his bargain to not touch her. That two-second hold had lit his body with sparks and sent blood rushing to his cock.

She wiped her hand across her sweaty forehead, unaware of the internal war raging behind her. "That's enough for today," he rasped, his voice gone gravelly.

Thankfully, she didn't seem to notice, her shoulders sagging in relief. "Getting scared, huh?" Her sarcasm shone through her grin, but yes, Sikthand was terrified.

"I'll think on what weapon might be best for you, and I can show you how to use it next time." A distant rumble of thunder had him peering outside.

"Shouldn't I learn how to fight without a weapon first?" she asked through deep pants.

"In a perfect world where we had years to train, a team to practice sparring with, and no other responsibilities." He gave her a tight smile. "You don't have enough awareness of your body yet. For now, I just need you to know how to swing a blade hard enough to give you time to run away."

Her lips pulled into a frown, but she nodded.

She slogged toward the study rather than the exit, and he stopped her. "Not today. This was all I had time for."

"Oh, I was looking forward to it since we didn't get to meet yesterday." His luscious little walking nightmare had the gall to look deeply disappointed, and his damned stomach lurched. He shook off the sudden urge to cancel every one of his plans and ushered her toward the door.

"Too many malginash are injured, and this storm will be particularly bad. I need to help with the seeding." As if to punctuate his point, a clap of thunder rattled the windows behind his bed.

He, too, had mourned their missed meeting the night before. News of her rocky visit to the mines had been relayed to him, and all he'd wanted to do was crash through her door and wipe away any trace of the foul fear Lindri had described pouring off her in waves. Protective instincts going haywire, he'd forced himself to keep away, instead standing sentry behind her mirror to soothe himself.

Sophia nodded and forced a smile, though disappointment was clear in her eyes.

"I may not see you tomorrow if the storm rages on," he said, a bit of his regret leaking into his voice despite his best efforts. "I want you to wear the armor for your tour of the schools and of the malginash clinic the following day if I'm not back by then," he added sternly. "You may not be able to fight in it, but it'll protect you from a flying blade."

"Okay, that's fair." She nodded again. "Have you memorized my schedule, *Your Majesty*?" she added, grinning.

Pulling open his door, Sikthand hid the shudder that quaked through him. She hadn't used that odd human address since their time together at the umbercree festival. "Yes. I've memorized it."

I've memorized it all so I know exactly where to find you when the pressure in my chest threatens to crush me.

She murmured some noncommittal noise and dragged her feet through his doorway. Was she… May the skies strike him down if she wasn't lingering.

Don't do this to me, little wife. His control was already threadbare without the added pressure of her behaving as if she didn't want to part from him.

"Why did you go on the tour with me today?" she asked slowly. Her features tightened, and she kept her eyes moving as if she were steeling herself for the cold answer he knew he should give.

It's my duty as king to make sure you don't embarrass the throne.

It was what he *should* say. It would make her leave.

But it would also cause a flash of pain to pass over her face.

"I thought…" He sighed, his will crumbling. "I thought you might feel more comfortable with me there."

A tremulous smile lifted the corner of her mouth and sent alarm bells ringing through his mind.

"The armor was too heavy for you. When I'm able, I'll make sure to accompany you until you're strong enough to wear it comfortably."

Her face didn't fall, but it contorted like she'd smelled something sour. "My armor. Yeah," she murmured. Her chest lifted with a deep breath, and she aimed a soft smile at him. "For the record, I liked having you there with me. And not just because I didn't have to wear the armor."

The sensation of his insides melting into a gooey puddle blotted out all reason. Feeling a bit lightheaded, he had to focus so as not to sway on his feet.

Lightning right outside illuminated his room, and her brows furrowed as her eyes flicked to the window.

Liquefied willpower slipped through his fingers as he tried to scoop it up and regain control of himself. He was still frozen when she placed a palm on his chest. Only the cloth of his shirt separated their skin. Goose bumps exploded outward from her small hand, and he fought with all his energy to keep his purr at bay.

He'd always had the least amount of control over his tail, a well-known weakness of the emotionless king, and it slammed against the door behind him despite his best efforts to keep it still.

She peered up at him through her lashes. "Be safe out there. It looks pretty bad."

His tail shot out, intent on wrapping around her wrist and hauling her against his chest, but he regained himself at the last second and instead managed to use it to nudge her out of his room. "I've flown through worse, human. Don't concern yourself."

He sent her a jerky goodbye nod and shut the door in her face. Listening past the deafening thrum of his heart, he waited until her footsteps had vanished down the hall, then piled on his armor and fled toward the rider's launch bay.

He was in trouble. Sophia was under his skin more permanently than his askait ink.

Soon whispers of the king's growing obsession would circulate, and he'd be too busy with said obsession to hear them before it was too late. He'd already hired a handful of spies to take over the surveilling he didn't have time for. But how long before he stopped trusting them?

How long before he forgot he shouldn't trust her? Politics and power and time would warp her as it did everyone. Would he be too afflicted with affection to take notice when it did?

Even the idea of riding through storms didn't hold as much appeal as normal. He studied his hands, still free of mate marks, before pulling his gloves on. He didn't know why he continued to check. It had been over a month, and they'd spent time alone together often. By all accounts, if he was going to recognize her, it would have happened already.

Sikthand adjusted his helmet, strapping it into his armor so it would stay in place as he entered the cavernous launch bay. Exhausted riders soared in on the right, practically falling off their mounts. To the left, new squads shot out into the clouds in formation.

Ahea was saddled and waiting for him already. He checked and rechecked her stays to make sure they were secure before calling for a cannon. Cloud chasers in training dashed about, arming waiting riders with cloud cannons containing the tightly packed chemical explosions that would wring the clouds of their moisture.

His mount swayed on her feet as though impatient to be off. At least one of them was looking forward to this, he supposed. As soon as a cannon was in his hand, they dove into the violent night sky.

Clouds thicker than sand obscured the sky in all directions. Rain pelted his armor as Ahea carried them higher and higher.

A bolt of lightning slashed to their right, and Ahea swooped out of the way. His grip on her reins tightened. That was too close. Were his tumultuous moods affecting her?

Her wings wobbled before she found a stable pocket of air and glided through. Cloud chasers and malginash spotted the sky, backlit against the glowing clouds and flashing lightning.

Sikthand took up a role as a cleaner and focused on shooting the patches of cloud that had slipped through unseeded.

Another flash of lightning sizzled right in front of Ahea's antlers, and she reared back. Sikthand barely managed to keep hold of the saddle, his tail cramping with the effort to stabilize himself.

Something was wrong. The storm was worse than he'd anticipated, yet he and Ahea had flown through fiercer weather without concern. She wasn't sensing the bolts like she normally did.

He craned his neck, calling her name until he could see her eyes and found them a muddier gray than normal.

Worry shot through him, and he yanked her reins, guiding her back toward the tower. They dove through glowing green dye, and Vrulatica emerged in the distance. "Hold on," he bellowed, heart thundering in his ears.

A deafening crack split open his head as blinding light set every cell ablaze with agony. He tipped forward in his seat, consciousness blinking in and out.

A dark moment of nothingness passed, then he peered at his hands and found them empty.

No reins. No saddle under his thighs.

He was falling. A peek of the blood red ground zooming up to meet him was the last thing he saw before it all went black.

25

Sophia. Sophia.

Something grabbed her leg, and Sophia bolted upright with a shriek, scrambling back into the dark confines of her bed.

The shadow of a man loomed in the narrow entry to her bed, but he was backlit and unrecognizable.

"Sophia."

"Alno?" she panted, pulse roaring. "What the fuck? Why are you—"

"The king's been hurt."

The air emptied from her lungs. "Wha…what?"

She clambered out of bed and saw Alno's golden skin had dulled. Nausea roiled her gut. "What happened? Is he okay?"

"I don't know. The Guild asked me to wake you up because if he's…"

No, no, no. Sophia couldn't manage to blink or swallow. She dressed in a daze, throwing on whatever Alno handed to her.

He can't be dead.

"He's alive?" she asked for the tenth time, even though Alno had repeatedly told her didn't know.

"He's been hurt in the storm. That's all I'm aware of."

She couldn't keep her body from trembling as she tried to breathe normally. They jogged toward the Guild chamber, only making it halfway before Commander Roldroth intercepted them. He spun her around with his tail on her arm and forced her back to the royal wing. "They're bringing him," he growled.

Her heart lurched into her throat. "What happened?" she demanded in a wheeze.

He shook his head, and she assumed he didn't know, but then he answered. "He was struck by lightning."

Sophia tried to process that. "No. That's not possible because—"

"I know," Roldroth cut her off, waiting for Alno to unlock the doors to the wing, then stomping inside so fast she had to run to keep up. "It shouldn't have been possible. His armor should have insulated him even if he was hit." He glanced behind him at Alno, then at her warily. "They believe someone may have tampered with it. And they've taken Ahea to the clinic. There's something wrong with her too."

"Somebody *tried* to kill him?" she bellowed, rage wiping away all fear. "This wasn't a cloud-chasing accident?" Sophia pictured Sikthand's guarded expression, which had been permanently affixed to his face after a lifetime of betrayal and heartache. Someone had tried to kill her future husband, and she was *livid*.

Roldroth paused, scrutinizing her boiling expression, his brows furrowed. "Too many coincidences," he answered simply.

Clattering from above made their gazes shoot skyward. They sprinted to the stairs but were blocked as a gurney with an unconscious Sikthand lowered down the spiraling steps. The rest of the Guild waited on the landing below, drenched as if they'd flown through the storm.

Sophia tried to stay out of the way, but her eyes were glued to Sikthand's unconscious face. The rest of him was covered. He looked unharmed, not at all like someone who'd just been struck by lightning.

"Is he okay? What's going on? Shouldn't we be flying him to the medical outbuilding?" she shouted up the stairs.

The medic, Vezel, poked his head out from above. "We just came from there. He's alive. He'll survive."

Sophia inhaled deeply and followed as they carried Sikthand to his room and transferred him to his bed. The doctor, Alno, and the Guild piled in, all bickering.

Vezel kept close to Sikthand, clearing off a small table and carrying it over to the side of his bed. He began extracting vials and sprays from his bag, setting them on the small table while ignoring the squawking group behind him. He said something to her, but she only knew so from the direction of his gaze and his moving mouth.

"What?" she yelled, cupping her ears.

He leaned over a little and tried to speak again, but there were too many voices sounding at once. Madam Kalos stepped to the side, arguing with Yalmi about something, and bumped into a pedestal, causing Sikthand's formal askait helmet to crash to the ground.

The clanging made something inside her snap.

"Out!" she bellowed, her voice booming across the stone walls.

Silence fell, and the Guild looked at her as if noticing an irritating barking dog. Sophia was undeterred.

She pointed to the door. "You can talk all you want, but you'll do it out there." Sikthand would hate having them all in here. He hated it when *she* was in his private space. Sophia couldn't imagine how upset he'd be if he knew the whole Guild was in his sanctuary while he was unconscious. Her throat swelled. He didn't even have a lick of armor on.

"Sophia," Madam Kalos began gently.

"Not only was I not notified immediately," Sophia hissed, staring the Guild down one by one. "But now you come into *his* space, a place that he has expressly said is off-limits to you, and scream and shout. This is my future husband, and I will not let his recovery be impeded by you lot disturbing his peace. Out."

She crossed to the opposite side of the bed as the medic and had to crawl onto the mattress in order to get close enough to see the steady rise and fall of his chest under his blanket. As she watched him breathe and saw his brows twitch in sleep, her pulse finally began to slow.

"Respectfully," Speaker Besith began with a sneer in his voice, "they discovered a malfunction in the lining of his armor."

Sophia spared him only a quick glance. "And?" she spat.

"*And* there are only a few people with access to this wing."

That got her attention. She stared, and they stared back. Their gazes weighed her down.

"You think *I* could have done this?" The notion was ridiculous, and yet…what else were they supposed to think? They were right. Not many people had access to the royal wing. Sikthand had explained he kept it that way so that there were fewer suspects in case of something like this. Knowing they would be jailed immediately if anything happened to the king ensured the handful of people with keys to the wing were cautious and less likely to betray him.

She was the stranger here. She understood why they suspected her.

But what had her breath lodging in her throat was not their suspicion. It was the knowledge that Sikthand would likely think the same. He'd suspect her.

A bit of her heart cracked.

She tried to scoot off the bed to give him some space, but something trapped her wrist in place. A choked sound escaped her throat when she found his tail wrapped securely around her wrist.

Her attention flashed to his face, but he was still unconscious, eyes closed, brows furrowed as though in pain. The Guild stared at her trapped hand uneasily, like she were the one holding his tail in place and not the other way around.

She tried to gently slip her wrist through the coiled tip of his tail, but it tightened painfully. A lump swelled in her throat.

Someone had done this to him, and she was determined to find out who before he woke up.

Slowly, her gaze rose, but not toward the Guild or the doctor. She let it settle on Alno, who was already staring back at her, eyes wide and terrified. "I didn't," he said quietly, shaking his head.

She gave him a sad smile. "I know. But…"

Alno gulped and stared down at the floor.

"We'll get to the bottom of it, but for now…" she urged. He nodded, gaze still trained on the floor. Tensing her jaw, she raised her chin toward the Guild. "Take Alno to the dungeons. Don't *hurt* him." She glared. "Question him. Figure out who else could have gotten in here. Go find everyone else with access and do the same with them." Her stomach turned. "Lindri can stay to keep an eye on me as it doesn't look like I'm going anywhere anytime soon." She wiggled her trapped hand for good measure and winced when his tail tightened instantly. "The rest of you need to leave." Her gaze locked with Vezel's, and she thought she saw approval behind his eyes.

The Guild lingered, unsure whether they should take orders from her or not.

She took a deep breath and glowered in their direction. "If you don't listen to me and he doesn't recover, then you're all in the clear. But if he *recovers*, learns that you ignored the future queen's orders and snooped around in his room while he was unconscious, what do you think he'll do?" A spike of concern passed over each of their expressions, and Sophia knew she'd won.

"I'm staying. Not Lindri," Roldroth declared while eyeing her. He clearly didn't trust her, and she didn't care.

The rest of the Guild grumbled amongst each other and slowly filed out of the room. Besith wrapped a hand around Alno's arm to escort him out. Alno lifted his key so she could see it, then placed it on a shelf near the exit before allowing Besith to lead him away.

Her heart clenched, her stomach hollow. She hated locking Alno up. He wouldn't have done this. She couldn't accept that. It wasn't that Alno was *incapable* of doing something like this, it was that he was too smart. Anyone with a key knew they'd be a prime suspect.

Whoever had tampered with Sikthand's armor didn't care that the small number of staff that serviced the royal wing would be the ones blamed. Fury simmered inside her once more.

"Why is he asleep?" Sophia kept her voice low and studied Vezel. She ignored Roldroth, who shuffled around in the corner of the room. At least he had the decency to look uncomfortable about being in the king's room.

"The lightning penetrated his armor. He was burned. Horribly." The doctor shook his head, his nose wrinkling as if he was remembering the smell of charred flesh. "We were able to get him into the healing chamber before it was too late. The functioning bits of his armor kept him from dying instantly, and we were able to repair the internal burns quickly enough. We gave him an elixir, and it's working, but there are still a few bits of his mind repairing themselves that need more time. I'd like to keep him sedated for a few days. I know if I don't, he won't rest the way he needs to."

It was almost laughable how true that statement was. If Sikthand woke up and learned there had been yet another attempt on his life, he'd tear through the tower. *Rest* would be his lowest priority.

"What about Ahea?" Sophia blurted, suddenly remembering someone saying the malginash had been taken to a clinic.

"Saved his life," Roldroth rasped from the corner, his voice thick. "They think she'll be okay, but she was poisoned. She's recovering now." Sophia could hear cold fury leaking into his voice at the idea that someone would harm a malginash. "We won't know what happened until he wakes up and tells us, but Ahea collapsed at the infirmary with the king in her claws. She carried him straight there, brilliant girl." His wide throat bobbed, but he kept his chin raised as if to honor the malginash.

"Remind me to bring her all the minata wood she wants."

Sikthand's tail twitched on her wrist, his chest rising and falling a little faster like he was having a bad dream.

"We should let him sleep," the medic said.

Sophia nodded. "Will you stay?"

Vezel shook his head. "There's no reason. He's stable, and I need to get back to the infirmary. I'll come back tomorrow. I've given him nutrient packs to keep him hydrated. Someone will just need to inject him with another in about six hours." Vezel demonstrated injecting one of the vials into Sikthand's arm, then held up a spray bottle. "This will keep him sleeping. One spritz to his face every ten hours should do it, but if he starts to get fidgety, up the frequency to every eight hours."

Sophia forced herself to pay attention to the doctor's instructions, but her focus kept drifting to Roldroth. If anyone had the power and sway to gain access to the king's quarters, it was the Guild. What if one of them had planned this?

Roldroth was commander of the storm chasers as well. He had access to the malginash, and he'd have a detailed knowledge of the specialty armor used during storms. She inched closer to Sikthand. What if he'd done this, and she was about to be left alone in a room with him?

It would make her feel infinitely better if she could grab one of Sikthand's many weapons. Sophia tried to pull out of Sikthand's reach when the doctor got up to leave, but a deep groan rumbled from his chest. She tried to avoid Roldroth's eyes as heat rose to her cheeks.

Sophia wouldn't be going anywhere, and if the situation weren't so serious, she was sure her belly would be flipping at the idea that the king unconsciously wanted her close. She scooted farther up on the bed, sitting against the stone wall just under the window near his head.

"I want to be clear that I can't move away from the king, and I have no weapons, so if anything happens to him…" Sophia shot a meaningful glance toward Vezel before retraining her glare on Roldroth. "You can logic out who's to blame."

Vezel nodded, and Roldroth scowled. The medic left, leaving them alone in the tense silence.

"When was the last time he went out?" If she had to be locked in a room with the commander, at least she could do some interrogating of her own.

"Out?"

"Whoever planned this knew when to drug Ahea," she explained. "They knew that he was going out today, which means—"

"His armor might not have been affected the last time he rode," Roldroth finished for her. "He was out two nights ago." His tail flicked behind him. "His armor could have been tampered with before. Perhaps they decided to take their plan a step further and poison Ahea when they realized damaging his armor hadn't been enough."

"Either way, it's clear to me that whoever did this had access to the launch bay and knowledge of when he'd be flying," Sophia said, keeping her face expressionless.

Roldroth caught her insinuation, but rather than appear offended, he nodded. "True. But they'd also have to have access to *this* room when he wasn't here."

His returned insinuation was reasonable in theory. "Do you really think I know enough to not only understand how to damage his armor in a way he wouldn't immediately notice, but also how to poison a malginash so exactly that she would still be able to fly him into a storm? That's ignoring the ridiculous assumption that Sikthand shares his schedule with me ahead of time. And apart from all that, what would I have to gain? How would his death benefit me?"

"You'd be queen," he growled.

"I'm only queen if I marry a king. If he dies, I'm nothing. If you really think that's my motivation, then my timing makes no sense. Wouldn't I wait to attempt murder until I'm enthroned?"

"Somebody could have asked you to do it. Maybe you did it just because you hate him. People have tried killing him for more pointless reasons than that. Perhaps humans are a vengeful species. Besides, the point remains that you have access. All you needed for an attempt is an accomplice with a plan—and that door." Roldroth hiked a thumb over his shoulder toward the ornate door behind him. The one that led directly to her room.

Her focus zoomed to the door. "That door is locked. Even if they went through the one in my room, they wouldn't be able to get in here."

"Unless he left the door *unlocked*." Roldroth held her gaze, and when the suggestion of what that meant hit her, heat raced to her face.

"Not that it's any of your business, but we don't…" Her cheeks burned hotter. "That passage isn't used."

"Traditionally, the queen is the one to call on her husband. I'd guess based on the way he's reacting to you now that it's not unlikely he unlocked it in the hopes you'd come to call."

"Then you don't know him very well," she argued. "He would never leave himself vulnerable like that. Not for me," she said, shaking her head.

Something worked behind Roldroth's expression, and his jaw tensed and relaxed as if he were deciding how to say what he wanted to say. "The king has been acting oddly lately. I think if there were ever a person he'd leave himself vulnerable for, it'd be you."

Shock had Sophia's mind going blank. She leaned forward, intending to argue, but as if to punctuate Roldroth's claim, Sikthand's tail slipped from her wrist. He groaned and rolled toward her.

Sophia lifted her palms up in front of her, not sure what he was doing. In sleep, the king wrapped his arms around her legs and nuzzled into the side of her upper thigh while his tail traveled outside of his blanket and curled around her ankle. The movement pulled his covers down since he was under them, while she sat atop.

Her face flamed from the intimate position in the not-so-intimate setting, but then she caught sight of his unclothed torso and her breath froze in her chest.

"No," she whispered. Forgetting herself, she reached out and brushed her fingers over his pale skin. His *clear* pale skin. "They're gone." She said the words to herself, forgetting Roldroth was watching, as sadness set in.

"His skin was…" The commander shook his head, his mouth contorting. "They couldn't heal it without also removing his tattoos. He can replace them." He stopped on an awkward note as if he'd almost added *don't worry* before remembering he was suspicious of her.

She fell into a mini spiral as she argued internally over whether it would be better to get Khes to redraw all of his tattoos while he slept, or if deciding something like that for him made her just as bad as the aliens who'd decided to remove all of her tattoos without her consent.

Brushing his white hair away from his forehead, she decided against sending a message to Khes. She continued to brush his hair back, even though she knew she shouldn't touch him.

A purr rumbled out of his chest, vibrating over her skin, and she snatched her hand back.

Her chest filled with butterflies, but she knew Sikthand wouldn't want anyone to hear him purr. Who would he be more uncomfortable with hearing that sound, though? Sophia or Roldroth?

Sophia's teeth ground together, and she braced herself. "Can you check?"

Roldroth was still gawping at the gently purring king as though he'd just bolted upright and started spouting slam poetry. "Check?" he asked absently. He followed her gaze to the passage door and nodded solemnly.

What did she hope? Sophia had no idea whether she wanted Roldroth to find the door locked or unlocked.

If it was locked, it would help confirm she had nothing to do with this attempt and her assumptions about Sikthand's wariness were accurate.

But if it was unlocked?

It would mean someone had likely used her room to gain access to his, which was a horrible thought. Yet it would also mean that he'd unlocked it. That he'd…

Roldroth reached toward the door. She held her breath.

"Locked," he growled.

It was stupid, but a piece of her that, despite the awful circumstances, had hoped Sikthand might've left the door open for her deflated. Roldroth retrieved one of the chairs from the study, and she was relieved to see it was the plush one she normally sat in. She didn't think she could abide him sitting in Sikthand's chair.

They fell into silence after that, both deep in thought.

Something fearful and protective had taken hold of Sophia. Sikthand had almost been killed, and though she should've been upset about that for a myriad of reasons, the only one she seemed to care about was that she didn't *want* him to die.

Sikthand was complicated and beautiful and honorable. Even if he never allowed anything more to bloom between them, and even if his paranoia amped up to an all-time high after he woke up, she still wanted to be near him.

Sunrise streamed through the windows, but the spray kept Sikthand unconscious. After a few hours, Sophia slipped her legs under the blanket. Roldroth eyed her, but she ignored him. This was the only way to keep his body covered since she couldn't get his tail to unwrap from her ankle.

As hours stretched by, his hold proved to be a problem. Her bladder screamed at her, and her muscles cramped from sitting in the same position for so long.

She finally broke down and asked Roldroth for help. They worked together to give him his medicine and also reapply the sleep spray. His body slumped deeper into sleep after that, and though it took some prying, Roldroth was able to unfurl Sikthand's tail from her ankle despite his growls.

After she was through in the bathroom, she found Roldroth waiting for her on the other side of the door. "One of us needs to retrieve food. I don't trust the guards to do it at the moment."

"Go ahead," she said, hands on hips. If he thought she would leave Sikthand alone to go grab food, he had another thing coming. A loud rumble from her stomach echoed through the room, undercutting her words.

He let out a frustrated growl, peering between her and Sikthand, but finally pointed his tail at her. "Do not go near him until I'm back."

"Fine," she snapped.

Roldroth stomped out of the room, leaving her alone with Sikthand. Her shoulders slumped in relief. She stared at the king's still form, and dread clawed at her over what would happen when the medic woke him up tomorrow.

She trailed around his room, eyeing his shelves but not really seeing anything. Would he lock her up in the dungeon with Alno? She recalled the hatred in his eyes that night he'd told her the Guild wanted them to be married. Heart clenching, she hoped he wouldn't look at her like that again.

She ran her fingertips over the tools in his small workshop, memorizing every piece. She doubted she'd be allowed in here again anytime soon.

Papers were spread out around a bench by his hearth, and she scanned them. Sophia's eyes narrowed. She squinted down at the papers, and her heart skipped a beat.

It was information from the human database. Sikthand *had* known about it. Why had he acted like he hadn't yesterday?

She shuffled the papers around, trying to figure out what he'd been so interested in that he'd felt the need to bring hard copies of the information back to his room.

Her lips parted.

Mouth kissing is a human cultural practice that is often romantic or sexual in nature. The act produces oxytocin and is…

Her gaze flashed to Sikthand's sleeping form, her chin dropped in an open-mouthed smile. She shuffled the papers a little more and found handwritten notations and circled bits of information like he'd been studying technique. Sophia exhaled a miserable, desperate sigh. How long would it be before he let her kiss him again?

They'd been so close.

He'd been researching kissing, for God's sake. What if he'd planned to do it again? She moaned while rearranging the papers so they looked untouched and continued dragging her feet around the room.

Roldroth entered not long after, and she tried her hardest not to look guilty. He set a few plates of food down, then lifted a coded tube. "A messenger delivered this this morning."

A private message? For her? She took it from him. Besith had given her a private code she could use for her mail, but she hadn't had time to send or receive anything yet. "Why wasn't I given this hours ago?"

"Everyone with access to these quarters is either locked in the dungeon or sitting in this room," Roldroth said dryly.

She took the tube and a plate of food to a stiff bench, input her code, and unrolled it. What she saw had her brain short circuiting for a moment.

English. Written English was scrolled in clear feminine script across the paper. She hadn't read a single word yet, but seeing the familiar writing brought happy tears to her eyes. It was silly how something as simple as a few words on paper could cause such intense emotion, but she welcomed any warm feelings right now.

It took her a moment to read the note, her mind so used to translating Clecanian these days.

It was from Heleax. She scanned his letter and learned that he hadn't returned to Tremanta. After getting in touch with a few of his soldier friends back home, he'd decided he'd be more useful outside the city. He'd traveled to Roborh, the city his brother had settled in, and met with the ruler there. Apparently Roborh was beautiful and even more advanced than Tremanta.

Sophia was happy for Heleax. It was clear from what he said that he had found a renewed sense of purpose. She peered at Sikthand as he twisted in the bed and began shoveling food into her mouth. Maybe it was a stretch to think he was squirming because she wasn't there for him to hold, but she let herself think it anyway.

Heleax had met a human in Roborh and had gotten her to write this message for him. Sophia frowned when Heleax relayed how appalled the human had been to learn of what had happened to her. She could just imagine the overdramatic nonsense Heleax was feeding her, and a protective part of Sophia lit with anger at the thought that Heleax was insulting Sikthand.

I've found a way to get you out of Vrulatica.

The words made her chewing slow.

King Cueyar thinks your plan to become queen is a good one. Roborhians don't want to submit to Vila either, but they didn't see any other option until I explained what King Sikthand has planned. Cueyar thinks the idea is brilliant, and he asked me to offer you the position of Queen of Roborh.

You could accomplish everything you want here. King Cueyar is kind, and his people are gentle. He is loved, and I'm sure you would be too. Vrulatica is a volatile place. Vrulans are harsh and explosive. You aren't safe there.

Sophia's gaze drifted toward the unconscious king and the heavily armed commander watching her. Ice slipped down her spine. She hated that Heleax wasn't that far off-base.

King Cueyar has agreed to all the terms you set forth with Sikthand and more. He wants a real marriage, if you're amenable. He's young and attractive to many females.

He says he'll give you until the week before the Leaders' Summit to decide and then he will attempt to find a human elsewhere. Margaret, the human translating my note into English for you, isn't interested as she's chosen to remain with her current husband and become a demskiv.

I know you have your principles, and you may feel that you should honor your deal with the Vrulan king, but I beg you, take the time to think this offer through.

Sikthand can be a cruel male. How long before you're the target of his paranoia and he locks you in the dungeon? How long before a citizen disagrees with something you've decided and tries to kill you?

Your life will be hard there, and as a human, hasn't your life been hard enough already? You can do more good for your people here. If Earth opens, I am very certain humans will prefer to live here rather than Vrulatica.

Take time to think this through and make the right *decision. I'll be waiting for your reply.*

Sophia scanned and re-scanned the words, a pit widening in her stomach. She'd come to accept her fate here, and now this?

She stared at Sikthand, and her insides warmed.

At this exact moment, she didn't want to leave. But how would he treat her when he woke up?

The turmoil in her heart didn't lessen as the day wore on. She remained by Sikthand's side, only moving to relieve herself or eat, and her breath always hitched whenever he reached out for her in sleep.

Late during the night, after Roldroth had finally fallen asleep in his chair, she'd stared at Sikthand. Though she missed his tattoos, she couldn't help but sigh at how he looked without them. His skin was as pale as marble, his black hood cutting over his face like a shadow.

There was a moment when she'd left his side to renew his sleeping spray, when she'd been halted in place. He'd lain in the bed, blanket scrunched to his waist, arms and legs relaxed in a way that put his body in stunning repose.

Moonlight cut through the window and glowed against his skin, so pale that pastel shades of blue and peach were the only other colors to speak of. He was like some kind of tragic Greek sculpture. All chiseled muscle and perfectly formed features, but even in stillness there was a devastating drama to him.

She wouldn't draw this. The memory would just be for her, and she would keep it close.

The next morning, when Vezel arrived, Sophia pulled out of Sikthand's tight embrace, and, swallowing the hard knot in her throat, left his room.

Though she desperately wanted to be there when the medic woke him up, she thought it would be better if she wasn't. She didn't know if she could look into the angry, accusatory gaze of the man who had tucked her against his chest all night in sleep. It would be too painful.

26

Sikthand's mind came back to him slowly. There was some confusion niggling at his brain, but he chalked it up to the same confusion one always got in the moments between sleeping and waking. The scent of Sophia wrapping around him made him want to drift back into slumber. Had he been dreaming of her again?

The memory of falling flashed through his mind, jolting him awake. His limbs were weak, sluggish, and his vision danced as he tried to keep his head from spinning.

There were people in his room. Commander Roldroth and Medic Vezel and…

He swung his head around, sure he'd spot the human nearby since her smell permeated his senses, but she was nowhere to be found.

He refocused on the two males standing a healthy distance away and tried to get his mind to catch up. Why were they here? What was the last thing he remembered? The storm. Pain.

His head snapped up. Falling. He'd been falling.

Each second that passed had his fury building. His eyes slid closed.

Again. He'd almost been killed *again*.

Sikthand rose from his bed, tail swiping against the floor, fangs pulsing for blood. "Who?" The snarl in his voice held the promise of pain. Both Vezel and Roldroth had the good sense to take a step back.

"We can't say for sure yet, but—"

He launched the metal table by his thigh into the wall. Stone crumbled inward and rained down over the crumpled metal. "Who?" he roared.

Vezel skittered to the door. "I'll leave you to…your…uh. Call on me if you need a medic."

Roldroth eyed the retreating doctor as the door slammed shut. He straightened. "Word from Lindri came through not five minutes ago. Did you take your armor for repair in the last week? They found a metalsmith dead. We're working on a theory that someone coerced…" Roldroth's voice was low and careful, but Sikthand couldn't focus on it.

Her smell. It was *everywhere*. He turned in place, trying to find her.

Muscles thrumming, he brought his hand to his nose. *He* smelled like her. His skin, his fingers, the air.

"Where is she?" He turned on Roldroth, who was still rambling. "Why is her scent all over me?"

The commander swallowed. "She stayed with you while you slept."

Sikthand prowled forward. He must not have heard the commander right.

"I don't believe she had any part—"

Before Roldroth could flinch, Sikthand had thrown him against the wall, one foot trapping his tail to the floor. A blade grasped in Sikthand's own tail, pressed into the soft expanse of Roldroth's neck. "In. My. Bed?" He bared his fangs. "You allowed her to sleep in my bed while I lay unconscious?"

Roldroth sputtered, flattening his spine against the wall to keep the blade from puncturing his skin. "You wouldn't let her go, sire."

Sikthand froze. "What?"

"You gripped her in your sleep. Your tail kept her trapped. You growled whenever she moved away. I stayed and watched over her the entire time—I vow it."

He backed away, tossing his blade to the floor. His breaths were deep, and for a moment, he thought he might be about to rage, but then he laughed. It began low and dry, then worked its way into his belly until he was all but wheezing.

Roldroth slipped out of his room, throwing him a horrified look, but he couldn't stop himself.

He'd been betrayed by nearly everyone he'd ever cared for. Sikthand had grown into a master of control. Always keeping himself locked down, always holding back and staying hard.

But how could he have prepared for this? His unconscious body had betrayed him.

A deep, ringing emptiness filled his chest.

He sunk onto his bed and buried his face in his palms. Almost immediately, he tore his hands away. His fingers twitched as if they could still feel the ghost of her. Where was she?

Fury sparked through every cell, but he couldn't tell if he was livid because he suspected her of something nefarious, or because she wasn't here now. He wanted to hunt her down and…what?

Throw her in a cell? Question her? Wrap her up in his arms so he could ensure her scent on his skin remained heavy for the rest of time? He didn't know what he'd do when he found her, only that he needed to. More than breathing, more than seeking vengeance, more than anything, he needed to get her in his sights.

All of a sudden, he noticed his hands. He'd been looking before, but he hadn't really *seen* them.

He pulled them back, twisting them in front of his eyes. His tattoos were gone.

He peered down and realized he was nearly naked, clothed only in thin medical pants.

Stalking toward the mirror, he tore the pants away and took in his reflection. He was unrecognizable. No scars. No marks. Just pale, clear skin.

The sight turned his stomach. The image didn't match, and it made his battling emotions more muddled than ever. *This isn't me. I am not pure. I am not unmarked.*

He stomped into his study, ironically the room that smelled the least like Sophia, and snagged the jug of renwaeder off his desk. Sikthand didn't know if the spirit would help or hurt, only that he needed a reprieve from reality.

27

Sophia stared at the text in front of her, trying again and again to read it but losing focus. Sikthand had been woken up yesterday morning and yet nothing at all had happened.

The stress of waiting for the shoe to drop was starting to get to her.

Things were too quiet. Too calm. She hadn't seen the king at all, and as far as she could tell, no one else had either.

Was he planning something awful? No longer able to pace in her room, she'd hidden in the archives and planted herself in front of a familiar reference book.

A listing about Roborh laid in front of her. It seemed as wonderful as Heleax had described, but her chest constricted just looking at the page.

She jumped when someone on the second floor snapped a scroll closed. She breathed deeply to slow her pulse. Any second now, she expected guards to barge in and drag her away. She'd been waiting for it for over a day. Every time she passed a soldier, her insides cramped up and her shoulders affixed themselves to her ears.

Her own entourage of guards waited outside, thankfully. It was the reason she'd fled to the archives. This was one of the only places where she could force them to wait by the entrance.

The archives were quiet at this time of night. Calm. But she grew more jittery with each peaceful moment that passed.

Where was he? What was he doing?

Sophia didn't believe the king would hurt her. Even if he believed she'd played some part in this assassination attempt, she didn't for one second think he'd set out to cause her pain.

But she had a horrible feeling that he'd *hate* her, and somehow she dreaded that more.

Focusing on the words before her, she tried to take them in. If the worst came to pass, she'd decided she should probably give Roborh serious consideration. Sikthand's effect on her was just too all-encompassing.

She'd been frantic when she'd thought he'd died. She hadn't realized she cared so much until he'd almost been taken from her.

And the way he'd held her... Could she live without that while knowing how it felt?

Damn it. She'd zoned out again. Groaning, she slumped back in her seat.

Her lungs seized and her joints locked.

Sikthand stood a dozen feet away, watching her.

She scrambled out of her seat, tipping her chair over in the process. She spared it a look, wondering for a split second if she should pick it up before refocusing on the king, who'd gotten closer.

"You're awake," she breathed.

"Were you expecting different?" His tone was odd. His stare too. She couldn't decipher his mood.

She took a step back. "No." She couldn't think what else to say.

Her initial shock at seeing him wore off, and she noticed he wasn't wearing any armor. Not even any metal. He was clothed in a soft, rumpled shirt and clutched a nearly empty jug of renwaeder. The same one from his study.

She took another look at his odd expression and gasped. "Are you drunk?" she hissed.

He tilted his head to the side like a predator. "I was drunk yesterday. Now?" He lifted the jar to his eyes and swirled the white liquid. "I'm currently on my way to drunk again. I think I've more than earned it."

Sudden concern for him spiked, overwhelming any concern for herself. "You shouldn't be wandering around the tower drunk and alone, without any armor or weapons. Not after someone just tried..." Her throat went dry at the flash of emotion in his silver eyes. But *what* emotion?

He took another step toward her. "I was sober, wearing armor, and had a weapon the last time I almost died."

She clicked her tongue, eyes speeding over his rigid muscles and slowly moving feet. "So what? You've decided not to even try protecting yourself anymore? Come on, my soldiers will walk us back to our wing, and you can be as drunk and defenseless as you want there."

A dark laugh bubbled up from his chest and sent shivers skittering over her skin. "I'm far from defenseless, little human." He rounded the table separating them, dragging the bottom of his glass jug over the wood as he prowled toward her. The scrape made her hair stand on end. "Besides, I sent them away."

"You what? Someone wants you dead." Her gaze flashed to the closed doors of the archives. "Did anyone see you come in here? If the wrong person—"

"I wanted to speak to you. Alone."

She continued to back away from him as he closed in. His eyes trailed over her open book, and her insides shriveled. She tried to keep the guilty expression off her face. He had no way of knowing why she was reading about Roborh.

He took a slow drink from his jug, keeping his gaze trained on her, then finally rasped, "Was it you?"

Movement from above had her attention lifting. A man leaned against the railing, watching them. Her steps halted. "Do you really want to talk about this here? What if you aren't safe?"

"I'm never *safe*." He followed the direction of her gaze and growled.

Steps faster, he moved toward her until she was forced to back up to keep from colliding with him. After a few clumsy steps through a row of scrolls, she realized he was herding her deeper into the dustiest section of the archives.

"Was. It. You?" he asked again.

"No." Her voice was breathy.

"You had access," he pressed.

She jerked her head around as he forced her around a corner. Panic rose in her throat, and she threw up her hands. "Just s-stop." Sucking in a short breath when he paused his steps, she steadied herself. "I have no reason to want you dead. Why would I try to kill you before we're married? It does me no good." Every time she'd put forth this argument, she cringed, knowing it didn't make her sound all that great, but it was the most convincing reasoning she had. Why *would* she try to kill him now and not later?

His eyes roamed over her face. "Perhaps you changed your mind about becoming queen. Maybe you realized how thankless and dangerous it is to be a ruler and wanted a way out."

"I didn't—" Sound from down the hall had her slamming her mouth shut.

A familiar voice floated into their dark corner, but she couldn't make out what they were saying. She pricked her ears up. "Is that Besith?" she whispered.

Sikthand looked unconcerned but turned his head infinitesimally. Besith's voice grew louder, as did footsteps from more than one pair of feet.

"Wha—"

Growling in annoyance, Sikthand swooped behind her, slapped a hand over her mouth, and began pulling her into the corner. He stepped back. And back. And back.

Her mind couldn't process it. They should have hit the wall already. Was he somehow stepping through the shelves?

The space around them turned black, and a wall slid into place in front of her nose. Somehow they'd slipped behind the bookshelf lining the back wall and were now standing in a dark, cramped alcove.

She tried to speak through his hand still covering her mouth, but he pulled her flush against his chest and breathed a deep "Shh" into her ear. His mouth brushing over the shell of her ear had all thought soaring away.

The air shifted, and she was abruptly very aware of each spot their bodies touched. Voices sounded from the other side of the bookshelf, but suddenly she didn't give a rat's ass about them. Her heartbeat pounded so hard she worried he'd be able to feel it through her spine.

His fingers loosened and retightened in a wave over her mouth. Could he feel her unsteady breath puffing from her nose on his hand?

Her shoulders twitched back without her permission, brushing against his firm chest. Using his hold on her mouth, he angled her head back a little so their eyes could meet. There was something challenging in his gaze, like he was waiting to see if she'd try to squirm away.

The voices still droned on from somewhere nearby, and his attention flicked out through the gap in the shelves in the direction of the sound.

He dipped his mouth back to her ear, whispering, "Roldroth said you slept in my arms."

She gulped, trying to think how to answer, but her mind went fuzzy when he swept her hair over her shoulder, exposing her neck. His upper body curled against her back as he forced her head to dip to the side further and ran his nose up the length of her throat.

Biting her lips together to keep her whimper in, she squirmed in his hold. Should she be trying to wriggle free? Or should she do what she really wanted and rub against him like a cat?

"Do you know how cruel that was?" he growled, brushing his free hand over her ribs and down her waist till it molded over her hip.

Her heart rate was soaring now. Heat pulsed through her belly, and her lashes fluttered. This wasn't the time or place, but she couldn't seem to make an argument rise in her throat. His hand drifted up her stomach higher and higher until finally, his fingers brushed over the swell of her breast. The deep rumbling groan he exhaled against her neck at the contact made her tremble all over.

Liquid heat flooded her sex, her pulse now thrumming steadily in her clit.

"Your smell is *everywhere*," he continued. "Do you know what it's been like for me to smell you in my sheets?" The front of her dress lifted slowly, and she realized his tail was dragging her skirt up, skimming her thigh as it climbed higher. "I can't wash you away."

Should she try to pull it back down?

Hot and firm, his tongue slipped over her pulse, and she moaned. His fingers tightened over her mouth, and he nipped her ear. "Quiet, little human."

Her dress was bunched around her belly now, his tail wrapped around the fabric, holding both it and her tight to his chest.

His hips rocked against her back. The unmistakable solid bar of his cock pressing into her spine had her eyes sliding shut and her panties growing damp. Her hips arched as he traced his fingers over her exposed inner thigh, teasing her.

"How am I supposed to stay away from you when you react like this to my touch?" His words were somewhere between a groan and a defeated sigh.

Sophia hooked her fingers around his wrist near her mouth. She rested her other palm on the top of his teasing hand. The pad of his thumb traced over the curve of her inner thigh, coming torturously close to brushing against the hem of her underwear.

She had just enough pride left not to drag his palm where she needed it to go, but her fingers twitched on his hand as she kept herself under control.

He pulled out from under her touch, and she almost let out a cry against his palm. But then he slung his forearm across her front, trapping her arm at her side beneath his.

No longer teasing, his hot palm cupped her sex over her panties.

She sucked in a ragged, surprised breath and rose to her tiptoes. His forefinger and pinky firmed against the edges of her pussy lips, gently massaging in a heavenly rolling motion.

When she rocked her hips in time with his touch, his purr vibrated through his chest, rumbling into her spine.

She let her head fall back against his shoulder and whimpered into his palm. "That's right. Melt into me." His hand slid upward, before delving beneath her panties.

Her belly trembled in anticipation, her core squeezing around nothing. She arched her back against his shaft, loving the way the steel bar of his cock dug into her spine and sent electricity sparking down the backs of her thighs.

He slid his middle finger down the seam of her pussy, slipping between her lips and tracing a devastating circle around her opening before sliding upward again. In the back of her mind, she knew there were people moving about on the other side of their dark hiding spot, but her eyes were unseeing. Each cell in her body hung on Sikthand's every movement.

He circled the pad of his finger around her clit, and she jolted, her moan against his hand loud and high. A flash of pain made her shiver when he nipped her ear again, this time using a bit more fang.

She squirmed, rising higher up onto her toes, wanting to feel his teeth on her neck. The king hissed out a curse and obliged, scraping his fangs down the column of her throat.

His fingers dragged over her skin up to her hip, leaving a wet trail of her own arousal on her belly. He balled the strap of her panties in his fist and gave them a vicious tug. When he released the fabric, it fell to the side, hanging limply on her right leg.

All at once, his tail coiled around her right leg just above her knee. Using his tail's grip, he hoisted her thigh up so she was balancing on one leg. Gently but firmly, his tail pulled her lifted thigh back until she was spread wide for him.

He gazed down her front at her exposed lower body and released a rumbling sound of satisfaction. "You said it made no sense for you to kill me *now*."

His fingers began slipping over her sex again. The muscles in the leg she balanced on tensed as she tried to keep her knee from going weak.

"Tell me, human," he growled into her ear. "How soon after we're married will you try to kill me?"

His thumb brushed over her clit, sending hot arousal flooding through her core. His middle finger returned to her entrance, and she shook as he forced the thick digit into her sex deeper and deeper until his palm pressed flush against her skin.

He pumped his finger inside of her, curling it in firm sweeping motions and making her breath stall out. "Will you let me have you once before I go? Will you take my cock before you take my throne?"

The embarrassing sounds coming out of her throat were muffled, but her quivering body showed him exactly how he was affecting her. Her bent right leg kept jerking forward when his fingers moved to slip in dizzying circles around her clit. The muscles of her left leg trembled as she rocked within his hold, sinking and rising in time with his delicious movements.

He plunged two fingers inside her, forcing a ragged moan out of her at the stretching sensation. "Do you want me, Sophia?" His growl held a twinge of desperation. She nodded as hard as she could with his hand on her mouth still holding her head in place.

She knew she must be soaking his fingers from the vulgar wet sounds filling the dark space. Her orgasm coiled tightly, her muscles tensing. Her breasts ached to be touched, but she didn't dare move as he rubbed against the perfect spot.

She went still, shaking as she held her body in place.

"Are you going to come on my hand already?" His purr vibrated through her body, and her orgasm broke. She cried out into his palm, shivering as waves of pleasure barreled through her. "What a sensitive cunt you have," he groaned while slipping his tongue over the shell of her ear.

His fingers continued to lazily explore, making her squeak and shudder whenever they hit a sensitive spot. His hand finally left her mouth and swept down to lock across her torso. "What am I going to do with you now?" he rumbled.

She was lax against his chest, letting him support her weight with his strong arm and tail. Her lids went heavy as he ran his hands boldly over her body. He rumbled an approving hum when he possessively squeezed her breast in his large palm and she arched into his touch.

"I really *will* have to fight for my life if I drag you through the halls." He sucked his fingers covered in her come between his lips and released a rumbling purr. "Every male who passes will want a taste of that nectar leaking from between your legs."

Heat bloomed in her sex once more, but Sophia was too stunned to speak for a moment.

He peered out through the shelves before them, scanning for any signs of movement. "Perhaps we'll go the back way."

"Back way?" she whispered in a cracked voice.

The corner of his mouth lifted. "Close your eyes, Sophia."

28

What have I done?

Sikthand walked through his tunnels back to the royal wing with Sophia clutched in his arms. There was a deep sense of dread stirring in him below the surface, but it was pushed down and hidden from view at the moment. Her taste in his mouth, her smell on his skin, and her warm body in his arms put him in an unmatched state of tranquility.

She leaned against his chest as he walked.

This was a bad idea. He'd revealed, at least in part, that he had a way to secretly move through Vrulatica. Even if he *had* blindfolded her, she now knew where one tunnel entrance was, though not how to get into it.

Her palm brushed over his collarbone, gripping his shoulder as he bent under a low bit of ceiling.

"You know it wasn't me." Her voice was barely a whisper, like she didn't want to ruin the moment but couldn't hold her words back.

His stomach hollowed at the reminder of his current reality. He didn't know for certain whether she'd had any part in this latest attempt. He didn't think she had, but he'd been wrong before.

The scent of her arousal still clung to their clothing, and he breathed it in. The world had seemed so pointless an hour ago.

He'd languished in his room, wishing news of a Tagion invasion would ring through the tower so he had a good reason to rip someone apart. He'd kept himself locked down, the furious futility of his life making him want to set the tower ablaze.

But her smell had reeled him in.

She was everywhere, no longer confined to his study. Sophia lit every corner of his room. Her scent made his chest ache and his insides boil with anger. He'd betrayed himself and revealed such a colossal soft spot.

He wanted Sophia desperately, and now the Guild knew. *She* knew.

If he turned cold toward her again, they would all know he was lying. And it wouldn't be long before news trickled down through the tower. Even if it traveled through whispers as a rumor, sooner or later, whoever had tried to kill him would learn that the king had a staggering weakness.

Not knowing what else to do yesterday, he'd gone to his study, poured a glass of renwaeder, and drank. Nothing resolved after his cup was empty, so he'd poured another and another and another, until he'd convinced himself that going to find the human was the best answer.

He'd lied, telling himself that once he found her, he would interrogate her. But in truth, he'd just wanted to see her. His hands had ached to touch her as though they recalled the feel of her body and were bereft. He'd known it was a mistake to go in his current state, yet he couldn't seem to care.

Sikthand had sought her without armor or soldiers or weapons, and part of him had agreed that if he died on his way, then that's what was meant to happen.

So what if she turned around and plunged a knife in his belly? He could be killed at any moment. It might be worth getting stabbed by her if it meant he could clutch her to his chest and take her mouth in a kiss as he drifted away.

"Where are we anyway?" she asked, head turning blindly in all directions. Her exhale ghosted over his neck, making his cock swell.

"A shortcut back to our wing."

She hissed in a breath. "Someone is trying to kill you. You're telling me there is a secret entrance to our wing and you aren't barricading it? What if they know about it?"

She couldn't see him through her blindfold, so he allowed himself to smile. "Only I have access, little wife."

She stiffened ever so slightly at the murmured name. "I don't understand you," she sighed.

He stepped onto an ancient lift and waited as the mechanical cogs rotated and clicked, carrying them up through the tower.

"I'm sorry," she whispered. Her hands tightened on his shoulders.

"So you did try to kill me, then?" he rasped.

Her lips pursed adorably. "No. I'm sorry *someone* tried to kill you. I'm sorry so many people went into your room without your permission. I'm sorry I slept there. I thought…it seemed to help you." She exhaled through her nose, and her brows furrowed. "I'm sorry that once again, someone has given you cause to hate the world."

His chest constricted with emotion. He brushed it away. "No need to be sorry. You've just allowed me to vent my frustration. It's hard to hate the world when I have a keening female writhing underhand."

A pale flush lifted on her cheeks, and the muscles of her leg under his palm tensed as though she were pressing her thighs together. His cock stiffened uncomfortably. He'd have to go relieve himself before he really lost his mind and stalked her into her room.

He activated the locked panel between this tunnel and the royal wing and stepped through. After walking through the halls of their wing in a few rambling directions so she remained unaware of where the panel was, he lowered her at her door and pulled off her blindfold.

The makeup on her eyes had smudged over her cheeks from the cloth. He didn't like it. It reminded him of how her face looked after she cried.

"I have to go," he said, holding his regret back.

She nodded gravely. "Go figure out who did this and run them through."

His mouth twitched. "As you wish, my queen." He gave a teasing bow, then frowned to himself. How was he so calm? Anger still lingered at the edges of his mood, but it was more of an irritated anger since now he had to go through the arduous and often unsuccessful process of unearthing a culprit.

When normally he approached the task full of gloom, he now merely wanted it done with so he could ensure his evenings were free for their meetings again.

She caught his arm before he turned to leave. He peered at her, but she only chewed on her lip as if working up the nerve to say something. Finally, she gave a tremulous smile. "I want you to know I'm here for you. You know…if you ever need to *vent*."

He wanted to growl and groan and bellow all at the same time, but what roared out of his chest instead was a purr.

She shrugged and backed toward her door. "I mean, allowing a sexy alien king to finger fuck me in a library will be difficult, but I can soldier through if it helps you, *my king*." She grinned wide, knowing exactly what effect her words had, before she slipped into her room and closed the door.

He stood rooted in place, every cell screaming to follow her. With a start, he noticed his tail had begun swaying from side to side an inch off the ground. He frowned and wrapped it around his thigh to keep it still, then forced his protesting feet to move.

This was bad. Sophia was like an oncoming sandstorm. He'd had time to prepare for it before. To run or hide or barricade himself underground.

But now the sand swirled just ahead, and it was too late for him to avoid it. All he could do was let it hit and hope he survived.

29

"What have we learned?" Sikthand asked the Guild. He tried not to let his gaze drift to Sophia sitting on one of the benches running along the back wall of the Guild chamber and failed. He didn't like her sitting back there where the Guild subordinates scribbled notes and exchanged gossip. She should be up here, next to him.

The throne room was Bavo and Besith's first priority. The Master of money and the Speaker of the people had deemed it appropriate to remodel the throne room before they tore apart the Guild chamber to build her a seat of her own. The public weren't allowed in the Guild chamber. It made sense to start with the throne room, but Sikthand was impatient.

The Summit was in four weeks, and his wedding would be soon after. Unease should've coursed through him at the mere thought, but he found himself swelling with warmth every time he imagined it. The *warmth* was what made his mouth go dry.

"Zommah the metalsmith was found dead." Sikthand's gaze flicked to Lady Lindri. He didn't enjoy the fact that she'd thought to investigate her metalworkers in lowcity after seeing some old pieces of warped armor strewn about his room. He'd pummeled his suit the night after he'd cut Sophia to pieces with his marriage proposal. Embarrassment at his lack of self-control had moved him to covertly drop off the salvageable bits of armor for repair. Just another way in which his human bride muddled his mind.

The fact that Lindri had conveniently found Zommah dead made his tail twitch with suspicion. Who better to plan an execution via failed armor than the Lady of Metalsmiths herself?

He'd had one of his spies begin tailing her the minute Roldroth had relayed the discovery of Zommah to him.

"We're still searching for his missing apprentice. We're hoping the young male may know something," Lindri announced.

"Secure his family. Lock them up, and they'll say where the boy went," Besith drawled.

Sikthand's instinct was to agree, but he caught sight of Sophia's stricken expression and found his resolve wavering.

He sighed inwardly. She made him weak. He'd already released those with access to the royal wing far sooner than he would have otherwise. Seeing her pained expression when she'd asked after Alno had made his skin itch. With one word, he could free the male and bring a smile to her face. How could he not do it?

Knowing that his bride had been the one to lock Alno away in the first place, despite their friendship, made the decision easier. She'd put Sikthand's safety before the comfort of her companion. It may be a small thing to some, but to him, it was everything.

"That seems a bit harsh." Madam Kalos glared at Besith. "Whoever did this, didn't work alone. The culprit had access to the king's mount and had enough resources to take advantage of an unforeseen opportunity to corrupt Zommah with an impressive swiftness. Someone like that would cover their tracks. I'm positive the boy is dead somewhere. We just haven't found him. Jailing his family would be piling cruelty on top of their heartache."

"What do you suggest, Sophia?" Sikthand almost glanced around before realizing it was *he* who'd spoken. The king didn't ask for opinions. He heard opinions if his Guild was bursting to share them, but he didn't *seek* them.

Sophia jerked in her seat, eyes widening. She stood slowly, glancing around at the Guild. "I think we should keep a close eye on his family and his house but do so covertly. If I were him, I'd hide until the coast was clear. But you said he's…" She peered down at her notes, and her brows knit with sadness. "He's only sixteen. If he's alive, it'll be only a matter of time before he tries to go back home."

"I agree," Lindri chimed in.

Sikthand nodded, trying to ignore Sophia's downcast eyes. "Speaker Besith, Commander Roldroth, arrange your people thusly. Stay stealthy."

They moved on to other topics, and he was relieved to see Sophia shake off some of her sadness. She was a resilient thing. And determined too. She sat quietly, taking notes, her brows furrowing on occasion as she listened to the Guild spout their opinions.

Madam Kalos complained once again about the trade agreements with Mithrandir. The formidable Swadaeth queen was offering cascades of money for an increase in delicate scuhowin metal. It was a tricky metal to mine as it lay beneath thick layers of askait.

A heated argument arose between Madam Kalos and Speaker Besith. Lady Lindri had all but given up fighting Kalos at this point, and Sikthand was surprised to see Besith take up the mantle.

"The safety of our people seems to be incidental to you, Madam."

"Think what we could build with that money," she insisted. "We could commission a secondary reservoir."

"And you could have a new accomplishment to boast about to your friends in Tremanta," Magistrate Yalmi grumbled, exposing her fangs in her irritation.

Madam Kalos puffed out her chest like a ruffled bird. "Well, why not? Why should Tremanta be praised and lauded as the most impressive city? If we devoted our time and resources to a space elevator or the Oasis—"

"Not this again." Roldroth groaned. "This is our city. We are proud not to be reliant on the technology the rest of the world obsesses over. We will not build a secondary city out in the desert where our malginash refuse to nest."

The bickering continued, but Sikthand occupied himself with watching Sophia. When her eyes rolled, his mouth twitched. When she sucked her lip into her mouth while thinking, other parts of him twitched. And when she yawned, he found himself cutting off Madam Kalos' vicious critique of Master Bavo's fund distributions and calling a close to the meeting.

Bavo corralled him while everyone shuffled to leave. Sophia glanced toward Sikthand. He could see the moment she decided to leave the males to speak, and he wanted to throw Bavo out of the Guild chamber by his tail. She sent him a small smile before slipping into the hall.

30

"This floor is dedicated to our husbandry school campus. The floor above is the uxorial school campus, for of-age females."

Speaker Besith sounded as if he'd rather be anywhere with anyone else rather than giving her this tour. She couldn't disagree. Sophia had been touring the coed primary schools with Besith as her guide for about two hours, and her professionalism was wearing thin. It was clear he didn't care for her or the idea of a human queen. It was also apparent, though, that he was snide to absolutely everyone, so she tried to convince herself that she wasn't special. He was just an unpleasant person.

"Is the husbandry school curriculum any different than the Tremantian curriculum?"

Besith sighed and held his hand out behind him. His poor aide dug through his overflowing bag and slapped a large stack of papers into his waiting palm. Besith flipped the papers toward her without a word. Her helmet hid her scowl. It took everything in her to gently take the papers from him and not snatch them away.

She rifled through the pages, a curriculum guide. "Thank you. I'll look over this later."

He continued walking on, lazily waving his hand in one direction or another, pointing out testing rooms, instructors, training yards. Sophia took sloppy notes as they walked, mostly scribbled thoughts on how human elements could be integrated.

They came to an open door, and Besith trailed inside. Sophia followed, her walk still embarrassingly loud, though she was getting more comfortable in her armor. "One of our classes in session."

Sophia peered around at the room full of owl-eyed men staring at her. She froze when her gaze landed on an extremely detailed diagram of a Clecanian vulva. It was a good thing she was wearing her helmet, or the dozen or so men staring at her would see her face turn beet red. *It's just anatomy. Calm down.*

"Hello, my queen." The female teacher gave a small bow. "We were all just discussing how interesting it will be when we get new anatomical studies for our human counterparts."

Sophia spotted one man nod eagerly. "Yes." She nodded back. "I'm excited to work with the schools to…uh…make sure the new curriculum is…uh…informative," she finished weakly. "Sorry for the interruption." Without waiting for a response, Sophia sped out of the classroom.

She was still cooling her embarrassment and resetting the unfazed queen persona she wanted to embody, when a large grinning man lumbered toward them. The soldiers at her back closed in. She appreciated the protectiveness, but she was still unused to them always being there and had to apologize when she flinched.

"Sophia, this is Sesnot. He is the massage instructor," Besith drawled.

Sesnot frowned at the man, then grinned toward Sophia again. "I am also the royal masseuse, my lady, though the king rarely employs me. I'm hopeful that you'll call on me often. I've been studying human anatomy, and the musculature on your lower back is fascinating. I'm excited to work on a tailless species."

"Oh?" Sophia was a little taken aback, but why wouldn't there be a royal masseuse? "That's interesting. How is a tailed person's musculature different?"

Sophia grinned behind her masked helmet as Sesnot brightened. He turned eagerly and pulled his shirt up, using his own back to point out a set of thick muscles bulging from his spine.

"I think my bride has seen enough of your body, Sesnot."

Sophia's hidden smile turned sappy. Sikthand stepped into view from behind her, yet again appearing at just the right moment. A shiver ran through her at his venomous glare. She didn't think she was the type of person to enjoy possessiveness, but for the cold king who'd barely given her the time of day for the past month to now look like he was going to rip this Vrulan himbo's tail clean off? Well, she now knew she liked possessive Sikthand very much.

***

Sikthand had known he'd seek her out as soon as his eyes had popped open. His neck ached fiercely from the odd angle in which he'd fallen asleep, tipped back in his chair behind her mirror.

He'd just been too relaxed watching her sketch in her small book. Smiling, her supple leg slung over the arm of her chair bouncing as she hummed some foreign tune.

They'd been parted for too long, the investigation into his assassination taking up all of his time. But today there was finally a spare bit of time. His spies were in place. His spies' spies were also in place. Ahea had recovered and was safely tucked into her nest with more minata wood than she could ever hope to eat.

And his night was open. He was too eager—he knew he was. Clamping down on the urge to drag her away from the male not so innocently showing off his large tail muscles, Sikthand peered down at her. Would she be upset he'd interrupted her meeting? Upset he was admonishing a male on her behalf?

Sikthand held his breath as she struggled to remove her helmet. She wobbled toward him, still clanging clumsily in her armor. When she finally tugged the helmet off, revealing her flushed cheeks and bright smile, his heart throbbed, and he had to smother his rising purr.

"Hello. I didn't know you were joining me on the tour today."

He forced his gaze back to Sesnot, who had blanched guiltily and covered himself up. Sikthand's fingers clenched. The male had been trying to entice her.

In truth, Sophia could employ whoever she wanted, but it was also true that Sikthand would ensure royal masseuses went missing often if they looked at her even half as enthusiastically as Sesnot.

She glanced between the males, noticing Sikthand's stare. "Uh, Speaker Besith, I think we're done with the tour, yeah? Thank you so much for showing me around. I'm going to get my thoughts on the additional human coursework together and present it to the Guild soon."

"I look forward to your notes." The sour sarcasm in Besith's voice had Sikthand's scowl darkening, but the male had already walked away before he could decide what to do about it.

Sikthand caught Sesnot's arm before he could leave and whispered low enough that Sophia wouldn't hear. "If you ever expose yourself to my wife again, I'll slice your tendons and leave your tail limp." The male shuddered.

With a hand on her back, Sikthand swept her away from the stammering male. "What did you say to him?" she complained, peering at the masseuse over her shoulder while he forced her forward.

Sikthand's jaw clenched shut. All the responses he'd normally give seemed lacking. Choosing his words in order to elicit a specific reaction had never been too difficult for him. He knew what to say to make her annoyed, scared, angry, disgusted. But what words did he choose to make her like him?

He hadn't concerned himself with being liked before, and he found himself on unsteady ground trying to decide how to speak to her now. Or how to act with her. He cringed, realizing he was still pushing her through the halls, forcing her to trot to keep his pace.

He slowed, suddenly worried about all the other unconscious things he did that might dismay her. They walked in silence as he brooded over the best words to use and whether he should reschedule their meeting until he could decide.

"Where are we going?" she asked above her clanging.

"We lost time looking over the candidates. We'll meet early tonight and get through more of them," he answered absently.

"Okay. I'm pretty hungry, though. Could we get some something to eat first?"

Pondering what types of compliments human females might like, he waved a hand. "I had Alno gather food for us to have in the study." *I enjoy how empty your face is without a hood.* He frowned. Describing her captivating, beguiling, hoodless face as *empty*? Idiotic.

"Oh. Okay, great."

Suddenly, he realized that while he'd been lost in his head, he'd ended up dictating what she would be doing, when she would be doing it, and what foods she would be eating.

His steps paused, and he peered down at her. "I… If you don't want to…" He wasn't used to this. He was used to ruling, telling people how things would be. He caught sight of her soldiers exchanging unreadable glances, and his fangs ground together. "Is that plan acceptable?" He tried not to growl his words.

The corner of her mouth lifted. "Yeah." She studied his eyes, her grin widening, and her head tipped down a little. "Dinner and an activity. Sounds like a date."

Romantic engagement. His translator chirped the translated meaning of *date* in his head. Sikthand's mouth went dry.

31

Sophia couldn't help but stare at Sikthand.

She'd studied him as they'd quietly walked back to their wing. While she'd bathed, changed out of her armor, and selected an outfit, she'd pictured his tense jaw and even tenser posture. And now, sitting across from him in his study, she watched his tail flick back and forth as he silently pre-read the next candidate file.

No matter how much she tried to convince herself otherwise, she kept arriving at the same conclusion.

Her future husband looked nervous.

She wanted to sigh.

A knock sounded at the door, and Sikthand shot out of his seat like there were hot coals underneath him. She waited, cheek resting on her fist, and tried to decide how to handle the jumpy king.

They hadn't talked about their little encounter in the library, and despite her lying awake at night, hoping he'd come to *vent*, he hadn't. Was that why he was nervous? Did he think she had regrets? Or was he nervous because he didn't want it to happen again?

Alno stepped into the study carrying two trays of food, and they exchanged glances that silently communicated, *He's acting fucking weird.*

Sophia was beyond happy that Alno was back. She'd apologized to him over and over, and he'd waved her off each time. Apparently, the stint in the dungeon had only made Difila keener toward him, and she'd had to clap her hand over his mouth to get Alno to stop relaying the *greeting* Difila had given him when Sikthand released him.

Alno gave her a significant look when he set the trays down and said, "Ezros was thrilled when I went down there and demanded some of this fruit."

Sophia peered at her plate and found a large chunk of the unnamed purple-leafed fruit they'd tried on their tour of the farms. Had Sikthand made Alno go all the way down to the farming floors to get this for her?

She peered at the king. He was staring hard at her as though trying to gauge her reaction, but then glanced away when she caught his eye.

Fuck a duck. Heat seeped through her insides. She was going to get into the king's pants tonight if it was the last thing she ever did.

"Thank you, Alno. You can go." She shooed her grinning chaperone out the door and waited till she heard the bedroom exit close before turning to Sikthand.

He was back in his chair, staring hard at the file. She narrowed her eyes and broke off a piece of the fruit. His pupils weren't moving up and down the page as they should've if he were reading.

She popped a piece of fruit into her mouth and let out an exaggerated moan. "This is *so* good." Sikthand's body tensed at the throaty sound. She broke off a few more pieces and casually strolled closer to him. "Did you ask him to get this for me?"

"I mentioned it was a food you enjoyed," he rasped, blinking at the paper in the same spot he'd been staring at for a while now.

She squinted at him and popped another piece of fruit into her mouth. Was he trying to be modest? Did he not want her to know he'd ordered Alno to go get this?

She'd grown pretty close to her chaperone, and she knew he complained about traveling down the tower far too often to have retrieved this fruit for her without being expressly ordered to do so.

She pursed her lips. "You only *mentioned* it? And he took it upon himself to go all the way down to the farming floors and get it for me? Wow, Alno really is a thoughtful male."

Sikthand's jaw tightened, and his eyes raced from side to side. Poor man was thinking very hard about something.

She stepped in front of his chair, close enough to invade his personal space. His silver gaze flashed up to meet hers. Sophia let the mischievousness she felt seep into her expression and smirked when he caught sight of it. His eyes narrowed suspiciously. She held a dripping piece of fruit out just before his lips. "Want some?"

He looked at the fruit, then back at her. She pressed closer, brushing the wet edge against his lower lip so he couldn't mistake what she was doing. Ever so slowly, he opened his mouth, allowing her to press her fingers between his teeth.

His fang scraped over her thumb as his tongue swirled across the tips of her fingers. Her breathing hitched at the deep sound that rumbled out of his throat. Their gazes remained locked.

Sophia lifted her fingers to her mouth and slid her forefinger in up to her knuckle to lick off the rest of the sticky juice that had run down her hand. Crumpling paper sounded from near her hip.

"Sikthand?" She turned slightly and tugged the destroyed paper out of his stiff fingers.

He let out a dangerous growl that seemed like the closest version of *What?* she was going to get at the moment. When she stepped between his now empty hands and lowered herself across his lap, his growl burst forward, then morphed into a purr. His hands slid back to grip the arms of his chair. Always the bit of him to be the most emotionally revealing, his tail silently wrapped around her ankle, pulsing and squeezing.

"You forced Alno to go get me that fruit, didn't you?"

His chest heaved in deep breaths, and his gaze kept falling to her mouth. He gave a slow, deliberate nod.

Bringing her mouth close to his, she smiled wide. "Thank you."

Sophia gave him a chaste little peck.

He broke—his body lunged forward, and his mouth crashed over hers. She was still sitting across his lap, but he'd curled forward, her shoulder blades flattening against the arm of his chair. His right hand fisted the hair at her crown as he delved his tongue into her mouth, and the other hand slipped under her back, pulling her body against his. The right side of her waist wedged in the crook of his arm.

Sophia quickly lost control of the situation. He kissed her with such ferocity, his tongue slipping over hers slow and deep. The moans and whimpers rising from her throat finally hit her own ears. She'd just managed to catch her breath when his grip in her hair tightened, and he took her mouth again.

He's been studying, she realized with a shiver.

His hand slid out of her hair and gripped her nape while his thumb curled under her jawbone. He forced her head to fall back, exposing her throat. Heat raced to slick her core. His other hand rubbed up her belly, then her ribs. He hooked his fingers over the edge of her sweetheart neckline and wrenched it down, dragging the bunched fabric until her breasts popped out.

Her head was still forced back, her long hair sweeping across the ground. All her soft parts were exposed to him, her tender throat, her chest, her breasts, and stiff nipples. He took advantage.

She writhed under his mouth. Tongue, lips, and fangs brushed over every inch of exposed skin, licking and nipping, and making her moan out some ungodly sounds.

She lost her breath altogether when Sikthand's thick tail grazed up her inner thigh under her dress and slipped over her sex.

"Wait," she breathed, trying to shake her head to clear it. "Wait," she said louder, eyes shooting open when the reverberation of his purr began buzzing through his tail. She shuddered as the vibration hit her sensitive clit.

For a second of bliss, she almost said fuck it and let her knees spread wide. But he stopped.

His fingers snaked back into her hair, and he pulled her head forward, none too gently. "Are you asking me to stop?" His voice had turned guttural, and an embarrassing whine tinged her shallow breaths.

"Yes," she panted.

A muscle ticked in his jaw, and he inhaled a growl of frustration before dragging himself back against the chair.

She licked her lips, heat pulsing between her legs. Sophia was commanding a king…and he was letting her.

He tipped his head to the ceiling and slid his eyes closed as though trying to regain his control. She bit her lips together in a grin when he huffed out another irritated snarl and tore his tail, which was still slipping up and down her leg with a mind of its own, away. He clutched the wriggling appendage in his fist.

Shakily, she sat up on his lap. "Don't worry, Your Majesty." She tipped forward against his chest and kissed the tight cords of his neck. Her lips buzzed from the answering purr running through his vocal cords. "*I* don't plan to stop."

His gaze shot toward her, and she grinned at his wide, confused eyes. After first tugging at his shirt until he got the hint and pulled it over his head, she shifted her legs and began sliding down his body. She dragged her hands over his torso as her knees lowered to the floor between his feet, loving the way his muscles jumped under her touch.

Her hands came to rest on the tops of his thighs. She grinned up at him again, her fingers inching toward the stays of his pants. A large unmistakable bulge strained against the fabric, making her lick her lips.

When she'd untied the last knot holding him in place, his cock surged forward, and her eyes nearly crossed. Her pussy pulsed desperately around air. She was so empty and hollow. Sikthand would stretch her out so deliciously if she asked. She could climb back up his powerful body and lower herself on this divine dick so easily, but she held herself back, locking her thighs together to relieve the worst of the pressure.

His cock was just as beautiful and devastating as the rest of him. Enormous and ridged. She'd almost thought the raised sections running along his shaft were thick veins, but they were too perfectly spaced for that. The king's dick was fucking ribbed. She nearly moaned.

Her hands slid farther up his thighs until her fingers formed a diamond around the base of his cock. She glanced up and found his stare blistering in its intensity. Shivering, she wrapped one palm around him.

His big body quaked, and he hissed out a vile curse. The subtle sound of fabric ripping was muffled beneath his hands. His clutching fingers had pierced the arms of his chair.

Sophia pumped her fist over him and whimpered at the way his chest and stomach rolled like a wave with her actions. Her free hand stretched to run over his gorgeous abs as he rocked in her hold.

It was beyond uncommon for Clecanian women to take their men into their mouths. Had he ever been given head before? There was a veritable puddle pooling under Sophia's dress, fantasizing about what reaction Sikthand would have to what she planned next.

Her breath came out in shaky pants as she moved her fist lower. She gripped the base of his shaft, then gave the thick head a long slow lick.

Sikthand jerked within her hold. "Sophia." His voice was pained and rougher than a sack of tumbling rocks. She glanced up at him, ensuring her breath ghosted over the wet crown. He shivered.

He didn't say anything else. He just stared at her, his chest not even moving to take in breath. She paused for a moment longer to make sure he didn't want her to stop, then gave him another thick lick.

This time his whole body seemed to melt, deflating, then violently inflating as he sucked in a ragged breath. Never in her life had she been more turned on by this task. She took him into her mouth, sucking him in as deep as she could.

Each one of his loud moans and growls had electricity sparking across her nipples and pulling at her clit. He didn't touch her as she sucked him deep, letting her saliva pool so her mouth slipped more easily over his enormous shaft. She glanced up and found his tail thrashing in his crushing grip.

"Let go!" she cried, releasing him from her mouth. "You're going to break your tail."

The king looked down his nose at her, his dark hood making his silver eyes glow more brightly than normal. "Are you sure, little human?"

She nodded.

The domineering look in his eyes had her insides melting. His thighs were spread, his greedy stare possessive and oh so hungry.

The hand not crushing his tail went to her mouth. He slipped his index finger between her parted lips, placing the pad against her bottom teeth. She whimpered as his strong finger pressed down, hinging her jaw open wider and wider for his use.

By the time she felt his tail snaking around her neck, she was trembling all over, her hips torturously rocking against nothing. "Swallow me deep, wife. I want to feel the grip of your throat."

His tail on her neck dragged her head down while his finger kept her lips open wide. He fed his cock into her mouth inch by inch until it hit the back of her throat. She moaned around him, her eyes rolling when a deep masculine purr of satisfaction buzzed through his shaft.

His fingers brushed over her cheek, and before his tail slid away from her neck, he gently rocked into her throat, releasing a drawn-out shuddering groan as though he'd never felt anything better.

Her mouth worked over him once more. She bobbed, firming her lips and pulling hard as she rose, then sucking him deep. Her jaw ached from his size, but she wanted this to be as seared into his mind as it would be in hers. She wanted the memory of this blow job to keep him up at nights as he was trying to fall asleep.

Tears burned in the corners of her eyes, her sex throbbing, weeping for attention. As though he could sense her need, his tail shot between her legs and nearly lifted her off the ground like she was straddling a hook.

The embarrassing garbled sound of her cry while her throat was stuffed full of his cock couldn't be helped. He was purring, *loudly*, and the vibration rumbling through his tail buzzed into her skin everywhere it touched from her low belly, to her clit, to between her pussy lips, and up through the cleft of her ass.

All she could do for a few moments was quiver with his dick deep in her mouth as waves of vibration pulsed through her. Moaning with each strangled exhale, she slipped her mouth over him again. She rode on his vibrating tail, his skin slick and dripping with the hot liquid arousal leaking from between her legs.

She swallowed him deep as she humped his tail into a delicious orgasm. He called her name, urging her on and groaning his praise. His body tensed under her, his cock swelling until it was so hard she might as well be sucking on a metal pole.

The end of his tail wrapped around her thigh in a bruising hold, and he roared to the ceiling. His chest quaked, his body pulsing with great big throbs as jets of cum coated her throat. She swallowed as much as she could, her hips still absently rocking over his tail.

She drank him down, then licked him clean while he gazed at her as if she were the most glorious thing he'd ever seen.

Sophia stayed kneeling on the ground between his knees, her head resting in his lap as his fingers scraped through her hair, massaging her scalp until her lids drooped. His tail remained locked between her legs, and though she no longer rubbed herself against it, there was something comforting about the firm pressure.

The next morning, she woke up in her own bed, though she couldn't recall getting there. As she went about her day meeting with Bavo and Lindri to approve the designs for her throne, she felt a twinge of sadness that she hadn't woken up with Sikthand's arms wrapped around her and his tail firm between her legs.

She tried not to let it bother her. Clecanian couples didn't usually sleep together, and she knew Sikthand was less likely to break that tradition than most since the bitch-who-must-not-be-named had injected that ink into his eyes after they'd fallen asleep together.

Still, Sophia hoped beyond reason that she was special to him. Maybe one day she could defy the odds and be the one he allowed to cuddle with him late into the night.

Any trepidation she might have felt evaporated, though, when Sikthand led her into the study the next night.

She halted in her tracks and stared at the towering piles and piles of purple-leafed fruit burying his desk.

32

If someone barged into his room at this exact moment and placed a blade to his spine, Sikthand didn't think he'd be able to lift a finger to defend himself. How could he when he needed all ten to hold down Sophia's bucking hips?

Together, he and Sophia had developed a glorious routine. She came to his office, he gave her some gift or another, and she thanked him with access to her sensitive little body. Currently, he had his face smothered between her thighs, his tongue working hard to teach her what techniques were normally implemented with Clecanian females so she could ensure the information she gathered for her human database was accurate.

Though the bundle of nerves that made her come was not located nearly as deep as a Clecanian's, the deep thrust of his tongue inside her channel had her orgasm shuddering through her all the same. He'd found that his purr made making her come dangerously easy.

Normally, he did everything in his power to hold his purr back. It was a show of weakness, and every time he let it out, she knew just how intensely she affected him. But the flavor of her cunt on his tongue never lingered long enough, and knowing his purr could keep her wet and wanting was the only motivation he needed.

Yet he still held back. He hadn't allowed himself to fuck her. It was a line he had enough control not to cross yet. Something about their looming marriage unnerved him. Though he often thought of her as his wife, she wasn't. Not yet.

Burying himself inside her would be the sweetest oblivion, one he knew he wouldn't come back from. If he fucked her, he'd bite her, and if he bit her…

His life would be changed. He didn't know how, but it would alter him. Fear was a difficult thing to break, and it had buried its claws in deep a long time ago.

Her soft moans echoed through the study from the top of the desk where she was perched. Her body continued to twitch in his hold as he lapped at her core, purring and flicking his vibrating tail over her nipples in the way he'd discovered made her eyes roll back.

He hadn't revealed to her what brought his purr to the surface so strongly. Sikthand let her go on believing it built when he was aroused. That was partially true. The scent of heat coating her sex did make him purr, but the thoughts that powered the deepest purrs, the ones that reverberated through his whole body were not sexual.

They came not when she palmed his cock, but when she rested her palm on his cheek. When he needed to call it forward, he imagined holding her in his arms in sleep. He thought of the moment days ago when they'd been sitting in front of their people in the dining hall, and she'd reached for his hand, holding it while they ate as if it had been a simple thing.

Or the moment when he'd been training her with the retractable spear he'd collected for her. She'd nicked his elbow. She hadn't even been trying to fight—she'd simply lost her grip on the weapon while they'd been discussing strategy, and it had grazed his arm.

She'd raced toward him with a horrified gasp to examine the sliced skin. Recalling the worry in her eyes and the gentle way she'd pressed a cloth to the cut while wincing…that made his purr roar to life.

The ways in which he called his purr forward haunted him.

He'd dodged sex so far by ensuring he thoroughly pleased her into a stupor each night, but he knew she was aware of his avoidance. Even now, still sprawled on his desk, she pulled him close, kissing him in a way that made him dizzy. His hips were wedged between hers, and though he remained unmoving, she rocked herself against him.

He could scent her arousal rising in the air once more, and he tried to decide how he wanted to sate her this time. Fingers? Mouth? Tail?

The heat of her seeped into the seam of his pants. He groaned against her mouth. A few tugs at his laces and he could be pressing himself into her needy cunt. His tail thrashed at the prospect.

A bell echoed through the room, a signal that someone without access was waiting to speak to him at the royal wing entrance.

Sikthand pulled back and stared down into her dilated pupils. He gripped her chin, running a thumb over her swollen bottom lip. He growled as the bell sounded again.

Her lips twitched. "Go." She pressed a quick kiss to his mouth, then pulled her dress down and patted her hands over her hair. He readjusted his throbbing cock and took in a deep breath before opening the door and stomping toward the exit.

***

Sophia tried to put Sikthand's desk back to normal, but he'd broken a few things as he'd swept it clear. Carefully, she picked up the largest pieces of glass from the ground and dumped them in the trash. She'd need to ask Alno to get the cleaning staff to sweep this area.

Steps sounded in Sikthand's bedroom. She spun and found…Difila?

Her gaze shot between Sikthand and Difila, who was covered in beautiful armor. Heat rose on Sophia's neck when the subtle wrinkle of Difila's perfect silver nose told her that this room must stink of sex.

"I need to have a private word with Difila," Sikthand announced.

Hurt swelled in her chest like an overfilled balloon. Sikthand never took meetings in his rooms. In fact, he very rarely, if ever, met with anyone one-on-one at all unless they were guildmembers. What private word could he need with a low-level cloud chaser like Difila?

"About what?"

Sophia should just leave. Sikthand was a king, and he was allowed to have whatever meetings he wanted, but not knowing what this was about had irrational possessiveness rising like acid in her throat. She tried to remind herself that the woman spent a staggering amount of time with Alno.

Perhaps the dread seeping in was because he and Difila had flirted at that party as if they were familiar with one another. The cloud chaser's eyes didn't move around the room curiously. Had she been here before?

"Doesn't she report to Commander Roldroth?" Sophia added, trying desperately to keep her voice casual.

Difila didn't appear affected by the exchange. She silently waited, watching the king as he eyed Sophia. Jaw tensed, he stepped toward Sophia slowly until he stood just before her. If she didn't have implanted birth control, she'd think she was about to start her period. What else would make her irrationally emotional enough to have tears rising to her eyes for no good reason?

Please don't scold me in front of her. Please don't make me leave.

He didn't appear angry, though. He tipped her chin up with the tip of his tail, staring down into her pinched expression as she tried to get ahold of her emotions. Cogs moved behind his eyes as though he were deciding something important. Sophia had no idea how to decipher his long sigh.

"Difila is one of my spies. She's discovered something about the attempt on my life." He spun to face Difila again but leaned back against his desk next to Sophia and pulled her into his side. Her chest expanded with warmth, fireworks erupting in her belly before the meaning of his words took hold.

"News?" Her gaze shot to Difila, who appeared uncaring of the fact that the king was allowing Sophia to stay.

She nodded. "I found the boy, the apprentice." Sophia tried to hold back her gasp. Difila's gaze flicked over her before she stoically continued. "He was hiding in the dump on the Xuu levels, surviving off scraps of food others had thrown away." The first flicker of emotion Sophia had witnessed from the woman passed over her face in the form of a wince. "He's badly injured. Someone ran him through with a blade, then threw him down the trash chute. Luckily, they'd emptied malginash-pup bedding a few days before, and he only broke a few bones when he landed. I've dressed his wounds the best I can, but I need permission to take him to the infirmary if he's to survive for further questioning."

"Yes," Sophia burst. "Yes, obviously, take him there." Sikthand was stiff at her side, and she paused. "What's the problem?"

Difila and Sikthand exchanged knowing glances. "He lost consciousness a few minutes ago. There's no way to get him to a launch bay unseen. The Xuu levels are near lowcity."

"I can get him as far as the shops in midcity without coming out into the open," Sikthand added, peering at Difila.

Did he have more secret tunnels than just the one he'd taken her through? "But after that, we'd need to carry him through the busy streets to get him up to the royal launch bay. Can he hang on until the streets are empty late tonight?"

"He won't last that long." Difila's throat bobbed.

Understanding crashed through Sophia. Whoever wanted the king dead was still out there. If anyone at all caught sight of that boy and learned he was still alive, whoever had tried to kill him would be desperate to finish the job.

Not only would the boy be in even more danger, but they might never learn who wanted Sikthand dead.

The king nodded. Voice tight, he said, "Take him. We don't have another option."

"No, wait." Sophia's mind whirred.

"The boy will die," Difila argued, the faintest anger lingering in her voice.

Sophia frowned. "I realize that, but there's a smart way to do this. Just let me think." A plan formed in her mind. She glanced between Difila and Sikthand. "Where can a person find some fake blood around here?"

33

"Okay, where do I have to run again?"

Sikthand kept his lips sealed.

Sophia huffed out an annoyed sound. "We talked about this. I'll be fine. You said Roldroth is the best shot in two centuries."

She glanced over to the commander, who looked as if someone was holding a pair of hedge clippers to his ballsack. Sikthand glared at the man.

"I'd rather not show off my skills in this way, sire," Roldroth grated through clenched teeth.

"Yeah, better leave the wounded, dying boy in a tunnel," Sophia said, with a heaping scoop of deadpan sarcasm.

Roldroth grumbled something under his breath.

Sikthand hauled her away from the commander. He stared at the man with an intensity that would have her cowering. "Do not be modest. Do not be boastful. Can you do this?"

Roldroth's jaw moved as he ground his teeth together. His gaze drifted to Sophia, then down to the crowded square once again. They were crammed into a cubby high above the square in midcity.

Sophia had thought this was merely an overly decorated bit of wall, but as it turned out it was another covert hiding spot. The dotted metal latticework gave Roldroth just enough room to fire a bolt from his odd crossbow-style weapon. "If she doesn't move…I can. But I want confirmation that I will not be held responsible if this goes wrong," he rushed to add.

"You won't," Sophia agreed.

"If something goes wrong and she is injured, I will—"

"You will do nothing." She stepped in front of Sikthand, glaring at him. Then she clicked her tongue at his unmoving scowl and spun to Roldroth. "If I don't move and you end up killing me because you aren't as good of a shot as you thought you were, I give Sikthand permission to push you out of a launch bay. Sound fair?"

Both men grunted at each other, and Sophia pulled Sikthand back to scan the square below. "Where do I go again? There?" She pointed to an alleyway that disappeared around a sharp corner.

"Yes," he grumbled miserably. "Alno and Difila have already dressed the boy."

"Okay, then, we're all good. Let's go."

Before Sikthand could haul her back, she sped out of their concealed spot with a whispered "Aim good" toward Roldroth, who groaned.

Sophia clanged a little more loudly in her armor than normal, drawing the attention of the evening shoppers. She kept her helmet tucked under her arm and gripped it for courage. They reached the area near the alleyway and spotted Difila and Alno canoodling nearby.

She grinned around at passersby, pretending she was having a great time being escorted through midcity by the king.

"I don't understand why I can't be shot at."

Sophia glanced at Sikthand and frowned. He was standing directly where he shouldn't be, blocking Roldroth's line of sight.

"Because you are not the size of a sixteen-year-old boy. Now, move." He didn't, and Sophia sighed. "I'll be okay, I promise. I'm good at pretending to be injured. I've been killed during almost every LARP event I've gone to, and I make it look good every time." She kept her fist closed around the leftover blood pellets from the umbercree festival costumes, hoping they were still there since she couldn't feel much through her thick gloves. "Besides, Roldroth is only going to shoot close enough to make it believable that I was hit. No big deal."

"I don't like this," he growled.

Sophia did a double take and noticed the deep panic in his eyes. She reached for his hand, wishing they both weren't wearing so much armor. "I don't like that there is someone out there who wants to kill you. I want that boy to survive not just because it's the right thing, but also because I want to kill whoever he tells us tried to get you electrocuted. Okay?"

As though he were dragging himself back through gale-force winds, Sikthand moved to her side. She pointed her body in the agreed-upon direction, pretending to peer through a Flesh Forge window and worked up the nerve to give the signal.

Khes appeared in the window, catching sight of her. His expression was as grumpy as ever, but his eyes had narrowed on her even more than usual, like he noticed something was wrong. Well, this was the perfect excuse to signal to Roldroth.

Fingers trembling under her glove, she lifted her hand toward Khes and waved.

Stay still. Stay still. Stay still.

She heard the sound of the zooming bolt whiz by her ear and her heart stuttered out. She'd almost been shot. That had been a real bolt. A few inches to the right and...

The moment's shock wore off, and she crumpled to the ground, slapping her palm to her temple and wailing fiercely.

A scream rang out nearby, and she felt Sikthand hauling her up while bellowing. As they'd planned, Sikthand began theatrically dragging her away, making sure that everyone got a good look at the blood oozing down her face from her skull. She made a show of nearly passing out as he hauled her into the safety of the alley, ordering their guards to block the entrance until they could find the shooter.

Alno and Difila sprang into action. Difila helped block the alley with the soldiers while secretly ensuring they didn't go to check on Sophia, and Alno ran through the square, searching for the imaginary assassin.

Sophia leaned against the wall of the alley as Sikthand opened the secret passage where an armor-covered filthy boy was slumped. Her stomach hollowed at his splotchy steel-blue skin. He looked much younger than sixteen.

Dizziness plagued her vision. Though she wasn't injured at all, a deadly projectile zooming past her head had had more of an effect on her than she wanted to admit. Her adrenaline was spiked, the fake blood dribbling down into her eye, confusing her body even more.

She breathed deeply, trying like hell not to pass out. If she passed out, Sikthand would never run off with the apprentice clutched in his arms like he was supposed to.

"Is he alive?" Her voice trembled furiously from the adrenaline. Her hands shook as she tried to wipe the fake blood out of her left eye but only managed to scratch herself and smear the blood over her metal gloves.

Sikthand's eyes were wide and filled with something akin to fury. "That was far too close."

"I'm okay, I promise. Not a single scratch. Just a ton of fake blood. We had to make it look bad, right?" Her gaze trailed back down to the apprentice, and something foul rose to her nose. He already smelled like death. "You need to help him."

Sikthand breathed through his nose, the muscles of his jaw bulging, and checked the boy's pulse. "Alive," he grunted, as though he couldn't access more words than that. He snatched her helmet from her loose fingers and plopped it over the boy's head, then hauled him out of the passage.

Sophia stumbled inside in his place. Sikthand crouched down to her level when she collapsed against the wall, disguising her dizziness as a mere trip over her armor. "Go, go. I'll come out as soon as the coast is clear. Sikthand…" She gripped his hand. "Stay with him and make sure he's safe. I promise I'll be in my room by the time you get back."

Bellowing from the square hit her ears, and her chest constricted. It was Khes' voice, and he sounded livid. "Stay out of sight. You won't have any guards or a helmet. You wait for Alno—"

"I *made* the plan. I *know* the plan." Sophia nodded, tugging the passage door closed before any onlookers could break through Difila's barricade.

She met Sikthand's gaze one more time before the door slid closed, and blinked through the blood dribbling into her vision.

Were the corners of his eyes black?

34

Alno and Difila were sleeping in a corner of the landing bay when Sikthand arrived back in Vrulatica.

They roused at the tapping of Ahea's talons as she landed. Both shot to their feet, their raised-brow expressions asking a million questions while their mouths remained closed.

"He lives. He's somewhere safe," Sikthand explained in a rush. "Where is she?"

"Back in her room. She's fine," Alno croaked, his voice still raspy from sleep.

He nodded, gave Ahea a few grateful scratches, then tossed her reins to Difila. "See to her."

Without another word, Sikthand stalked out of the bay.

Hours had gone by. Hours and hours of picturing nothing but Sophia's pale, blood-streaked face flash over and over through his mind. He needed to see her, feel her body under his hands. She wasn't hurt—, it had been fake, but he hadn't been able to calm his racing heart since watching Roldroth's bolt soar by, inches away from her face.

Glancing down at himself, he caught sight of his filth-covered armor, and turned on his heel so he could first visit his room.

The apprentice had survived, but just barely. Sikthand had had to help Vezel remove the armor before he could be loaded into the healing tube, and the stench from the boy's infected belly wound had nearly brought both males to their knees.

Sophia's plan to sneak the boy out of the city had been overly dramatic and dangerous and a bit silly, but it had worked.

Vrulatica buzzed with the news of the future queen's assassination attempt. No one questioned whether she was the one Sikthand had carried off through the tower and flown to the infirmary with. As she'd planned, Vezel had even cleared a whole floor of the infirmary as he always did whenever there was a royal visiting. The male had been beyond surprised when Sikthand had removed her helmet and revealed a dying young male.

The apprentice was safe, stashed in a covert location. Vezel was sworn to secrecy, and though the boy was still too terrified to speak, Sikthand was certain he'd be able to name the person who'd done these vile things to him in time. Thanks to Sophia's quick mind, she'd kept an innocent Vrulan safe.

The threats he'd spat toward Vezel and the singular sentinel tasked with guarding the boy had been harsh, but Sikthand didn't regret them. For hours, his insides had felt like they were being slowly pulled in half.

All he'd wanted to do was return to Vrulatica and confirm with his own eyes that Sophia was okay. She'd been shaky when he'd left her in the passage. Shaky, but perfectly healthy. Still, having a bolt shot at her head had made bitter fear waft off her in a way that had his gut twisting.

He tossed his armor into a pile in the corner of the room, bathed, then paused in front of his mirror. More than anything, he wanted to go to her and pull her against his chest, but he knew how she'd act. She'd wave away his concerns. She'd pretend everything was alright.

How did she really feel?

Sikthand stepped into the secret passage and crept behind her mirror. His eyes found her instantly, as if they'd already known where to look. She sat in a comfortable chair, and he was pleased to see someone had started a fire for her.

Muscles loosening one by one, he let his gaze roam over her. Blood no longer oozed down from her head. Color had returned to her skin. She was clean and healthy and safe.

He let himself relax as he watched her. She held up a mailing canister, extending it so she could read a letter. Early on, he'd kept track of what she mailed and what she received, but her correspondence had been sparse and innocent. Whatever she read now would likely be more of the same, but the way she stared at the paper, gazing at it as though she'd read it before and was admiring the words, had tension building in his shoulders. What did it say?

His tail flicked anxiously and hit the chair behind him. It scraped across the floor for half a second. The sound should have registered mildly with her, but she flinched, practically jumping out of her seat.

Her eyes flew to the door, and she shoved the message between her thigh and the chair, hiding it as she held her breath and waited for someone to come through the door. Sikthand scooped his tail up to keep it from moving and swallowed past the tightness building in his throat.

After moments of silence, her brows knit and she glanced around the room like she'd just realized the sound hadn't come from the hall outside. Pulling the letter from its cramped hiding spot, she re-rolled it and stuffed it into a low drawer behind bundles of bedding.

His eyes fixed on the drawer as she moved about her room. He wanted to tell himself it was nothing. Being protective of a private message didn't mean anything.

His heart was on the verge of splintering, like glass hit by a piece of hail. The cracks hadn't formed yet, but the integrity was compromised.

He'd read that letter as soon as he had the opportunity, and he'd give himself a good smack when he found it to be a simple message from one of the Tremantian humans.

That's all it will be.

***

A knock sounded low on her door, and Sophia sprang to answer it.

Her heart leapt when she found Sikthand waiting for her. She studied his expression, noting the tightness around his mouth and the way his hood seemed to grow into a sharper triangle when he was tense. Her gut roiled.

She pressed a hand to her heart. "He's dead."

Sikthand shook his head and stepped in. "Alive, well, and eating more food than a starved malginash."

Sophia cried out in relief. "Oh, thank God. You looked so down I thought he must have… Did he tell you anything?"

"Not yet. He needs time to understand he's safe. He's too scared to speak right now." Sikthand stepped toward an enormous barrel filled with purple-leafed fruit.

"Oh yeah." Sophia rushed over to the barrel and grinned. "This worked too. I was really nervous about it. It was like something out of a sitcom. After the streets cleared and Alno got me out of the alley, I stuffed myself into the barrel and he covered me with fruit. I was sure the guards at the door were going to dig through it. I mean, it's so absurdly large, but they just peeked in and moved the top layer of fruit around a bit then let him through." Sophia sidled closer, giving him a coy look from the corners of her eyes. He still looked stiff. "The fact that you had demanded *two* barrelfuls just a few weeks ago helped. Alno said the soldiers made some comments about how obsessed with this fruit I am. They joked that they should start stocking up in case any more human females came to visit."

"Perhaps Ezros will name the fruit after you."

Sophia's brows knitted. "Yeah, maybe." Sikthand had tried to make his voice light, but she'd heard the strain. His tone sounded way too similar to polite small talk. Should she mention the weather next or some shit? "Is everything alright?"

His mouth tightened, his jaw working. "It's been a long day. My nerves are worn." His fingers lifted and brushed across the area of her scalp where the fake blood had been. "I just wanted to check in on you before I went to sleep."

Disappointment welled in her throat. Sophia shook it away. *He's tired, so he's going to sleep. Stop overanalyzing it.*

Still, Sophia couldn't keep her mind from reexamining his shuttered expression late into the night. It hadn't been angry or suspicious or cold, even. It had almost been sad. But what sense did that make?

Even before they'd saved a boy's life—with an incredible performance on her part, if she did say so herself—they'd had a good day. She'd finally began to narrow down the candidates she liked, he'd dived face-first between her thighs showing her just how deep Clecanian women needed to be licked, and she'd even caught him smiling absently a handful of times.

What had happened at the infirmary?

35

Hours had never passed so slowly. Sikthand's eyes burned. His insides had that hollow feeling from lack of sleep, and every muscle in him was restless. A million possibilities had played through his mind since he'd seen Sophia reading the letter two nights before.

He'd spent the previous day hosting meetings with the Guild and lying about Sophia's assassination attempt. The Guild had scrambled to assure him that the culprit would be caught. He'd allowed his broodiness over the letter to shine in his expression and kept quiet. Everyone had seemed to attribute his silence to a simmering thirst for vengeance, which worked out well for him. At least he didn't have to concentrate on pretending everything was normal.

Sophia had remained locked in the royal wing, which had also helped his swarming mind. He hadn't had to worry about running into her. He'd sent word through Alno that he'd need to remain out for the night and that he'd miss their meeting.

It was a lie.

He'd returned to his room through his passages and slipped inside quietly, then he'd come here, to her mirror.

Until he saw what was in that letter, he wanted to keep his distance. No point in acting oddly toward her if it turned out to be nothing after all.

It was morning now, and she was nearly ready to leave for the day to tour the cloud chasers' training yard. They'd announced to the people that she would go on her tours as normal, which had had the unforeseen benefit of building a bit of respect in the Vrulans' eyes. From *their* perspective, their future queen had been shot and nearly killed, yet she was holding her head high and carrying on.

At long last, Sophia clomped out of her room. Sikthand remained in place until he could no longer hear the metal clanging of her armor, then stepped into her room and retrieved the message canister from her drawer.

He typed in her code, which he'd ensured he'd known as soon as she'd decided on one.

The canister popped open. Sikthand had one hand on each edge of the scroll, but he couldn't seem to make his hands pull it open. He'd wanted nothing more than to read this for over a day, but now apprehension set in.

It's likely nothing, he argued, before pulling the scroll wide. His mind shorted when foreign scribbling met his eyes. What language was this?

Paranoia building in his chest, he sped back to his room, retrieved a translation reading glass, and rushed back. Dark thoughts kept filtering into his mind, and he struggled to keep them under a net of rationality. Just because the message was written in a foreign language didn't mean it was willfully coded.

Fury had his muscles stiffening harder and harder as he passed the glass over the words and watched them translate into familiar Clecanian. What had Heleax done?

This king *thinks he can steal my bride away?* Sikthand would tear out his throat for the insult. And he'd tear out Heleax's for carrying this insidious offer to Sophia.

Sikthand's anger hardened like metal quenched in oil. This letter was old, the delivery date long past.

And Sophia had *kept* it.

Was she considering this offer? Why had she tucked the message away behind bedding? Why was she so nervous about someone walking in while she read it? Why was she rereading it at all?

His heart swelled in his throat. King Cueyar of *Roborh*.

She'd been reading about Roborh when he'd sought her out in the archives. Had she been considering his offer even then? Sikthand couldn't blame her if she had. At the time, he'd just nearly avoided assassination and she'd probably been worried he'd suspect her—which was fair, since he had, in fact, suspected her.

But now? After all their nights talking and touching? Was she still considering this?

He says he'll give you until the week before the Leaders' Summit to decide and then he will attempt to find a human elsewhere.

Sikthand rolled the scroll away and replaced it in her drawer before he accidentally crushed it in his palm.

The week before the Leaders' Summit was in eight days.

Sikthand stalked through the halls. He didn't know what to think or how to feel. She hadn't done anything, and yet the familiar taste of betrayal was bitter in his throat.

The world was a blur around him, his mind a tangle of rational and irrational thoughts. He reached the messenger station closest to their wing and searched until he spotted the male in charge. Focused on sorting through piles of waiting message canisters, the male didn't hear him approach. He caught sight of Sikthand's shadow falling over the table and jumped, letting out a startled bellow as he whirled.

"Sire," he breathed, gaze zooming around while he tried to gather himself. "I didn't—"

"I wanted to confirm that you are still notifying me of all messages sent to or from the human." Sikthand tried to recall whether he'd been told of the message from Roborh or not, but couldn't. He had no idea exactly when it had happened, but Sikthand had stopped making a point to read her correspondence.

Though the word was something shameful in his family, he'd started *trusting* her, and reading through her mail had felt more and more like a betrayal. It was an immensely hypocritical feeling considering he had no reservations about stalking her throughout the castle and watching her in her room.

The male was quick to nod. The metal headpiece he wore jiggled with the action. "Yes, sire. I've been sending a notification, then holding the mail for one day before delivering it, as you instructed."

"You sent a message when a delivery from Roborh arrived?" he growled.

The male's dark bronze hood paled. He scrambled over to a small book hidden under a stack of empty canisters and flipped through. His eyes slowed on one entry. "Yes. I sent word on..." The male swallowed. His hood was nearly gold now, the color continuing to drain. "Sire, I... On the day..."

Sikthand's anger built as he stammered on. "Spit it out."

"We were very busy that day and I set the message aside, but..." He licked his lips. "I now realize you were recovering from your...from the attempt on your life. I'm so sorry I didn't think harder on it. The time period passed, and I hadn't been given an order to continue to hold the mail so..."

Sikthand glared, his metal gloves scraping as his hands drew into fists. He wanted to release some of his pent-up aggression on the male, but he held it back. "If I can't count on you to use your head in a situation like that, then perhaps I need to employ someone new."

The male was shaking his head wordlessly.

Sikthand continued in a dangerous hiss, "If the human sends *any* mail, you will hold it until I have seen it. Do you understand? If that takes ten days, a year, then so be it."

"Yes," he squeaked.

Sikthand made to turn, but another squeak had him pausing. His gaze settled back on the nearly quivering male. "Is there something else?"

"It's just…the queen sent out a letter to Roborh weeks ago. I sent word. I didn't receive an order to hold, so…"

Sikthand's stomach bottomed out.

He left without another word, trying to force breath to resume moving through his lungs.

He was furious. With King Cueyar, with Heleax, with the messenger, with Sophia.

But most of all, he was disappointed in himself. As soon as he'd met Sophia, he'd known she was dangerous to him. Nothing about this situation should feel like a sucker punch.

He'd deluded himself into believing that he was building something with her. Something that would last, even though nothing lasted. Nothing good anyway.

He trudged out of sight until he was sure no one was watching, then disappeared into a passage. It was dark in here. And quiet. His mind whispered words of encouragement, but they felt hollow, empty.

There was no way to know what she'd said apart from asking. But if he asked, she'd know he'd breached her trust and read her mail. Even if she'd turned down the king, she could still change her mind after hearing that. She could decide that his invasion of her privacy was the final blow and send another letter accepting the king's offer.

What if she had already accepted? What was she waiting for, if so? Wasn't her continued presence in Vrulatica proof that she'd turned him down?

Unless…

What if she planned to leave after the vote? What if she was staying only to ensure he voted for her pick and then planned to vanish in the night? Off to live in Roborh where flowers sprouted thickly from the earth and the clouds were fluffy and white?

No. Sophia wouldn't do that. His chest ached as he earnestly tried to believe those words.

Their relationship had started roughly, but they'd turned a corner. She sought him out, tried to get him to smile. She'd taken him in her mouth and let him kiss her lips. She acted upset when he didn't have time for her, as if she *liked* spending time with him.

That couldn't be fake. Not all of it.

She wasn't going to leave. This paranoia was just from old wounds turning his thoughts malignant. Sikthand rose and stepped quickly toward their wing.

He set his mind to burying the cynical whispers that told him to study and spy and suspect. They reminded him he'd been blindsided before. He could be wrong now. The same way he'd been wrong about Japeshi.

He pressed the memories back. He'd been happy a day ago. Blissful. He wouldn't let his past taint the only good thing in his miserable life.

Sophia would stay. He would go to the Leaders' Summit and submit their vote in two weeks. Then he would come back, she would happily marry him, he would finally allow himself to fully take her body with shaft and fang, and he would win her affection.

Hours later, he sat with Sophia in his study and knew all his efforts to put the letter from his mind were in vain.

What would he do without her? Like an infection, weakness had snuck into his heart without him knowing and silently spread. He was dependent on her. On her scent and her presence and her taste. He honestly didn't know what would happen if she betrayed him. With a terrifying uncertainty, he wondered whether his mind would break.

She scrunched her nose at something in the file she was reading and peered up at him.

If she was planning to leave him, how could she sit there so casually? She had either turned down the king, or Sikthand had been fooled by someone who had no heart to speak of. She'd said she was a good actress, but how good?

"Sikthand." He brought his vision back into focus and found her watching him with knitted brows. "Are you okay? It's like you didn't even hear my question."

Had she asked him something? "What was the question?"

Pressing her lips together, she moved the file aside and crossed to him.

His body tensed fiercely as she lowered into his lap. She'd done this on a few occasions now, and he loved it. She'd usually kiss him while sitting here.

But the purr in his chest didn't rise.

She hooked her hands around his neck. A wave of intense possessiveness crashed through him, and he nearly pushed her away. All he wanted to do was claw at her dress, force her neck to his mouth, and bury his fangs so deep no healer could ever remove his marks.

With shaky hands that wanted to restrain, he guided her to rise. The look of hurt and confusion in her eyes scalded him, but his old wounds threatened his control. "We need to get through these last few candidates so we can discuss your pick for the Summit. We don't have much time left." He forced a smile, hoping she'd believe his weak excuse.

Her lips pursed and she studied him suspiciously, clearly not believing a word. "Alright," she said, apparently deciding not to press him for now.

They sat back down, and Sikthand's tail swished over the ground. She eyed the movement with furrowed brows, then peered back at her file.

If she were planning on leaving, she'd tell him.

Stupid. No, she wouldn't. If she even had a fraction of an inkling of how he would take that news, she'd try to fly herself out on a malginash before telling him.

But we were growing closer... he thought. Surely Roborh and the vote weren't good enough reasons for her to betray him.

It's only the vote that will decide which powerful Clecanian will guide the very lives of her species.

He hated the voice hissing through his mind, and he hated how effortless it was for him to believe the worst rather than give her the benefit of the doubt.

"What if I don't vote for who you request?"

Sophia's head snapped up. "What?"

"Say we go through all the candidates, and I don't agree with who you pick, so I vote for someone else. What would you do?"

Her jaw dropped open, and fire lit behind her eyes. "We had a deal, Sikthand! Are you saying you aren't—"

"Hypothetically," he interrupted. "If I didn't vote for your choice, what would you do?"

Her jaw snapped closed, and she glared at him for a moment. "Well, *hypothetically*"—she said the word with a sneer—"I'd be really fucking pissed off. And *hypothetically* I'd take that shiny retractable spear you gave me to train with, and *hypothetically* I'd shove it up your ass." She fell back in her seat with a huff and flipped through the pages in front of her.

"You think you could shove that pole up my ass, little human?" He couldn't help but allow the warmth to chase away some of his misery and grinned at her ridiculous statement.

At his raised brows, she shrugged. "*Hypothetically.*"

"And in reality?"

Sophia let out a huff and flattened the papers in her lap. "What is going on with you? Are you seriously thinking about reneging on our deal?"

Sikthand said nothing. It was completely out of line, but he wanted her to tell him that it wouldn't matter. That she'd marry him regardless.

When he only stared, waiting for an answer, she shook her head and peered up at the ceiling.

Her eyes scanned the lights above while she thought. "I honestly don't know. I'd be really upset. That's all I know for sure."

"Would you still marry me?" he asked, the emotion bubbling inside came out as a growl, though he wasn't feeling angry.

A line appeared between her brows. She tilted her head at him, seriously considering his question. "I don't think I can answer that. My instinct is no—unless you had a very, very good reason. You'd be breaking my trust. Why would I marry someone who does that?"

Sikthand's insides were crumbling. She wasn't wrong. Sophia respected herself. Why would she marry someone who broke their word?

"But it's not that simple, is it?" She sighed. "Marrying you and becoming queen would still mean I could help my people. So, I suppose I don't really have a choice. But it would be a cold marriage, like you said." Her gaze rose to his. "Do you still want that? A cold marriage?"

Sikthand swallowed. King Cueyar had offered her a romantic marriage. He'd offered her the vote and a throne. Roborh was also a gentler city. Humans would be much more excited to live there than they would in the stormy, technologically bare city of Vrulatica.

If Sophia's decisions were solely driven by where she could make the most impact and give the best life to humans, he'd be an idiot to think she'd remain here. Even if she felt something for him, it would be in her best interest to go, and there was no argument Sikthand could make for why he and Vrulatica were the better choice. He could only hope she was honorable enough to keep her word.

So, did he want a cold marriage? *No.* His insides screamed for him to say the word aloud, but revealing the change of his heart would leave him vulnerable.

Sophia's lips pulled down the longer the silence stretched. He didn't know what to say.

"I think I'll head out for the night," Sophia murmured, gathering her things. Before she left, she turned to him, her eyes glassy. "Don't do anything foolish, okay?"

He wanted to burst out laughing. He'd fallen in love with his future wife. He was the biggest fool of them all.

36

"Nothing?" Sophia questioned.

Alno shrugged from his relaxed spot on a couch in the archives. "No. Not *nothing*. The king has plenty of reasons to be acting weirdly, but none of them are things you don't already know. Maybe the boy said something to him that freaked him out. Maybe he truly doesn't think you're going to pick a good candidate. Think of how difficult of a position that would put him in."

"Thanks for the vote of confidence," Sophia grumbled.

"He could be pushing you away for countless reasons." Alno crossed and recrossed his legs which were extended on an ottoman. "And I don't mean to offend, but didn't you say he wanted a cold marriage? Maybe he's trying to reinforce that relationship before the wedding."

"That's what he said early on, but after we…" Sophia crossed her arms over her chest. "I just thought things had changed. I mean, we haven't exactly been *cold* to each other." She gave Alno a meaningful look.

He thought for a moment. "Have you had sex?"

Sophia sighed, her head pulsing from all the overanalyzing she'd been doing. "Well…no. But…" She shook her head. "There was more to what we *did* do. It didn't feel…I don't know how to describe it, but it wasn't casual. There was something there. I don't want him to push me away." Her voice was almost a whine, and her neck heated in embarrassment. *Grow up, girl.*

Alno chuckled humorously. "Look, you asked him whether he wants a cold marriage. He said yes."

"No," she rushed, pointing her finger. "He *didn't* answer, so that's…" Her grinning nod fell as she heard her own argument out loud. "That's closer to yes than no, isn't it?"

"You can't force it either way. You think I don't want to decide how Difila feels about me? I can shower her with gifts and orgasms and compliments as much as I want, but if she doesn't want to marry me, I can't control that."

Sophia slumped back in her seat, the scroll she was meant to be reading sat untouched in her lap. She was confused and heartsick. A deep ache had taken up residence in her chest since two nights before when she'd left Sikthand's study.

She'd only seen him once since then, when he'd come to tell her that the young apprentice had finally started speaking. The boy had revealed that a cloaked male had given him a vial of notak venom from the icy city of Aqoneron and made him inject it into Ahea's thick hide the next time he went to see his friend who saddled malginash.

The poor thing hadn't wanted to hurt the creature, but the male had threatened his father. When the boy had rushed back to Zommah's shop, too ashamed of himself to go home, he'd walked in to find Zommah spitting up blood, and the cloaked man standing over him. The boy had run, but the male had caught him.

Sikthand had walked into Sophia's room, dropped this news, then left, claiming he had meetings to go to concerning a Tagion sighting in the Choke. His twenty-minute visit had been so…formal. Civil. And yet so serious.

Sophia had wanted to reach out, grip his hand, and assure him they'd figure out who this assassin was, but she didn't know if she was allowed to anymore. Would he pull away if she tried to touch him? She didn't think her pride could handle that.

The day wore on, and Sophia remained lost in thought. Sikthand had sent another message to Alno to tell her that he wouldn't be meeting with her again tonight, and she'd deflated even more.

"Time for dinner?" Alno asked, yawning and stretching.

"You go ahead. I'm not hungry. Just make sure my guards are still outside when you pass them."

After a few minutes of urging Alno to leave while he pretended—poorly—that he'd rather hang out with her mopey ass, he finally sped away to the dining hall.

The archives were so quiet tonight. The silence *should* have been relaxing, but her mind was far too loud. She needed a distraction.

Sighing, she got up and gathered her things. She walked down the stairway leading to the second floor, then paused halfway to the door. She surveyed the large room for any signs of life. Confirming she was alone, she crept toward the back wall of the archives until she casually loitered near the corner where she knew a hidden panel lay.

She searched for it but, unsurprisingly, found nothing. Pulling scrolls and running her fingers over the woodwork revealed no secret buttons or latches. Leaning in, she placed her chin on the edge of a shelf and breathed deeply, shutting her eyes.

She pictured the darkness of the little cubby. The recalled sensation of Sikthand's breath on her neck and his hands dragging down her belly made her shiver in the warm air.

Though heat curled in her stomach, it was quickly overtaken by a hollow ache. She was falling for the king.

If she was honest with herself, she'd already fallen for him.

It was true that he'd never reciprocated her affection out loud, but she'd thought she'd been able to read between the lines. Had she been naïve to think she understood the damaged alien king?

She'd thought he'd sought her out far more often than she did him, but had she been imagining that, too? Though Vrulatica was vast, he always seemed to appear wherever she was. That couldn't be a coincidence. She could chalk it up to him checking in on the troublesome human to make sure she stayed alive, but the way he looked at her made Sophia believe there was more to it.

She pulled away from the shelves and peered inside. "Do you follow me around in those tunnels, Sikthand?" Sophia whispered the words, but she kept squinting into the cracks of the wall. They appeared solid from this direction.

After a minute more of perfect stillness and silence, Sophia sighed and left the unassuming corner before someone caught her lingering and started poking around. She stepped out of the archives and waited for her guards to gather around her.

She didn't know where she wanted to go exactly, only that returning to her lonely rooms made her chest tighten. Where else could she explore?

She glanced up and down the corridor and considered for a moment how interesting Vrulatica was. In any other circumstance, the width and openness of the space in front of her would be called a street, but it was an interior and had no transportation. Paved with gleaming stone and mosaic, it was simultaneously a busy pedestrian thoroughfare and an enormous castle hallway. Weird and wonderful.

She smiled gently. Not only had she grown to care for Sikthand, but she loved Vrulatica too. It was a bit more violent than many places, but she found that to be riveting. People were passionate here, and artistic and unconcerned with how the rest of the world felt about them. She started walking down the street, nodding to Vrulans as they passed by.

A few stopped to tell her how happy they were that she'd survived, and her chest warmed with fuzzy heat. A bittersweet thought curled in her heart, and she let it linger. She could pour her love into the city if Sikthand wouldn't take it.

"How do you get to the Heroes Hall from here?" she asked one of her soldiers, who straightened as though surprised she'd spoken to him directly.

They guided her through midcity, then down almost all the way to lowcity. The memorial area called Heroes Hall occupied an entire floor and was only accessible through a grand stairway.

Above the stairway was the open core of the tower stretching ten stories high. A hanging sculpture of clouds, deadly thrashing malginash, and falling warriors were suspended in the jaw-dropping area.

A large light shone from the ceiling far above and broke through the hanging sculpture, shooting beams through the clouds as if she were staring up at a deadly but beautiful battle taking place in the sky. Sophia removed her helmet, needing to see the artwork unimpeded.

"*The Taming of the Malginash*," one of her guards provided when she remained frozen in place, her mouth open and her neck craned back painfully. "The name of the work."

"Wow." Sophia smiled. "It's incredible."

She continued down the steps, mentally laying out a large back piece depicting that sculpture. Maybe on her way out, she could find a nice spot with a good perspective and sketch out her design. She'd brought her book with her after all.

Sophia had always enjoyed going to museums on Earth, finding a quiet spot and drawing one piece of art or another. *I'm going to see SAM,* she'd tell her friends. Whenever she said that, they knew not to expect to hear from her all day because she'd be parked somewhere in the Seattle Art Museum until it closed.

Towering sculpted Vrulan historical figures lined the hall like massive sentries. Some were simple likenesses, while others were glorious works of forged art. Sophia paused her meandering at an enormous statue of a golden soldier astride his malginash.

The body of a four-armed Tagion was hanging limply from the malginash's antlers. Gored, but left on display. It was like many renaissance paintings she'd seen, gruesome but somehow also created with enough movement and drama to make the gore beautiful. The musculature of the dead Tagion was spectacular.

Sophia breathed out a sigh. Had Ahea ever gored anyone? Probably.

She continued on a few steps, then froze when she spotted another visitor. Madam Kalos. Sophia groaned. She really didn't feel like company tonight, but Madam Kalos had already spotted her. She couldn't slink away now without being rude.

Sophia crossed to the woman and her guard. "Good evening, Madam Kalos."

"Good evening, Sophia. What brings you to the hall?" The madam's eyes flicked over Sophia's armor. Though the tradition of rulers wearing armor had been in place for decades now, Madam Kalos had been quite vocal about her dislike of the practice. *A ruler should not shield themselves from their people. It sets a precedent of suspicion.*

"The artwork. It's incredible. It seems ridiculous that I didn't make a point to come here sooner." Sophia slipped off her helmet again and glanced up at the statue Madam Kalos was admiring.

Madam Kalos nodded absently. "Isn't he magnificent?"

The man, molded in iron and steel, was tall and sturdy and wore a pompous expression. Sophia didn't think he was particularly magnificent compared to the other sculptures, but she nodded anyway.

"He was my grandfather," Madam Kalos whispered conspiratorially, as though telling a stranger she was related to a celebrity.

Sophia tried to feign excitement. "Really? Wow. Who was he?"

Madam Kalos gave a satisfied smile and turned back toward the statue. "He was the head of trade too. He did so much for our city. His clever trade deals funded the restoration of our schools, you know?"

"That's...incredible." It wasn't. Sophia regretted coming down here. Now, instead of sketching the statues like she'd wanted, she was engaging in polite forced conversation with the dull woman. After an awkward moment of silence, she tried to escape. "Well, it was nice to run into you. I hope you have a pleasant night."

Sophia began walking, squinting, and hoping she could get away without a fuss. She'd made it a few feet when Madam Kalos called out to her. "Sophia, since I have a moment with you, I wondered if you've narrowed down your selections any further."

It took everything in her not to groan as Kalos and her guard sped up to join her on her walk. "I've narrowed it down to five, but I still have two more candidates I need to research."

They rounded a corner, and the statues became simpler and less refined, as though they'd all been built from the period of time in Vrulan history known as the Warp. War, contaminated reservoirs, and a decade-long drought had ensured everything to come out of the Warp was solemn and lacking in extravagant detail.

Sikthand's oldest ruling ancestor had taken power during that time. Sophia scanned the statues, wondering if that relative was among them. She was half tempted to ask Madam Kalos, but she didn't want to encourage conversation more than she already was.

"And what of Maddar? Have you revisited her file as I requested?"

Sophia kept her groan inside and plastered on a fake smile. "Yes. I looked at her file again." She hadn't. "I just don't think she's a good fit. She's very…spirited about the projects she fights for." Translation: *impulsive*. "But her follow-through isn't great. I'm worried she'd get big ideas in her head and work toward them without thinking. We can't afford to be hasty."

"She is passionate," Madam Kalos argued. "She may have grand ideas, but she follows through. Aqoneron is in the process of building a space elevator because of her."

Sophia sighed, growing more and more irritated. It was clear Madam Kalos was in no way objective. After Sophia had complained about the way Madam Kalos had been hounding her about the candidate, Sikthand had revealed that she and Maddar were longtime friends who shared unrealistic visions for their cities.

Both women had an *act now, worry later* state of mind. "She's building a space elevator in *Aqoneron*? The city notorious for its near-constant blizzards? You see how that might seem to some to be…poorly…planned…"

Her blood rushed to her head, and Sophia nearly stumbled a step forward.

Aqoneron?

Based on the description of the liquid Zommah's apprentice had given, combined with what the veterinarian knew of how it had affected Ahea, Sikthand had determined that the poison used was notak venom. The only city in the world to produce that was Aqoneron.

Madam Kalos' voice came back to Sophia after a moment. "…the world will be in awe when the elevator is completed. The fact that the city isn't ideal will make it all the more impressive, and the revenue it will generate will be city changing."

As they walked, Sophia furtively inched away from the woman. She couldn't be responsible, could she?

Madam Kalos had always been a little intense, but she cared. She'd always tried to show Sophia a bit of kindness. Then again, her kindness had usually come with remarks about her species, as though she were gracing the dumb human with her benevolent compassion.

"I thought Maddar was from Huvuita," Sophia said, trying like hell to keep her expression normal. How should she look again? Relaxed? Vaguely annoyed? "That's what my file said."

"Oh, she had to relocate recently. Huvuita is a backward place. They rage against change even more than we do, if you can believe it."

Sophia caught sight of Madam Kalos' guard walking on her far side and realized he was staring at her, studying her.

Was she being paranoid? She covertly took a deep breath and forced herself to relax.

"Are you feeling alright, dear?" Madam Kalos stopped her with a raised brow. "You smell like something has startled you."

Shit. She gripped her helmet a little tighter, and wondered if there was any good excuse for her to put it back on.

She pointed to a grisly statue of a man tearing out another man's innards. "That caught me off guard. It's a bit brutal, no?" She gave a little chuckle and tried to make sure it didn't sound flat. She had no idea whether she'd succeeded.

Everyone except for the madam's guard peered over to the statue. The guard stayed focused on Sophia. Alarm bells flared in her mind. Fuck, how could she control her damn smell?

"Oh, yes. One of your future husband's kin." Madam Kalos turned back toward her, and Sophia saw a flash of repugnance she'd never caught before.

An idea suddenly lit in her mind. "Yes. I *know*. Back on Earth things like that don't happen too often. Every time I think of Sikthand's family and what might happen to me as his queen, I can't control my reaction." She shook her head and made a show of peering over to the statue and shivering. "Humans are much gentler. Probably since we're so much weaker."

Her insides rejoiced when Madam Kalos gave her a sympathetic smile. Sophia had to keep herself from flinching when she reached out to gently pat her arm.

Her answering smile fell when Madam Kalos didn't remove her hand. "Aklin?" she said.

Sophia didn't have time to figure out what *Aklin* was before the guard rasped, "She knows."

Quicker than she could process, Madam Kalos and her guard drew weapons.

Sophia's poor soldiers were just as surprised as her. The one closest to her flew backward as though someone had pulled his legs out from under him. The second guard reacted a second too late, and Madam Kalos snuck her long thin blade through the sliver between his helmet and chest plate, sinking the blade into his throat. Blood flowed out of his neck, painting his bright silver armor red. The other guard, who'd been tripped by Aklin's tail, was now struggling to free his axe from its holster as Aklin raised a blunt hammer and smashed it down against the side of his helmeted head twice.

Sophia stumbled away but tripped in her clunky armor. Falling to her ass, she crab-walked backward as she watched the double homicide unfold—soon to be triple.

Madam Kalos turned her attention to Sophia and was prowling toward her, a disgusted look on her face. "Did you really think I wouldn't be able to sniff out a lie? You puff up like an angry cethid every time I call humans weak, simple girl." The woman sighed and peered down at the blood dripping from her weapon. "What a waste. I was really excited about you. The prestige of a human queen." She raised a reverent palm into the air, then dropped it with a sneer. "A few more drops of notak venom, and that useless king would finally be dead." She shook her head sadly. "I would've made sure a better male took the throne. One worthy of a human queen. One who would strive to make our city the most glorious place on Clecania. You and I could have worked together. But now..." She gestured disappointedly at her as Sophia freed a small blade from her hip and brandished it. "What a waste," she repeated.

The soldier's legs stopped moving, and Kalos' guard, who must've been named Aklin, rose to his full height. Sophia let out a strangled whimper.

"Sikthand!" she yelled as Aklin drew closer.

Madam Kalos looked behind her while laughing. "Did you hit your head when you fell, or are humans really that thick? He's not here." Her cruel smile warped into a scowl. "How did you know? It must have been something I said."

"Aqoneron, Madam." Aklin holstered his hammer and lifted the dead soldier's axe. "That's when her scent changed."

Sophia tried to scramble away, but it was like something out of a nightmare. Her armor was so cumbersome she felt like she was moving through mud.

"Hmm, I'll have to remember to play down my friendship with Maddar in the future." She waved a dismissive hand. "Go ahead, Aklin. Before anyone sees."

Sophia screamed as he advanced.

A whoosh sounded in the air a second before an axe sliced into the armor covering Aklin's chest. The guard sailed across the room, only stopping when the axe had buried itself in a charcoal-gray statue, spearing Aklin through and through.

Sophia whirled around. Her heart nearly exploded at the sight of Sikthand. He was shrouded head to toe in armor, and his frame swelled with deadly rage. The light shining behind him sliced off his razor-sharp antlers.

Madam Kalos stumbled back but seemed to realize there was no way to outrun him. Disgusting metal-on-metal scraping came from Aklin's jittering form as he died skewered to the statue of a glaring warrior.

Kalos gripped her weapon and, in a last-ditch effort, threw it hilt over blade at Sikthand's chest. Sophia shrieked, throwing herself onto her knees and trying to bolt toward him.

He caught the blade in his metal-gloved hand and tossed it away like a bit of trash. Like a predator beginning to charge, his steps picked up speed.

Madam Kalos snarled at him. "You were always a foul excuse for a—"

Sikthand's tail slashed out, and Madam Kalos blinked. For a moment Sophia couldn't understand what had happened, but then a bright red line appeared across Madam Kalos' neck. Blood seeped out of the slice and dribbled down her teal dress. She coughed, spraying blood across Sikthand's armor.

He rotated away from her as she crumpled to the ground, gurgling and clutching her throat.

In two long strides he was in front of Sophia. He knelt and tore off his helmet. His nostrils flared as he inhaled uneven breaths. It looked like he was just managing to hold himself together, his face stonier than she'd ever seen it.

He reached out toward her cheek, but his hand shook. He pulled it back, curling his fingers into a fist to still his trembling. "Are you…" His voice was strangled, both words an effort to push out.

"I'm fine. Totally fine," she assured in a whisper.

Her insides were rioting, and tears sprung to her eyes. She didn't know what to do in this moment. She didn't know what to say or whether to say nothing at all. He was scared and full of aggression.

Her words remained trapped in her throat. Finally, she roused, pointing down the hall. "My guards. Can you check if they're alive?"

Sikthand stared at her for a moment longer, his neck muscles bulging, then gave a short nod and walked away. He glanced between her and Madam Kalos' body when he neared it. Seeming to worry that she'd suddenly wake and attack, Sikthand dug his fingers into her coiffed hair and dragged her limp form along behind him as he made his way to the downed soldiers.

Nausea rose in Sophia's gut at the action, and she shot her gaze to the floor.

What do I do? What do I do?

Panic sparked in her chest, making the nausea worse, but it had nothing to do with the four dead people lying in bloody pools all around her. It was because she'd seen Sikthand's eyes up close when he'd removed his helmet…and they'd been solidly black.

He'd recognized her—at least with initial recognition.

Sophia peered up and watched as Sikthand checked on the two men. A silver gaze met hers.

I can't tell him.

***

Foreboding slid through her veins like askait ink. Sophia paced her room, trying to decide what to do.

It had been hours since a troop of soldiers and Alno had escorted her back to the royal wing at Sikthand's command. There was a rather large mess to clean up, figuratively and literally. When Sophia had asked to help explain to the Guild what had happened, he'd taken her by the arm, and said, "I need you to be somewhere safe. I *need* to know that, or I won't be able to function."

At any other point in time, she might have argued, but she'd realized that even Sikthand wasn't aware how true his words were. A mated Clecanian was protective to a maddening degree, especially right before they got their marks.

Sikthand is my mate.

Initially, when her mind had really taken that fact in, her stomach had exploded with heart-shaped confetti. But then she'd recalled that his eyes had turned black once before, and he'd been left devastated and altered by it. The king was unmatched in the *trust issues* department.

No one else had seen his eyes change, and even if they had, Sophia didn't think he'd believe them. The betrayal last time had been so vile, so utterly sickening, that telling him about his eyes felt oddly cruel.

But was it right to keep something like that from him?

She couldn't decide.

Sikthand *was* her mate. Though she didn't know how, she'd felt it from the moment she'd first laid eyes on him. He was hers, and she refused to do anything to hurt him. The only thing that would truly convince him the recognition was real this time would be when the true secondary recognition occurred and marks appeared on his hands.

She could wait for that. Sophia would be patient, and apart from that one detail about his eyes changing, she wouldn't hold anything back from him. No more uncertainty, no more wondering whether he wanted her or not. This proved he did even if he fought against it.

She collapsed onto her couch and stared into the cold hearth. Though she wished there were a fire so her eyes had something to watch while she thought, she couldn't ask Alno here to start one. She'd sent him away as soon as they'd arrived, needing time alone to think.

She rubbed at her chest and thought of Sikthand. The ache had deepened into something nearly untenable. Where was he?

She slipped her sketchbook out of her bag and flipped to an empty page. Though it was dim in her room since she hadn't bothered to turn the lights on, she began sketching the memory of his body when he'd arrived in the Heroes Hall. A glorious, vengeful monster. *Her* monster. Her shadow. Always emerging from the darkness when she needed him.

He'd appeared again. She'd called him, and he'd appeared.

Had he been watching her already? Had it just been luck?

She huffed out a breath, scribbling over the sketch and slamming the book closed. *Where is he?*

It'd been hours. He'd told her he'd be back by now.

Sophia caught sight of herself in the mirror and smoothed her nearly dry hair. Her hands froze. She stared at the mirror.

Thoughts zoomed through her mind, and she forced her eyes to the floor.

He had passages *everywhere*. He always seemed to know where she was, and he'd known other things too.

She'd always just assumed they were coincidences or that he was incredibly intuitive, but…what if it was more than that?

The first night she'd been here she'd examined her battered back. The next day Sikthand had demanded she go to the medic. When she'd decided to go to the Flesh Forge, he'd appeared at the Flesh Forge.

Sophia stared around her room, recalling the items that had appeared right when she'd needed them.

She'd always attributed it to Alno, thanking him though he'd continued to claim he didn't know what she was talking about. Sophia peered down at her sketchbook.

Had Sikthand been watching her this whole time? Had he seen her cry and throw her sketchbook into the fire?

Tears welled in her eyes. Her chin wobbled and her brows furrowed.

Did he get me a new book and leave it in my room?

Her heart skipped. She sniffed. She should be mad. Furious.

If she was right, it meant he'd been watching her all along, spying, invading one of the only places she'd thought she could be alone. But she couldn't seem to feel anything less than heart-wrenching love.

Though he must fight against it with every fiber of his being, he was her mate. Of course he watched her.

She set her sketchbook aside and rose. Her bare feet were silent as she stepped toward her reflection. She didn't look at herself, though—she tried to look *through* herself.

There was one other trick she remembered from Claire's safety PowerPoint. How to check for two-way mirrors.

Breath stalled and heart thundering in her throat, she stepped right up to the mirror and lifted her finger. If it was a normal mirror, when she pressed the tip of her finger to the glass there would be a gap between her fingertip and her reflection's fingertip.

She touched the mirror.

No gap.

Her palm flattened on the glass, and she stared at her reflection, wishing she could see him. She peered above her head toward where his eyes might be. Was he back there?

Her fingers slipped away from the glass. She might not be able to tell him he was hers yet, but she couldn't go another minute without seeing him.

37

Sikthand raised his palm to Sophia's. He didn't know what she was doing, but his throat bobbed at the near contact. She was so close. Less than an inch away.

He'd been here for hours now, just staring and trying to get this screaming lighting every nerve to calm before he went to her. Even watching her, which usually soothed him, had only managed to muffle the scream to a fuzzy roar.

She'd almost died.

And worse, she'd almost died at the hands of two people he hadn't been suspicious of at all. It felt like a personal failure. His instincts were too disordered as of late. Did he no longer have the skill to sniff out dissension within his city? How could he ever hope to keep his fragile human safe?

A vise had wrapped itself around his chest as soon as he'd understood the danger she'd been in. The only peephole in the Heroes Hall had been far away. The minutes it had taken him to dash to the secret exit a few halls down were the worst minutes he'd ever experienced. Each crunch of his boots against the ground had filled him with fear like he'd never known.

He'd prayed they'd question her, torture her, anything to give him more time to get to her. Luckily, they had.

She was alive and whole and standing right in front of him. Less than an inch separated their palms. His body nearly shook just from looking at her.

If he hadn't been so overcome, so mindless, he would've spent more time ripping those two apart.

He would've made it last.

He would've made it hurt.

Tail wrapped around his thigh to keep it from thrashing about, it squeezed his leg, sending spikes of pain through his bones. All he wanted to do was walk into her room, but he didn't know that he was safe for her right now. He felt too out of control. What if he dragged her into his arms too aggressively and hurt her?

He'd wondered before whether his mind would break without her. He had his answer.

Even now, with her standing right in front of him, his mind was close to unraveling. She couldn't see him like this. He'd scare her away.

Her eyes lifted to his, and his breath froze.

No. She wasn't seeing him. She couldn't be.

Sophia's palm slipped away from his, and his fingers curled against the mirror. It took much more willpower than it should've for him not to punch through the glass and pull her hand back.

Confusion filtered in through his chaotic thoughts as she stepped purposefully around her room. She grabbed two glass bottles from her desk and crossed to her door.

Misery carved out a space in his chest when she angled one bottle against the door the way she had on her first night here. As a booby trap to alert her to unwanted visitors.

She was scared again. Not able to feel safe even in their wing with him just down the hall.

She placed the second bottle against the door that led to his room, then stepped back to her mirror. Sikthand's brows knit. Her expression didn't look scared.

Her breaths were coming fast, a rising flush hit her cheeks. What was she doing?

He had to bury a choked growl when her fingers slipped under the hem of her sleeping gown and she pulled it over her head, baring herself. A pop sounded from his hip as his tail constricted, pulling his thigh in an unnatural direction.

Sikthand blinked. He shouldn't look. He should turn his back or run to his room. Anything but look at her naked body while she was unaware.

A purr rumbled in his chest, the allure of her body no match for the battle waging inside. He was unable to move, unable *not* to look. His cock swelled beneath his armor, and his heart throbbed at the sight of her exquisite body.

What are you doing to me, my love?

Though she was only a foot away, it might as well have been another galaxy. His fingers brushed over the glass, tracing along her curves.

"Are you watching, Your Majesty?"

In that instant, there were statues more capable of movement than he was. Had she just…

She must have been talking to herself.

Her eyes lifted again and landed eerily close to where his were. Sophia's chin raised in challenge, and she turned away. His shock still rocked through him, his mind torn between working out whether she knew he was behind her mirror or admiring her round backside as she sauntered away.

His growl broke through when he realized where she was headed.

Sophia stopped in front of the door to his room. His heart thundered to life, but he was still too enraptured to breathe. Her hand lifted—not to the latch of the door, but to the switch that would send a bell dinging in his room.

A bell that meant she wanted him to come to her. His fangs pulsed in time with his shaft. A bell that meant she wanted him to fill her.

She didn't pull it right away, and Sikthand thought he might die of anticipation, but then she peered over her shoulder, at the mirror…at *him*, and pulled the switch.

Sikthand's mind whirred. The bottles, her words, her focused stare.

She knows.

He finally sucked in a breath as he watched her walk to the center of the room, stopping under the bright beam of light that made her skin glow.

An odd calmness spread over him as he gazed at her. She was not staring at either door. Her focus was utterly and completely on the mirror. Sure, he could leave, go to his room, and make a show of entering through the passage, but he didn't want to.

"I need to see you, Sikthand." There was a desperation in her voice that clawed at his chest.

This was the end.

His hand lifted to the latch. The control he'd been scratching and clawing for with bloody fingers and bared fangs was dissolving before his eyes. He couldn't fight anymore.

She was inevitable.

If he'd ever had any power, it was hers now. *He* was hers now.

***

Every cell in Sophia's body was lit with electricity. Apprehension, arousal, love, excitement. They all swirled and sent shivers through her. Was he here? Would he reveal himself?

Staring at her own naked body in the mirror built up her edginess. Her nipples were tight and sensitive in the cold air. She shifted from one leg to another, her limbs too restless to stay still. She felt her pulse thrum through her all the way to her toes.

The mirror shifted.

Sophia wobbled on her feet. Was she about to pass out, or had the mirror actually moved?

Her inhales shallowed as the mirror swung open inch by inch. Her reflection warped, then disappeared from view. Goose bumps raced over her exposed skin as the towering frame of Sikthand filled a black cavity where her mirror once was.

Ever so slowly, he stepped through the threshold. She was so sensitive that she jumped as his heavy boots hit the ground and sent vibrations through her bare heels.

Once he was through, he straightened again. Her fingers went numb as she caught sight of his black eyes.

"You called," he rumbled in a deep, otherworldly growl.

Heat sliced through her belly and pooled in her core. She took in a shaky breath through rounded lips. "I knew it." The whisper was for her, but it seemed to spur him on.

Eyes black, he prowled toward her. Each light clink of his armor sent electricity skittering down her spine.

The king stopped right before her, and though she couldn't tell for sure when his eyes were black like this, she thought he was running his gaze over her figure. Her pussy throbbed.

The fact that she was completely naked and shaking under his black stare while he was clad to the neck in thick armor made the difference in their size even more unnerving. She had to crane her neck up to meet his eyes.

His sharp weapons glinted at his hips, and her gaze locked onto the sticky blood splashed across his chest.

He hadn't even changed. He'd come right to her mirror.

Though the sight of Madam Kalos' blood should unnerve her, it didn't. She licked her lips and felt the insides of her thighs dampen. This alien king—her mate—would slit anyone's throat if they threatened her. The knowledge was as heady as any aphrodisiac.

Though she didn't mind the blood, she needed to get to him, and from the rapid rise and fall of his chest, she thought he needed the same. With shaky fingers, she undid the straps and ties holding his armor in place.

He remained still, a muddled purring growl reverberating through him as he watched her undress him with greedy molten askait eyes. Each time she freed a piece, the rumble in his throat would deepen, and he'd slip it from her fingers, then toss it aside. She jerked every time the clang of metal thundered through the room.

When his upper body was free, she knelt to work on the armor on his legs. His ragged groan had her peering up. He stared down from his towering height like the vulnerable sight of her kneeling at his feet while he presided over her was filling his mind with horribly indecent thoughts.

Her mind filled with indecent thoughts of her own, and she pushed her thighs together to ease the pulsing in her core. He'd taken care of her, kept her safe, and now she'd take care of him.

After the last of the metal was removed from his tail, Sophia rose and watched with uneasy breaths as he slipped off his cooling suit. He kicked it to the side, and his impressive, beautiful dick bobbed.

Sikthand stepped toward her slowly, the tip of his cock pushing against her belly as he moved in close. Already slick with a bead of precum, the head of his shaft slipped up her skin when he drew her against his chest.

The scalding bar of his cock burned a line down the middle of her torso where it lay flat and hard against her stomach and ribs, the tip resting just below her sternum. His tail wrapped around her spine and forced her closer.

Running her palms over his sculpted pecs, she craned her face up to him. She studied his dark eyes, trying to hide the tears threatening to rise at the overwhelming fullness in her chest. "You saved me."

A hungry grin made his fangs flash. "Are you my reward, then?"

"Yes," she answered seriously. "You can have me any way you want."

His smile faded, but his grip around her back tightened.

"I knew you'd be there." Her voice came out breathy. "You're always there, aren't you?"

Sikthand's palm lifted to her cheek. A line formed between his brows as he scanned her face solemnly. "I shouldn't be," he whispered back.

She laid her palm over the top of his and urged, "But you are."

He stared at her, pain that mirrored the ache she felt in her heart, tightening his eyes. "But I am," he agreed.

Sophia lifted to her toes and brushed her mouth over his. He let out a deep sigh as if he'd just slipped into a hot bath before he kissed her back. His hand on her cheek tightened in time with his tail.

His lips were slow at first, sensual and firm, but as soon as his tongue slipped through her mouth, his movements changed.

His steel cock pressed into her belly so hard she could only suck in quick gasps. The soft fingers on her cheek snaked into the hair at her neck and firmed, his grip tight and commanding. Sophia whimpered when he forced her head to tilt to the side so he could deepen the kiss, consuming her with rough swipes of his tongue while his hips rolled, sliding his trapped shaft between their bodies.

His left palm came down hard on her ass, kneading until she cried out against his mouth. Nails sliding across his muscular back, Sophia wriggled in his hold. His cock was not where she needed it, and the slippery liquid leaking out of him had fire shooting through her veins.

He snarled at her attempts to wriggle free and bent further over her, forcing her back to bend. He spun them in place, then guided her back with deliberate steps. His relentless kiss rendered her a limp mess and she could only stumble backward in the direction he walked. Only his coiled tail kept her upright.

Suddenly, he pulled away. His hands, his mouth, his tail—they were all gone.

Sophia swayed forward with a whining moan. The black in his eyes swirled and darkened. He bared his fangs as he raked his gaze over her.

He reached one palm toward her chest, and her back arched in anticipation, her nipples crying out to feel his rough fingers. But he pressed his hand to her upper chest and sent her an evil grin.

With a firm push, she fell back. She cried out as she tried to get her balance, but his tail had wrapped behind her knees, and she tumbled over it. With a soft thump, she landed on her back in her bed.

Her heart thundered through her, then pulsed a steady maddening beat in her clit. She lifted to her elbows and watched his dark figure loom in the narrow opening of her bed. His face and body were nothing more than a backlit shadow from this angle. An enormous, hulking shadow that blocked her only escape from the bed.

A deep pulsing growl rumbled from his outlined form, and she trembled. His fingers slid behind her calves. He wrenched her toward him, kneeling simultaneously, so by the time her ass had slipped off the edge of the bed, his waiting tongue impaled her.

The cries and moans that burst from both of them at the connection fused and rang through the air. Sophia's knees pulled up and fell wide when his thick tongue dragged deep through her core. His rough fingers scraped up her ribs and flicked at her nipples until her eyes rolled back.

She lifted to her elbows again so she could watch him devour her, and moaned at the sight. Her hips jolted and rocked in time with his rolling tongue. Sikthand flattened a palm to her belly to keep her steady, and the pressure almost made her climax burst out of her.

"Y-Yes. Sikthand, yes. Please. That f-feels…" She couldn't take in air fast enough to get her words out.

Her shoulder curled in, and her hand reached down to grip his hair. She rode his tongue, her thighs clenching around his ears. He purred, and the vibration shot through her.

It was as if she were being electrocuted with pleasure. Her muscles seized, freezing and spasming as the vibration from his lips and tongue zinged through her clit and deep within her cunt.

Her thighs jerked around his ears as she came, and she let out a long high-pitched cry.

The two hard curves of his fangs pressed against her mound while he lapped up her come. Sophia fell back against the bed, running her hands down her face while letting out breathy whimpers. She jerked every time his tongue swept over her sensitive clit.

"This bed is too dark." His purr made his words choppy.

Her body moved like jello as Sikthand dragged her off the mattress and spun with her in his arms. He laid her on the soft rug beneath him and pinned her thighs open with his palms. "I will see your eyes roll as I split your little cunt."

Sophia nearly choked on her tongue. Her hips heaved forward with a mind of their own.

Sikthand stared down at her pelvis and released a dark chuckle. "Such a needy thing."

He scooted forward and gently but firmly replaced his hands holding her thighs open with his knees. Sophia's ass muscles clenched as her core gripped around nothing. He tilted his head, watching her body squirm under him as he palmed his shaft with his now free hand.

An ache built within her body again when she took in the sight of the thick head of his cock bulging out from the rough grip of his palm. She fondled her breasts, squeezing to relieve some of the pressure.

He pumped his hand over his shaft, swirling his palm across the head to spread his thick precum over the rest of him. His intense gaze seared into her pussy as he did this, his hips pumping slowly into his hand like he was imagining himself sliding into her core. He was making himself slick for her, she realized.

A desperate moan broke from her chest. She rose to her hands, but she could only lean so far forward with her legs trapped under his knees as they were. "Let me."

***

Sikthand took in Sophia's wide pupils. *Let me?*

A groan quaked out of him when she licked her lips, and he followed the direction of her gaze to his cock. His balls tightened painfully. He was practically strangling his dick to keep himself from shoving inside her like he wanted to.

"Stay put," he demanded, forcing her back down with a hand to her chest. The thundering beat of her heart pulsed through his palm, and his own heart seemed to change its tempo to match.

Lifting his knees off her, he lined up the head of his swollen shaft with her entrance. She was so small there, his tongue barely had room to delve. Her thighs shot up, her heels digging into his ass to spur him on. He slipped forward just barely and felt the first touch of her hot soft cunt.

Sikthand shuddered and let out a low growl. She lifted her hands, but before she could touch him, he wrapped one palm around her left bicep and the other around her throat and held her to the ground. "I said stay," he barked, his control slipping when her hips jerked, and she tried to press herself further onto his shaft.

Tension knotted his belly when he backed his hips up and she cried out. "No. Please. I need your c—"

Sikthand bared his fangs and squeezed her throat until her words cut out. He loosened his hold and watched her silently breathe. The scent of her arousal burst more heavily into the air, and Sikthand's arms shook. This female would be the end of him.

His words were guttural and groaned out of him. "Bride, I'm going to squeeze my cock inside you. Do not move until I'm done. You need to adjust before I fuck you. You understand?"

Sophia's head flapped up and down wildly. Her palms flattened against the ground and her muscles tensed as though she were going to try with everything she had not to move. Sikthand grinned at her enthusiastic submission.

He rewarded her by pressing against her core. There was a moment of resistance before her lips spread around his head and the wet heat of her cunt greeted him.

He hissed in a breath as he ever so slowly drove his cock deeper. Unable to tear his eyes away from the spot where their bodies connected, he watched as her soft belly trembled. Sweat lifted on his skin while he worked to keep his hips moving slow, waiting until her insides relaxed then clenched as if they were ready to drag him in further. Sophia's throat flexed under his palm as she whimpered and moaned.

If she had claws, they'd be buried in the stone floor from how hard her fingers clenched. Her eyes were squeezed shut, and a tear slipped down her cheek. He sank an inch deeper, and her body began to shake, her small breasts jiggling so exquisitely his fangs ached to bite into them.

"Just a bit more, then I'll make you come. Would you like that, my queen?"

"Y-Yes." A sob ripped from her throat, and her core gushed with liquid, making his cock slip into her more easily. Her head tipped back, her throat pressing more firmly into his palm. "Please, Sikthand. I can't keep still anymore." Her brows knit, and she opened her eyes to plead up at him.

He shoved into her the rest of the way with a growl, and her legs tensed as her eyes rolled back. She released a long throaty moan that made a knot tighten in his belly.

He needed her more slick before he fucked her. He needed to know he'd done everything he could to keep her from being hurt when he finally allowed his hips to move. His tail unwrapped from her leg, and the tip settled over her clit.

He gave Sophia's neck a little shake until she aimed her bleary lust-filled gaze at him. "My fangs will be inside you before this is through," he grated. "Do you understand?"

Her eyes widened. "Bite me," she begged breathlessly. "Bite me everywhere." Sikthand could feel his purr rising at her words, and his hips began to rock. She grinned wildly. His chest heaved. "Bite me so everyone can see the marks."

His control snapped at that. His purr thundered through his chest, and he pounded into her with hard heavy slaps. His tail, vibrating with his purr, curled and flicked over her clit, and he felt her insides clamp down as she came.

Her nails scratched over his arms as she screamed and shuddered in his hold. Her back bowed off the ground, her legs squeezing where they cradled his hips. He shot his hand under her back, gripping her ass to keep her body stable as he drilled into her. With his other hand he fisted her hair and lifted her head from the ground.

He pulled her neck to his mouth and buried his fangs in her tender throat. She writhed in his hold, her core convulsing around him again as though his bite and his vibrating tail slapping against her slippery clit had forced another orgasm to tear through her on the heels of the last.

The coppery tang of blood exploded on his tongue, and he groaned. She clutched his head to her neck, gripping his hair to keep his mouth in place. He lifted her hips a fraction higher so he could drive down deep into her.

With one hand still in her hair, Sikthand pulled her head back to take in the sight of her beautiful bloody throat and the angry evidence of his teeth. Her eyes were wide, and her lip was pulled in between her teeth. Her attention was rapt as she watched his cock slam in and out of her cunt.

He groaned down at the vision beneath him. She was more perfect than he could have dreamed. Whimpering and bloody and using her toes on his calves to gain purchase and meet his driving hips as though she couldn't take him deep enough.

His mouth came down over hers. She didn't turn her face away from the blood on his tongue—she licked and nipped and nearly drew blood of her own. He weighed her down, his chest crushing her into the floor, but she merely clutched his back and moaned under him.

"Come inside me. Bite me and come inside me. I need to feel it."

He groaned out a string of curses, his hips growing jerky. He pulled her head to the side with one hand in her hair. He gripped her hip with the other, pulling her down as he rammed up into her. His tail wrapped around her other thigh, holding her in place.

He purred and growled and panted against her shoulder as his cock pistoned into her. The knot in his stomach tightened and his dick swelled, her tight core clenching so hard it almost pained him.

He bit down on her shoulder, purr building at the sensation of his fangs dipping into her supple skin. She stiffened underneath him, then screamed as she came. His mind dimmed at the added pressure of her cunt spasming in time with her climax.

With his tail and his hand, he wrenched her down and buried himself as far as he could go. Sikthand quaked and roared against her shoulder, his cock shooting jets of cum into his bride's squeezing cunt.

His breaths shuddered out of him as the waves of pleasure tore through and made his vision go spotty. Curling forward, then relaxing, he softly pumped in and out of her.

When she began petting his back and gently moaning, his purr reemerged soft and nearly keening.

If he was to die, let it be now, while he was still buried in such paradise.

***

Sophia awoke to the sensation of being carried. The king's scent and his strong chest under her cheek had her insides fluttering. She was so happy she barely registered the soreness running through her body.

He crawled into her bed with Sophia tucked in his arms and laid her down. He crouched over her, his silver eyes just bright enough for her to see them within the dark confines of her malginash canopy. Brushing his fingers over her cheek, then smoothing her hair back, he rumbled, "Sleep well, Sophia."

Panic had her shooting out to blindly grab his hand when he made to leave. "No, stay." Her heart clenched. "Please. Will you stay?"

He remained silent and unmoving. She wished she could see his face, read his expression. After a nauseating amount of time had passed, his hand relaxed. He crawled into bed beside her, and she curled against his chest. "Thank you," she whispered.

Sikthand pressed a kiss to the top of her head and pulled her close, running his fingers gently up and down her thigh draped over his hips.

His hand flashed in and out of a small bit of moonlight as he caressed her, and she frowned down at it. *No marks yet.*

She put her disappointment out of her mind and closed her eyes. She would wait an eternity for them to appear if that's what it took.

38

The last week and a half had passed in a daze. Sikthand's mind was clouded over.

Every moment that he spent with Sophia was utter bliss. No longer torturing himself with the delusion he had the ability to stay away from her had left him happier than he'd ever been.

They did everything they could together. Talked, fucked, ate, bathed, worked. The only thing he couldn't seem to do was sleep.

The exhaustion was wearing on him. Each night she writhed underneath him, begging for his touch in a way that filled him with unparalleled satisfaction. When they'd fucked themselves out of all their energy, she'd ask him to stay.

Sikthand wanted to sleep with her. He closed his eyes each night with Sophia clasped in his arms, his purr heavy in his chest, and tried and tried and tried. But sleep never came.

Thoughts would creep into his mind in the black of the night. He ignored them, but couldn't keep them from affecting his subconscious. Every action of hers told him she wanted him, that she might even love him, but he couldn't quite settle the building dread the closer they got to the Leaders' Summit.

One day he would heal, he tried to convince himself. One day, he would hold her close and take in her smell and fall asleep. The morning that he woke up with her wrapped in his arms would be the beginning of a new life.

Perhaps today would bring him one step closer.

Sophia sprawled out on his bed as he packed and dressed for the Leaders' Summit. His heart ached just looking at her.

"Remember, you have to make sure to argue my case to everyone else too. I know it's a long shot, but I really think Asivva is the best choice. Not only is she super smart and super accomplished, but she's already familiar with humans, and—cherry on top—she has a freaking half-human niece! She's perfect."

Sikthand grinned down at her.

A knot twisted in his gut, dimming his smile. Two days was too long to be gone.

His jaw clenched. Why couldn't he just let go of these vile dregs of distrust? Sophia was nothing like Japeshi. She was warm and open, and she didn't hide her anger or her dislike. Whenever he pissed her off, she told him.

His idea to close their wedding to the public had been short-lived. He'd announced the decision to the Guild without first confirming with her, and she'd seethed at him about it that night.

Running his decisions by another person was a new concept for Sikthand. He'd been a solitary king for so long, it was second nature for him to believe his choices were final. Sophia had let him know differently.

Though his chest had puffed indignantly and the instinct to shut her down burned bright, he'd forced himself to remember that she would be his queen. Sophia was his partner now. And more than that. He loved her. He valued what she had to say. Even if he didn't ultimately agree with her position, hearing her out and compromising was the right thing to do.

It helped that they never critiqued each other publicly. Throughout the tower they presented a solid, unified force. But when they were alone, they were free. Their wing was for fighting and lovemaking and laughing. In here, honesty reigned.

He'd told her everything. How he'd watched her, how he'd followed her, how he'd taken himself in hand each night and thought of her mouth and her tailless ass as he'd pumped himself dry.

He'd revealed his maze of tunnels and walked her through the hidden bowels of Vrulatica, describing his childhood and grinning as she'd told him about hers.

He wished he could have met her then, when they'd both been young. A gangly prince mostly known for vomiting an impressive amount while getting tattooed, and a pimply, bespectacled girl, who spent her time dressing in silly outfits and acting in plays.

She would have made his life brighter even then.

The only thing he held back from her was the fact that he'd read her mail. He'd tell her after their wedding. After it was clear beyond a doubt that she'd turned down King Cueyar. His chest constricted.

She *had* turned him down. He knew it. Old wounds just wouldn't let him believe it yet. She'd prove it to him in two weeks at their wedding. He refused to give in to his paranoia any longer. He'd fight against it for her. She deserved his trust. She didn't deserve to be questioned and forced to prove her loyalty.

His eyes fell to her neck, and his insides heated.

Not when she strolled around their city with a tattoo of his bite marks proudly displayed on her throat for all to see.

Khes' eyes had nearly bugged out of his ancient head when she'd described the tattoo she'd wanted. She'd waited until the bruises from Sikthand's bite had mostly healed, then forced Khes to outline the marks in a way that must have hurt like hell.

He stepped toward her and gently pulled her head to the side so he could kiss the marks. Sikthand did this often, and he loved the way she shivered and sighed each time.

He sat on the bed next to her as she sketched out a back-tattoo design she was creating for him. His tattoos were almost replaced. Khes came up many evenings to work on them, and having Sophia there always made the pain oddly manageable.

Everything was better when she was there. There was no part of his miserable life that her mere presence didn't improve.

If anyone other than leaders and their right-hand officials were allowed to go to the Summit, he'd be dragging her along. But alas, she was not yet enthroned.

She glanced up at him, then did a double take, noticing his inner turmoil in his expression. She rose to her knees, her brows drawing together. "What's wrong? Are you nervous? Don't be nervous."

"I love you, Sophia." Though he didn't know why, the words came out like a plea.

He watched her chest rise, then go still. A slow smile lifted her face, her eyes glassing over with tears. "I…" Her voice cracked, so she swallowed and tried again. "I love you too."

Sikthand swelled with happiness until he was sure his metal armor would crack. He had the oddest instinct to undermine her statement, to excuse her from her words and remind her that she didn't have to say them just because he wanted to hear them. But his throat closed.

He searched her beaming face, hoping to the skies that her words and the warm glow of love shining from her smile could be believed.

Before he could think what more to say, she bolted into his lap and kissed him so deeply, his tail curled.

It took him many hours to pry himself away from Sophia, and by that time, he was late. He flew with Ahea away from the city limits to the area where cruisers worked. Commander Roldroth was already waiting for him, a slight look of annoyance tightening his hood.

The two males stuffed themselves into the tight metallic transportation orb others called *cruisers*—but Vrulans called *sightless prisons*—with twin scowls.

How the rest of the world preferred this confined space with no view of the sky was beyond him. Even before they took off, nausea built in Sikthand's gut.

With each moment that passed, he had to fight with himself not to turn the cruiser around. Moving in any direction but toward Sophia felt…wrong. He was meant to be wherever she was.

"Are you troubled, sire?" Roldroth asked after about an hour of silence. "We believe most of Madam Kalos' underlings have been located, Zommah's apprentice is back with his grateful family, and the new Madam of trade has surprised us all with how quickly she's adapting to the role. The threat is neutralized. Is there something else weighing on you?"

He glanced toward Roldroth and found his hood had lost some of its color. Maybe it was his exhaustion, but he suddenly found himself too tired to hold back his words. "I dislike leaving Sophia."

"Are you worried she'll exercise more power than she yet has a right to?"

"No," he barked immediately. Sophia would make a wonderful queen. Fair and firm and more compassionate than any Vrulan.

Roldroth hummed out an unsurprised sound. "Then perhaps the rumors are true and you are besotted."

Sikthand eyed the commander. "Rumors, huh?" He sighed. "Is that what they say? Besotted?"

Roldroth tipped his head from side to side. "They say *love*." The commander studied his reaction, seemingly trying to gauge how much truth there was in the statement. When Sikthand didn't answer, Roldroth went on. "They wonder when your marks will appear."

He scoffed, glancing down at his gloved hands. He'd hardly allowed himself to ponder such a thing. He wanted too badly for it to be true, for Sophia to be his mate. He didn't allow himself to dwell, though. If hope infected him and the marks never came, it would hurt all the more. Still, he didn't deny Roldroth's words, and the male shifted forward in his seat, a tempered awe lighting his expression.

"What does it feel like?"

"I have no marks," Sikthand grated.

"Then your love." Roldroth shrugged. "Even that is so rare these days. Females don't usually allow it or reciprocate it, but Sophia watches you as if her heart will stop if you don't gaze back."

A small smile tugged at his lips. He glanced at the male, not the commander, not Roldroth—just a male. He saw a familiar loneliness behind his eyes. Perhaps it was Sophia making him weak, but he decided to consider an honest answer.

"My life has been…wrought. Each day is filled with dread and suspicion and fixation." He glanced at the floor, his brows knitting. "She brings me silence." Sikthand swallowed down the tightness in his throat. "The clouds are not so heavy when she's near."

Roldroth let out a deep exhale and sat back in his seat. He fell into silent contemplation after that.

A sick feeling lingered in Sikthand's gut. He tried to will it away, but as they drew farther and farther from Vrulatica, it grew.

39

Sophia, and the remaining members of the Guild still in Vrulatica, sat in the communications outbuilding waiting for the broadcast of the vote to begin. Sikthand had only been gone for two days, yet she missed him fiercely.

Her spirits lifted when she reminded herself he'd be home tomorrow. Close to vibrating with excitement at the thought, Sophia hid her wide grin and stared hard at the space where the broadcast would begin.

She supposed it was a good thing he'd gone away. Maybe he'd finally get some sleep. Though he'd agreed to stay with her through the night as she slumbered, she'd kept waking to find him already peering down at her.

At first, she'd thought nothing of it, but as his hood had faded, and his eyes sagged with exhaustion, she'd realized he hadn't been sleeping. Sophia had started making flimsy excuses to go on long drawn-out trips through the city with Alno so he could sneak in naps.

How she should interpret his refusal or inability to sleep, she didn't know. It cut at her insides to think he still didn't trust her, but she hoped that would all change in time. Maybe after their wedding. Maybe after they'd had a child.

Eventually, he'd lie with her through the night and not worry that she'd slip a knife into him or fill his eyes full of ink.

His uneasiness validated her decision not to tell him about his eyes, and luckily they hadn't changed in front of anyone except for Khes.

The moment had been an odd one too. Khes had been replacing Sikthand's tattoos, as he did often. Almost three quarters of them were back now. Sophia had commented on how difficult the skill was to learn, and Khes had offered to let her try on Sikthand.

Initially, she'd scoffed, but Sikthand had smiled and urged her on, curling her toes when he rumbled how much he'd love to be marked by her. She'd drawn one of the thin lines he'd had on his back, but it had come out all splotchy and wobbly.

As it turned out, Vrulan tattooing was much harder than she'd imagined. If she moved too slow, the ink following her pen tip pooled and made blotchy marks, if she moved too fast, the ink fell away from the magnetic tip and she had to go back to grab it again. The pressure of the pen was important too. She'd felt bad pressing so hard into Sikthand's skin, but he'd barely even twitched with discomfort.

"Showing off for your future wife?" Khes had joked, scooting forward to peer in Sikthand's eyes as he teased him.

What he'd seen had made his smile fall. Luckily, she'd guessed what he'd seen and, from behind Sikthand's back, had caught Khes' attention and put a silencing finger to her lips.

Khes had slid his chair away before Sikthand could catch the shocked expression lingering on the inkmaster's face. After a few moments, the line between his brows had softened, and they shared a wordless conversation in which Sophia had been somehow sure Khes understood exactly why she was keeping Sikthand's eyes a secret and approved of her decision.

One painful, swollen beat of her heart passed as she recalled the way Sikthand gazed lovingly at her ugly squiggly line in the mirror. He hadn't let Khes fix it, and Sophia had internally squealed. No longer was Japeshi's name scrolled on his chest—now he had *her* mark on him.

And he *loved* her.

She still couldn't believe it. He'd told her he loved her in such an out-of-the-blue, heartfelt, sincere way. Though she'd said it back, Sophia itched all over feeling like she hadn't said it hard enough, hadn't said it in five different ways so he really heard it and believed her. Maybe when she did, the damn stubborn marks on his hands would finally appear.

Lindri finished up her conversation with Magistrate Yalmi, and Sophia jumped at the opening. "Lady Lindri," she called.

Lindri peered over to her and smiled. "Yes, Sophia?"

She leaned close and whispered, "Is everything on track for my throning dress?"

"Yes," Lindri squeaked with a wide grin. "I've shown your designs to my favorite metalsmith, and he believes he can make the pieces in time. You'll truly cause a stir, I think."

"Good." Sophia grinned. She'd sketched out the design after Sikthand had left and had grown more and more excited about it as she'd added bits and pieces here and there.

Her outfit for her throning needed to work double duty since her wedding was on the same day, a compromise they'd made after Sikthand had nearly imploded at the idea of two separate public events during either of which she might be killed by some unknown foe.

Though she loved Sikthand, she couldn't quite work up any excitement for their wedding. For one thing, weddings on Clecania were not typically romantic. Normally, they were small, simple ceremonies in which both parties agreed to a temporary marriage. Though her marriage to Sikthand would be permanent, the ceremony itself was still likely to be a more cold, efficient, and formal affair than a celebration of love and commitment.

Sikthand's initial recognition was another reason she couldn't muster too much joy for her upcoming nuptials. If his damn marks would just appear already, a wedding would be unnecessary. Matehood superseded marriage. Matehood superseded *everything*. It was beyond sacred. Knowing what she did about Sikthand's eyes, marrying him felt oddly…deceitful.

Sophia sat back in her chair, the one Sikthand normally sat in. But the wedding would make her alien king happy, so she'd put on a smile—and a devastating lingerie set—and go through the motions for him.

A projected figure emerged in the center of the room, and Sophia sucked in a noisy sound of disgust. It was…gloopy. Its shape was something between an octopus and a rhinoceros, and it had sticky gobs of what looked like snot dripping off it onto the ground. It didn't leave a mess, though, as its suctioning feet began to move, slurping up the goop. Sophia jumped when the repulsive noise of the slurping translated in her ear.

That's *how it talks?*

She tamped down her queasiness and tried to listen to what the creature was saying. If her prepping had been right, this was Irgh, the Intergalactic Alliance representative from the planet Gninzol who was acting as an impartial moderator for the vote.

How did this being belong to a Class One species? It was incredibly impolite of her to even think it based solely on its appearance, but *damn*. Irgh was like an animated booger, yet their kind was light-years more evolved than humans and Clecanians combined.

Sophia's lips curled down as sloppy gurgling echoed beneath the translation chiming through her ear. Irgh outlined the events of the past two days for the audiences who might have never witnessed an Alliance vote before.

The first day had been spent introducing each candidate and letting them convince the leaders why they should receive their vote. Sophia wished *that* part had been broadcast, but the Leaders' Summit was incredibly private. Only those in attendance knew the extent of what was said.

The next time one was scheduled, Sophia would be attending, she realized with mild surprise. She kept forgetting that in a week's time, she would be a queen. A *fucking* queen! It still left her a bit dizzy when that reality slipped in.

Goodbye to LARP, hello to…LAR?

Irgh described how on the second day, the leaders of the planet—barring any who were also running as candidates, such as Vila—had met and discussed the candidates. Sophia could only hope that the hours of prepping she'd done with Sikthand had paid off and he'd convince enough other leaders that Asivva was the right choice.

A twinge of fear flickered in her heart, but she ignored it. Sikthand would vote for who she'd selected. He wouldn't change his mind at the last minute and betray her trust. The fear was just an intrusive worry. She could count on Sikthand.

Sophia sat forward in her seat as Irgh announced that the votes were being tallied now. A screen popped up with an enormous list of names. Numbers began appearing next to their names, showing how many votes they'd received so far. Names rose and dropped quickly, reordering themselves based on who was winning.

She still wasn't proficient enough to decipher the names before they moved on her, but she could read the name at the top since it hadn't moved.

Her fingers curled around the arms of her chair. *Vila.*

Votes continued to come in, and a second familiar name appeared under Vila's name. Sophia sucked in a shaky breath. Asivva was gaining.

Squinting at the constantly changing tallies next to their names, she tried to understand how far apart they were. She didn't know for sure, but she thought it was close.

Sikthand had done it. He'd argued in Asivva's favor well enough that she might win.

Sophia scooted to the edge of her seat as the votes started to slow. The names no longer shifted, and the only votes coming in were between Vila and Asivva.

The room fell into a breathless silence as Asivva's named jumped ahead. Sophia clutched a hand to her mouth.

The numbers next to their name flicked to the same number.

Tied.

Her body stiffened.

Sophia blinked when Vila's name flashed back to the top of the list, and the numbers remained unchanged. She waited, and waited, but nothing changed. Her heart sank.

Vila had won.

Sophia's head drooped in time with her pitching stomach. Sounds of upset echoed through the room, mirroring her own dread.

She lifted her chin as Irgh explained the tally was being confirmed at that moment. Time to be queenly. "It's okay," Sophia reassured the Guild. "We knew this was the most likely outcome. That vote was so, so close. That means there are a ton of cities that just pissed Vila off. Those are our allies. If she gets out of hand—"

A thundering bang echoed through the room, and everyone shot to their feet. Sophia's ears buzzed, the blood rushing in her veins cooled to ice as she spotted the bowed center of the heavy metal door. It looked like it had just been hit with a battering ram.

Guards crowded in front of her and the Guild as something enormous slammed into the door again. It flew open, still on its hinges, then rebounded off the wall and swung closed.

In that moment, her fear morphed into confusion. In the split-second view, a familiar red, horned giant had appeared. "Rhaego?" Sophia called.

The Guild all looked to her.

"You know—"

Bavo's words were cut short when a smoking canister slipped through a mangled crack in the door. The room began to quickly fill with gas. The guards near the door heaved at it, trying to drag it open, but Sophia knew that if Rhaego was holding it closed, there was not a chance in hell they'd get it to budge.

Sophia stumbled into her seat as a wave of dizziness hit. Her lids drooped.

No. Panic seized her chest. It was sleeping spray. She stumbled forward onto her knees and started to crawl toward the door as she fought to stay conscious.

One by one, guildmembers and soldiers crumpled around her.

Sophia gave her face a hard slap and continued dragging herself to the door. "Rhaego! Open…the…" Sophia's cheek hit the ground, and her words slurred out of her. "Door."

40

The sight of Vrulatica stretching into the clear, star-strewn sky had never looked so beautiful. Sikthand greeted Ahea, who was waiting next to the commander's malginash.

The Leaders' Summit hadn't been a success. But it hadn't been without merit. He'd spoken to many rulers who felt the same as they did. Disgust for the Tremantian Queen's bribery was high. And though many had resolved to vote for her despite their disgust, many had seemed to be seeking any reason not to.

Sikthand had given them that reason. He'd made his case, speaking at length of his bride and relaying her clever reasoning for favoring Asivva.

King Cueyar had looked on with a smug expression. It could have meant nothing, but Sikthand had avoided the male so he could, in turn, avoid ripping the king's head from his shoulders.

He itched to get back to Sophia. Thoughts of her haunted him every waking moment. No matter how much bedding he piled on at night, he couldn't recreate the lovely weight of her arm draped over his torso.

He climbed into Ahea's saddle before Roldroth had even clambered out of the cruiser, and jettisoned into the sky. It was late, and he hadn't been scheduled to arrive home until tomorrow, but he couldn't wait any longer. As soon as the doors to the Summit Hall were unlocked, he'd dragged Roldroth out to a cruiser, and set it to the highest speed it could go.

Would she be waiting for him in his room? She *should* be.

He'd sent word ahead, notifying her of his arrival. As long as that imbecile messenger had given her the communication, Sikthand believed she'd be waiting in his room. He'd rather not search Vrulatica for her and make a public scene of hauling her back to their wing.

The air cooled as they soared parallel to the tower, swerving by sturdy nests and zooming between buttresses. Ahea's wings flared wide to halt their breakneck ascent when they reached his landing bay, and he lifted an inch out of his seat. He activated the robust gate blocking access to the royal wing and swooped under the metal bars before they'd fully risen.

He hopped off Ahea, pulling away the stays of her saddle a little more roughly than normal, but then the scents of unwelcome visitors caught his attention and he spun.

Alno, a troop of wary, tense soldiers, and the Guild all waited on the opposite side of the landing bay.

Ice slid down his spine.

They didn't speak, though each one of their faces held a look of such pity and torture.

"Sire, during the broadcast, the queen…Sophia…"

An iron clamp wrapped around his belly, and his insides threatened to empty. He rocked forward and backward as his chest caved in. Ahea clicked angrily from behind him.

"Is she alive?" Sikthand's voice was unrecognizable to his ears.

"Yes."

A droning buzz rang in his ears. *Not again. Not her.*

His mouth twitched back, pulling almost to his ears as pain lanced through his brain. "Is she… Is she *gone*?" His voice broke.

The answering "Yes" was quieter this time.

His eyes slammed shut. The intensity of his agony was so visceral that he wondered if his body was collapsing in on itself like a dying star becoming a black hole. He wanted to wail and scream, but he couldn't get any breath to fill his crumpled lungs.

She's gone.

41

Sikthand's face swam in her mind, and Sophia's chest filled with warmth. Her mate. So handsome.

She walked closer to him, and his features warped, they pulled taut like he was being tortured. She reached out but she couldn't get to him. A blood-curdling scream pulsed through the air, and he collapsed.

Sophia bolted upright, her heavy clothing dragging across her skin. Was she soaking wet?

Breathing labored and head pounding, she tried to get her eyes to focus, but they were waking up much slower than her limbs.

Hands grabbed at her arms, holding her in place, and voices called out muddled words. She tried to wrench free of the fingers gripping her shoulders, but they were too strong. She screamed and struggled, but then a figure came into focus before her, and she stilled.

Sophia squinted and blinked at the woman. Sound began to grow coherent in her ears. "Meg?"

Meg, her human friend, and one of the women who had been on the world tour with her, grinned wide. "Hey! I thought you were about to take Rhaego out."

Sophia tipped her head up and up and up and peered behind her at the enormous, horned demon holding her shoulders down.

"Good eve to you, Sophia. I apologize for my force, but I could not allow you to injure yourself in your confusion," Rhaego rumbled in his deep voice. She blinked at him.

Memories flooded back to her, and dread had her throat closing. Rhaego allowed her to shrug out of his hold. She tried to shoot to her feet but fell backward instantly.

"Ope!" Meg lunged forward to catch her, but Rhaego was already at her back, gently holding her until she could maintain her balance.

She glanced around the room, trying to figure out where in the tower she was. The walls weren't made of metal or stone. They curved gracefully without any dour embellishments.

Her heart thundered. She caught sight of another figure in the corner and recognized the familiar form of Maxu, Meg's mate and the one who'd aided her group in their escape from Vrulatica.

A sinking, awful worry had tears springing to her eyes. "Where am I? What am I doing here?" She glared at Meg, whose head snapped back in surprise.

"Wha... We rescued you," she said, tipping her head down and furrowing her brows as if Sophia didn't understand. "I told you I'd come back for you, and I did. It wasn't easy—let me tell you. There was a lot of planning. But when we heard the announcement that you were getting married to that tyrant, we knew we had to get you out of there."

Fury roared to life in her veins. She took a step toward Meg but stopped when the urgent scrape of a chair sounded, and Maxu stalked over.

Sikthand. Sophia's gaze went out of focus. "No!" she shrieked to the room at large. She crushed her skull between her hands and breathed through the clenching of her heart. He'd be devastated. He'd come home and find her gone. Would he think she'd left?

Her palm curled into the wet fabric of her shirt. *Sweat,* she realized. She was sweating everywhere.

"I need to get back. Now." Sophia spun in place, looking for…something, anything. She spotted a door and dashed to it, but Maxu stepped in front of it, blocking her path. "Move," she growled.

"Do you know how much shit I had to go through to retrieve you for my mate? Thank. Her." Sophia and Maxu glared at each other.

Meg stepped in front of her mate and rested a calming palm on his chest. "I don't get it. You *want* to marry him?"

"He's. *My.* Mate." She seethed in Maxu's direction and lifted her brows at him, hoping her sharp words would cut at his insides. Maxu knew what it felt like to be separated from his mate—he'd spent months chasing Meg down before finally getting to her.

The angry lines of his scowl went soft, and his face paled. He exchanged a wide-eyed look with Rhaego behind her shoulder.

"What?" Meg breathed.

Sophia's glare shot toward Meg. "If you'd sent me even one goddamned letter before deciding to *Ocean's Eleven* me out of there, you'd know that."

"We…" Meg's voice failed, and she tried again. "We've been in hiding. We couldn't risk it. You have no idea what's been going on. You aren't the only human we've rescued. Rhaego has been running all over the planet setting up safe houses for when Vila FedExes us across the planet."

"Does he know?" Maxu's voice cut in, and an intense look of concern crossed over his face.

Fucking good. He *should* be concerned. *Sikthand won't rest till he finds him and…* But fuck…

What if he thought she'd left with them? Sophia let out a strangled whimper and clutched a hand to her forehead.

"She must return," Rhaego boomed behind her. "Mates must not be separated. It's unthinkable." He stepped forward and comically slid an unmoving Maxu away from the door. He struggled against it, but it was as if Maxu were trying to hold in place a slowly moving bus.

Sophia could kiss the demon. "Thank you!" She dashed through the door and scanned the room for an exit.

"Does he know?" Maxu bellowed, running after her.

Sophia sucked in a calming breath and scowled back at him. "No. His eyes changed, but knowing about his past, I decided not to tell him until his marks appeared. And now, thanks to you, he will *never* trust me again and they might never appear. He'll just go crazier and crazier while in that awful in-between state. Thanks a lot. I need to get back ASAP and try to undo some of this damage. If I hurry, maybe I can get there before he gets back."

"We took you three days ago," Meg squeaked.

Sophia froze, horror swept through her stiff limbs, and she rotated on the spot. "What?"

Meg winced apologetically. "We had to use a pretty intense sleep spray that we invented. It's strong enough to knock out most Clecanian races, which means it really, really knocks out humans. It's safe, but you were out for about three days."

Fuuuuuuuck.

42

Okay, almost there. I'm just going to explain myself, and we'll have a good laugh about it. Sophia gnawed on the quick of her nails, her knee bouncing uncontrollably.

Every second was moving far slower than it should've. How many eternities had passed in the time it had taken them to hike to a secure location, find a cruiser, go to a busy city, find another cruiser that Maxu had insisted on hacking into to further hide their whereabouts, go to another city, then load Sophia into a *final* cruiser that would take her to Vrulatica.

She'd now been gone for four damn days.

When she'd said goodbye, she'd been mildly apologetic, and she'd parted with her friends on good terms. She'd told Meg that while she appreciated the thought of her rescue attempt, next time she'd prefer a letter. Meg had promised to send one as soon as Maxu gave her the go-ahead.

It had helped their moods immensely when Sophia explained the ways in which she planned to make Vrulatica a haven for humans. All the safe houses Rhaego was establishing were just dandy, but if they didn't work out, she'd make sure Vrulatica could protect them.

She stared at the small dot on the cruiser screen. It pulled closer and closer to the Vrulan outbuildings. Once there, she was sure she could get someone to fly her to the tower.

Sophia was too eager when the cruiser stopped, and she ended up tripping and tumbling out of the transport as she climbed over its slowly lowering door. She dragged herself up through the sand, and tripped into the first building she saw—the infirmary.

A wide-eyed male leapt away from her with a cry when she crashed into him headlong.

"I need a ride to the royal wing."

"Wh-W…" He peered down at her dirty, sweat-stained clothes and sniffed. "My lady, are you—"

"I need a malginash. Call someone to fly me!"

With a look of horror, the man sprinted away. A door down the hall opened, and a familiar, though bewildered, face popped out.

"Vezel!" she screeched, sprinting over to him.

"Sophia." His eyes widened, and he took in her bedraggled appearance. "We all thought you'd left."

"Shit," she wheezed while clutching a stitch in her side. Three days asleep had made even that short run exhausting. "Does he think I left willingly?"

Vezel's jaw softened. "You didn't?"

"No! Does he think I did?" Tears threatened to fall. Only the panic to get back to Sikthand kept them at bay.

"I believe so. We're nearly at war with Roborh. He's demanding King Cueyar return you, though the king continues to claim you aren't with him. Were you?"

"King…" Sophia froze, vision going out of focus as she thought. Sikthand must have read Heleax's letter and assumed she'd run away to Roborh. Sophia winced, squinting her eyes shut and letting her head fall back. *Stupid. Stupid. Stupid.*

She knew she shouldn't have kept that letter. She should have thrown it out as soon as she'd sent her response turning down the king, but it had brought her a weirdly powerful sense of comfort. Written messages weren't common on Clecania. Everything was sent electronically. The sight of handwritten English after months of torturing herself learning Clecanian had made her heart swell, and it had somehow made her feel closer to Earth to see it. It could have been a grocery list and she would have felt the same. Had her fucking nostalgia started a war?

"I have to get up there," she begged, desperately.

Vezel nodded. "Proit," he called down the hall.

The timid male from before popped his head out of a doorway. "I'll be back soon—look after Rider Huth until I return."

Vezel stomped ahead, and Sophia followed in a trot. "Thank you. Thank you. Thank you."

Outside, around the back of the outbuilding was a sleeping malginash. Vezel let out a short whistle, and its cloudy eyes popped open. Sophia waited to approach so as not to frighten it, then clambered onto the saddle. Vezel hopped on behind, and they were off.

"Can you get into the royal landing bay? I don't want to cause a scene. I need to see him alone first," Sophia yelled over the howling wind.

Vezel pulled the reins, guiding his malginash to soar higher toward the royal landing bay. "Are you sure that's wise? The king has been…distraught."

Sophia nearly choked on the boulder lodged in her throat. She silently nodded.

When they reached the bay, Sophia slid off the malginash. "Don't tell anyone I'm here yet. I need some time to calm him down first before the whole Guild shows up with questions."

Vezel nodded, then took off into the sky.

Anxiety keeping her heart hammering in her chest, she raced to Sikthand's room first, testing the handle before banging loudly on the door.

"Hey—who gave you permission…" Alno came running around the corner, but his voice died when he saw her. He put his hands on his hips and tilted his head, expression livid. "Where the fuck have you been?"

"Where is he?" she breathed.

Alno's gaze flitted over her disgusting clothes. A line formed between his brows. "I don't know. I'd guess the Choke."

She lifted off the door. "The Choke. Why?"

"Because there's a hoard of invaders right now, and he's burying his pain by ripping Tagion warriors apart. The amount of dried Tagion blood I've had to clean up…" he complained, almost to himself.

Sophia swallowed. Her poor mate. All she wanted was to drop to her knees and convince him she hadn't meant to leave. "When will he be back?"

"No idea. He doesn't speak to anyone apart from Khes except to bark commands. Do you know how many Vrulans are locked in the dungeons right now just because they might know someone who knows someone who knows where you went?"

Something in Sophia finally broke. A deep, painful sob wrenched out of her chest. She buried her face in her hands and wailed miserably.

Alno let out a long breath and wrapped an arm around her shoulders. "Okay. Okay. You'll be alright. Come on. Let's get you fixed up."

Still sobbing into her hands, she let him lead her down the hall to her room. She peered around the space, expecting it to be torn apart. It somehow hurt worse that it wasn't. Everything was exactly how she'd left it.

In a daze, she let Alno guide her about. She jumped at every little noise, even going so far as to stumble out of her bath when a crash sounded from her bedroom. Throwing a towel around her body, she'd stumbled into her bedroom only to find Alno had merely dropped a tray of food.

"Nothing yet," he said sadly.

Hours passed and still no sign of Sikthand. Eventually, she sent Alno off, though he initially refused, arguing that he'd never forgive himself if the king accidentally killed her in a rage upon returning.

When Sophia had quietly explained that she didn't believe it was possible for Sikthand to harm her considering he was her mate, Alno had crashed back into a chair, shocked.

After he finally left, she snuck to her mirror and activated the switch that would make it swing open. Her heart quivered like a scared rabbit as the secret passage was revealed but grew cold when she didn't find him hiding there.

Bottles littered the ground around his chair. A deep gash in the stone floor confused her for a moment until she realized it must be the path the point of his swiping tail had carved. She made her way to Sikthand's mirror and let out a miserable sigh at the sight.

He hadn't touched a thing in her room, but the same couldn't be said for his. The mirror was shattered and lay in pieces on the ground. The bedding was shredded. Weapons of all kinds were embedded in the walls, and his study looked like someone had set off a bomb.

Tears falling fast, she crawled into what remained of his bed. She closed her eyes and listened intently for any sound—

the click of Ahea's claws on the stone landing bay far above, the clink of Sikthand's boots in the hall.

She held his bedding close to her nose in balled fists, the scent of him clinging to the fabric.

While trying to convince herself over and over that he'd come back, hear her out, and forgive her, the calming scent of him lulled her into sleep.

***

A loud roar had her shooting awake and scrambling out of bed. She turned in place, expecting to see Sikthand in the room ready to rage at her, but he was nowhere. The sky outside was black, and lightning cracked across his windows.

Shit. It had been midafternoon when she'd come in here. How long had she been asleep?

More yelling echoed from the passageway leading to her room, and she silently followed it. Sophia kept her steps quiet as arguing voices grew clearer.

She choked back a pained sob when she heard him. Furious and deep, Sikthand's voice carried to her.

"Get out! If you won't do it, then leave."

Sophia stepped around the bottles and peered through her mirror. Khes was there, standing in the center of her room, but she couldn't see Sikthand.

Khes clutched his tattoo bag and looked toward her open bedroom door with such a worried expression. She'd never seen anything close to the look on the inkmaster's face before, and it tore at her insides to imagine what was bad enough to put it there.

"Out! You're of no use." Sophia tipped her head forward, but it sounded as if Sikthand was standing in the hall, waiting for Khes to leave. Her knees wobbled at the wrath in the king's voice.

At last, Khes trudged out of the room.

Suddenly not brave enough to face her mate, she lowered into the chair. She needed to see him first. The bedroom door slammed shut, and Sikthand pounded into the room.

One hand lifting to her mouth, the other to her heart, she took in the sight before her. He was gazing down at her sketchbook, a wretchedly hopeless look pulling his features tight.

Except for a snug pair of shorts, he was nearly naked. Sophia's eyes scanned his body. He'd covered himself with tattoos, more than she'd ever seen on him before.

But they were different.

Sophia clutched at her throat, tears streaming down her cheeks as she studied the tattoos traveling from his chin all the way down to the tip of his tail.

They were *hers*.

She had no idea how he'd withstood it, but he'd changed every one of his tattoos and added tons more, and they were all things she'd drawn.

Every tattoo she'd ever designed—along with sketches, notes, abstract scribbles. They covered every inch of his skin. The only piece that had remained unchanged since the last time she'd seen him, was the wobbly line she'd drawn on his back.

Sikthand dropped the book on the ground and sank into a chair, his head dropping into his hands. A deep, anguished moan ripped out of his chest, and she stood. Her hands shook as she reached for the latch and silently opened the mirror.

The crash of his chair hitting the ground rang through her ears. By the time she'd stepped through the mirror, Sikthand was on his feet, blood-crusted blade held behind his shoulder as if he were about to hurl it at her.

She took a step toward him, then stilled. The ramming of her heart pulsed all the way down to her toes.

His eyes were wide and unblinking, his axe clutched in his hand. He stared at her as if unsure whether she was real.

"Sikthand," she said, starting to walk toward him again.

His chest heaved in a colossal breath, and he blinked.

She took a few more steps.

The axe clattered to the ground behind him, and he sank down to his knees, staring up at her as she stopped just before him.

There were so many things she wanted to say, but she couldn't get her throat to work. "I—"

His tail slammed behind her thighs, and he hauled her against him. His shaking arms and tail squeezed her lower body tight to his torso. His face nuzzled against her belly, sniffing and sucking down deep breaths.

"She's real. She's back. She's here." His arms tightened painfully, and he muttered words to himself as if to reassure his own shaky mind.

Sophia wanted to get to the ground and pull him in, but she didn't think it was wise to try to wriggle out of his iron hold at the moment. She hugged his head to her belly instead, running her fingers through his hair.

Without warning, a growl built in his throat, and his fangs sank into the soft flesh of her hip, spearing right through her clothing. She held in her squeal of pain when she heard the groaning sound of relief rising from his chest and felt the shuddering in his arms subside.

He released a moan and lifted his mouth, pulling back just enough to see the blood blooming over the fabric at her hip. Sophia took the opportunity to slide through his arms until she slammed to her knees in front of him.

She had to rub her lips together to keep her sob in when she saw his eyes were utterly black. His expression was so torn. He looked at her like he hated her but would die if she pulled away. His gaze ran over her face, his brows drawing together in pain. "You left me."

"No. *No.*" She shook her head, tears streaming down her cheeks. "I didn't want to go. They *took* me. I *never* want to leave you. Ever. As soon as I woke up, I ran back as fast as I could." She was pressed tight to his chest, and she had to crane her neck back so she could talk to him.

"You didn't leave?" Hope lit up his face, he smiled and sucked in a joyous breath. His nostrils flared, and he shook his head, peering around for a moment as though something unseen had brushed past him.

He eyed her again, and his brows furrowed. "But the king—"

Her head thrashed back and forth. "I turned the king down weeks ago. I only kept the letter because it was written by a human in English, and it reminded me of home…Earth. It reminded me of Earth. Meg took me. She left me behind when they escaped, and she thought she was rescuing me. She was wrong."

"That vermin! Maxu! This was his doing?" Sikthand's features darkened with rage.

She clasped his face in her hands. "Hey, listen to me. It was nothing but a mistake. I'm back. I will *always* come back."

His gaze was still so tragic, like he wanted to believe her but couldn't.

"I love you," she croaked. "So, so, so much. I would never leave you. Please believe me." She pressed kisses against his mouth though he didn't respond. "I was so furious when I woke up. All I wanted was to get back here."

"You didn't choose to leave me?" he repeated. She watched his thumb brush over her shirt collar. He pulled it back so he could check for the tattoo of his bite.

"No." Sophia eyed his hand and swallowed, trying to decide what to say. "Sikthand, I will *never* leave you." His thumb brushed over the tattoo on her neck. She licked her lips. "You're my mate," she whispered.

His body stilled. She stopped breathing, waiting for his reaction.

"Don't say such things," he growled low.

Gathering her courage, she shifted her head to the side so the mirror at her back was visible. Sikthand did a double take at his reflection, seeing his black eyes. "I..." He shook his head.

"Don't you feel it?" she urged. "*I* feel it. Sometimes I think I'm going to die if I don't see you, touch you."

"How are you doing this?" He blinked at his reflection.

She shuddered out a breath, pressing her lips together. Hugging him close around the neck, she brushed a kiss against his ear and whispered, "Look at your hands."

She felt his arm shift behind her back and lift. A tremulous smile spread over her lips. She didn't know exactly when, but his marks had appeared. She'd seen them when he'd pulled her collar aside. They clashed with the tattooed designs he'd taken from her book, overwhelming them.

He jostled her in his arms when his other hand flew up to meet the first. She looked over her shoulder as he turned his palms back to front, staring at the black marks, the same color as his hood.

Suddenly, his palms zoomed to clutch her face. Smooshing her cheeks in his firm hold, he forced her gaze to meet his. "You're my mate?" he asked, still not believing his eyes.

"Yes." She tried to smile, though the heels of his palms clenching her face made it difficult.

"You didn't leave me?"

Her body wiggled more than her face when she tried to shake her head. "No—never."

"We're mated." The words were no longer a question. "You're my mate." A glorious, wide, beaming smile broke over his face as his eyes flicked over her.

"I'm your mate," she agreed, grinning through a happy sob.

He kissed her squished lips. "You're my mate." He repeated the statement over and over while pressing toothy kisses to her lips.

Finally, he loosened his hands enough for her to throw her arms around his neck again and kiss him properly. It was sloppy from her tears, and her blood still on his mouth, but his grinning lips against hers nearly made her heart burst.

Epilogue

Sikthand stared at the throne room doors, wishing he could see through the metal. After his mating marks had appeared on his hands, his strength and speed and eyesight had improved exponentially, yet he still couldn't see through walls—and at the moment that angered him.

How was she? Anxious? Excited?

Sikthand scanned the packed space, mentally threatening each citizen to behave themselves during Sophia's throning.

The conversations happening around the room all seemed to be hushed, but there were so many impeccably dressed Vrulans packed into every spare foot of the space that the noise in the room was cacophonous.

His hands itched beneath his gloves. He, the Guild, and Sophia had decided that they would reveal his mating marks to the city after Sophia was enthroned. The moment could not come fast enough. He abhorred covering his marks.

His marks. His *mating* marks. Sikthand still couldn't believe it.

All his life he'd been told that Vrulatica was his purpose. He'd suffered and toiled for the sake of his city because that was what he'd been born to do. But he had a new purpose now. His mate.

He would still rule his people, but he would do it with the most glorious female he could have imagined at his side, and his life would no longer be one of loneliness.

His hands clenched around the arms of his new throne, and he peered at Sophia's covered throne next to his. He needed her to make her entrance and join him. She'd been apart from him all day, and though it was easier to manage than before, he still hated being separated from her.

The soldiers at the door slammed their tails against a golden slab of metal, and a high-pitched ringing echoed through the space. The room fell silent, all eyes pointing toward the massive double doors.

Sikthand blinked to hydrate his dry eyes. They ached to see her.

A loud creaking echoed through the room as the doors opened an inch. Sikthand's chest swelled as bright red fabric came into view. They opened further and further, and Sophia was unveiled.

Emotion welled in his throat at the sight of his queen. She didn't wear armor but a combination of soft fabric and metal décor. Her headpiece was constructed of sharp askait antlers like the ones on his helmet and stretched high above her head.

The fine fabric of her blood red, floor-length gown was voluminous and delicate like the material of the dress she'd worn during the umbercree festival. But on her bodice, her bare arms, and crawling up her shoulders to her neck, were black metal designs. They'd been forged to fit her body exactly. Each piece of askait molded over her and highlighted the soft curves of her hips and breasts in a sharp corset.

Sophia hadn't allowed him to see her outfit before tonight, and now he knew why. The unmistakable inspiration for the metal designs decorating her dress were his tattoos. Geometric thick lines and curves in the same style he favored.

Love swelled inside him until every pore was gorged with it and he thought he might burst. He removed his helmet, though he wasn't supposed to. He wanted her to be able to see his eyes so she knew how much her choices meant to him.

She'd been peering around the hall at the thousands of Vrulans sizing her up, but then she glanced toward him. When she saw him staring down at her from his perched throne high above, she smiled. As the tension from her shoulders relaxed, so, too, did the tension in his.

Her grin warmed him for a moment longer before a look of determination crossed over her features. She tilted her chin up and stepped forward, walking the long distance to the base of the throne steps.

A slit in her dress opened, and her long lean leg appeared clad up to the knee in an extravagantly forged metal shoe that looked like a beautiful filigree cage on her foot. The shoe had a very tall base and the height it gave her, combined with the height of her antler headdress, made her look statuesque.

Muttered gasps and excited grins were exchanged as she strode by, and his brows knit together. What did her back look like to make everyone she passed so giddy?

Sophia arrived at the base of the long staircase where Madam Ostra, the new Head of trade, waited.

There were six landings on the staircase. Six stops and six sets of vows from the six sacred heads of Vrulatica, before she'd finally make it to him and take her rightful place.

"When you are queen, do you vow to hear me, Madam Ostra, sacred head of trade?"

"I vow to hear you, Madam Ostra." Sophia answered loud enough that her voice carried through the acoustically miraculous throne room.

After receiving a nod from Madam Ostra, Sophia proceeded up the steps until she reached Lady Lindri's level, then made her vow again.

Each time she rose from a level, he watched one of his guildmember's faces light up at the sight of her retreating back. His tail flicked across the floor, impatience to see her up close forcing movement out of him.

As the most senior guildmember, Speaker Besith's landing was last. Sikthand was nearly vibrating with pride and eagerness as she neared, her expression calm.

After the assassination of his father, Sikthand's ascension to the throne had been a rushed, dour affair, and he'd been racked with nerves while climbing to his seat. The head of defense had had to ask him to repeat his vow, he'd been stammering his words so badly.

Sophia repeated her vow to Besith effortlessly and grinned at Sikthand in triumph. He tried not to grin like a fool back.

As she ascended the last few steps, Sikthand stood.

"Hello, my handsome king," she whispered for just the two of them. "How do you like my dress?"

His chest swelled with warmth again. It happened so often these days he must walk around looking like a puffing desert weaver.

"When deciding on what visage of the queen they will sculpt for the Heroes Hall, our metalsmiths will surely choose this one."

A flush stole over her cheeks, and she slipped her gloved hand into his. He grinned down at her glove—the long, pointed claws extending from her fingers gave her hands a deadly look at odds with the gauzy skirt of her dress.

With a squeeze, she let his hand go and made her way over to stand before her veiled throne.

Sikthand sucked in a breath at the sight of her back. Her dress was open, dipping all the way down to just above her tailbone. The expanse of soft pale skin curving over her spine would have been reason enough to catch his attention, but the glint of metal made his lips curl upward.

Attached at her neck and running down the length of her back were interlocking askait vertebrae. The metal bones continued over her ass all the way to the ground, giving her a skeletal Vrulan tail.

His clever, creative mate was announcing to the city that although she was human, she was also one of them.

Sophia tugged at a knot, and the white fabric covering her chair fell away. The room cheered when the glimmering throne was revealed. It was nearly a twin of his own, with its hollow askait tail plate and inlaid silver metalwork, but the designs were softer, more beautiful and less angular than his.

Taking in a deep breath, Sophia lifted a chain at her hip which attached to the tip of her tail. Rather than using the delicate mallet carefully hidden by her throne for this purpose, she tugged on the chain until her metal tail thumped against the hollow plate. Two booming clangs echoed around the room, proclaiming to the city that she approved of her throne.

Cheers rang out, and the Vrulans tapped their tails on the ground and against plates inlaid in the rows and rows of benches lining the room.

Sophia pulled her lips down, attempting to rid her face of her beaming smile before spinning to face her people. She turned and Sikthand saw she managed it, but just barely.

She took in the booming cheers for a proud moment before peering over to him with an excited smothered grin. Lifting her tail out of the way, Sophia lowered onto her throne.

"Vrulatica," Sikthand roared into the crowd, brandishing his hand toward her. "Your queen!"

The cheering in the room doubled. Sophia's eyes grew glassy, and her lips shrunk into nothing as she tried to keep her regal expression in place.

Sikthand lowered into his seat and thanked the skies their thrones were close enough that he could hold her hand.

***

I'm a queen.

Sophia surveyed the cheering Vrulans in the throne room and tried to keep herself from crying. She knew there were likely those out there who didn't want her to be sitting here, but all she could see was beaming faces and thumping tails. It made her heart melt into a gooey warm mess in her chest.

She caught sight of Khes hammering his tail on a golden plate, a suspiciously wet twinkling in his eye, and it almost broke her composure.

Sikthand's hand wrapped around hers, and a tear finally slipped free. "They're happy," she choked out.

"They'd be stupid not to be." He surveyed the crowd, then focused back on her. "Are you ready to see them even happier?"

Her heartbeat picked up again, and she nodded. At long last, it was time to announce their matehood. Finally, Sikthand would get to feel safe. She might not be very strong or know how to fight, but her existence and the marks on his hands protected him, and she was the reason they were there. The knowledge had her spine straightening, her Vrulan spine straightening along with it.

The king rose, pulling at his gloves, and while he was distracted, Sophia quickly slipped off her own.

"Another cheer for your queen and…" He paused for a tension-filled moment, then lifted his bare hands to the sky. "My mate."

There was a dead-silent pause, like life itself had screeched to a halt. Then, beginning with a buzz and building to an ear-splitting, throne-shaking barrage, the city of Vrulatica exploded. The sound in the throne room was louder than clapping thunder.

A vise locked over her chest when Sikthand glanced at her and caught sight of her outstretched hand. His expression blanked.

He took her palm in his and ran a thumb over the matching mate marks she'd had Khes tattoo on her a few hours ago.

He swallowed, and the inner corners of his brows lifted as he gazed in pained happiness at her marked hands. "I love you, Your Majesty," he rasped, loading the words with more adoration than she knew was possible.

"I love you too," she choked out through a tight throat.

Shirking tradition, Sikthand used his grip on her hand to haul her against his chest and kiss her.

The Vrulans continued to cheer, the sounds of celebration only getting louder as the reality of the king's marks sank in.

But to Sophia, all noise grew muffled, the world slowing as though it knew she and Sikthand needed time to exist in this moment together.

I am so damn lucky.

About the Author

Victoria Aveline is the USA Today bestselling author of The Clecanian Series. She lives with her husband, dogs, and about sixty thousand badass honey-making ladies. When not writing or fantasizing about future characters, she enjoys traveling, reading, and sipping overpriced hipster cocktails.

www.victoriaaveline.com

Printed in Poland
by Amazon Fulfillment
Poland Sp. z o.o., Wrocław